THE MARITIME

BETRAYAL

BY

CHARLES BARKER

Published by KDP Amazon 2020

Edited by John Cairns

First Edition

ISBN: Paperback: 9798646032608

www.charlesbarker.club

Dedication

To the wonderful and dedicated people who, often at great personal risk, continuously and selflessly strive to protect the oceans and all the magnificent creatures dwelling in them.

Table of Contents

Characters

Claire Armstrong	Marine conservationist and former Captain in the Special Boat Service
David Armstrong	Father of Claire and marine conservationist. Runs the NGO, Protection of Sea Creatures (POSC)
Queenie Ho	David Armstrong's housekeeper
Ronald Ma	Deputy director of Environmental Protection, Hong Kong
Vivien Armstrong	Claire's mother
Sir Iain Campbell	Chairman of Campbell's Trading Company and head of Demesne
William McMahan	CEO of Campbell's and deputy head of Demesne
Clement Huang	Chief of security for Campbell's and head of Demesne's enforcement team
Kevin Lim	Huang's deputy
Winston Lau	Leader or dragon head of the Xuè yuèliàng (Blood Moon) Triad in Hong Kong.
Mr Kim	Lau's deputy
Chuck Bailey	Chief Executive of POSC
Debbie	Member of POSC board

Gaby Saunders	Head of POSC, Costa Rica
John Teach, aka Blackbeard	Head of POSC, Japan, and former Special Air Service sergeant
Namika	Teach's sidekick and lover
Kage Kuraim	Head, or *oyabun*, of the Yakuza syndicate Boryokudan
Rai	Kuraim's deputy
Miguel Sanchez	Leader of the Barrio 18 crime syndicate, Costa Rica
Simon	Senior triad enforcer
Philip Wong	Director of Environmental Protection, Hong Kong
Micky	Chief engineer of the *Hiyo Maru*
Lt. Col. Richard "Dick" Bennett	Deputy CO at Special Boat Service Regimental Headquarters in Poole, England
Jason Chan	Former Special Air Service captain
Chris Turner	Newspaper editor of the *South China Morning Post* (*SCMP*)
Albert "Bertie" Tsang	Head of Hong Kong's Independent Commission Against Corruption (ICAC)
Wan Kuok-koi	Leader of the 14K Triad in Hong Kong

James Russell	Senior assistant police commissioner and director of B Department – Serious Crime and Security, Hong Kong
May Kwok	Russell's personal assistant (PA)
Miko	Waitress at the New York Lounge, InterContinental Tokyo Bay Hotel
Andy Tyler	Captain of the *R/V Seven Seas*

Crew of the *R/V Seven Seas*:

Olafur Jonsson	First mate
Jock	Engineer
Kevin	Assistant engineer
Miles and Chris	Deckhands
Knowledge	IT and communications
Muscles	Security

Captain Saito	Captain of the *Nisshin Maru*, a whaling vessel and factory mother ship
Kenichi Shinoda	*Oyabun* of the Yamaguchi-gumi Yakuza syndicate
Bertrand Favre, Olivier Viger and Philippe Lapointe	French assassination squad
Stanley Fong	COO of Campbell's Trading Company

"The sea, the great unifier, is man's only hope. Now, as never before, the old phrase has a literal meaning: we are all in the same boat."

Jacques Yves Cousteau

"How inappropriate to call this planet 'Earth' when it is clearly 'Ocean'!"

Arthur C. Clarke

"For years we thought that the oceans were so vast and the inhabitants so infinitely numerous that nothing we could do could have an effect upon them. But now we know that was wrong. The oceans are under threat now as never before in human history."

Sir David Attenborough

Prologue

A New Millennium Begins

"Sharks have no sense of humour," the girl's father told her. "They are unlike dolphins, who like to clown about and wear perpetual grins on their faces. Sharks all have mouths that turn down at the corners and give the impression they are constantly miserable. You'll soon see when we meet some."

But they are not constantly miserable. Rather, they are supreme masters of their environment whose behaviour solely focuses on survival through eating and procreating. The first happens most efficiently, their large mouths possessing rows of constantly replaceable, sharp, triangular teeth with which they saw up their prey. The latter is managed less efficiently, at least judging by numbers. This inefficiency posed no problems for the first 400 million years of their existence. That is, until mankind became interested in them for commercial reasons.

Now sharks are caught for their cartilage and oil for medicinal purposes, for their meat, for sport and by mistake as "by-catch" in fishermen's nets. Lack of proper fisheries management also hastens their decline, and as a final nail in their coffin comes the insatiable desire by many Asian countries, especially China, for their fins in soup. Slaughter of these magnificent creatures accelerated with demand until their extinction looks inevitable. Sharks simply cannot reproduce fast enough, and their numbers have diminished at an alarming rate.

Although only 12 years old, the keenly interested girl was tall for her age and totally relaxed in or under the sea in a way unusual for someone so young. She had passed various scuba-diving certifications and, despite her youth, already showed the maturity to train as a dive leader.

This morning, though, she was going with her father on her first shark dive. They were in Oman and heading out from the capital, Muscat, towards Fahal (meaning "shark") Island, a popular dive location known for its large variety of sharks. The island actually was no more than a big rock sticking out of the ocean, covered with sea birds and little else.

As agreed in their dive plan, they went to shallower waters west of the island. They entered the water and descended gradually to the seabed, just four metres below their dive boat. There, they rested quietly on the bottom, breathing gently, and waited. The warm water stayed reasonably clear, and the girl, with her heart pounding, peered to the edge of visibility some 30 metres away. In these food-rich waters, a profusion of reef fish fed busily among the corals and rocks that were their home, and she marvelled, as always, at the diversity of sea life.

Suddenly the reef fish scattered and hid away, and then there it was. The girl held her breath, her pulse racing, and remained motionless as a two-metre-long, black-tipped reef shark cruised silently along the bottom with barely a perceptible movement of its tail. Curious, it swam towards the girl and cruised by, just inches from her face.

She looked straight into one of the shark's steely grey, unblinking eyes as it passed and observed the glum expression caused by its down-turned mouth, just as her father had described. She saw the black tips on its pectoral, dorsal and caudal fins which gave the species its name, before watching the creature swim away unhurriedly into the gloom.

The girl exhaled, just as a movement to her left caught her attention, and she saw two more of the soundless creatures approaching her. Before they came close, though, another appeared and then another. Soon she counted at least 10, all probing to investigate this new bubble-blowing entity lying on the seabed.

Each shark came towards her and then, like the first, veered away at the last moment before heading off into the haze beyond. As the "meeting" went on, the girl's confidence grew, and she reached out and briefly touched one of the passing inquisitors. It jerked away in surprise, leaving her with a feeling of having brushed her hand against sandpaper.

The entire episode lasted little more than five minutes until the sharks were gone. Silent, graceful and elegant, these magnificent creatures had given her easily the most wonderful and thrilling experience of her young life. Sure, she felt a huge adrenaline rush, but at no time had she been afraid. As her father had explained earlier, she herself would have resembled a large fish, with her diving fins making her nearly as long as the sharks themselves and her scuba gear and tank adding bulk to her frame. Accordingly, the sharks reacted to her only with curiosity and posed no threat.

The girl's father caught her attention and signalled that they should ascend slowly to the surface. Without realising it, she had used most of her air reserves during the short dive, the adrenaline rush boosting her oxygen requirements. She obeyed reluctantly, wanting to stay forever among the fish and other sea creatures, feeling totally absorbed by their colourful, bustling and peaceful world.

When the two divers broke the surface, the girl ripped the regulator out of her mouth, and words poured forth in her excitement. The sheer thrill of the experience felt almost overwhelming, and she talked continuously about it all the way back to their mooring at the Muscat Boat Club.

The girl's passion for the sea and its wonderful treasures pleased her father. As more years went by, they dived often and explored many riches of the deep. He wondered if she would follow in his footsteps as a marine biologist and oceanographer, but he never tried to pressure his wilful daughter. She would choose her own path in life, and that suited him just fine.

PART 1

*

SHARKS AND DOLPHINS

Chapter 1

Introducing Claire

Adding women into the sharp end of the British Armed Forces was a long and tortuous journey. This especially applied to the elite regiments, whose official position always had been that women were a distraction at best and a dangerous liability at worst.

Yet the most enlightened men in high command understood that benefits resulted from having women as elite troops. There were no compromises on eligibility or training, and the same vigorous selection processes applied as for their male counterparts. But as long as women could survive the gruelling tests on their own merits, tests which traditionally had attrition rates above 90 per cent, they became eligible to proceed into training.

The trend began with the Royal Marines, the Parachute Regiment and the Royal Armoured Corps. Before long, it extended to the Special Reconnaissance Regiment, the Special Air Service (SAS) and, perhaps the toughest of them all, the Special Boat Service (SBS).

*

Claire Armstrong stepped forward as one of the earliest and most successful female recruits to join the SBS.

Tall at almost two metres, Claire was a slim and wiry brunette. She possessed her mother Vivien's good looks and stubbornness, but also inherited her father's determination and adventurous spirit. She spent as much time with him as possible during school holidays, wherever he happened to be working.

David Armstrong was a renowned marine conservationist whose work kept him travelling all over the world. Claire excelled from an early age as an outstanding swimmer, and qualified as an open-water scuba diver when just 12 years old. From such early experiences, she developed a love and passion for the oceans.

Stubborn and determined always to have her own way and to succeed at any challenge, she had been a rebel at Canford, a highly regarded co-educational, private boarding school that she had attended in Dorset, England. However, she outshone her peers at sports and extra-curricular activities like outward-bound programmes, shooting and swimming, but disliked the academic side. Rather a "Tom Boy", she always enjoyed competing with boys, and later men, never easily accepting second place.

Anticipating Claire's indifferent A-level results, an enlightened tutor suggested that she should join the army, an idea that took root, and she was selected for officers-training at Sandhurst. Within a year, she had won the Sword of Honour, awarded to the best recruit of her intake. Ever wanting to stretch her achievements, she successfully applied for and joined the elite Royal Marines. After two years of intense action in several military theatres, she applied to join the Special Forces, particularly the SBS, despite the fact that no women had entered this exclusive unit before. Following a highly secretive review process, and to her considerable surprise, she was allowed to proceed, and six months later, she successfully passed the extraordinarily demanding selection process, outperforming most of her male peers.

Claire served with distinction in various conflict regions and, after three years, sought three more. Again, she was accepted and later gained high commendations for her roles in some extremely secret and hostile actions, most of which were unknown to the world at large. Although internally recognised, her skills and bravery could not be acknowledged publicly, as is the way with the Special Forces.

By then, Claire ranked as a captain but, as with almost everyone in the Special Forces, such an occupation cannot last indefinitely. She was 30 years old and, sensing that her military life held little long-term future, she accepted her father's suggestion to leave the military and join him in Hong Kong. There, beginning in 2017, she worked on his latest ocean-conservation projects, striving to halt the gruesome trade in shark finning and to ban inshore bottom trawling.

David Armstrong persuaded Claire to enrol in an oceanography-degree course at the University of Hong Kong, explaining that she could do this in tandem to her work with his NGO, Protection of Sea Creatures, or POSC as it was better known. At his suggestion, she also studied Cantonese and Mandarin, reasoning that to really help in this region, she needed the languages.

*

Initially, Claire didn't realise just how difficult marine conservation could be and how many forces ranged against those who tried to protect the oceans and their wonderful creatures. She began to learn about the pillaging of the oceans by organised enterprises, many of them criminal.

She heard about the dreadful global practice of shark finning for the Asian, but mostly Chinese, markets and the destructive practice of bottom trawling. The latter happens when trawlers weigh down their nets to scrape along the seabed and drag up everything in their path, destroying all bottom-dwelling creatures from corals to sea ferns or juvenile and unsellable reef fish. She discovered the process of electrofishing, when electric currents are deployed in the water to disorientate entire shoals that then swim towards the source and are scooped up in massive nets.

Claire learned how commercial whaling continues, despite treaties and conventions to restrict or prohibit it. And she discovered with horror about the annual dolphin culls in Taiji, Japan, and the massive slaughter of tuna in the Mediterranean and other oceans, these huge fish targeted by spotter planes to maximise catches. Elsewhere, indiscriminate long-line nets catch everything and anything, wanted or not, and as if that isn't enough, the unimaginable pollution of the oceans worsens.

The destructive list seemed endless, with oceans and the precious lives within them being systematically betrayed and eliminated. Claire quickly began to feel determined to do something significant about it all.

Simultaneously, she grew frustrated at the university and impatient with her father, unable to understand why everything on the path towards progress seemed to take so long and why he appeared to tread so carefully. She had operated at high-octane levels for years, usually with clearly defined targets and enemies, and she found this new, slower way of life increasingly unbearable.

*

One evening in late 2018, as David and Claire sat on the balcony of his home in Hong Kong's Shek O district, gazing out as the sea crashed its breakers into Big Wave Bay, her father tried to explain the dangers of pushing too hard and about the particular problems they faced in Hong Kong.

He stressed that the shark finning business was not simply a matter of private initiatives with which reasonable negotiations could take place. Rather, it was an organised criminal enterprise, managed and controlled by the locally based triads whose tentacles circled the planet. Frustratingly, though, in most countries, wildlife crimes don't fall under organised and serious-crimes ordinances, so the authorities, in turn, are little interested.

"Well, shark finning should be totally illegal," spat Claire, somewhat naively.

"Sadly, shark fins are harvested not only from Third World waters by destitute fishermen, although this is probably the largest source collectively, but also from the waters near so-called 'civilised' countries," her father said. "Blue and basking sharks are killed in Cornish waters in the United Kingdom, and Spain makes a huge contribution to the trade. Tens of millions of sharks have been systematically hunted from the waters of North, South and Central America, Australia and Southeast Asia. There are pitifully few marine protected areas where sharks theoretically can live in peace, but even there, poaching still claims plenty of them."

"But that's outrageous!" said Claire. "Can't anything be done anywhere?"

"The trouble is," explained David "and, of course, I'm stating the blindingly obvious, there's no way you can tell a shark to stay in a particular area for its own safety."

This brought the first grin from Claire all evening. "Do you mean that we can't place underwater signs saying, 'Hey, sharks, no swimming beyond this point'?"

"I'm afraid we can't, Sweetie," replied David, glad to see his daughter relaxing a little.

"So, who are the triad leaders? Can't we reason with them, talk to them, I don't know, show them the harm that they do to the order of nature...?" Claire fell silent as she realised the stupidity of her questions.

"The only thing we can do, Claire, is try to educate the public and persuade people to stop demanding shark fin soup. We need to team up with other environmental agencies and forge strong partnerships. We want to bring in allies, such as international hotel groups, clubs or restaurant chains and organisations that arrange banquets, like local governments, and encourage them to use sustainably sourced seafood and to take items like shark fin soup off their menus.

"Furthermore," David continued, "we need effective public-relations campaigns, conferences and public platforms to promote the message that eradication of the oceans' apex predators will lead to a complete system imbalance in nature. We've got to keep chipping away at it, gradually proving that human practices will lead to the eventual destabilisation of the seas and all the creatures living in them. And that this ultimately affects mankind."

"So not much of a challenge then," jested Claire. After a pause, she continued, "Perhaps we just need to play dirty. When faced with a problem in the SBS, we'd consider all the reasonable options and then, if it couldn't be sorted out, we'd resolve it unreasonably." She smiled, recalling instances of such resolutions.

"But the culprits aren't doing anything particularly illegal, and that's an obstacle," reminded her father. "Shark fin soup isn't an illegal food, and the methods of harvesting the fins are illegal only in some countries, not all. Many countries call finning illegal only if the fins are collected without the whole shark, which should be sold separately for food.

"Strangely enough, Hong Kong actually signed up to the convention banning the practice of finning, yet still most of the world's product is channelled through here." David paused for a moment of reflection. "Besides, if you want to confront illegal enterprises at sea, plenty of other things happen."

"Don't tell me about it," replied Claire. "We had a lecture today about whaling and the nonsense concessions that the International Whaling Commission (IWC) has been granting to just about every whaling nation."

"Did your professors also tell you that organised crime is behind most of that too?" asked her father.

Claire sat up rigidly. "No, they did not," she replied.

"Well, connections to criminal enterprises lurk behind much of the whaling industry. Not just whaling, but all aspects of immoral fishing, from tuna, to dolphins, to bottom trawling. Name it, and they're there."

"But if that's well known, why isn't anything being done about it? I can't believe this."

"Well, for a start, it isn't all that well known. For another thing, despite a UN and Interpol report calling crime against wildlife equally as serious as other major criminal activities, it just isn't deemed important enough for overstretched law-enforcement agencies the world over to seriously tackle. They focus on the war against drugs, on terrorism, on cyber-crimes and so forth. I'm sorry to say that fish, no matter how big, just aren't a high enough priority."

"They are as far as I'm concerned, and they should be, and I'm going to make sure they are," said Claire stubbornly.

"Be careful, young lady," cautioned David. "Crossing the triads, or any crime organisation for that matter, can turn very dangerous. People get hurt, or worse, killed, so please don't start getting adventurous, Claire. You're not in the Service now, you know."

"I suppose you're right, Dad," she conceded. What her father said made perfectly good sense, but she remained upset and was damned if she'd just sit back and do nothing.

Evening had turned into night, and the humidity seemed to be rising. A storm looked likely, so David and Claire went inside to the cooler air-conditioning and to their dinner.

"Bloody good job that amah of yours didn't serve up fish," said Claire sulkily.

David smiled at thoughts of what his truculent daughter might have said then. "Cheer up," he urged her. "It's not all bad. I've got a meeting tomorrow at the ministry, and I'm hoping for good news. The people there have looked at my latest proposals to tackle the finning issue here, and the early indications appear promising."

"Can I come along?" asked Claire.

"Sure, why not? It's good for you to see how the mechanics of government and diplomacy work."

That seemed to appease Claire. Soon the subject changed and, to David's considerable relief, the mood lightened.

Chapter 2

Father Stonewalled by Government

The next morning, the two Armstrong conservationists left together for David's appointment with the director of Environmental Protection, a department under the auspices of Hong Kong's Environment Bureau which, in turn, reports to the Executive Council. They arrived at the relevant government office in the Wan Chai district just before 10 o'clock.

They were met by a harassed-looking government secretary who said how much he deeply regretted that the director could not attend the meeting, but added that a deputy had been briefed and would see them shortly. Minutes passed, and "shortly" stretched into a wait of more than an hour, by which time Claire was chomping at the bit.

"Just try and relax," said her father, who during a lifetime of dealing with government offices, had learned to accept such delays. "This is the way it works, and getting angry doesn't help you or anyone else. It's simply the way of things."

"Well, it's not the way I do things," stated Claire grumpily.

"Just be quiet please," admonished her father, "and let me do the talking when we meet the man."

She was about to argue more when the secretary reappeared and asked them to follow him down an exceedingly tatty corridor some distance past the director's office and remote from the comfortable waiting room. "Some hope for the environment," whispered Claire grimly, "if this is the quality of the workplace."

They were led into an equally shabby office where the secretary introduced them to Mr Ronald Ma, deputy director of the Environmental Protection Department. Ma was a small, balding man with a comb-over hairstyle and with little piggy eyes exaggerated by his thick-lensed glasses. He did not stand, nor show any greeting or apparent courtesy, so the visitors merely took a chair each and sat opposite his cluttered desk.

"We understood that this meeting was scheduled just with you, Mr Armstrong," said Ma.

"This is my daughter, Claire, who is taking an oceanography degree at the University of Hong Kong while also assisting me with my work here. I trust that her presence isn't a problem?"

"In point of fact, it is a problem, so she should return to the waiting room," stated Ma rudely.

Claire had already taken an instant, intense dislike to the man and now felt inclined to drag him across his desk and pummel him. Her father intervened and quietly asked her to leave.

"I'll see you at home later," she answered, glaring at the little human-pig before storming out of the office without another word.

"Sorry, Mr Ma," offered Armstrong, "but the director never had a problem before with me bringing along advisors or assistants to our meetings."

"That was before, Mr Armstrong. Things have changed."

"How so?"

"It seems that you have badly upset some important and high-ranking members of Hong Kong society with your continual preaching about the trade in shark fins. Also, the smaller traders are angered by your behaviour and have made representations to the bureau."

"This all seems very strange, Mr Ma," responded Armstrong uneasily. "When I last spoke with the director, he seemed quite optimistic that progress was happening, even at the Executive Council level, and beyond that...."

"You clearly misinterpreted the director's courteous nature," interrupted Ma, "no doubt deliberately, so as to advance your agenda."

"That's outrageous. How dare you suggest such a thing?" retorted Armstrong, raising his voice, his usual good temper suddenly evaporating.

Ignoring the outburst, Ma continued, "You have abused our hospitality here in Hong Kong, and the director's good nature too, with your rhetoric and unfounded accusations for long enough. Accordingly, it has been decided to revoke the permit for you and your NGO to work in the Hong Kong Special Administrative Region. That is all."

"I can't believe that I'm hearing this!" said Armstrong, standing up angrily. "My NGO has worked for years to improve the quality of your seas and the environment as a whole. What you're saying is outrageous!"

Ma seemed unfazed. "Our position is clear and irreversible," he stated bluntly.

Preparing to leave, Armstrong turned back towards the other man. "I'll be obliged to take this up with higher authorities. You probably are unaware that Hong Kong's chief executive is a friend of mine, and I most certainly will discuss this matter with him, along with telling him about your rudeness and unacceptable conduct."

"That would be extremely inadvisable," bristled Ma. "Seriously, please consider that you have been sternly warned."

Without another word, much like his daughter moments earlier, David Armstrong whirled and left the room, distrusting himself to respond again.

Once the conservationist had departed, Ma reached for a mobile telephone and called his non-government, less-official boss, a man who headed up the largest of Hong Kong's triad gangs. "How did it go?" asked the person receiving the call.

"Armstrong did not accept our decision well and threatened to take up the matter with so-called higher authorities, including the CE. Naturally, I warned him against that. He also brought along his daughter to the meeting. In the brief time before I told her to leave, she seemed most hostile."

"I believe the Armstrongs pose a serious problem, one with which we must deal."

The communications link ended, and Ma, who ranked as just one among many junior, but useful, minions within the Xuè yuèliàng (Blood Moon) Triad's hierarchy, returned to his more routine work, knowing that he likely had heard the passing of a death sentence.

*

Telephoning his daughter, David Armstrong asked without preamble, "Have you left for home yet?"

"No, I'm just walking around outside the building and trying to let off steam. Why? How did the rest of the meeting go?"

"Meet me in The Captain's Bar at the Mandarin Hotel. I need a drink," he said, terminating the call.

"Not well then," muttered Claire into her suddenly unresponsive mobile phone.

*

"What happened?" Claire asked immediately when they reunited some 20 minutes later. She found her father already seated in the bar where he was several gulps into his first whisky and soda.

David Armstrong related what had transpired. "It must be the triads," he concluded. "They heard about what we're doing and perceive a threat to their business interests, which frankly is very perturbing."

"I disliked that little shit, that Deputy Ma, from the moment when I clapped eyes on him," said Claire. "But can't we go higher up and appeal?"

"I already had reached higher up, remember? No, this is a serious warning, and we need to re-group and think this one through very carefully."

With a series of phone calls, David Armstrong then arranged an online meeting with his NGO colleagues for the afternoon. Next he and Claire talked through aspects of the problem, while munching on a lunch of light sandwiches, before heading to his office.

Chapter 3

Shark Finning

The decades-long Chinese economic miracle had taken the world by storm. Truthfully, average Chinese people felt just as surprised as anyone else. Suddenly they could afford much more, and countless millions of them indulged collectively in an unprecedented spending spree. Entrepreneurialism became a new order of the day, and more dollar-billionaires emerged in China than in any other country.

Dining out became wildly popular, and new restaurants proliferated nationwide. Despite the vast country's varied regional tastes, everyone sought one particular item. Traditionally a rarity that only the elite enjoyed, shark fin soup suddenly fell within reach of the general population. Everyone could afford to eat it. Soon all wedding banquets featured it, whether in poor, rural communities, industrial neighbourhoods or high-tech city centres. People flaunted their money, and social pressures made this soup a "must have" on many social occasions.

That the fins were gristly and tasteless, adding nothing to the flavours of the soup broth, made no difference. Eating shark fin soup was all about status, and so its popularity and prices soared.

Of course, all this came as bad news for sharks. They had received a bad press ever since 1975 when Peter Benchley's novel, Jaws, became a wildly popular Steven Spielberg film that badly misrepresented them. Among more than 500 species of sharks, the largest is a gentle ocean giant, the whale shark, which grows up to 20 metres long, innocently surviving on a simple diet of plankton and small fish. In more predatory classes, the large bull, tiger and great white sharks lead the way, down to thresher and smaller whitetip or blacktip reef sharks. But in their respective environments, all are masters of their domains atop the oceans' food chain

Historically the only real danger posed by mankind to these magnificent creatures came through sports fishing. They are not easily caught and never before formed a viable target for commercial fishing. But when news spread of China's intense demand for shark fin soup, every poor fisherman possible received instructions and sailed in pursuit of sharks just for the lucrative fins.

Usually the fishermen did not land their catches. That was too dangerous in small boats. Instead they baited and hauled in sharks alongside their vessels, leaned over the sides and hacked off the dorsal and pectoral fins, all easily picked up in nets. Then they tried for the most valuable of all, the caudal fins, or tails, definitely much harder to remove. Next they cut the lines holding the sharks, allowing them to wallow, sink and die. Sometimes the dying sharks would be attacked, killed and eaten by other emboldened predators, but often they simply drowned, unable to maintain momentum through the water to aerate their gills.

As with any high-value item, shark fins rapidly attracted the attention of organised crime, starting with the triads in Hong Kong. That city became a holding and staging post where almost all the severed fins were gathered, dried and forwarded to buyers across China. The triads coordinated with regional crime syndicates and partners internationally. With incredible speed, the management of a new industry took shape.

Since the shark fin trade didn't endanger people or threaten legitimate businesses, governments took little notice, making just occasional token seizures in ports, mainly to keep up appearances. Only environmentalists, oceanographers and the underfunded organisations representing them screamed in protest, but their cries fell on deaf ears.

The plunder accelerated. Soon most sea-bordering nations contributed to the slaughter. Any shark became fair game, and the balance of nature wobbled as tens of millions of sharks were killed annually. On the rooftops of triad-controlled warehouses across Hong Kong, hectares of shark fins dried in the sun in preparation for soup dishes.

Sharks badly needed a human champion. Otherwise they'd become extinct, irreversibly changing the order of nature.

Chapter 4

Demesne and the Crime Syndicates

Organised crime exists to a degree in every corner of the world. Sometimes it operates as gangs with a small community focus. Often it reaches wider with names feared by the masses. For example, the Mafia began in Italy and crossed the Atlantic to North America. Back in Europe, the less-well-known Union Corse, from its power bases in Corsica and elsewhere in southern France, developed a heroin trade from the Golden Triangle in Southeast Asia, among other enterprises.

Asia spawns its own brands of criminal organisations, like Japan's highly disciplined and ordered Yakuza, or Hong Kong's triad societies, whose tentacles span the globe. Elsewhere, the Russian Mafiya, although newer to international crime, may be the most brutal of all, along with its associated Eastern and Central European brotherhoods. Then, of course, vicious and pitiless drug cartels prowl South America.

Wherever people exist to be corrupted, extorted, suborned, bullied, blackmailed, assassinated, robbed, bribed, coerced and threatened for financial gain or influence, criminal enterprises appear to exploit them. But one organisation, known only to the most senior leaders of the criminal underworld, holds power and influence second to none while coordinating the activities of all other syndicates and ensuring their smooth running for its own vast gain. It has no public name or known leaders, but anyone challenging this mysterious force finds that negotiations never happen and that rapid, violent death forms the only alternative to total compliance. The few people in the know call this dark organisation simply "Demesne".

When unknowingly meeting the head of Demesne, a name derived from the hubris of its founder, meaning essentially "the realm of the monarch", it is hard to imagine him as one of the world's most dangerous and ruthless individuals. Sir Iain Campbell came from Scottish ancestors, who had ventured into Shanghai with the East India Company to capitalise on vast fortunes arising in opium and tea trade during the late 18th century. His predecessors enjoyed spectacular success and switched their base to Hong Kong before the mid-20th-century takeover of China by communism's dark forces.

Once in Hong Kong, then a British colony, they consolidated their power and influence and soon controlled much of its major commerce and industry. The name Campbell became synonymous with wealth, success, influence and authority, and everyone in the business, political and trading communities stood either with them or against them. They projected power from Campbell's Tower, a 25-storey office block, long ago one of Hong Kong's tallest buildings and still among its most prestigious, near the harbour in the Central district. The growth and stability of individuals or companies aligned against them tended to be short-lived.

Small in a physical sense, Sir Iain stood just 1.5-metres tall. But what he lacked in height he made up for in strength. He exercised regularly and stayed fit, both physically and mentally. Aged 67, he had a full head of combed-back, grey hair and a permanent light tan that set off his piercingly blue eyes separated by a large beak of a nose. He dressed impeccably and exuded a sense of power and purpose that, when he chose to use it, could be overwhelming.

One of Sir Iain's past success stories was the creation of his own container-shipping line, which soon became one of the world's largest. He always believed in the importance of dominating the sea-trade routes, so during the Chinese Renaissance that continued into the early 21st century, he ruthlessly took advantage of the many opportunities, both legal and illegal. Commerce in and out of China boomed, and he fully capitalised.

To Sir Iain's way of thinking, shark finning was an easy enterprise to manage because most governments showed little concern about the long-term implications of the likely mass extinction of sharks. Nobody he knew liked the creatures much, so who cared what happened to them?

He had reached out to his felonious triad connections and suggested a new side-line business to them. Encourage fishermen everywhere to catch sharks, remove the fins and send them to warehouses in Hong Kong. Fair market prices would be paid and then, having dried and packed the fins, the triads would sell them at hugely inflated prices into the ravenous China market. Demesne would receive healthy "facilitation fees", or commissions, from all the participating concerns. Considerable sums of money changed hands, and the mobs set about their new venture with enthusiasm.

Everyone involved felt happy, from the fishermen and their dockside controllers to the regional crime bosses and on up the chain. The end users exalted, as millions of Chinese people boasted to each other about enjoying shark fin soup. Graft multiplied, and money flowed.

Everyone felt happy, that is, except for the environmentalists, and, of course, the sharks.

Chapter 5

David Armstrong's Nemesis

A formidable man, Winston Lau had inherited leadership of the Xuè yuèliàng (Blood Moon) Triad after a bloody turf war in 2011 and 2012 against the Wo Shing Wo Triad, Hong Kong's oldest, if not largest, triad society. The Xuè yuèliàng became the undisputed leading society with expanded dealings and influence. Its global reach blended almost every form of vice, notably drugs, trafficking, extortion and murder. Winston Lau commanded with absolute authority, ruling his triad with a ruthless grip. After all, he answered only to the mysterious head of Demesne.

The power of Demesne had supported Lau's ascent and allowed him a free reign, for doing so served its purposes. It fully encouraged his most adventurous illegal activities, and he appreciated his enigmatic benefactor.

It was Winston Lau who had passed sentence on the Armstrong duo.

*

The assassination team consisted of five members, all experienced killers. They scouted the Armstrong villa in Shek O when its occupants were away. Then they planned their assault.

At three o'clock the next morning, four of them stealthily approached the house, leaving the fifth team member to keep watch and stay in reserve for any unexpected contingencies. They had decided that the easiest means of entry would be through double glass doors leading in from the slightly elevated ground-floor balcony. Silently they climbed onto the structure.

A lock yielded, an old latch quietly lifted, the doors opened and all four men entered the house almost without a sound.

Once inside the living room, they split into two pairs, one for each target. Their orders called for being lethal and quick. On this mission, no drawn-out, personal, sadistic indulgences were permitted. Each killer carried a pair of traditional Chinese *duandao*, 18-inch short-swords ideal to stab or slash, and each assassin knew well how to use them.

The first bedroom door stood open. Judging by the masculine tone of snoring from beyond, this was David Armstrong's room. Two killers approached the soundly sleeping man, quietly slashed his throat and then stabbed him several times on his torso. David awoke gurgling in his own blood and made a weak, gasping sound before succumbing. He died quickly without even realising it.

At the same time, the other two assassins moved in on Claire, but they failed to reckon on facing an ex-Special Forces operator. Always a light sleeper, Claire had awakened as the assassins breached the balcony doors. Although the noise was all but inaudible, her highly developed sense of danger alerted her. She rose from bed to investigate just as the two executioners entered her room.

Hard-earned training took over, and Claire automatically went into combat mode. Enough ambient light existed for her to see and operate in the darkness. She struck the first person she saw with a full-force, right-hand chop to an extended sword arm while almost simultaneously delivering a left fist to his neck, just below an ear. Two snaps of breaking bone sounded almost as one.

All that the second assassin saw was his shadowy partner dropping like a stone. Suddenly the woman confronted him too. Despite his *duandaos* held at the ready in front of him, nothing in his martial-arts training prepared him for the speed of Claire's attack. Even in the tight confines of the doorway, Claire jolted him with a roundhouse kick to his head and then pivoted to deliver an equally hard snap-kick to his upper torso, one of her feet flying neatly between his swords. He fell backwards into the passageway, crumpling to the floor with the air forced out of him.

Pulling him forward again, Claire grasped the back of his neck with one hand and his chin with the other. Jerking her arms in opposite directions, she snapped his neck.

The other two assassins, emerging from David's bedroom, quickly sized up what had happened and charged at Claire. Even for her, two more-alerted men with swords confronting an unarmed person in a small space amounted to bad odds, so she turned and ran for the large kitchen at the rear of the villa.

On reaching the kitchen, she grabbed a large meat cleaver, the preferred utensil of all Chinese cooks, and a frying pan. She kicked the kitchen table against a wall and turned to face her attackers. They needed to enter the room in single file, and she confronted the leading one immediately as he approached, already slashing at her with both *duandaos* in a rotating windmill motion.

The frying pan absorbed most of his first few strikes. Suddenly ducking to the floor, Claire swung the cleaver at the man's ankles, connecting solidly with one and cutting lightly into the other, evoking a loud scream of pain as the intruder crashed to the floor. But he wasn't quite done and continued to slash out weakly with one sword.

Springing clear, Claire refocused on the second man as he more cautiously approached her, arms stiff out in front of him. He tried some experimental stabbing motions, forcing Claire

28

back. Then with more space, they slowly began to circle each other.

So far, the entire intrusion had generated few sounds, other than the scream from the man at the kitchen doorway and the clang of sword strikes hitting Claire's frying pan. But those were enough to alert the lookout.

Discarding his orders to stay out of sight, the fifth assassin cautiously approached the balcony. He had just reached the living-room door before hearing a blood-curdling scream from somewhere deep inside the villa. No one expected to hear such a noise on a routine, clandestine mission, so he hesitated, troubled by what might have happened, yet he couldn't imagine his colleagues faltering against an old man and one woman.

The source of the sound was Claire as she stood tall, opened her guard and screamed like a banshee. The movement and the noise distracted her attacker just enough. She launched herself at him, slamming one blade away with the pan and hurling the cleaver into his chest.

The tip of his second sword pierced an inch into Claire's torso as she threw the heavy cleaver, but it was too late for the attacker to capitalise. He died instantly as the cleaver punctured his rib cage and pierced his heart. Claire barely glanced toward the trickle of blood running down her left side from just below her ribcage and ignored the slight pain that the stab wound caused.

One intruder still sat in the kitchen doorway with a smashed left ankle and a badly bleeding right one. From his seated position, he continued pointing a *duandao* at Claire, but they both knew it was a feeble gesture.

Claire wanted to interrogate the man, but just as she advanced towards him, he turned one of the blades on himself and plunged it into his body, slashing downwards into the gut. This time he did not cry out, and he died as Claire watched.

Hearing a muted whisper from the living room, Claire realised that at least one more intruder remained. She quietly put down the pan and, taking one of the dead man's swords, stepped over him and crept silently towards her prey.

Another whisper came, with a note of anxiety this time. The increasingly puzzled man could not see his brethren, and everything had fallen as silent as a grave.

Just as he cautiously advanced farther into the room, the lights illuminated. All he saw before losing consciousness was a bloodied apparition flying at him and slashing at his forehead in a sweeping cut. Next a hand-chop to his neck left him senseless.

A slash across a forehead makes an extremely efficient method to immobilise someone. If the cut goes deep enough, the muscles, which essentially hold the skin and flesh of the lower face in place, are severed. So, the man's eyebrows, eyelids and cheeks lost their hold and drooped over his face. That caused a loss of sight, considerable anxiety and disorientation, as well as pain, and quickly rendered him pliable for interrogation, something Claire fully intended to conduct.

But first she urgently needed to check on her father and then secure the premises. Calling the police could come later.

With a sense of dread, Claire went into her father's bedroom, seeing at once that he was dead. Her training and experience kept her adequately detached from the awful scene, so she quickly went to the balcony and down the steps into the garden. She crept all around the villa, she too now with a *duandao* in each hand, and peered into the street.

Seeing nothing of additional concern, Claire returned inside, satisfied that she was alone with the remaining assassin and that any other attackers had fled. Ripping up a bedsheet, she made a pad and secured it in place over her wound which was still bleeding slightly. She realised that she was lucky the sword had not penetrated deeper. With the rest of the sheet, she tightly bound her prisoner.

Now she could begin an extreme interrogation with this piece-of-shit criminal who so violently had entered her life. As the man regained consciousness, he found himself kneeling on the floor with his hands and legs tied firmly behind him. He started to gabble in discomfort, realising that he couldn't see, and the strange feeling of blood, skin and flesh askew over his face sent him into a panic.

"Silence!" ordered Claire loudly. But he continued his panic-driven rant.

Claire kicked him in the groin so forcefully that he fell forward onto his damaged face and vomited. When his retching stopped, she leaned over him and spoke in a whisper.

"I hope for your sake that you understand me because I have some questions, and you will answer them," she hissed. "If you don't speak to me, or if I dislike your answers, then I'll slice open your intestines and watch you die. That's a most-painful death lasting up to three hours, if I'm careful where I put the blade. I've killed all your companions, so I won't hesitate to kill you too. Do you understand me?"

The assassin nodded, causing the wayward sections of his face to sway grotesquely.

"Say it," Claire shouted. "Do you understand me?"

"Yes, y-y-yes," he stammered. This woman was crazier and tougher than the triad chiefs for whom he worked, and that really scared him. He completely believed her threat and decided to tell her anything she asked.

The interrogation lasted for almost 20 minutes, during which time the man passed out twice, before becoming clearly spent.

Splashing water on the remains of his face no longer revived him, but at least Claire had extracted the information she needed.

*

The whole deadly event had taken less than an hour, so it was a sleepy night-desk sergeant in nearby Stanley, site of the nearest police station, the one covering Shek O, who took the emergency call. Startled into wakefulness, he hastily set things in motion for law enforcement to investigate what had happened at the villa.

Initial crime-scene investigators were horrified at the carnage and quickly concluded that it involved a triad hit squad. As to why, that would take time to determine.

The investigators also needed to decide what to do about Claire, who wasn't saying much of anything. They wondered how she alone could fend off the entire team of attackers. After allowing medics to properly examine and treat her wound, the detectives took her to the police station, where formal questioning began.

All Special Forces troops receive a hotline number when leaving the service. The simple fact is that trouble frequently follows them after they depart or, often for noble reasons, they find trouble because they can. Claire asked a detective inspector interviewing her to place the call. Within an hour, lines buzzed and very high-ranking authorities in the UK and in Hong Kong cleared the way and arranged to transport Claire to a safe house. A debriefing there would take more of a military slant with the police kept in the loop as necessary.

Claire was escorted, now with great courtesy and a considerable measure of respect, out of the Old Stanley Police

Station and taken to a highly secure residence on the Peak. There, she received some hot tea and biscuits (the British answer to every crisis), a room, some fresh clothes and instructions to rest.

In the early dawn, the views over Victoria Harbour and much of Hong Kong were spectacular, but they were lost on Claire. Now that all the adrenaline had evaporated, she felt exhausted, deflated and overwhelmingly sad.

She lay on the bed in her room. As she drifted off to sleep, she swore to herself that those responsible for the night's actions would pay dearly.

Chapter 6

Winston Lau Hears Bad News

Receiving no word from his team of assassins, Winston Lau initiated discreet enquiries and was astonished to discover that four of the five hitmen were dead with the fifth in a hospital under police guard. Astonishment soon turned to anger, mitigated only in part when he learned that at least the meddlesome David Armstrong also had died. But he was mystified by how the daughter could not only survive the hit and inflict such damage, but also disappear without a trace.

Winston Lau issued two orders. One, find the woman and kill her. And two, spring the fifth assassin from his custodial hospital bed. Triad minions set about their tasks with enthusiasm. After all, four of their own had perished, and the hunt for the Armstrong woman had turned personal.

The second task was relatively easy. That night, a squad of 10 Xuè yuèliàng enforcers visited the Hong Kong Adventist Hospital on Stubbs Road. After threatening and guarding first the reception staff and then the night nurses on the secluded fifth-floor ward where their colleague was incarcerated, they quickly overpowered the two policemen on protection duty. They placed their invalid and disfigured associate unceremoniously in a wheelchair and brazenly pushed him out the hospital's front doors to a waiting, innocuous, green mini-bus before fleeing at speed. By the time the police responded to an emergency call from the hospital-reception area, the triad members were long gone.

The first task proved more daunting. The triad's usual sources in the Hong Kong Police Force couldn't help because they didn't know where Claire was taken. They suspected that

Department B of the Criminal Intelligence Bureau was involved, but beyond that, they were equally in the dark.

Department B, responsible for security issues and battling organised crime, operates secretly and independently of the regular Hong Kong Police Force and, more interestingly, of the Chinese Ministry of State Security's Bureau Four, which oversees state-security matters pertaining to Taiwan, Hong Kong and Macau. Essentially, the department had inherited the British Secret Intelligence Service's activities in the region, although they too remained covertly present.

All this posed a big problem for Winston Lau. The Armstrong woman clearly had very high-level connections. If he stirred up this particular hornets' nest, he knew that he could expect serious consequences. He would need to play a waiting game while trying to learn more about the enigma that was Claire Armstrong. When she surfaced, as she eventually must, then he would decide on the appropriate action.

*

In a luxuriously appointed office on the top floor of Campbell's Tower in the Central district, Sir Iain Campbell peered pensively out over Victoria Harbour as he received early-evening briefings from his various enterprises. When other executives had finished and left, the organisation's CEO, William McMahan, remained behind to discuss extra matters with his boss. Two days had passed since the mayhem at Shek O, about which Demesne was as fully briefed as possible.

McMahan had worked together with Campbell for almost as long as anyone could remember and had been instrumental not only in securing Campbell's Trading Company's considerable legacy, but also in building on it and ensuring the company's continued spectacular growth. He was also the indispensable deputy head of Demesne.

A large man in his early sixties, McMahan had thick, black hair, a fleshy face and humourless, black eyes that seemed able to stare through a person and reach into the soul. His height, at a little beyond two metres, could not disguise his sizeable paunch, but what he lacked in physical agility he more than made up for with his mental acuity. He could be charming at times, which was seldom, and ferociously ruthless when he chose, which was often. Indisputably, he was Campbell's hatchet man, both in boardrooms and on the streets. People crossed him at their extreme peril.

"What is it, Billy?" asked Sir Iain.

"Some interesting developments regarding the Shek O incident," began McMahan.

"What have you found out?"

"It seems that Claire Armstrong was among the first in a pioneering programme secretly to introduce women into the British Special Forces. She served six years in the SBS."

That got Sir Iain's attention. "Good gracious, I didn't know that plan had been implemented yet."

"I didn't know either," continued McMahan, "but evidently she left the service a year ago and came to Hong Kong to join her father's NGO, Protection of Sea Creatures. She's also doing a degree in oceanography at the Hong Kong University."

"Protection of Sea Creatures, that's the outfit tediously trying to stop shark finning, isn't it?" Sir Iain asked, adding with a chuckle, "Fat chance, eh?"

"That's the one," replied McMahan. "But Armstrong's NGO must have made enough noise and become enough of a nuisance to attract our friend Winston Lau's attention. He put out the word to rescind the visa for POSC to operate here and, when Armstrong heard, he threatened to pursue the matter at the Executive Council level, even with the Chief Executive whom he apparently knew quite well."

"So, Winston Lau, impulsive as ever, sent out a hit squad," completed Sir Iain. "Obviously, the assassins didn't reckon on meeting a member of Her Majesty's Special Forces." He laughed at the thought of it. "She must be pretty bloody good to have killed four experienced assassins and maimed another."

"Well, technically, ex-Special Forces," corrected McMahan. "In any case, she's been spirited away and is now out of sight, as is the surviving killer, who was broken out of the Adventist Hospital last night and whose whereabouts officially are unknown."

"Meaning that she's probably in the safe house on the Peak, and the killer is busy spilling his guts to Winston Lau before inevitably following his four colleagues into death," completed Sir Iain.

"Yes, that's about the size of it. Do you want me to talk to Lau?"

"No, not yet. Let's wait and see how all this plays out. Ms Armstrong may leave Asia, and then the entire issue goes away. If not, then we can step in, but I'd prefer to keep out of it for the time being."

McMahan wondered about the wisdom of such a strategy. He considered Winston Lau just a bit too unruly for his liking and would have preferred to nip the whole matter in the bud. However, the boss had ruled so he kept his opinion to himself.

Chapter 7

Who Believes in Mermaids?

After a debriefing at the safe house, it was deemed prudent to move Claire out of Hong Kong and beyond harm's way. In the days following the attack, her father's body was repatriated back to the UK, and POSC shut up shop and left Hong Kong to consider its future.

Claire saw the good sense in this, but stayed silent about what she really intended to do. For the moment, she would play along with the authorities, go and stay with her mother at their family home in Lyme Regis, Dorset, and help with her father's funeral arrangements, all while personally regrouping.

On the night after David's funeral, the mother and daughter walked quietly together along the beach and out onto a harbour breakwater known as the Cobb. There was a chill in the air, but otherwise, it was a peaceful, beautiful and clear night. A full moon illuminated a path towards the beach. They sat down on an old iron bench and gazed out over the sea.

"Do you still believe in mermaids, Claire?" asked Vivien, breaking into her daughter's reverie.

"I wasn't aware that I ever did, Mum," replied Claire, puzzled by the unusual topic.

"Oh, yes, you certainly did. When you were about eight years old, we lived in Brighton and employed Justine, an *au pair* girl from France. She was a very lovely girl, rather willowy and with long, golden hair, who always seemed to be immersed in daydreams, as if distracted by something. She was a bit strange altogether and, unfortunately, she didn't stay long with us, but you were captivated by her and the stories she told you.

"One summer night, she persuaded me to drive us down to the beach to see the full moon's glare on the water. It was late and past your bedtime, but she seemed so anxious to go that I relented, and off we went. Good job your father wasn't home, or else we'd never have gone!

"Anyway, all three of us walked along the promenade and watched the gentle swell lifting and dropping the moon's reflection on the calm waters. The moon hung quite low, and its light shimmered, seeming to stretch right to the horizon, just like now."

Vivien paused reflectively before continuing the story. "Justine then said it was a time when you might see mermaids basking in the moonlight. She spoke with such authority and described how mermaids always got up to mischief, how they lived under the sea, but enjoyed coming to the surface during a full moon and flapping in the reflection of its light. We were mesmerised by her story.

"Then quite suddenly she gasped, grabbed your hand and pointed. 'There,' she said, 'not far offshore'. We looked and perhaps in our imaginations saw an extra ripple that transcended into a mermaid.

"We both felt captivated under Justine's spell, and anything seemed possible. She sounded very anxious to know that we had seen the mermaid and, by that time, we were convinced that maybe we had.

"We didn't see any other mermaids that evening and, as we drove home, Justine regaled us with stories about the merfolk. It was enchanting, and for a time you absolutely believed in mermaids."

"What a beautiful story," said Claire, enchanted again, this time by the flashback to her childhood. "Now I remember that night. I thought Justine was a mermaid too. When she suddenly left us, I believed she'd gone back to the sea."

Inexplicably, tears welled in Claire's eyes as she recalled the mysterious *au pair* girl. "There are so many mysteries in the oceans, Mum. Why shouldn't mermaids exist?"

"Are you okay, Darling?" asked Vivien, until that moment not having seen her daughter shed tears at all over the recent tragic events.

"Of course I am," insisted Claire, breaking the spell as she wiped at her eyes. "Bloody hell, can you imagine if my buddies in the SBS could see me now? How embarrassing would that be for me?"

Vivien reached over and held her daughter's hand. "You're allowed to be human, Claire. Let go of all that bottled-up emotion, my darling, and have a good weep. You can do this with me, you know."

Suddenly the floodgates opened, and Claire wept with all the built-up stress, emotion and sadness that she'd repressed since joining the army, at the loss of comrades and at her father's death.

Eventually the crying stopped. Claire pulled herself together and, almost with a sense of shame, told her mother, "I haven't done that for a very long time."

"Don't worry, Darling. It's good to unburden."

"I saw and did some horrible things in the SBS, you know," Claire said, quietly opening up to her mother for the first time. "We saw action in places that were known about, like around the Middle East and the Med, but there were other places never spoken about, like North Korea, even Russia and China."

Claire paused. Then, with a half-smile, she continued. "We even did something very bad in US waters once against the members of a drug cartel, but they deserved what they got. We

had an 11th commandment, 'Thou shalt not get found out'."
She smiled wider at the memories.

Again, a silence ensued, one that her mother chose not to break.

Then Claire collected herself once more and continued. "Somehow I suppose that we became almost immune to it all. In the SBS, we knew exactly who the enemies were and what needed to be done about them. More importantly, we were sanctioned to do it.

"But now, with so many terrible things happening in the oceans, the task of doing something about it all seems insurmountable. Ruthless bastards are raping the seas and ravaging all the wonderful creatures in them, mostly with protection from nation states and criminal gangs. I don't know, Mum. The job of responding somehow is just overwhelming."

"You never doubted yourself before, Claire," her mother replied gently. "I have no doubt that you'll find ways to make a difference and become a champion for all the creatures of the deep who need you, Darling."

"Including mermaids, huh Mum?" said Claire with a lopsided grin and a final sniff.

"Definitely including mermaids," said Vivien, returning her daughter's grin.

Chapter 8

Claire Plans Her Comeback

With aspects of the tragic events in Shek O somewhat buried along with her father, Claire sought out his former colleagues from POSC. Most of them had attended his funeral, where they agreed to keep in touch with her and invited her to attend a board meeting at their British headquarters the following week.

Although relatively small, POSC had gained global appeal as the tides of public opinion rose on environmental issues, like the oceans. So POSC was reasonably well funded and operated programmes around the world. It was based in David Armstrong's hometown of Brighton, a bustling British city on the south coast an hour's train journey from London.

After Claire arrived for the board meeting, she discovered a certain sense of apathy on the management team, a sentiment festering since David's death. He had been a driving force behind POSC, and his absence left a big void. The directors' morale languished, and they actively wondered if their NGO had a future.

Although still running busy operations in the Philippines, Hawaii and southern France, they fretted about two other missions, one in Costa Rica, dealing mainly with shark finning, and another in Japan, concerning whaling and a yearly dolphin cull in Taiji. Attempts to establish a base in Vladivostok to oversee the whaling activities based there had been repulsed vigorously by the Russian authorities.

Since the Hong Kong calamity, POSC employees in Costa Rica and in Japan had received threats. A Costa Rican staff member was beaten up and told to stop working for the NGO. The criminal gangs responsible doubtlessly felt inspired by the events in Hong Kong, if not actually directed by Winston Lau's organisation.

So the POSC directors expressed great concern for their people's safety. They viewed the organisation's prospects gloomily.

Indignant at much of what she heard, Claire would have none of it. Although not officially one of the board members, she reacted like a human tornado in their midst, trying to reinvigorate them with her positive approach and remind them of their purpose and responsibilities.

"If you quit now," Claire said, ending a rant, "everything my father fought for and believed in will have been for nothing. Then who stands up for our precious oceans and the marine life within them? And I'm not just talking about the big mammals, but also the small, less-popular sea creatures and corals. They're all equally important in the balance of nature."

For support, she looked to the NGO's chief executive, Chuck Bailey, a mild-mannered and kindly American marine biologist whose patient and experienced guidance had provided bedrock for POSC's early work. A long-standing colleague and friend of David's, he backed up the founder's daughter.

"Claire's right, folks," he affirmed. "This awful matter of what happened to David must serve to strengthen our resolve and make us more forceful in our work. David's death can work positively for us."

Suddenly he stopped, looking uncomfortable, and then said, "Gee, I'm sorry, Claire. That sounded bad."

"No, you're absolutely correct, Chuck," she responded. "Let's use Dad's death to swing public opinion against these bastards. I know it sounds awful to say, but this really can work for us."

"I hear what you're saying, Claire," offered Debbie, one of the organisation's early members, "but we still must look out for our people in Costa Rica and in Japan. It's become just too dangerous for them."

"Debbie's right," agreed another director. "We should close those two operations, at least temporarily, to let the dust settle."

"I couldn't disagree more," Claire stated bluntly. "If we run away now, we'll never go back, and the bad guys win. I think that we should ask our teams in the field what they think and then, if they want to pull out, so be it. But first let me go and talk to them and see more specifically what we're up against."

"That's all well and good, Claire," said Debbie testily, "but with all due respect, you're not experienced in the field, and these guys play rough. Our people aren't trained to handle such pressure, nor, I might add, should they be expected to handle it."

"Well, in case you hadn't noticed, Debbie, I play even rougher," Claire replied frostily. "So, let me go and see what's happening before you make any final decisions, alright?"

"Okay, okay, let's all calm down," interjected Chuck. "I don't see that a few days will make much difference and, in the meantime, we'll instruct the teams to keep a low profile. Claire can assess the local situations and report back to us, after which we'll decide. Is that okay with everyone?"

Following a chorus of assent, they reached the final agenda item, the appointment of a new chairman. Earlier, suggestions had surfaced that Claire should assume the mantle, more in an honorary role, because of her father. She had dispelled the notion straight away, stating rightly that the position required someone with the right experience and, in any case, she needed to be free to pursue other matters, about which she said little. With this clarified, there was no real contest, and Chuck Bailey was proposed, seconded and unanimously elected as the chairman and CEO.

*

After the meeting, Chuck took Claire out to Al Forno's, a nearby Italian restaurant where the NGO was well known. Over a glass of fine Amarone, Claire asked, "How do you manage to do all this bureaucratic meeting and organisation stuff, Chuck?"

"Every business or enterprise needs structure and organisation," he replied. "It's really no different from the army, if you think about it. There are the administrators and planners who dish out orders, and then the grunts carry them out. Some people do one thing better than others, and hopefully everyone finds the right fit."

For years, Chuck had known about Claire's association with the Armed Forces, but he never learned exactly what she did there, nor did anyone else at POSC, including her father. What she had accomplished in Hong Kong gave him a pretty good idea though, yet he did not pursue it.

"Well, I think it sucks," she said, just as a waiter placed a large bowl of steaming linguine carbonara in front of them to share. "But this food doesn't," she added with a grin. "It smells fabulous."

They tucked into their meal while Chuck explained the parameters and expectations for Claire's visits to the two projects. She now regarded those visits as a mission.

She would start in San Jose, Costa Rica, where POSC promoted an end to shark finning on both the Caribbean and Pacific coasts. It worked in close partnership with Bloom

Associates, a French NGO that also vigorously championed the cause.

Then Claire would fly to Tokyo and visit the project base at Taiji in Wakayama Prefecture, some 600 kilometres southwest of the capital. There, along with tracking the movements of Japan's whaling fleets, the NGO also monitored the grotesque annual dolphin cull, teaming with the well-established Project Dolphin organisation. She'd submit reports as she went, with observations and recommendations as appropriate.

"I want to pop into Hong Kong afterwards since I'll be in that neck of the woods," said Claire. "If that's a problem with expenses, I'll cover it myself," she added, seeing the astonished look on Chuck's face.

"It's not the expenses I'm worried about, Claire," he said. "I think it's a bit soon to show your face there. The triads are unforgiving, and they don't need especially long memories to remind them about someone of interest, namely you."

"They don't frighten me," she said defiantly.

"Well, they damn well should, young lady," replied Chuck with untypical heat. "You may think you can look after yourself with all that kung-fu stuff or whatever, but these people are not to be messed with at all. Do you understand me?"

"Got it," Claire replied calmly, "but I'm still going, Chuck, with or without your blessing." With a lopsided grin, she mysteriously added, "There are some people I want to look up, and I never did say goodbye properly to my university pals when I dropped out of the course."

Resignedly, Chuck said, "Well, I can't stop you, but please be careful. POSC couldn't survive the loss of another Armstrong, and frankly, neither could I." By this point, his eyes glistened with unshed tears at thoughts of his friend and colleague, Claire's father.

She placed a hand on one of his before saying gently, "Don't worry, Chuck. I'll be fine."

Claire poured the remains of the wine bottle's contents into their glasses. Raising her drink, she proposed a toast. "To POSC," she said. "Cheers, Chuck."

"Cheers, Claire," he said quietly. "To POSC, but just take care, d'you hear?"

Chapter 9

Claire's Induction Trip – Costa Rica

As the sun dipped below the horizon, an old Grady-White Marlin 280 fishing boat made its weary way past the smart Marina Pez Vela in Quepos on Costa Rica's Pacific coast. It headed into a creek to the north, passing the fine hotels and restaurants sprouting up to welcome a newly discovered tourism industry. Chugging slowly up the channel for a few kilometres, the boat finally reached its destination, the fish-processing facility of Pescaderia La Cristal.

The old man and two younger crewmen on board had endured a long and hard 10 days. Relieved to be back, they tied up alongside the dock to unload their catch where people on several similar boats were in various stages of doing the same.

Some carried buckets full of sardines. Others offloaded larger fish, snapper and wahoo being the most common. An occasional roosterfish could be seen and even the odd small yellowfin tuna. But these fishing boats usually did not land the bigger game fish, like sailfish. Those were the realm of more well-to-do boat owners who managed game-fishing for the tourists.

No sooner did the newly arrived boat's crew members make fast to the dock when the dockside foreman marched over to inspect their catch. A brute of a man, he represented Barrio 18, the most prominent of the region's organised crime syndicates. Lagging behind on his quota this month, the foreman faced pressure from his boss in San Jose, so the burden inevitably passed onto the fishermen obliged to fish for special prey.

At last, the gangster smiled at what he saw, for this boat's catch would not go for local consumption. Instead it would be packed up and sent halfway across the world.

The old man gave the foreman a worn, but satisfied, smile. Having made up the shortfall on this trip, maybe now the old man and his crewmates could take a break. They had set off 10 days ago for Cocos Island, some 550 kilometres to the southwest. Cocos was designated a National Park and the waters surrounding it a protected marine-conservation area. Fish of all descriptions thrived there, including nine species of sharks. It took three days to get there, but the pickings were rich. In the ensuing few days, they had hooked and finned no less than 17 sharks.

After drawing each of the thrashing, rearing and snapping sharks alongside the boat, the two younger lads had the dangerous task of leaning over the side with long machetes and chopping as quickly as they could at the fins. The near-side pectoral fin wasn't difficult to chop off, but the outside one involved high risk. With those removed, a shark's ability to balance in the water suffered, and removal of the dorsal fin became easier.

The severed fins all needed catching before they sank. The old man would reach out into the water with a net at the end of a long pole and land the precious limbs. In doing so, he made sure to avoid the wild and flailing creature's deadly jaws and thrashing tail.

They also would try to hack off that caudal (tail) fin since it was the most valuable fin of all. But because it was the hardest to remove, they often failed to catch it. The larger species also had secondary dorsal and pelvic fins to remove. With luck, they could cut six fins plus the tail from a large shark.

Their biggest catch had been a tiger shark. That one gave them a bloody and bruising fight, and it took them more than an hour to render it fully helpless. After the last fin had been hacked off, the wretched creature was cut free and, totally unable to propel itself, slowly sank as prey for other predators before it drowned.

They also caught several scalloped hammerheads and a rare Galapagos shark. The others had been smaller blacktip and whitetip reef sharks.

All considered, they had made a good haul. After cleaning up their bloody and foul-smelling boat somewhat, the two lads set off for a bar and some well-earned beers. The old fisherman sauntered home to sleep.

*

Following nearly 15 hours inside packed airplanes and cramped economy seats, with just a brief leg-stretch in Miami, Claire finally reached San Jose, Costa Rica. Despite the early-morning hour, she was met at the airport by the local head of POSC, a pleasant and softly spoken, middle-aged Canadian woman named Gaby Saunders. Gaby had been with the NGO since the beginning, and her quiet demeanour masked a valuable role as a very determined and able trooper.

Considering Claire's short stay, Gaby suggested that they visit Quepos on the Pacific coast straight away to scout out the area where much of the shark finning activity happened. "You won't witness much, I'm afraid, but at least you'll get a sense of the place," she told her guest. Claire readily agreed.

After a quick shower and a change of clothes for Claire at her hotel, the two women left on a two-and-a-half-hour drive to the coast. On the way, Gaby briefed Claire about the work the POSC team did in Costa Rica.

"Essentially, we monitor the shark finning, counting boats and the people involved, catches if we can, that sort of thing," she explained. "Officially, shark finning is banned here, but nobody seems to take any notice. It's a seriously dangerous country with drug cartels, from Mexico to the north and Panama to the south, controlling everything. They use Costa Rica as a drug-trafficking staging post. Since there's no effective law enforcement here, they do pretty much whatever they like. I tell you, Claire, we need to be very careful here."

Claire sensed the tension in her host, so she asked about the threats and beatings some members of the POSC team had received.

"Maybe the latest incidents weren't as bad as they sounded," Gaby said. "But the thing is that the levels of violence here generally are unimaginable. We have more rapes, kidnappings and killings than almost anywhere else on earth. If the gangs thought we really interfered in any way with their activities, we'd be dead meat."

"But I assume that would be true only if you interfered with their drug trafficking," said Claire. "Surely, shark finning doesn't attract the same level of attention."

Gaby smiled resignedly. "After Spain, Costa Rica is probably the world's biggest supplier of fins. It's a huge business here. Remember, we have two seas. Limon, in the east, handles finning from the Caribbean, and Quepos, where we're going now, is the centre for the Pacific. Both places control huge fleets of boats, and the slaughter runs rampant."

"And this is all controlled by the cartels?" Claire asked.

"Here, it's one main player, Barrio 18. Its people are utterly ruthless, and we take great care not to cross them. Apparently, they recently executed a group of fishermen in Limon for failing to reach their fin quotas. You know what they did? They took the fishermen out to sea and hacked off their arms before throwing them overboard. They let one guy live so he could tell the other fishermen what happened."

Claire was not easily shocked, but that story appalled her. "My God, that's terrible."

"The biggest difficulty for fishermen on the Caribbean side is that they've killed so many sharks that the numbers are seriously dwindling, especially for the once-common Caribbean reef sharks and even tiger sharks. So the fishermen face big problems getting their quotas, and when they fail, they're in serious trouble."

Claire had thought she knew all about shark finning. But she rapidly realised that the problem was much bigger than she ever imagined.

"What are we actually going to do in Quepos?" she asked.

"We'll pose like a couple of tourists at the fish market on the docks where they land their catches. A little farther along is where the finning boats dock, and we'll play it by ear and see what we can." Gaby looked over at Claire and asked, "That alright with you?"

"Sure, but I'd like to see a bit more than that," Claire said, starting to feel slightly testy. "Where do they take the fins? What happens to them after they're landed and counted? How about that sort of thing? There's not much point in me being here if all I see is just a quayside."

"Honestly, Claire, it's much too dangerous to start poking around. I just want to show you the scene so that you get a flavour of the place."

"Okay, I understand," replied Claire stubbornly. "Let's see what happens when we're there."

The pair lapsed into silence. Gaby worried that Claire could get them into serious trouble, while Claire thought about being somewhat more adventurous than her host wanted.

Finally, they came into Quepos and parked at the Bahia Azul, a small restaurant near the fish-processing quayside where Gaby seemed to be no stranger. She was known to come to Quepos from time to time, ostensibly to do some game-fishing, and she was warmly welcomed, as was her friend. They ate an indifferent lunch and then wandered off towards the Pescaderia La Cristal.

The quayside resembled such places worldwide. Fishing boats of various sizes came and went, unloading their catches and then casting off to make room for others. On land, workers sorted the catches by size and type, weighing the fish, placing them in large, open, plastic containers and covering them with crushed ice. Other workers transported the fish to a warehouse, presumably to be packed up and trucked off to fill orders. Fishing-industry officials recorded the catches from the boats and credited the skippers accordingly. There seemed to be nothing untoward.

"Where are the fins?" demanded Claire.

"You see that tatty building farther up the quayside," said Gaby, indicating it with her head. "That's where they're landed and processed. I see a few sport-fishing boats alongside, so probably they're unloading a catch now."

"Let's go take a look," said Claire, walking in the direction of the building.

"For Christ's sake, Claire, didn't you hear what I've been saying?" hissed Gaby angrily. "Nobody is allowed too near the place. Do you see those two thugs by the dockside and that big bastard near the building? They won't take kindly to you poking your nose in there. Do you understand?"

Claire looked at Gaby, realising that she could not expect her companion to come with her. "I'll meet you back at the restaurant, Gaby," she said kindly. "But I've come a long way to investigate this problem, and I need to get up close and personal with these characters. Don't worry. I can look after myself, but it would be best if you stayed out of it. Besides, if I get stuck, I'll need you to call in the cavalry."

Claire grinned, but Gaby appeared unamused, so before the Canadian woman could respond, Claire marched off towards the building. As she approached it, the big man saw her and started walking towards her, shouting something and gesturing with his hands for her to go away. Claire continued walking, keeping watch on the two men by the dockside, who now looked up to see what was happening. As the big man came closer, Claire took in his battered and scarred features. He was about two metres tall, thickset and had a huge waist around which a large, leather belt held a long filleting knife. His ragged T-shirt did little to hide several scars and tattoos, and his shaven scalp, above a much-broken nose, topped off a look of thorough nastiness.

The other two characters were leaner and smaller, but equally piratical in appearance. They too carried knives, and before they turned toward her, Claire noticed that one of them also had a pistol tucked into his jeans at the small of his back.

Claire kept striding towards the big man, who still shouted at her, and shrugged her shoulders in a helpless gesture of not understanding him. "I'm a tourist," she explained. "Do you speak English?"

"You not allowed here. Go away, stupid tourist bitch," he bellowed in broken English, seemingly incapable of speaking normally. The other two men now moved to join the bellowing giant. Fishermen on the boats stopped what they were doing and watched the scene unfold.

"I'm sorry," said Claire with a lopsided smile. "I think I'm lost. Can you help me?"

The big man stopped just in front of her and turned to his colleagues, all of them now with lecherous grins on their faces. "Oh, you lost, huh?" he shouted. "Okay, we can help. You come with us."

As he spoke, he grabbed Claire by her shirt and pulled her forward. Claire put on a frightened face.

The other two men came closer. Claire needed them altogether. "Please," she pleaded, "let me go."

"Sure thing, tourist bitch, we let you go afterwards," replied the brute. He laughed coarsely as he started to drag Claire towards the building.

As the other two thugs came alongside, leering in anticipation, Claire suddenly straightened, grabbed the man's hand holding her shirt and brought her other arm around in a stiff clubbing movement that snapped the brute's arm with a loud crack. As he roared in pain, she chopped him hard in the throat. He sank to the ground, gasping for air through a shattered windpipe.

The other two were taken completely by surprise. Before the man with the gun knew what was happening, he took a massive kick to his crotch followed by an open-handed uppercut to his face, and he doubled over, falling unconscious to the deck. The third man pulled his knife and jumped back out of the mad woman's reach. He swapped the knife between his hands, back and forth, hoping to confuse his opponent before striking, but he never had the chance. Claire moved at lightning speed onto her left foot and delivered a powerful right-leg kick straight to the man's chest. He flew backwards and crumpled, the air knocked out of him.

Quickly, Claire looked around for any other threats. She discounted the fishermen, who simply stared at her, their mouths open in amazement. Seeing no more danger, she removed the weapons from her attackers and then bent over the man she'd kicked. He clearly had suffered some broken ribs and gasped for breath.

"Where are the fins?" she asked quietly. The thug was no hero and did not need to be overly bright to understand what Claire asked. With difficulty, he pointed at the warehouse. Claire moved behind him and locked his neck in a vice-like grip, squeezing until he passed out. Then she approached the two fishing boats ready to ask the same question. But there was no need since the decks of both boats were covered in baskets of fins.

"Throw them overboard," she ordered, pointing.

When nothing happened, she repeated her order, this time more loudly and accompanied by more gestures and waving the pistol. Language posed no barrier, and the fishermen obeyed, muttering as they threw their precious cargoes overboard.

Claire turned and headed for the building. It was only one storey high and not large. Finding the door open, she entered. An awful smell of decaying fish assailed her nostrils. Suppressing a gag, she toured the dimly lit interior, seeing all the usual clutter and paraphernalia found in fishing warehouses everywhere. There were old nets and coils of rope, broken and rotted oars, an upturned rowboat, pots of paint and brushes, jerry cans of diesel and petrol, and a long workbench covered in old rags and odd tools. But standing in the middle of the warehouse were several sealed crates, each about a cubic metre in size. There were also some empty ones with lids to the side.

Claire found a claw hammer and jacked open a crate to discover inside a bunch of tightly packed and partially dried shark fins. They smelled terrible.

Continuing her inspection and finding little else of interest, Claire climbed a set of rickety wooden stairs at the far end of the room that led out onto a flat roof. What she saw there revolted her. Laid out across the entire surface were rows and rows of shark fins. Hundreds of them were drying in the sun.

Stunned and appalled at the implications of her discovery, Claire was damned if the people responsible for slaying so many wonderful creatures would profit from their prizes. She climbed back down to the ground floor and grabbed a jerry can full of petrol. Looking around, she also found a box of matches and a Zippo lighter beside a half-full packet of cigarettes.

Returning to the roof, she showered many of the fins with petrol, emptying the entire jerry can on them. Then, standing ready at the top of the stairs, she applied the lighter to a rag and threw the burning cloth out onto the roof.

Fire spread fast as Claire descended the stairs. She hurriedly spilled some diesel onto the crates and, after igniting them too, this time with the matches, she hastily retreated from the burning building.

In nearly no time, angry flames consumed the entire structure. Thick, black smoke billowed into the clear afternoon sky.

As Claire considered her next move, she heard a truck speeding towards the building and realised it was time to escape while she still could. Looking around, she noticed that one boat had departed, but a fisherman on the other was just casting off, so she dashed forward and jumped onto the boat's deck, just as it left the quayside. Brandishing the gun, she told the boatman to move them away quickly, and then she crouched below the level of the boat's side. Disinclined to argue, the fisherman put the throttle down.

As they sped away from the quay, an open Toyota Land Cruiser skidded to a halt near the burning warehouse, disgorging a team of armed men. From the front of the vehicle, a tall man stepped out carrying a small automatic machine gun. Grimly, he observed the fire and the three men sprawled nearby. As the area gang chief, or *capo*, he gave terse orders for his newly arrived men to fan out and check the vicinity before attending to their fallen colleagues.

There appeared unlikely to be any clues about the attackers and arsonists until the injured men revived and could be questioned. The *capo* needed to be patient, not something that came easily to him. Definitely, he didn't believe the frantic fisherman who had called in to alert him because a lone woman could not possibly cause all this mayhem.

With a loud roar and a final blast of fire and sparks, the warehouse collapsed. There would be some very unhappy people in San Jose when the *capo* reported the loss of property and merchandise, something he did not look forward to doing.

*

Claire and her reluctant companion travelled fast down the creek. Shortly after passing Bahia Azul, she saw the outer arm of a marina ahead. Using words and gestures, she told the fisherman to take her into the main marina basin.

There were few sailing boats, the moorings being mainly occupied by launches and large motor yachts. A sign proclaimed the presence of a harbour office at the land end of a long pontoon, so Claire directed her host there and jumped off.

As soon as she landed, the fisherman reversed, turned his boat and quickly fled.

Claire opened her mobile phone and called Gaby, who was sitting and fretting at the bar in Bahia Azul, as instructed. When her phone rang, she was pondering the likelihood of Claire's connection to a huge pall of smoke visible in the direction of the quay and wondering what to do. Claire explained where she was, telling Gaby to come quickly and fetch her.

Without delay, Gaby arrived, and Claire hopped into the car, ordering a hasty drive out of town. As they departed, Claire insisted on taking a different route. "I don't want to go anywhere near the way we came in here. I'll explain later." Then she lapsed into silence, repeatedly peering out the windows for any signs of pursuit.

Although relieved to see Claire still in one piece, Gaby felt alarmed by the terse instructions and what they must mean. Still, she obeyed, and soon they motored along a longer route back to the capital, heading initially southeast before taking a loop and continuing towards San Jose, arriving back at Claire's hotel just after dark.

Over drinks in the hotel bar, Claire explained what she had seen and done about it. She didn't elaborate on how she had "persuaded" the guards to allow her access to the building, just that she had taken decisive action. She advised Gaby to stay well clear of Quepos for a while.

Gaby needed no second bidding. The next morning, she drove her mystifying guest back to the airport. Claire had not even seen the NGO's local offices, nor met the other staff member.

Chapter 10

"Black Diamonds" and Beyond the Cove

From the public viewing balcony, Kage Kuraim quietly watched preparations for the auction. It was the beginning of the New Year, and the annual tuna auction for 2019 was about to unfold in Tokyo's vast new fish market at Toyuso. The catches diminished year-on-year, especially for bluefin tuna, now officially an endangered species. Both the quantity of catches and the sizes of individual fish trended smaller, but Kuraim still hoped for better auction results than last year.

Adeptly, Kuraim had fought his way up through the ranks of the Yamaguchi-gumi, Japan's largest Yakuza "family". Then in a rare move within such a disciplined and structured organisation, he had split away to become the *komicho*, or syndicate boss, of his own more dangerous and harmful crime family, known and feared as Boryokudan. His reputation grew, and soon he challenged his former family for territory and influence within Japan and beyond. Japan's vast whaling and other fishing industries were the most recent activities to fall under his sphere of control. Naturally, Demesne assisted in his extraordinary rise to power.

To the auctioneers, the bidders and the viewing and consuming public, it was a matter of complete indifference that they contributed to exterminating one of the largest and most powerful fish in the oceans. Pacific bluefin tuna teetered on the brink of extinction, and yet the fishing fleets, extolled by their syndicate masters, hunted down the creatures wherever possible. Spotter planes searched the known migration routes of the once massive shoals and summoned fishing vessels with powerful engines to move neatly onto the paths of the great fish.

The deceased creature now going under the hammer was slightly smaller and lighter than last year's record-breaking fish, this one weighing in at 278 kilograms, but the bidding climbed steadily. It was less about size and quantity than about the kudos and the wonderful ensuing publicity to promote the successful bidder's sushi-restaurant chain. Indeed, the final bid set a new record with the hammer falling at the equivalent of US$3.1 million for that single great fish.

Hearing the impressive price, Kuraim smiled happily to Rai, his *saiko komon* or deputy. As a man of exalted rank and position, Kuraim could look forward to being offered the first taste of this so-called "Black Diamond", the giant fish with a huge value.

*

Among the tourists on the balcony, another person watched the sale without smiling. She felt disgusted by the whole spectacle, not only by the sight of the specific fish just auctioned, but also by the many hundreds of no-less-impressive giant creatures still waiting to sell.

Claire turned to her companion and said, "Come on. Let's go. I've seen enough."

Having left Costa Rica, Claire had flown to Tokyo where the head of POSC in Japan had whisked her straight from the airport to the fish market. "If we bustle, we should just make it," declared John Teach, a dark-bearded and rugged campaigner with many years of experience with Greenpeace.

Now in his fifties, Teach had lived life at the sharp end, first with the British Army and then Special Forces and afterwards in ocean conservation. His legendary escapades on the high seas, coupled with his swarthy appearance, inspired his friends to nickname him "Blackbeard" after the infamous pirate.

Word of Claire's fiery "incident" in Costa Rica had travelled ahead of her, along with the stories from earlier in Hong Kong. So Teach looked forward to spending time with someone he regarded as a true kindred spirit. "Well, if you didn't like the auction, you'll really hate the rest of our tour," he said.

As they approached the main exit-gate, a group of about 10 men pushed through the departing crowds, clearing a path for two other men strolling nonchalantly through the masses of people. Initial shouts of indignant protest abruptly fell silent when the remonstrators saw who it was, and the privileged pair passed through the parting melee quite untroubled.

"Who is that?" asked Claire, as she followed Teach out onto the pavement.

"That's Kage Kuraim and his sidekick, Rai," replied her guide. "They're unruly brutes with whom even you don't want to tangle."

"I'm intrigued," said Claire, grinning mischievously. "Can you introduce me?"

"Very funny," Teach retorted, "and no, I can't. Kuraim leads the Boryokudan, the nastiest of all the Yakuza syndicates in Japan, and believe me, that's quite an achievement."

"Then what's he doing here?" she asked.

"Among many interests, he controls all the rackets associated with Japanese whaling and fisheries. He'll take a large cut out of all the tuna sales today, and I mean that financially as well as on a dinner plate."

"Does he also control the dolphin cull at Taiji?" queried Claire threateningly.

"Absolutely, so when we get there, we'll observe only, okay?"

"What's the point of simply watching dolphins get slaughtered?" she asked. "We already know it happens. It's about time to do something about it."

"You're right, of course," replied Teach as they approached his car. "But to be blunt, Claire, and if you'll excuse the expression, 'You can't fart against thunder'. The only way we'll ever get things to change here is through the force of public opinion."

This brought the first big smile that Teach had seen from Claire, and they both relaxed as they set off for a long drive to the coast. Initially, she'd wanted to fly to Taiji to save time, but he had persuaded her that the seven-hour car ride would allow him more time to brief her on the many issues that POSC faced in Japan, including keeping tabs on the relatively small, but highly active, whaling fleet, so she'd acquiesced.

*

Years before, POSC had purchased a cottage in Taiji on a hill overlooking the harbour and near the notorious bay where a cruel annual hunt of some of the planet's most sentient and sensitive creatures happens. Hundreds of dolphins are trapped and caught, then either sold for use in amusement parks or slaughtered for their meat. Fishermen, or more appropriately, dolphin hunters, "drive" the mammals to their capture or deaths using physical violence and tortuous acoustic techniques designed to confuse the aquatic creatures.

The cottage served as POSC's Japanese headquarters and as home to a small, impassioned team working there. Claire had arrived more than halfway through the culling season, which typically began in September and ran until the end of February. It was dark when she and Teach reached the cottage, so not until morning, after a jet-lagged, sleepless night, did she see the town and its infamous bay.

There seemed to be activists and protesters everywhere. They appeared in the streets waving placards, on the water in all sizes of boats adorned with banners and as close as they could get to the harbour facilities. Almost in equal numbers was a formidable police presence, tasked to preserve the local fishing community's rights to go about its fearsome, yet lawful, business.

Although Claire knew beforehand what to expect, she watched in horror as the awful events unfolded before her eyes. The dolphins, of all species, faced ongoing harassment and abuse, being chased, injured, run over, manhandled, dragged alive and taken captive or slaughtered. Entire pods of dolphins were decimated. Frames, with tarpaulins strung between them, were positioned in the water, under which the creatures were dragged to be killed or captured. There were "banger" poles around the mouth of the cove, which when hit created underwater noises to confuse and frighten the dolphins, making them more pliable to direct to the waiting nets, tarpaulins and harpoon-and-hook-wielding fishermen.

The dolphins caught alive would be supplied to marine parks and aquariums, satiating people's appetites for dolphin shows. Many would die in transit and others surrender the will to live in captivity, leading to sad and solitary deaths in the aquatic theme parks. The freshly killed ones would be packed, frozen and sent to Japanese fish markets, while some of the meat filled the ice-covered slabs of local stores. And all the while, dolphin hunters worked alongside dolphin trainers, a bizarre alliance of one group aiming to kill and another to capture.

Perhaps the most-terrible sight of all was the bright-red colour of the sea there, the natural blue replaced by the rich red life-blood of so many slaughtered animals. Claire had seen more than her fair share of blood-letting and brutality, but this reached an altogether different scale and against innocent, intelligent creatures. She turned away from the scene, sickened to her core and feeling helpless, at least momentarily, to do anything about it.

*

"We can't just sit here and let all this happen," Claire forcefully told members of the POSC team gathered around their kitchen table. "We have to do something."

The group consisted of Teach, a young Japanese woman called Namika, whose petite physique, yet determined countenance, perfectly complemented her boss, and two younger campaigners, students, scheduled to spend six months collecting data in Taiji.

"Just what do you have in mind?" asked Namika. "So many people participate in this massacre, which is legal actually, and the police protect them."

"We've debated this for years, Claire," added Teach. "As I told you, public-relations efforts are our best weapon."

"That hardly sounds like the 'Blackbeard', that scourge of whalers and the champion of oppressed sea creatures, about whom I've heard so much," replied Claire.

Her comment drew light laughs around the table and a shy grin from Teach. "Now that I think of it, Teach," Claire continued, gently jesting, "didn't you help to sink two whalers in Iceland away back in the 1980s?"

"That was a long time ago when I was little more than a kid, even before I joined the army," he said quietly. "This is very different."

"I disagree," said Claire, serious again. "Something always can be done, even if it's simply disruptive. Maybe we can't stop this awful slaughter in its tracks, but I'm sure as hell going to guarantee that this year gets noticed as a turning point and is never forgotten."

They juggled ideas for a while, getting nowhere. Finally, Claire rose from her chair and said that she needed some fresh air, asking Teach to join her. Once they stood outside together, she told him that she needed for him to acquire a few useful items by nightfall, all inoffensive in themselves and easily available.

"I don't know what you have in mind, Claire," said Teach suspiciously, "but you really must watch out, you know. This place isn't lawless like Costa Rica. You need to be careful."

Claire simply smiled. "Don't you worry, John. Just get me those things that I need, and I'll do the rest."

As an afterthought, she added, "While you're at it, d'you think you could get one of those kids in there to book me on an early flight out of here tomorrow morning, going to Hong Kong via Tokyo?"

"From what I know about you, that's probably a good idea," Teach said. "There's an early flight at seven o'clock, that suit you?"

"Perfect," she said. "Now I'm going to scout around the town, so I'll see you later."

Watching her depart, Teach felt both apprehensive and exhilarated. Perhaps this sort of thing was exactly what they needed here.

Chapter 11

Claire Goes on the Offensive in Taiji

Among all the skills that Claire had developed during her time with the SBS, one at which she excelled was the ability to irreparably damage all types of watercraft, from small run-arounds to spy-ships posing as trawlers, right up to submarines and battleships. She just needed the right equipment, plenty of guile, a good plan and adequate luck.

Understandably, "the right equipment" was not all readily available in Taiji. Pistols and machine guns, let alone limpet mines and high explosives, did not sell at local hardware stores. In fact, Claire knew that Japan had some of the world's strictest gun laws, which was why she didn't even suggest to Teach that he try to buy weapons. He might have refused anyway, she thought with a smile. However, the vessels in Taiji's fishing fleet ranged from small, open-topped fishing boats to ocean-going trawlers, so Claire would improvise. The presence of a much larger vessel tied up alongside the outer harbour also had given her an idea.

When Teach returned with the goods that Claire had requested, he confronted her, insisting in no uncertain terms that whatever she planned to do, he was going along. At first she remonstrated with him, but soon realised it was futile. Blackbeard aimed to reclaim his reputation, and no slip of a girl would stop him. So Claire gave in, actually quite glad for his support. She told him the details of her plan and, after discussing it for a while, with Teach adding some useful amendments and refining it with her, they settled on a final strategy.

At two in the morning, they left the cottage, both dressed entirely in black and with balaclavas to pull on later. Each wore a backpack stuffed with some of Teach's purchases, plus a few extra items that he deemed useful. On rubber-soled trainers, they stepped silently into the night.

*

Taiji is a small fishing town with a permanent population of about 5,000 people. This grows considerably during the dolphin culls, the numbers swelled by domestic tourists sympathetic to the fishing practices, by protesters who are not, by police and other security personnel and by fishermen from elsewhere along the coast. Then there are the gang members, representing the interests of their bosses and ensuring that all appropriate dues find their way into the *komicho's* coffers.

The harbour faces east, protected by two stout overlapping walls. These, in turn, are guarded from the Pacific by a headland that curves from the mainland to the northeast. Three separate wharves jut out within the harbour walls, the outer one being the deepest and providing for bigger fishing vessels, through to the shallow inner wharf where small, open fishing boats tie up. As usual at this time of year, more than 200 boats of assorted sizes filled the harbour.

But the vessel that most interested Claire and Teach was a large, rusting hulk of a ship that Claire had noticed earlier, tied up on the southern side of the outer harbour, facing out to sea. Clearly, it wasn't part of the dolphin cull, and Teach had explained its history and presence.

At 143 metres long and weighing 8,725 tons, the *Hiyo Maru* once was the largest ship in Japan's whaling fleet, carrying fuel and resources while providing stock-storage space. In 1992, it was renamed and reflagged to Panama, but a dispute sent it back to Japan. After serving again, this time strictly as a fuel tanker for Japan's smaller whalers, it allegedly sold for scrap years ago. Yet here it was in Taiji and, according to Teach, still in service. To Claire, it looked perfect.

*

Along the well-lit waterfront, police officers patrolled, albeit somewhat drowsily at this time of night. A few lights shone from some of the bigger boats, their owners and crews living aboard at this busy time. Various all-night café-bars housed members of the Yakuza gangs, who took rooms where they could find them and local call girls to share them. Claire planned to visit a few of these mobsters first, for she needed weapons.

Crossing a small car park, Claire and Teach approached from behind the hostelry they had selected. It resembled a North American motel with a parking bay fronting each room. They waited in the shadows, listening and watching one particular unit that showed a light behind drawn curtains. Clearly, an intense party was underway because they heard a mixture of music, laughter, unintelligible guttural grunts and cries of apparent pleasure from more than one female voice.

The plan was to make a forcible entry and knock senseless any males they saw, silencing them and anyone else who made a sound. They would gag and secure everyone present before searching for available weapons. From the noises, they anticipated at least two males and probably two females. The raiders each carried a short wooden club.

Donning the balaclavas, they readied themselves at the door, counted down from three and then, with a hard, coordinated kick from each of them, broke in the door to find a frenzied scene. Two couples were intertwined, moaning to a rhythm on a double bed, the men heavily tattooed and the women not much less so. Seated beside the bed, semi-naked and with bottles of beer in hand, were two other men, apparently encouraging and extolling the four love-makers to greater heights of athleticism and gratification. Sweet and pungent smoke lingered in the air, and the combined smell of drugs, beer and sex hung heavily. The room's occupants, with their senses dulled by alcohol and marijuana, had not anticipated an assault.

One couple continued on, oblivious to the interruption, while the other paused and unravelled, curiously looking up at the intruders. A seated man sprang up in surprise, stumbled over his equally intoxicated colleague, and they both sprawled to the floor just as Claire reached them and chopped the first fellow hard behind an ear. She reached behind the second man and squeezed his neck until he joined his companion unconscious on the floor.

Meanwhile, Teach moved to the bed and clubbed both men there on the backs of their heads. One woman started to scream, but Claire quickly rendered her senseless and silent. The remaining female looked shaken, but stayed quiet, struggling to pull a sheet over her nakedness.

Teach looked outside, but they seemed not to have alerted anyone, so he returned, pushing the broken door shut. Reaching into their backpacks, they first removed some cable ties to act as PlastiCuffs to immobilise and restrain everyone. Then they produced cloth gags and, after stuffing these into their prisoners' mouths, taped them in place with wide packing tape.

With everyone quietly secured, Claire and Teach searched the room for weapons and were not disappointed. They found three Smith and Wesson M&P 9mm semi-automatic pistols and two Kel-Tec PLR-16s, dangerous 30-round semi-automatics. Both weapon varieties were popular among the Yakuza, who smuggled large quantities into Japan from the US mainland via Hawaii. Along with the guns were several knives, unremarkable in themselves but lethal in the hands of these street thugs, a pair of knuckle-dusters and a two-handled cheese wire, probably used as a garrotte. What a bunch of charmers we have here, thought Claire.

Two of the mobsters began to revive as Claire and Teach piled the weapons into their backpacks. After looking around the room one last time, the two conservationists quietly departed.

*

Avoiding detection, the stealthy prowlers crept silently at almost three o'clock into the shadows of the wharf where the *Hiyo Maru* was moored. No lights were visible on the ship, and Teach confirmed that he seldom saw any signs of life aboard. Still, at least they were armed now and ready for anyone inclined to impede their plans.

A ropy, old gangway suspended above the quay hinted that maybe someone was aboard. Otherwise how could it be lowered again? They studied the length of the ship, finally deciding that the best way aboard would be to climb up a mooring line, something that posed no problem for Claire, but would take the older Teach considerably more effort.

Claire went first, quickly scaling the thick rope and climbing over the gunwale. She squatted down and looked around to make sure she had not been seen. Then she waved for Teach to follow and kept a constant check on the surroundings as he laboured, struggling up the line. He finally made it, panting and sweating despite the cool air.

"I'm getting too old for this," he quietly exclaimed.

"Nonsense," whispered Claire. "Now let's search this place before we try to start the engines. We don't want any surprises."

Although the *Hiyo Maru* dwarfed most other whalers that Teach ever had visited, the layout and design were similar for reasons of function, so he led the way to what he expected would be the crew's quarters. It was very dark, but their strong torches provided enough illumination. They found a mess hall and a squalid kitchen adjoining it, both littered with dishes, pots and pans, discarded mugs and mostly empty bottles of spirits and beer. Passing through, they reached a narrow corridor from which sprouted the crew's berths, all apparently empty.

Just as they opened the last door, a light switched on and a gravelly voice challenged them in heavily accented, parrot English. "Who the fuck you? Me no' tol' anyone com' fo' one mo' week."

Raising their pistols in alarm, they spun around to see a dirty, pot-bellied and greasy little man, wearing filthy shorts and a vest, standing in the passageway. Certainly not Japanese, he still looked Asian and, from his speech, Claire surmised that he could be a Filipino.

Seeing the weapons, the little man raised his arms, stammering, "Don' s-s-shoo', don' shoo'."

Relaxing, Claire approached the man and lowered her weapon. "It's okay. We're not going to hurt you," she said calmly. "Please put your hands down, and let's talk. Do you understand me?"

The man did understand, for he lowered his arms and asked, "Wha' you wan'?" Puzzlement replaced his initial fear.

"Is there anyone else aboard?" asked Claire briskly.

"No, jus' me," he replied.

"Let's go into the mess," suggested Claire, "and we can talk, okay?"

"Okay, we talk in mess," agreed the man, and turning, he led the way back to the mess hall. Teach, meanwhile, remained tense from the unexpected encounter and followed, his gun still raised.

They all sat down, and it emerged that the man was the ship's chief engineer and, indeed, he did hail from the Philippines. Reeking of cheap whisky and gripping a large measure of it in a mug, he told his story.

He said that his name was Micky, and he had been living aboard the *Hiyo Maru* because he had nowhere else to go. But nowadays, he felt upset because the ship's Japanese owners were not paying him and, although there wasn't much work to do, he still felt entitled to something. He appeared to be a sad wreck of a man, bitter and lacking prospects.

Time elapsed, so Claire cut to the chase and told Micky what they intended to do. She felt sorry for him, but stressed that he was either with them or against them. He had to choose, and they needed to enact their plan.

"I guess all I go' to lose is my home," he said sadly, "but wha' the fuck? I don' owe the bastards anythin'. They owe me." He paused in contemplation before adding, "I'll help you."

"Good decision, Micky," said Claire. "Now how long before you can get the engines started?"

"It no' take lon'," replied Micky. "Maybe haf hour. You wait in brige, an' I call you."

They agreed that Teach would go to the engine room with Micky, partly to make sure that he did as he said and partly to find the ship's seacock valves. These turned out to be nearby and, when opened, permitted seawater to flow into the vessel.

Teach opened them fully and watched as the sea flooded in, reminding him of the time in Iceland when he and others from Greenpeace had done the same thing and sunk two whalers in Reykjavik before destroying a nearby whale-processing station. He wondered if tonight's adventure would stir up a similar firestorm and supposed that it would.

Claire found her way to the bridge and soon familiarised herself with the layout. She tried an experimental communication exchange with the engine room and, satisfied that everything worked despite being rather decrepit, waited while keeping a close watch for any unwelcome visitors to the wharf.

After almost 45 minutes, a bell sounded, and Claire answered instantly. The engines were ready to start, so she told Teach to go on deck to cut the mooring lines. Then she and Micky commenced the tricky process of preparing to move the ship carefully away from the quayside.

"Start her up, Chief," Claire instructed the engineer. Within seconds, a deep rumble began as the engines fired into life.

Teach slashed the forward mooring lines, allowing the ship's bow to drift slowly away from the side. He raced back to the stern mooring line and cut that too, just as Claire urged the engineer to go "slow ahead".

The *Hiyo Maru* vibrated and groaned as it reluctantly came under way, pointing towards the gap between the harbour walls. The incoming seawater had yet to cripple the ship's manoeuvrability, so Claire aimed the bow at the north harbour wall and ordered "full ahead".

Responding, the ship moved slowly at first, but then gathered momentum for its exceedingly brief and final journey. Moments later, the bow ploughed forcefully into the wall with fearful grinding and crashing noises, tearing metal and crumbling masonry.

All three people aboard had braced for the impact, but it still gave them a violent jolt. Claire maintained revs and steerageway, for now she sought to steer the vessel's stern to come around and wedge itself against the south harbour wall, creating an effective blockade. To her relief and satisfaction, the stern obeyed her instructions and quickly ground itself into the wall.

Being about 30 metres longer than the mouth of the harbour at its widest point, the ship created a perfect seal. Claire just needed to hold the vessel in position long enough for the seawater flooding in through the seacocks to assist with her plan. A substantial impact-driven hole in the bow just below the waterline hastened the flooding.

Claire tied the wheel in place just as she heard running footsteps. Teach appeared, shouting at her to leave the bridge and get off the ship. He was right, of course, so she followed him down to the main deck and started towards the bow.

Without houses on the north side of the harbour and with fewer patrols at the end of the quay, they had agreed earlier on this as an exit point. As anticipated, the south wharf now was abuzz with people, disturbed by the noises of the ship powering up and then crashing into the harbour wall. Sirens wailed. Public officials and curious citizens approached the crash site.

"Where's Micky?" Claire asked as she ran.

"He wanted to stay put in the engine room," replied Teach breathlessly, "but I persuaded him to at least come up on deck. The last I saw of him he was sitting in the stern holding a bottle of booze and singing to himself as the sea came in around him. I guess he'll simply float off, at least I hope so."

"Poor bugger," she said feelingly. "He's a sad little man."

*

With the bow sinking, now almost to the same height as the dock, it was an easy jump to reach dry land. Claire and Teach quickly scaled a low retaining wall and scrambled down the other side over the precast concrete blocks that formed the harbour wall's foundation. They slipped unobtrusively into the sea and began a long swim to a point a kilometre up the coast on the southern shore.

A few metres out, they dropped their backpacks. It wouldn't do to be caught with the guns and other items they had carried, which in the event had not been needed much anyway.

The water felt desperately cold, but they swam strongly and moved with purpose to a natural break in the rocky shoreline and the cliffs behind it. They landed and paused only briefly to catch their breath before cautiously climbing a pathway between the forested rocky bluffs. The top of the path emerged near a secondary coastal road that led into town, and they followed this route back to the POSC cottage.

A grey hint of the approaching dawn showed on the eastern horizon as they entered the quiet cottage. For the moment, its other occupants, all sound sleepers, remained none the wiser about what had transpired.

Claire took a quick, hot shower while Teach changed clothes and brewed some tea, preparing to drive her to the nearest airport. Gripping her carryall bag, Claire joined him in the kitchen, and they exchanged big grins.

"Well, Captain Blackbeard," she said, "I reckon we did a rather good job this morning." She raised her mug, and they toasted each other.

76

"I reckon you're right, Claire," acknowledged Teach. "That was bloody marvellous, and it will keep the boats locked in for ages. We just struck a big blow for the future of dolphins."

As they left the cottage, they could see the big ship wedged and sinking in the mouth of the small port. Crowds of onlookers still gathered to watch. Official blue lights flashed impotently as the authorities gazed helplessly at the wreck.

At the airport, Claire gave Teach a big hug. "Thank you, Blackbeard. I'll be seeing you," she said.

"Take care, lady. Do you hear me?" he replied. "This is a rough course you've set."

Claire just smiled and squeezed his arm. Then she walked purposefully to the airline check-in desk.

Chapter 12

Triads and Yakuza Lick Their Wounds

Bad news travels fast. Miguel Sanchez, the country head of Barrio 18 in Costa Rica, felt embarrassed and extremely anxious. Although the financial loss from the destruction of the shark fins at Quepos was not in itself so high, and certainly nothing to rival the massive revenues from his drug shipments in cooperation with the South American and Mexican cartels, the fact that it happened at all posed the problem. His men had been thumped and thwarted so easily that it caused a major loss of face. Enquiries had confirmed that, indeed, just one woman caused all the mayhem, which merely compounded the fragility of his position.

Already Sanchez lagged behind on his shark fin quotas from the Caribbean, and now his competence was being questioned from Hong Kong. The message conveyed by Winston Lau was clear. Barrio 18 in Costa Rica, and specifically its leader, needed to make up for the product loss and guarantee no more slip-ups. The consequences of failure needed no elaboration.

*

Another man feeling some unwelcome heat was Kage Kuraim's regional chief for the Wakayama Prefecture, who held responsibility to amass proceeds from the dolphin culls. After the incident in Taiji, the harbour was locked down and the entire fishing fleet unable to sail due to the wreck of the *Hiyo Maru* wedged firmly in its entrance. With the sunken keel steadfastly resting on the bottom and the decks and superstructure remaining above the high-water mark, not even the smallest boat could pass.

Some small fishing boats were lifted out of the inner harbour and transported overland to resume fishing from other towns. But they were too small and too few to continue effective culling operations on their own. Until the *Hiyo Maru* could be salvaged and lifted, there would be no more fishing from Taiji, let alone dolphin culling.

Protesters chanted and sang in jubilation. TV networks from around the world flocked to record the town's humiliation. Public opinion had never run stronger, and the entire event was hailed as a landmark victory for environmentalists. Nobody seemed to have been hurt, and the heroic perpetrators, whoever they were, remained a total mystery.

The Yakuza knew differently. After the four assaulted mobsters were found and released, a hunt began for the mysterious man and woman who had overpowered them so effortlessly, although it was reasonably assumed that the attackers had left the area, if not Japan. The gang members concerned then had to accept the usual harsh punishment meted out to those of the Yakuza who make a mistake. They all had to cut off one of their own fingers in front of their masters.

*

Inevitably, news of Claire's exploits reached the POSC headquarters in the UK and triggered rising levels of alarm. Contrary to her promises, the directors had heard nothing from her, and the trail of havoc floating in her wake troubled the NGO's leaders more than a little.

Soon after Claire left San Jose, Gaby had called in with details of what had happened in Costa Rica. Deeply distressed, she planned to suspend the NGO's local activities and temporarily close the local office. She reported that gang members from Barrio 18 had barged into the POSC office and trashed the place, roughing up the staff members and threatening her personally with unspecified consequences if they didn't stop their anti-shark-finning "propaganda". The gangsters lacked proof that the assaults on their men and the fire in Quepos were linked to the NGO. Otherwise their unpleasant visit would have been much worse.

Chuck Bailey had asked about police protection, but Gaby simply laughed, telling him that the police authorities were complicit with the crime syndicate and that no help could be expected from that quarter. Bailey reluctantly agreed with her decision and told her to pay off and release the local staff and for her to return to the UK.

A few days later, John Teach made contact from Taiji. He told Bailey about the sinking in the harbour, much of which the NGO chief executive already knew from TV news shows. Bailey asked how on earth that Claire had pulled off such an extraordinary assault, but Teach answered evasively, claiming that the perpetrators' identities remained unknown. Teach and his team had received a visit from police officers making general enquiries about the harbour incident, and later some other people, presumably Yakuza, had come by with similar questions. Both groups had continued on their way, none the wiser.

Teach turned increasingly defensive as Bailey asked him more questions about Claire. But he assured the UK-based leadership that everything was under control and that the POSC mission in Taiji remained operational. Bailey felt certain that Claire was behind the affair and that, in all likelihood, Teach had been too, given his past record for such reckless activities. Still, Teach was a valuable member of the POSC team so Bailey let it go.

Now Bailey urgently needed to speak to Claire, and he assumed that she was in Hong Kong.

*

The lady in question proved difficult to track down. Bailey had a mobile-phone number for Claire, but this never was answered, nor were the messages he left for her returned. He finally found her at her father's house, a place where he'd thought she never would want to return.

"You seem to have been busy, Claire," he said without preamble when they at last connected late one evening her time, Hong Kong being eight hours ahead of the UK.

"Actually, I seem to have spent most of my time on airplanes, Chuck. But I've had some interesting learning experiences," she replied.

"Oh, really, 'interesting learning experiences', were they?" he replied, exasperated. "Is that how you describe burning down a warehouse belonging to one dangerous criminal organisation and sinking a whaling ship, effectively halting an important income stream for another, not to mention beating up gang members of both mobs?"

Bailey ran out of breath and stopped talking. Had he been able to see Claire grinning mischievously at the other end of the conversation, he would have been apoplectic with fury.

"Come on now, Chuck, aren't those the sorts of things we're meant to do?" asked Claire, feigning innocence. "I thought that's what we environmentalists did."

"No, it bloody well isn't," shouted Bailey. "Confrontations happen sometimes, but it's the propaganda war that we're best equipped to fight. Swaying public opinion, peacefully protesting, petitioning institutions or governments, and working beside organisations like Avaaz, Project Dolphin, Bloom Associates and Greenpeace, those are our sorts of things. What you've done is much too dangerous and will get people killed."

"Well, I'm very sorry, Chuck," said Claire, "but I don't do peaceful protests. If you wait patiently for your messages to get heard and acted upon, there'll be nothing left alive in the oceans to save. So, I'm going after the ravaging bastards, with or without your help. If you can provide me with some backup and support, that's great. Otherwise, just stand aside and let me do things my way. Don't worry. I'll do nothing that links what I do to POSC."

Bailey calmed down and tried a different approach. "Claire, please listen to me. If this is about your father, I know he wouldn't want you to endanger your life to avenge him…."

"It's no longer about him, Chuck," she interrupted. "I've seen the results of this bloody finning. There are rooftops, mostly here in Hong Kong, covered in fins to dry out, thousands and thousands of them. You can keep talking to the Chinese authorities as much as you like, but by the time they get the message and understand the consequences, there won't be any sharks left. It's a similar story for whales and bluefin tunas, and so it goes. The only way to slow down the slaughter is forcefully."

"You don't need to lecture me," said Bailey hotly. "Damn it! I've been trying to save sea life since before you were born, and…."

Claire interrupted him again. "I know, and I'm sorry. So long, Chuck." With that, she disconnected the call.

Undoubtedly, POSC meant well, Claire thought. Over the years, the NGO had done plenty to promote the oceans and their precious creatures, bringing awareness to the public and mounting campaigns to protect the environment. She always had admired the work her father did, his patient and steady resolve never faltering. But what had it really achieved? Now he was dead, and the culprits who plundered the oceans continued unscathed. Well, that habitual plundering needed to change.

Chapter 13

Demesne Considers Reports From Costa Rica and Japan

News of the latest two incidents also attracted William McMahan's attention. He felt extra concerned because they had happened within a few days of each other, and it wasn't difficult to track Claire Armstrong's travel itinerary for the period in question. He saw a connection between her father's murder and these recent mishaps in Costa Rica and in Taiji. He shared his concerns with Sir Iain Campbell.

"Really, Billy, aren't you being a bit paranoid?" asked Campbell. "I can't believe that the Armstrong woman is on a global rampage to avenge her father. I would think she did enough here at the time he died."

"I think it's very unwise to underestimate her," said McMahan gloomily. "Her father's NGO maintains bases in both the places that were targeted, and she has the skill and resources to carry out exactly such attacks. That job in Taiji was quite extraordinary."

"You sound almost like you admire her, Billy," chuckled Campbell. "Anyway, supposing you're right and she's out for revenge, don't you think she's had enough of it by now?"

"If she wants revenge, I'd expect her to go after Winston Lau, at the very least," replied McMahan.

"Then why travel all the way to Costa Rica and Taiji to cause mayhem? Why not just return to Hong Kong and confront Lau here?" Campbell reasoned.

"I don't know, but I'm not happy, and I want to find out. If she does target Lau, then she gets that much closer to us. We should mitigate the risk and eliminate her."

Campbell felt faintly amused by his deputy's discomfort. "Oh, come on, Billy. You sound like you're in a board meeting." He paused and saw that McMahan remained disgruntled. "Okay," he offered, "brief Huang and have him find out what she's up to next. Let's see where she goes and who she sees, and then we'll decide what to do about it."

"Thank you," replied the ever-lugubrious deputy chairman of Demesne. "I'll put Huang on the case right away. I also think it's time we talked to Lau. He needs to stay alert."

"Okay, if you must, but tell Lau not to take any unnecessary actions as yet. We don't want him rocking the boat any more than he already did by ordering that attack on the Armstrongs."

*

Officially, Clement Huang worked as the chief of security for the Campbell's organisation. He also led Demesne's enforcement team and consistently showed himself to be a thoroughly callous and unforgiving individual. He kept his hair short and spiky and had inscrutable eyes set in a hard, angular face. Huang was big for a Chinese man, standing at just on two metres inside a compact and muscular body, the result of his obsessional use of a gym. He performed impressively in several martial arts and, when called upon by his masters, proved a merciless and enthusiastic killer.

Huang's first task required learning where the Armstrong woman was. He was pleased to discover quickly that having recently flown into Hong Kong from Tokyo, she once again stayed at her father's house in Shek O. Probably the place had been cleaned up since the slaughter there, he thought, but he also believed that it always would have bad *joss* after five people had died so violently there.

Having the woman followed turned out to be easy. She started each day early and, always dressed casually, took a bus into one of the many retail districts on Hong Kong Island, where she wandered among business stalls and into small shops. She never entered the big shopping malls in Admiralty or Central, preferring the back streets of Causeway Bay, Wan Chai, Lan Kwai Fong, Sheung Wan or Kennedy Town.

The shadowy figures trailing Armstrong stayed extra alert in Sheung Wan, where many of the shops offered the ingredients for Chinese delicacies, potions and medicines. These businesses sold shark fins, ivory, tiger testicles and other body parts from endangered species. But the wandering woman appeared to be unmoved by such offerings and simply passed by them. Once she visited the former location of her father's NGO office, but did not stay there long.

After several days of this random activity, Armstrong began to stroll among similar areas slightly off the most-beaten track across the harbour on the Kowloon Peninsula. She'd take a ferry from North Point to Hung Hom and walk for hours around there and Tsim Sha Tsui, stopping briefly at shops, cafes or bars before returning home usually well after dark.

Huang regularly reported his team members' findings to McMahan. They had followed Armstrong for more than a week and seen no signs at all of questionable activities. But McMahan was unimpressed and told Huang to have his men ask questions in the shops that she visited and find out exactly what she did inside, to whom she spoke and what she said or asked. He wanted more details.

The men working for Huang continued their surveillance and asked questions as instructed, but all the woman was doing was enquiring about the prices and provenance of goods that she never seemed to buy. They were bewildered by their task, for it seemed meaningless.

*

Thanks to Claire's military training, she had noticed her shadows almost right away on the first day, so she'd decided to lead them on a time-wasting dance. She did not know exactly who they were or to which gang they belonged, but she did assume them to be hostile, and so she prepared accordingly. Briefly she considered capturing one of them and interrogating him, but then decided against it. She would know more soon enough, and she planned to learn all the relevant details at her own convenience and according to her own agenda, not theirs.

After a second week of laying false trails, Claire decided it was time to shake loose from her tails and set about her real mission. She boarded a bus and rode to the Star Ferry Terminal in the Wan Chai district. From there, she travelled by ferry across the harbour to Tsim Sha Tsui, where she briefly mixed with the crowds. The watchers trailed close behind her.

Then Claire stopped to visit a public lavatory, where she changed her appearance when inside one of the washroom stalls. She pulled up her hair, put on a dull, lightweight jacket and a small, floppy hat and replaced her jeans with a frumpy skirt. A large shoulder bag that she had carried went inside a plastic shopping bag, along with her jeans and other items.

After emerging again into the crowds, she kept her head down and reversed course, re-boarding one of the Star Ferries and this time riding to Central back on Hong Kong Island. Behind her in Tsim Sha Tsui, the watchers waited and waited before apprehensively realising they had lost her. They knew that Huang would not be pleased.

Briskly, Claire walked a short distance to Sheung Wan and entered a shop which she had noticed on a previous stroll some days earlier. It displayed rows and rows of shark fins, ranging from just a few centimetres long to large dorsal fins nearly a metre high. The latter likely came from harmless whale sharks, Claire reckoned, and again she silently cursed the people engaged in this awful industry.

Feigning an interest in buying large quantities of fins for a restaurant chain that she allegedly planned to open on Hong Kong Island, in Kowloon and across the Chinese-mainland border in Shenzhen, she asked the shopkeeper about prices and long-term supply. He was an old man and automatically grew suspicious of such questions coming from a *gweipo*, or female foreign devil, as the Chinese liked to call Caucasian women. However, Claire's passable proficiency in Cantonese, a sizeable wad of cash and a promise of future commission payments on her purchases all helped to loosen his tongue. He explained that he was not a wholesaler, but he provided the name and contact number of his supplier.

After Claire left the old man's shop, he stood, scowling, near the glass door. Then he grunted, pulled a mobile phone from a shirt pocket and placed what he regarded as an important call.

Stopping at another public-convenience location allowed Claire to change back into her original clothes. After reverting to her previous appearance, she returned home, seen upon arrival by the determined watchers who had scurried back there hoping to pick up her trail again.

*

The next day Claire repeated the process of losing her followers, although this time she travelled to Kowloon and stayed there much longer. Using a fake name, she had phoned ahead and secured an appointment with the man whose contact details she had received at the shop selling shark fins in Sheung Wan. After finding the supplier's premises on Cameron Road, she climbed a stairway to his non-descript third-floor offices and paused outside just long enough to turn on the voice-recorder function on her smart phone.

Then Claire knocked and entered an outer room in which three young tough guys lolled around, smoking, while seated in tatty chairs. Tattoos covered their muscular arms and necks. Silently, they exuded an air of menace while studying her from head to toe.

"Hello. I have an appointment with Mr Kim," Claire said firmly. "Please tell him I'm here."

One of the thugs made a coarse remark in Cantonese, which caused the others to laugh. Then he stood and approached Claire, standing right up close in front of her intimidatingly.

"You the *gweipo* bitch wants to buy some shark fins?" he asked in English, still grinning from his little joke.

"No, I'm Father Christmas looking for fucking reindeer horns, asshole," responded Claire in equally coarse Cantonese, which wiped the smiles off their faces and straightened their postures. "So get out of my face and take me to see Kim."

The man glowered at her, looking like he wanted to strike her. Then he took a deep breath and appeared to relax.

"Huh, ho, very good, reindeer horns, eh?" With a silly smile, he stepped back several paces, and the others also relaxed.

"Mr Kim will see you now," he said. Then he opened an inner-office door and accompanied her into the next room.

Kim had watched the confrontation on a security screen and felt only partly amused to see such fools being made of his hired muscle. He had received firm orders from his boss, Winston Lau, to cooperate with Claire Armstrong, if at any time she appeared, and then to report back to him. Now he held no doubt that the woman coming to meet him, reputedly a Miss Jones, was indeed Armstrong, and he had instructed his men not to provoke her. They were told to be careful and respectful with her, so his henchmen's actions displeased him.

Once introductions were exchanged, Claire told her story about opening a restaurant chain. She explained about wanting to place large orders for shark fins.

"How many restaurants do you plan to open, Miss Jones?" asked Kim.

"My backers and I want to open 12 locations within the next 18 months and one per month after that to reach a total of 30. We will offer different shark fin soups, other traditional Chinese favourites and delicacies."

"Ambitious plans, Miss Jones," Kim observed, "especially with so much propaganda against shark finning these days. What, may I ask, are your thoughts on the subject?"

"Frankly, I don't care about shark finning," she retorted flatly. "Just tell me where I can get my supply and give me a good price with a bulk-volume discount. We can discuss the specific quantities in due course."

"Understood. Do you plan to talk with other suppliers?" Kim asked, innocently posing what he regarded as a trick question.

"Not yet, but I will, of course, look for other quotes. After all, it's simply good business sense," she replied.

"Normally, I would agree with you, Miss Jones, but this particular commodity is very rare, and only one organisation here really handles the product." Kim's face remained deadpan, despite what sounded to him like confirmation in her words that she was an imposter.

"Oh! Who would that be?" asked Claire. "Maybe I should talk directly to those people?"

"That won't be necessary, I assure you. I handle all the dealings for the organisation."

"Good, then I'll expect to hear from you with the details on prices and availability," Claire said, standing. "There is one other thing. I'd like to see some samples of the product first to ensure that it's fully dried and top quality. I assume there's no problem with that?"

"Actually, that would be most unusual," replied Kim. "But since you're here, I suppose we can make an exception."

He turned to his goon who still lounged against the door. "Simon here will show you now. Meanwhile, I'll make some calls and get back to you tomorrow with a proposal."

"That would be most kind," said Claire suspiciously, not having expected such helpfulness. "I look forward to hearing from you, Mr Kim. You have my number. Thank you for your time."

Simon escorted Claire out of the inner office and, accompanied by the other two ruffians, they climbed two more flights of stairs. They came to a padlocked door that was opened by Simon, who then preceded her onto a flat roof.

Surreptitiously, Claire pulled out her smart phone and changed its function to video-record before following Simon onto the roof with the device palmed in her hand. The roof space extended over several abutting buildings, and she viewed the now-familiar sight of uncountable numbers of shark fins of all sizes drying in the sun. Large tarpaulins rolled up along the sides of the roof waited to cover the fins in case of rain or perhaps in case of drone inspections by the police. Otherwise, just a few television aerials sprouted above the parapets.

Controlling her emotions, Claire simply nodded and looked around as if satisfied. She bent and picked up a few fins at random, confirming that they were indeed dry. They felt surprisingly light and coarse to the touch.

"Okay," she announced, turning back to the door. "That will do for now."

She led the way back down the stairs and, leaving her minders at the third floor, continued to the street. Then she went through her charade of formally changing from Miss Jones back into Claire Armstrong before travelling home.

*

Once Simon reported that the visitor had left, Kim called his boss, Winston Lau, who asked: "Was it the Armstrong woman, as we expected?"

"Yes, sir, I am sure it was," replied Kim nervously, for any discussion at all with the triad leader made him fearful. "Her cover story was too flimsy to be serious. She had only a superficial understanding of how to conduct such transactions. Regardless, I did say that I would call her tomorrow with quotations."

"And you showed her the fins on the roof as I instructed?"

Again, Kim replied in the affirmative.

"Very good!" Lau chuckled, almost gleefully. "Don't bother to call her. Just make sure that the place is well guarded and that you're ready for her next visit. Inevitably she'll come to try and destroy all the shark fins. When she does, kill her immediately. Is that clear? No mistakes this time, or it will be your head."

Nervous as he was, Kim wasted no time once the call ended. He spat out orders to his men and then, to calm his shaky nerves, reached into his bottom desk drawer for a bottle of cheap brandy, at which he drank straight from the neck.

Chapter 14

Claire Stirs Up a Hornet's Nest

Contrary to Winston Lau's expectations, Claire was not intent on mounting what could be a suicide attack against the rooftop on Cameron Road. Instead she determined to pick up where her father had left off, albeit with a somewhat more forceful approach to provoke the triad society. Too bad that she wasn't better at "diplomacy", she thought.

After much cajoling and generally making a nuisance of herself, Claire had succeeded to book an appointment for the next day with the director of environmental protection, Mr Philip Wong. She arrived punctually and was met by the same harassed government secretary as before. This time she faced no wait and was led straight into the director's office.

When Claire entered, Wong stood and greeted her courteously before offering her a chair. He was tall, thin and well-dressed with a constantly strained look about him.

To one side of the room, though, Claire saw the familiar figure of Wong's dreadful deputy, Ronald Ma, who sat there, looking glum. She gave him her frostiest glance and then ignored him.

"Miss Armstrong," Wong commenced, "may I begin by saying how very sorry we were to hear about your father's tragic death? On behalf of the Hong Kong government, I assure you that we are doing everything possible to bring the perpetrators to justice, but please accept our condolences."

"Thank you, Director," she responded, biting on her tongue to avoid saying anything rash.

"This is my deputy, Mr Ma," the director indicated, gesturing towards the repulsive little man. "I asked him to join us for the meeting." No explanation was offered as to why, and Claire did not ask. Wong continued, "I understand that since the regrettable incident with your father, his NGO has closed its offices in Hong Kong, so how may we assist you?"

"Well, Director, Mr Ma here told my father that the licence for the NGO was revoked because POSC apparently had made a nuisance of itself in trying to protect the environment. The attack on his house and his death followed quickly afterwards." No longer ignoring the culprit, Claire glared at Ma as she spoke. "However, the NGO remains very active and continues its work from its British headquarters."

"I'm glad to hear this," replied Wong smoothly. "I was away at the time and unaware of the decision to force his enterprise to close. Had I been here, I'm sure we could have straightened everything out amicably."

Yeah, right, thought Claire.

"So now, what can I do for you?" Wong asked.

Here goes, thought Claire. "Am I right in understanding that in principle the government here supports the concept of saving sharks by banning the sale of shark fins and, consequently, limiting the sale of shark fin soup in restaurants? Am I also correct that measures already have been taken in the Legislative Council to impose such a total prohibition?"

The two men swapped uncomfortable glances before Wong responded. "As you say, in principle we support an embargo, but there are many considerations. For example, the public fails to understand why a ban should exist, and many traders depend on the business. Even the big international hotels would suffer from the absence of shark fin soup if much of their wedding-banquet business then went elsewhere."

"And, of course, the triads would lose a lucrative income stream too," said Claire challengingly.

What a pin-drop moment this is, she thought amid the ensuing silence. Then she continued, "That aside, though, the government remains in agreement to prohibit the trade in shark fins, correct?"

"Well, yes, in principle," replied the director uncertainly. "Why do you ask?"

"Because there exists a thriving black-market trade in these fins, and nothing is happening to prevent, stop or even limit it," she stated bluntly.

"Are you certain of this, Miss Armstrong?" spoke up Ma for the first time. "These are very strong accusations, which should not be made lightly. Can you prove your allegations?"

"Absolutely," replied Claire, producing a USB stick from her shoulder bag and handing it to Wong. "Here's the proof. This flash-drive device contains a recording of a meeting I had with a Mr Kim on Cameron Road in Kowloon. He confirmed that he represents the sole trader of shark fins in Hong Kong and participates in the movement of shark fins here from around the world. There's also a video of countess fins drying on his rooftop there."

With his mouth hanging open, Wong accepted the USB stick, handling it as if it were a scorpion. Delicately, he placed it on his desk.

Ma recovered first and said, "Miss Armstrong, you play a very dangerous game here. We deeply regret the tragic death of your father, but you would be well advised to leave these matters to be dealt with by the appropriate authorities and not interfere."

"Do you mean that otherwise I might meet the same fate as he did? That sounds to me like a threat, Mr Ma. What do you think, Mr Wong?" she challenged.

The director looked shaken. "I think we must continue this meeting another time, Miss Armstrong," he said, rising from his chair. "I have another pressing engagement, I'm afraid."

"Understood, Director. Thank you for your time. I'll leave the USB stick with you since I have copies. You may wish to study it carefully and prepare a media statement because the details soon will appear in a story by the *South China Morning Post* newspaper."

This revelation clearly disturbed both men, but again it was Ma who recovered first. "I strongly advise you against publishing this, Miss Armstrong. Such a story could have unforeseen consequences."

"Gosh! That sounds like another threat, Mr Ma. How tedious you are!" Claire smiled brightly before turning towards the door. Hesitating, she spoke again. "Frankly, I think it's shameful that a government professing to be environmentally friendly and so understanding in banning this shark fin trade is, in essence, blatantly supporting it. That means there must be plenty of collusion between the government and the organisation responsible for the trade, and we know exactly who that is, don't we, gentlemen?" She paused, allowing the impact of the unsaid identity to hang menacingly in the air.

"Maybe I should send one of my USB sticks to Hong Kong's Independent Commission Against Corruption too," she added. "This could make a really good investigation for the ICAC."

As Claire left the room, she waved in farewell to the two men. When she did, her hand-held mobile phone, a useful recording device, came into view over her shoulder. The door closed behind her.

*

Ma reached for the telephone on the director's desk even before Wong had slumped back into his seat.

"Who are you calling?" asked Wong nervously.

"Who do you think?" spat his so-called assistant. "I'm calling Winston Lau, of course. This whole affair needs to be stopped once and for all. He never should have allowed that woman access to Kim, and now look at what's happening. She must be taken care of for good."

When connected to the triad leader, Ma told him the details about the meeting. Lau calmly instructed him to send over the USB stick and then to take no additional action. He would handle the matter.

Ma informed Wong what had been said. The deputy was about to leave the room to obey his triad instructions when Wong stopped him.

"Make a copy of the USB stick for me first so that I can review it and prepare a press release just in case," the director said. "I may need to brief the Executive Council too."

Wong also thought of another phone call that he needed to make. But for that one, he'd wait until he was quite alone.

*

"You were right to contact me," said McMahan over drinks in the Champagne Bar at the Grand Hyatt Hotel, near Wong's office. "Leave the USB stick with me, and I'll take care of things quietly with no fuss."

"But what about the possible newspaper article and the ICAC?" Wong asked. He still felt agitated by the entire situation.

"Don't worry about it," said McMahan reassuringly. "I promise you this matter will end now."

"How can you be so sure, William?"

"Because I say so! That's how! Shut up and enjoy your champagne, will you, Philip? Now I have to go."

McMahan asked for the bill, paid it and bade goodnight to Wong, who remained sitting pensively in the bar while nursing another glassful from the bottle of the excellent Krug that McMahan had ordered.

*

McMahan telephoned Huang and summoned him to meet an hour later. When they sat down together in McMahan's office, the Campbell's CEO asked for a full update on the Armstrong case.

At first, Huang explained that he had nothing remarkable to report. His team members had followed the Armstrong woman and checked on what she did and whom she saw, but so far, they'd discovered nothing unusual. He ended by saying that earlier the woman had visited the Environment Bureau and that he did not know yet who talked to her there or what was discussed.

McMahan fixed his most ferocious and penetrating stare on his security chief. "Now cut the bullshit, and tell me everything," he shouted, slamming his right hand onto his desk.

Instantly, Huang realised that something big must have happened during at least one of the two times when his team members had lost track of Armstrong, so he confessed about their lapses.

"Well, let me update you on exactly what she did when those incompetent fools working for you lost her," spat McMahan.

Before Huang arrived, McMahan had plugged the USB stick into his desktop computer and played the contents. Now he played them again for his security chief, twisting the screen to face the man.

Huang sat silently, embarrassed and seething that some of his best men had made him look so foolish. But that wasn't all, as McMahan continued: "Later at the Environment Bureau, Armstrong met with Director Wong and his deputy Ronald Ma, who as I'm sure you know, also work for Winston Lau. There, she confronted them about Kim's operation and threatened that an article based on these recordings will appear in the *South China Morning Post*. She also recorded the meeting there, during which that stupid little shit, Ma, threatened her with consequences if she didn't drop her enquiries so she threatened him back with the ICAC. Therefore, telling me that she has done 'nothing remarkable' would seem incorrect. What do you have to say now?"

Bowing in humility, Huang apologised for his failure and that of his henchmen. He vowed that such ineptness never would happen again.

"Too bloody right it won't," hissed McMahan, "or you'll be out, and with what you know about us and about Demesne, that could prove complicated and uncomfortable for you. Do you understand me?"

The threat and its implications were not lost on Huang. "I understand, sir. What are your orders now?" he asked, his head still bowed.

"Well, probably we can assume that by now Lau has renewed his order to have Armstrong found and killed, which is probably for the best. But his goons already tried and failed once, being very messy and public about it. So I want you to handle this quietly and discreetly. No trace, no mess, simply make her disappear quickly and permanently, okay?"

"Understood, sir," said Huang, grateful for a chance to redeem himself. "But what about Lau's men? They may be hunting for her too. We don't want to clash over this."

"Good point," replied McMahan. "I'll speak to Lau. His people shouldn't bother you. Now go, get on with it and let me know when the job's done."

Signalling an end to the meeting, McMahan turned his stare away from Huang and instead considered some papers on the desk. Thus dismissed, Huang quietly left the office and began making phone calls.

After the security man had gone, McMahan dropped the paperwork and telephoned Lau, reaching the triad leader at home. Making this particular connection was no easy task unless one knew exactly how, something that few people did. The chairman and the deputy chairman of Demesne were two of them.

*

Winston Lau lived in palatial, but somewhat solitary, splendour on Beijian Island, his own small, private island about 100 kilometres southwest of Hong Kong. Part of an archipelago, Beijian had been administered by Hong Kong starting in 1892 and later fortified for Second World War military purposes. In 1949, China reclaimed sovereignty over many of the islands, including Beijian, but left the smaller ones unoccupied. Being too remote for most people to live on and commute from, Beijian had stayed uninhabited until Lau took a liking to it.

For the triad leader, Beijian made a perfect lair, so he had leased the entire island from the government of China's Guangdong Province, which had no particular use for it. He restored and updated the facilities and turned the place into his impregnable home base and a headquarters for his extensive smuggling and trafficking operations. Officials on the Chinese mainland ignored him, and even the authorities in Hong Kong paid him little attention, mainly due to his regular and sizeable bribes to the people who mattered. As the owner of powerful launches and a helicopter, he came and went as he pleased.

When it suited Lau, he brought in people he wished to see, either for business or pleasure. Rumours abounded that certain people, having displeased Lau, had arrived on Beijian and never left again. Now the triad boss intended for Claire Armstrong to join this group. Explicitly, he ordered his men to find the woman and bring her to Beijian alive. He wanted to enjoy her final moments and her death up close and personally.

McMahan's call came through on Lau's SAT phone when the triad leader was busy frolicking in bed. Enchanted by the attentions of two talented girls who extravagantly entertained him in hopes of earning their freedom, Lau almost opted not to take the call. But maybe that would be unwise, he decided. Reluctantly, he shooed the girls out of his bedroom and answered his benefactor, realising that it must be something extra important for such a call to reach him at home and at night.

Impatient with pleasantries, McMahan began straight away. "I understand that Claire Armstrong has surfaced and seems to be turning into a nuisance, much like her father did."

"Oh, really, is that so, Mr McMahan?" Lau said, feigning surprise. "Please do tell me where she is. As you can imagine, I am most anxious to talk with her."

"Cut the crap, Lau," McMahan said bluntly. "She's been to see Kim and made a recording of her meeting with him and a video of the bloody fins on his roof. She also recorded a meeting at the Environment Bureau and threatened to send the whole lot off to the *SCMP* and maybe the police."

"I had no idea," said Lau defensively, seeking safety in a lie.

"Anyway, I'm guessing that you have ordered for her to be killed, shot down on sight. Is that correct?"

"Yes, it certainly is, Mr McMahan," Lau lied again. "She has caused more than enough trouble, and before she does anything else…."

"Hold it right there," McMahan interrupted, his voice rising. "I am telling you to order your men to back off from her. We don't want another bungled bloodbath. Am I clear? It attracts too much attention and risks exposing your links to us, all of which is unacceptable. We'll handle Miss Armstrong by our own means."

Never a tolerant fellow, Lau turned livid at being spoken to disrespectfully, even by McMahan. "How dare you lecture me?" he shouted back furiously. "I'm the one losing out to this maniac-bitch as she goes around like a one-person army. She already has killed some of my men, badly disrupted my supply chain from Central America, interfered with my colleagues in Japan and now threatens us here again."

McMahan disliked being shouted at too, but for the sake of expediency, he took a more conciliatory tone with the mobster. "You've got other businesses, Lau, certainly more profitable ones than shark fins. Why not just leave it be with Armstrong?"

"She has dishonoured us and must pay the ultimate price. But don't worry. We'll leave behind no mess on your precious streets. She will be brought here, and I will attend to her personally."

"That's what I feared." The unforgiving steeliness returned to McMahan's voice. "So I've instructed my people to take care of Armstrong, and I insist that you leave her alone. Do you hear me? Just remember how it happened that you came to be the big boss of the Xuè yuèliàng Triad, my friend. What a shame if we needed to make a sudden change!"

Lau started to retort before realising that the phone link had gone dead. He fumed and strutted around the bedroom, shouting and ranting. After a time, he calmed slightly and then called Kim, waking him.

"I want you to bag up all the fins from your rooftop and bring them out here to the island," Lau ordered. "Claire Armstrong has stirred things up, and now there's a risk that the police will raid you, so clear out the merchandise right away."

Prospects of a police raid appalled Kim. After all, the triad society paid large sums of money to certain people in the proper positions so as to avoid government or police interference in its activities.

"You also are instructed to leave Armstrong alone, at least for the moment," Lau added. "Her death right now would focus too much attention on us, so have your men stand down."

The triad boss had no intention to reveal to his subordinates that he had been ordered to halt the contract on Armstrong. He already had lost more than enough face because of her.

After Kim acknowledged the new orders, Lau ended their call. He still bristled from talking to McMahan and so needed to vent his anger and frustration. Reaching into a bedside drawer, he removed some handcuffs and a whip before calling for the two girls to be returned. He was a nasty, cruel man, and he would enjoy releasing some of his fury on those two beauties, he decided.

Chapter 15

Claire Calls For Reinforcements

Despite Claire's self-assurance, she knew that she now faced a considerable risk of being attacked and killed. It was only a matter of time until the opposition organised properly and overwhelmed her. She realised that she had been lucky so far, but having provoked so many hostile factions, the most recent being the triads with their obvious links in the government, her life definitely was in danger.

Ominously, Claire also wondered if the high-stakes game might include a third party, one whose identity and intentions remained murky. She felt surprised that the people following her for the past few weeks had done nothing aggressive and had taken no overt action against her, something that she believed the triads would have done and for which she'd prepared. All this required careful consideration.

Yet despite such grim realisations, Claire still wanted to press her advantage. She clearly had wrong-footed her enemies, and now would be a good time to follow through on her "attack".

But as a good soldier, she recognised her limitations. For a start, she lacked proper weapons, and the path she followed required a more forceful capability than she presently could muster. She also had no friends or comrades in support, no safe base and no exit strategy. Best that she drops out of sight for a time and work on improving her odds.

Reluctantly, Claire placed another phone call to her Special Forces hotline in the UK. Her call arrived at the SBS headquarters in Poole, Dorset. An officer took her number and told her that someone would call back on a secure line. Soon she was speaking with the regimental deputy commanding officer, Lieutenant Colonel Richard "Dick" Bennett, an officer Claire knew well and with whom she previously had served.

"Hello, Dick," she began, "got a moment?"

"Of course, always, Claire. What scrape are you in now?" he enquired kindly, remembering all too well the details and the aftermath of her last entanglement in Hong Kong.

"How long have you got?" she asked, more pleased than she had expected to be talking to a trusted colleague.

"As long as you need. From what we've picked up, you seem to have been busy again," he ventured.

Claire briefed Bennett accurately and unemotionally on everything that had happened since her father's funeral. She ended by giving him an assessment of her situation.

When she finished, he commented, "Well, I said 'busy', but that hardly describes it. Bloody hell, soldier, you've almost started a new war!"

"It wasn't planned that way," she replied rather defensively. "But I wanted to find out who ordered Dad's murder and get even, I suppose."

"And how do Central American drug cartels and the Yakuza factor into your plans for revenge?"

"I know, Dick, but the problem is that somehow they're all connected. It's like there's this big company, a multinational, so to speak, and each crime syndicate forms a different branch in its global operations."

"Well, that's the way of the world, Claire, and unless we're instructed by Her Majesty's 'powers that be' to do something about it, I don't see such crime structures changing anytime soon."

"Yeah, I know," she acknowledged.

Bennett always had regarded Claire as an outstanding soldier, but he worried that the way she was carrying on would land her in serious trouble. It happened sometimes with elite Special Forces soldiers. After leaving the military, they had difficulty settling into the "normal" world, their thirst for more "action" seeming almost unquenchable. "Well, what can I do for you?" he asked.

"Okay, for starters, how about sending me a fully armed troop of my pals and ex-comrades?" she asked mischievously.

"Ha! Ha! Seriously, though, and of course, remembering that this call is recorded." Although pleased to hear from his former teammate, Bennett began to feel slightly uneasy about the conversation's direction.

"Seriously," repeated Claire, "I'm going to need some support, Dick. I know perfectly well that 'the Service' can't condone my activities or actively help, but I wondered if you knew of anyone in my area who might be willing and able to lend a hand."

"Let me have a think about it, and I'll get back to you. Keep safe, and lie low until you hear from me." He disconnected without another word, and Claire was left pondering her fate.

*

Aware that staying any longer in Shek O was unwise, Claire threw some clothes into a lightweight bag, along with her laptop and some toiletries, and walked to the nearest bus route, quickly flagging down a green mini-bus to Central. Her departure was observed and reported upon, as she had expected, but this time she aimed to lose her followers completely.

Huang's latest orders to the surveillance team had been very clear. Observe the Armstrong house at Shek O, but do not try to launch any overt action there. If the woman leaves, the watchers were told, follow her and call for backup, which would stay ready and waiting. If a good chance arose, then Claire should suffer a severe "accident", like falling under a bus, but failing that, she was to be picked up, sedated and driven to a more remote setting in the New Territories to be killed and buried. Huang had assigned his absolutely toughest and best men to the task. Under no circumstances could there be a botched or bloody street fight. Armstrong's execution would be quiet and low profile.

After reaching a busy transport hub at the International Finance Centre (IFC), a skyscraper in Central district, and still making no attempt at concealment, Claire boarded an MTR (Mass Transit Railway) train to the Hong Kong International Airport on the outlying Lantau Island. There, she headed for the departure terminal. Then once again she ducked into a public washroom, this one a big improvement on those at the Star Ferry Terminals, she reckoned.

Emerging five minutes later in a drab disguise, Claire veered away from the departure gates, the airlines desks and all the airport shops. Moving leisurely, she went outside to a bus terminal and boarded a coach to Mui Wo, a community on the other side of the island.

By the standards of populous Hong Kong, Mui Wo amounted to little more than a remote village, a place where water buffalo and wild cattle often wandered in the streets. But the town had a few bars and hostelries, largely to serve the summertime tourists who arrived by ferry and liked to swim and sunbathe at the adjacent Silvermine Bay Beach.

Claire checked into a small B&B situated a block away from the waterfront. There, she lay down, holding a bottle of water, on the squeaky bed in her room and waited for Bennett to call her.

Back at the airport's departures terminal, Huang's followers raced about in a state of panic. Their orders could not have been clearer, but once again, the cursed *gweipo* had vanished from right under their noses. They had failed and knew well enough to expect serious consequences.

*

Claire had dozed off when her mobile phone rang. It was Bennett. Without any preamble, he asked, "Do you remember Jason Chan?"

"Yes, sure," replied Claire. "We were together on joint-selection training, but he headed for the SAS, as I recall. Haven't seen him since."

Selection training for both the SAS and SBS takes several months. All the candidates are trained and assessed together. Those who qualify advance to their respective regiments, with the SBS troops facing additional and intensive water-related training programmes.

"That's the guy," confirmed Bennett. "He left the service at about the same time you did, also as a captain, and for the last year he's done some private-sector security work in Macau. Apparently, it's doing his head in."

"Do you think he'd be willing to join up with me? I mean, if he's got regular work, however tedious, it's a big ask for me to make and certainly could be dangerous." The more Claire had thought about recruiting someone to help her, the more she felt that perhaps it wasn't the greatest idea after all, especially from the other person's viewpoint.

"Since time is clearly of the essence," Bennett observed somewhat caustically, "I had a word with him and sounded out his possible reaction. I didn't say it was you or give him too many details, but he leapt at the idea, and I expect that by now he may be at the Macau airport awaiting his battle orders."

"Good grief! Didn't he get enough excitement in the regiment?"

"So asks Captain Claire Armstrong, a survivor of five official campaigns and God knows how many unofficial ones, now embarked on a personal crusade to destroy organised crime in Southeast Asia. Come on, Claire. We're all alike, hard-to-cure adrenaline junkies, and you know it."

"Yes, I suppose you're right," she replied, quietly amused by his abridged summary of her career.

"Well, don't sound so bloody miserable about it," snapped Bennett. "Do you want his help or not?"

"Sorry, Dick," she replied more cheerfully. "It would be great to have him along, and thanks, really."

"Good, then here's his phone number." Brisk and all-business now, Bennett recited the digits. "He's expecting a call. Just be sure that the two of you take care, d'you hear?"

"Will do, Boss, and thanks again."

They disconnected without another word.

Never one to procrastinate, Claire promptly memorised the phone number and then called it. Jason Chan picked up on the second ring.

Unusually large and soft-spoken, Jason came from mixed parentage, with an absent father from northern China and an errant Hong Kong-expatriate mother. His mom died when he was a child, and so he spent his formative years in and out of orphanages or fighting his way around the back streets of Kowloon. A lucky break took him to England crewing on a cargo ship, where he absconded in the port of London. There, he drifted on the city streets for a few weeks before, out of desperation, making the best decision of his life and joining the army. He gave an impression of being a kindly, gentle giant, but many an enemy had miscalculated and not lived to regret it.

"Hello, Jason," Claire began boldly. "It's Claire Armstrong. Do you remember me?"

"Well, damn, that's a voice I've not heard for a while," Jason replied in his soft, barely accented English.

Suddenly, Claire recalled how flawless Jason's use of English was, with hardly a hint of the Chinese-mainland portion of his roots

"Is it you that Dick Bennett's been onto me about?" Jason asked. "Whatever are you doing?"

"Yes, I'm the one, Jason. I understand that you're in Macau and somewhat interested in a little adventure."

"Affirmative on both counts," Chan replied. "But let's not talk much on the telephone. Where are you holed up?"

"Mui Wo, Lantau Island," said Claire succinctly.

"I know the place. I'll get a chopper to take me from Macau over to Hong Kong and then catch a local ferry. Once I'm on the boat, I'll give you a shout."

"Helicopter's a bit flash, isn't it?" she queried.

"They pay me a heap of money here to direct security in a bunch of casinos, but I'm bored to tears. I'll see you soon," he said, disconnecting.

Claire looked at the now-silent mobile phone and shook her head in amazement. Only this morning she'd sent up a distress flare, and by evening she'd have reinforcements. How about that?

Chapter 16

Headless Chickens

One of Huang's men hastily left town rather than face his irate boss. He knew that Huang would prove most unforgiving after learning that they had lost the Armstrong bitch again and that this time she failed to reappear. His two hapless colleagues did report the bad news and were comprehensively beaten to within an inch of their lives by Huang himself.

After calming slightly, Huang used his extensive network to check if anyone named Claire Armstrong had left Hong Kong by airplane, ferry or train and was relieved at indications that she had not. She definitely seemed to have gone to ground, so the trick became to find her quickly. Huang mobilised his resources, including contacts in the police force, and put out word on the streets about an urgent need to locate the woman. Big rewards were promised for anyone who found her.

Joining the hunt was Kim's hatchet man, Simon. He had received a personal call from the big boss, Winston Lau, awarding him a lucrative contract to find and kill Armstrong. He was told to keep the arrangement quiet and not to share any details with Kim, whose position, Lau intimated, might fall vacant soon. Lau knew that he took a risk with Simon, for if things went wrong, McMahan certainly would react badly. Being willing to take that risk demonstrated to Lau just how badly he wanted Claire Armstrong dead.

Simon set about the hunt with enthusiasm, taking along his two fellow mobsters from Kim's premises on Cameron Road. They all went to Shek O where Simon reckoned that Armstrong would turn up again, sooner or later. Next time no one would fumble with swords or knives. Simon and his cohorts planned to go in shooting automatic weapons.

One unintended consequence was that when Kim tried to arrange for the packing and transport of the shark fins on his roof, no one was around to perform the grunt work. He cursed, fumed and eventually arranged to bring in other less-trusted men for the task, but all this took time.

Everyone on the hunt ran around like headless chickens and, however hard they searched, Claire Armstrong could not be found. But it was just a matter of time, Huang believed, so he took a short break from the waiting game by going to work out in his personal gym. There, fresh bloodstains still on the floor attested to how he nearly had killed two of his men a little earlier.

*

Meanwhile, Claire met up with Jason Chan, and they sipped beers together at the China Bear, a small bar on the Mui Wo waterfront. After briefly catching up on what they each had done since leaving their respective regiments, Claire began a detailed briefing, starting with the attack at Shek O.

Jason interrupted occasionally to clarify a point or a name, and when she finished, he blew out a long breath, ordered two more beers and then said, "By all the gods, Claire, what have you gotten yourself into? Cartels, Yakuza, triads and heaven knows who the hell else, all wanting to provide you with a creative exit from this world. This is some serious shit!"

Claire grinned wickedly at him. "That's about the size of it, Jason. Still want to play?"

"Just you try and stop me. Cheers." He smiled, and they clinked together their bottlenecks.

"So what's the plan," Jason resumed, studying her dowdy apparel, "apart from spending the rest of your life in that clever disguise?"

They talked late into the night, consuming some indifferent burgers and more beer. When the time came to turn in, they had hammered out a loose action plan, and so they needed an early start in the morning. Helpful management at the same B&B where Claire stayed had provided Jason with another room.

Claire had just stripped off, ready to sleep, when she heard a quiet tap on her door, followed by a whispered, "It's me. I've got something for you."

"Oh, no! You must be kidding me," she muttered to herself, rolling her eyes. Hoping that Jason wasn't going to try any unwelcome advances, she tied a large towel around herself and opened the door a few inches.

"Relax," Jason said, seeing her face twisted into a scowl. "I just thought you could do with this."

Through the narrow opening in the doorway, he handed over a bag, its open top revealing a compact and lightweight pistol, a Sig Sauer P228. There was also a suppressor, along with some spare 15-round ammunition clips.

"We can talk about other toys in the morning. Sleep well, Claire."

Jason pulled the door shut. Once he did, Claire forgot about holding the towel in place to focus on handling and checking the weapon. Doing so made her feel a whole lot better for the first time in ages.

Lingering in the corridor, Jason smiled as he heard the gun being loaded, a round chambered in the breach and the weapon cocked. Then he returned to his own room across the hallway.

*

After an early breakfast, Jason showed Claire the "other toys" he had brought and stashed in his room. There were two M16A2 compact assault rifles, the sort that had been a main weapon in the Special Forces when it came to special protection duties and keeping a low profile. Each of the 30-round weapons was light, compact enough to carry in a backpack and effective in combat. Along with a pistol for himself, Jason also had masses of ammunition, half-a-dozen flashbangs, other grenades and two lethal-looking knives. Completing the collection were 10 blocks of C4 explosives, detonators and two monocular night-vision devices, the state-of-the-art AN/PVS-14.

Claire expressed amazement. "How did you get all this stuff, and how could you carry it on the flight?" she asked, stuffing much of the ordinance into her own carryall bag.

"Well, if I insist on having plenty of stuff like this, the casino-owners tend to think it's a sign that I'm prepared for anything and doing my job properly." He winked, not really answering her question. "And I never did say what chopper I used. The company has one that I can ride in when needed, so it was quite easy, d'you see?"

"And how did you explain your leave of absence?" Claire asked.

"Well, it's my poor, old granny in Changchun, away up there in the far north of China, who has taken a tragic turn for the worse," said Jason, exaggerating his Chinese accent which became so pronounced that Claire barely could understand him. They smirked at one another and then set off for Kowloon.

Jason had argued that they should seize the initiative and immediately go on the offensive against the triads, starting with

Kim, rather than wait for something to happen. Claire had agreed, and now, having set aside her "disguise", she felt ready for battle and wanted to be seen.

A sharp pair of eyes did see her, and so an informant called, reporting to Clement Huang that the woman he wanted to find had appeared at the Kowloon Star Ferry Terminal and was moving north along Nathan Road, the main street in Kowloon. Galvanised in anticipation, he ordered that she be followed.

While leaving his office and rushing to the lift in Campbell's Tower, Huang told a team of his men to drive fast to Nathan Road in a plain-white Ford Transit van, the vehicle being needed to deal with Armstrong once they caught up to her. His men would pass through a tunnel under Victoria Harbour. But the MTR trains, which zipped through a different tunnel, always delivered passengers faster, so Huang himself set out at a run for the Central Station.

Seconds before Huang descended into the underground station, the watcher busy following Claire on the other side of the harbour in Kowloon called with an update. He advised that there appeared to be a man with Armstrong and that they both had turned right onto Cameron Road. Huang told him not to dare lose sight of her, and that he hoped to be there too within minutes.

*

Walking along a congested sidewalk to approach Kim's building on the opposite side of the street, Claire and Jason arrived just in time to see the last few bundles of sacks being loaded onto the back of an open-top lorry. No one made much effort to conceal the contents, and shark fins protruded from the sacks. A frantic, petulant Kim could be seen and heard regaling the men carrying the bags and, when the last of the cargo was loaded and the lorry's tailgate slammed closed, they all climbed into the vehicle's cab or onto its flatbed before driving away.

Without hesitation, Claire waved down a taxi. She and Jason climbed into the vehicle's backseat and, with the inducement of a Hong Kong $500 bill, urged the driver to follow the heavily loaded lorry. "You bet," he said, delaying only long enough to push the money into one of his trouser pockets.

Huang's watcher felt dismayed, but he too flagged down a taxi and persuaded the driver to follow the one in front. He, though, chose to encourage the driver by waving a pistol rather than cash, but this technique worked equally well. "Yes, sir," this driver intoned and didn't pause at all.

Again, the watcher telephoned Huang, who was just emerging from an MTR-station exit onto Cameron Road, and reported what was happening. "I'm nearly there," the rugged Campbell's executive shouted back.

Suddenly the surveillance man in the taxi saw Huang engaged in some impressive multi-tasking: yelling into a phone while running at full-pelt down the street. The watcher instructed the taxi driver to slow down as he swung open a rear door and leant out, waving to his boss.

With impressive agility, Huang jumped into the car and looked ahead to where his man pointed. Armstrong's taxi, easily visible several vehicles in front, moved slowly in the heavy traffic, following the lorry to which the watcher also keenly pointed.

"Alright, let's bring this situation under control," Huang said. He started by phoning his team members, now approaching in the Ford Transit van after an unusually quick ride under the harbour. He provided an update, telling them to push through traffic until they moved ahead of the taxi he was in, and when they did, he joined them in the van, and together they continued to follow Claire's taxi and the lorry.

The lorry took a circuitous route towards the old China Ferry Terminal. It headed a long jetty, alongside which small boats were moored, and pulled up beside a large, old Chinese junk moored stern-to at the jetty's end, about 200 metres from the entrance gate. A rickety gangplank connected the junk to the dock.

Immediately men sprang out of the lorry's cab and off its flatbed. At Kim's orders, they began offloading the sacks of fins and throwing them onto the junk where deck hands caught and stowed them in its hold.

Claire and Jason released their taxi at the entrance gate and proceeded on foot, keeping as low a profile as possible. "It looks like we need a boat to follow this lot," suggested Jason, looking around.

As his gaze turned, he noticed a white van pull up at the entrance and six men climb out. "Are these friends of yours by any chance?" he asked Claire. As he spoke, the men pulled out guns and ran towards them.

"No point in asking questions now," Jason said, opening his bag and removing his assault rifle. "You get us a boat, and I'll hold them off.

Without time to argue, Claire quickly selected a medium-sized Viking sport-fishing boat into which she jumped and hastily set about cross-wiring the engine, just as the familiar clatter of an automatic weapon opened up in repeated three-round bursts behind her.

Jason was gratified to see that his shooting had scattered the advancing men, forcing them to take cover behind what little protection they could find. A few half-hearted shots came back in his direction, but the shooters lacked the range of his M16 and, as things stood, they posed little threat.

At first, the gunfire had a paralysing effect on the men working at the junk. They dropped everything and also dived for cover. But seeing that the action stayed some distance away and wasn't directed at them, Kim bawled at his men to continue loading, and they set about hefting the bags with renewed fervour.

Changing his ammunition clip, Jason backed towards the boat that Claire had purloined, which now revved throatily. Sending another salvo toward the still-unknown enemies, he also jumped aboard. He cut the mooring lines, and they accelerated away from the jetty at speed, taking care not to go near the junk and risk being identified by Kim.

The junk's motor was running, and the men there also fired some rounds towards Huang and his team to discourage any approach, or other interference, before they cast off too. It was abundantly clear to Huang where Kim was going, and presumably Armstrong and her mystery associate would follow them, so the Campbell's security chief ordered his own men back into the van, and they all departed before the police arrived.

*

Claire and Jason pointed the Viking west, but then gently slid the boat into an empty mooring on one of the jetties serving the Western Wholesale Food Market in Sai Wan on Hong Kong Island. From there, they could see the junk and then follow it at a distance. Everything had happened so fast that they really had not worked out what was going on, so now they took stock of their position.

"Well, that was all very exciting to start the day with," offered Jason. "I can see why you need some support."

"That's the first time there's been any gunplay though," replied Claire thoughtfully. "And the shooters appeared unconnected to Kim."

"You said last night that you thought members of another group might be involved somehow. I guess that's them."

"Yes, I suppose so, but who the hell are they, and what do they want?"

"Well, dear lady, with all the enemies you've made, I suppose it must be tough to keep a count of them all." His black eyes twinkled, and his smile evaporated any slight that she otherwise may have felt at his words. "Anyway, one challenge at a time, so let's see what the guys on this old junk are up to, shall we?"

They observed the junk moving west at a fair rate, kicking up a large bow wave. They also saw two police launches, with blue lights flashing and sirens sounding, approach the scene of the earlier action, but the officers aboard looked unconcerned by the junk.

Claire and Jason watched the junk glide past and allowed it to make plenty of space between them before they slipped their mooring and started off after it. The junk rounded Green Island near the western tip of Hong Kong Island and then set a south-southwesterly course, making a speed of some 10 knots. The two boats soon passed Lamma Island on their port sides and entered open water.

Once settled into a remote pursuit, Jason rummaged around in the Viking's cabin. He came up with some tins of tuna, sardines and fruit salad, plus water and beer.

"Wow!" exclaimed Claire. "That's some feast you've knocked together. Good on ya', partner."

"There's also some chocolate, but I left it 'cos I'm worried about protecting my health," Jason joked.

"Yes, do be careful," she reposted. "Bullets are okay, I guess, but too much chocolate really kills."

They took turns at the wheel and tucked into the food and water. After three hours, they had travelled well out to sea. They had passed a few small islands on the starboard side, but were becoming concerned about the distance to their destination and fuel constraints. There was a spare tank aboard, so Claire calculated that they probably could go another two hours before needing to turn back.

"Alternatively, we could attack and commandeer the junk," suggested Jason, still sounding whacky, although Claire suspected that this time, he was being serious under the comic guise.

"Let's see if anything interesting happens within the next hour and then make a decision," she argued, a proposal that Jason seemed happy to accept.

A hazy sun did its best to warm them, but it was the wrong time of year for the oppressive heat of summer. They cruised on and swapped stories about some of their past combat experiences, many of which would have horrified anyone unaware of typical clandestine activities by the United Kingdom's Special Forces.

Just over an hour later, they consulted some nautical charts that Jason's earlier foraging also had unearthed, along with a good pair of binoculars. The distant junk continued to hold its course and appeared headed for a group of small, rocky and mostly uninhabited islands still below the horizon. Claire and Jason decided to keep following.

A distant smudge soon appeared, and gradually the small island group took shape. The charts showed the largest island as being Beijian. From a distance, it looked craggy and barren with no apparent place for boats to land or tie-up safely. But the charts did indicate the existence of a mooring of sorts on the northwest shore and a track leading to some old Second World War fortifications on the island's highest part. That mooring had to be the junk's destination.

At the wheel again, Claire throttled back on the engine and allowed the distance between the two vessels to grow. She and Jason needed to decide on their next move.

After some discussion, they increased speed, but headed instead towards Miaowan, a smaller island to Beijian's southwest. A tiny fishing community was located there, and so they could use that place as cover before diverting unobserved to Beijian's blind side intent on seeing what Kim was doing.

It was late afternoon by the time they sailed briskly parallel to the larger island, half a kilometre away from its south side, and quickly realised that the information on the charts was incorrect. A sizeable modern building, together with what appeared to be accommodation blocks and warehouses, had replaced the old fortifications on the highest point. They also saw watchtowers with guards. Motoring on, they rounded the end of the island and kept going. Beijian looked like a hostile environment, and they needed to plan their strategy very carefully.

So they returned to Miaowan and entered the small harbour that serviced the fishing boats based there. The few people nearby clearly weren't used to visitors, but Jason quickly dispelled their mistrust of strangers with his oddly accented Cantonese.

Soon finding themselves inside a grubby little tavern, Claire and Jason ordered some food, plus beers, and then engaged in gentle conversation with a friendly old woman who was seemingly in charge of the place. Claire asked about the people on Beijian, but to her surprise, the previously garrulous senior citizen clammed up and vanished into a back room.

"What happened there?" asked Jason.

"I don't know," replied Claire, "but as soon as I asked about Beijian, she went all weird."

A young girl, who had served their meals, came by and whispered briefly to Claire. Then she too disappeared.

"Bingo! It seems there are bad people on Beijian, lots of them, including the society chief, Winston Lau," said Claire, relaying what she'd learned. "When they come to Miaowan, they treat the villagers badly, and our waitress wishes they'd all go away and leave everyone in peace."

"I've always thought the term 'society chief' was a blatant misnomer," remarked Jason.

"I know what you mean," Claire said flatly. "It sounds much too gentle and civilised. But 'society' is a polite term given to the triads. Incidentally, Winston Lau is the same crime boss who ordered my father's death."

Jason nodded, and they lapsed into silence. He finally glanced at his wristwatch. "It's getting late, Claire, and it'll be dark soon," he said. "We should return to Hong Kong Island if we know what's good for us."

"Do we?" asked Claire.

"Do we what?"

"Know what's good for us?"

Jason took a deep breath and smiled. "Probably not," he conceded. "In which case, let's go and meet that society bastard."

Claire grinned back, but then expressed concern. "Are you sure, Jason? I mean, this isn't your fight. It probably will get messy…."

"Will you shut up, girl?" he interrupted. "Let's get back to the boat, top up its fuel and decide how to handle this. Now pay the bill, and let's go."

Jason rose from his seat and departed for the landing stage where the boat was tied up. Claire followed moments later.

Unseen in the rear of the café, the old woman placed a call on her expensive mobile telephone, a generous gift from a nice man called Mr Huang. He not only provided her with occasional gifts and regular cash payments, but also had asked her to inform him, on an ongoing basis, about anything of interest that she saw or heard concerning Beijian.

Chapter 17

Newspaper and Claire in the Crosshairs

Chris Turner, the editor-in-chief of the *South China Morning Post* newspaper, had just received an ordinary-looking USB stick from a mystery source. Such things were not uncommon in journalism, and so he passed it along to a junior intern to see what it contained. If events followed the usual form, the stick probably would end up in a rubbish bin.

To Turner's surprise, the intern soon returned to his office, almost tripping over herself with excitement and apprehension. Although new to the world of journalism, she knew that if the contents of the stick were true, then the potential news story would be explosive.

The editor-in-chief told her to calm down and leave the stick with him. He'd examine it later. When he finally did, he experienced feelings similar to those of his young intern, but with the benefit of experience, his apprehension far outpaced his excitement.

Turner realised that the mystery sender could only be Claire Armstrong, whose father was assassinated in a recent triad attack and who also nearly died. He believed that she had left Hong Kong, but the recordings linking the triads and the Environment Directorate suggested that she had returned and set out to avenge her father. This all made rather good material for newspaper headlines, but when triads and senior government officials were involved, one needed to tread very carefully.

As Turner reflected on whether to advance the story at all, he received a phone call from William McMahan, someone he had met in passing many times at receptions and high-level events, but really knew only by reputation. Successful newspaper editors generally aren't fearful or hesitant people, but in the case of interactions with Campbell's Trading Company, and with McMahan especially, Turner was most circumspect.

Answering the call, he began, "Good day, Mr McMahan. What can I do for you?"

Turner did not expect McMahan to devote any time to pleasantries or social graces and so felt no surprise when McMahan cut straight to the point. "Have you received a recording of a private conversation between some government officials and one Claire Armstrong?" he asked.

"Well, Mr McMahan," responded Turner cautiously, "I'm sure you can appreciate that any leads we receive for stories and their sources must remain confidential."

"Cut the crap," shouted McMahan into his telephone. "I asked you an important question: yes or no?"

Turner bridled at the man's rudeness. He resented intimidation efforts by the bully at the other end of the line. But he also knew of the influence wielded by the Campbell's deputy chairman and also that Campbell's held a large stake in the *SCMP* newspaper.

After a pause, as Turner wrestled to control his temper, he replied, "Yes, as a matter of fact, we have received such material, along with a recording of a meeting with the triads. Perhaps you could tell me how they're connected."

"You will destroy any copies you have of the recordings and publish nothing whatsoever about them. Do you understand me?"

"Yes, I hear you, MISTER McMahan," hissed Turner, emphasising the "Mister" and struggling for self-restraint.

"Good. Ms Armstrong has caused a lot of trouble and fabricated stories to satisfy a sense of payback for her father's death. We do not want to jeopardise perfectly good government people's careers with inaccurate and irresponsible press coverage."

"Excuse me, but are you suggesting that triad leaders are 'perfectly good government people', Mr McMahan?"

"Don't play silly buggers with me, Turner," replied McMahan nastily. "Should a single word of these meetings leak out, you will be out of a job, out of Hong Kong and your days in journalism will be done."

After the call ended, Turner pensively chewed over the conversation. The sensible thing would be to follow the directive. But his journalistic instincts twitched, and he was damned if he'd allow a brute like McMahan to ride roughshod over him, however fearsome this "business executive's" reputation was for destroying people and their careers. Turner would keep the USB stick and plan how best to use it. An interview with Claire Armstrong might make a good start.

*

McMahan's next call reached the head of the ICAC, Albert Tsang, an ex- chief inspector and a man long respected in the Hong Kong community. "Bertie", as he was known, had been classically schooled in England. He was always expensively well-dressed, which typically included one of his many signature bow ties with a matching breast-pocket handkerchief, and often was considered more British than most of the English expatriates living in Hong Kong. In as much as McMahan had any friends, Tsang was one of them, and they frequently lunched together, went golfing or attended regional sporting events.

"What do you know about Claire Armstrong?" asked McMahan after their next dinner date and bridge party had been confirmed.

"Apart from the fatal matter with her father at Shek O, you mean?" Tsang replied in urbane, unaccented English.

"Yes."

"As far as I know, she left Hong Kong soon after the attack, and that was that. Why?"

"Because she's back and intent on stirring up trouble. Rather than just accept that the whole incident when her father died was a burglary gone wrong, she visualises some big conspiracy involving the Environment Directorate and the triads, and she's out for revenge. She's created a few fake recordings of conversations with high-ups, rattled cages and made some people we know quite anxious."

"Well, that's no good," replied Tsang dryly. "Mind you, from what I have heard, you wouldn't want to be on the wrong side of her. But why are you asking, Billy? Campbell's isn't involved somehow, is it?"

"No, no, of course we're not," assured McMahan smoothly. "But the CE (chief executive of Hong Kong) has approached Sir Iain asking if we can use our influence to silence her. He doesn't want it to appear that the request comes from him, do you see? While I know it's not strictly your department, I thought that I'd run it by you and see if you have any ideas. Naturally, if there is a conspiracy lurking around, we'd want to see it exposed immediately, but I think this is just an emotionally distraught young woman making trouble."

"In that case, maybe the best thing is to revoke her visa and pack her off back home. I can arrange for that if you like," offered Tsang.

"Oh, that would be marvellous, Bertie," gushed McMahan. "I'll advise Sir Iain immediately. I know he'll be most grateful."

Unspoken was that Sir Iain's gratitude most often manifested itself in donations to the benefactor's Swiss bank account. Tsang's account number had been known to Campbell's for many years, as had many others belonging to Hong Kong's most senior and influential citizens.

"Right, I'll get onto it straight away," Tsang said. Although curious, he wondered if it might be best if he didn't know the full details, whatever this was really all about. "Plausible deniability", as the Americans called it, could be a wonderful thing.

*

McMahan listened to Huang's latest report and then asked the security chief what he planned to do next about Armstrong and her new associate, now that she had evaded him yet again. The detail that his own men had faced gunfire from an automatic weapon bothered McMahan not at all.

"It depends if you want me to avoid conflict with the Xuè yuèliàng," began Huang. "If you don't mind, then I'll take a unit to Beijian Island and destroy the two targets there, along with anyone getting in our way. But if you want us to avoid such a risk, then we must wait for Armstrong and her sidekick to return to Hong Kong. Already I've sent out some people on sampans and other boats to watch for their return, so we'll know immediately when they come back."

McMahan thought for a moment. "I suppose there's a good chance that Lau will kill them on his island. The woman may be lethal, but she can't take out his entire triad headquarters.

Initially I didn't want Lau involved because he and his thugs make such a mess, but out there it doesn't matter, I guess."

"Armstrong and her accomplice may return without getting involved in any action, though, in which case we can take them at sea," suggested Huang. "Alternatively, the woman actually might kill Lau, and then you'd have a power vacuum in the triad, which I don't imagine you want."

"It seems like there's a risk either way, so let's play it by ear. However it goes, though, just make sure that one way or another, Armstrong and her friend disappear. As for the 'mountain master' (another term describing a triad boss), I'm sure there'd be plenty of volunteers to take over if Lau fell to Armstrong's sword."

Once Huang had left him, McMahan considered briefing Campbell. Although bothered by Armstrong's recordings, he believed that he had nipped any press problem in the bud by talking to Turner. Normally he wouldn't withhold important information about Demesne's operations from Campbell, but given the man's attitude the last time, he decided to leave it be and simply tell his boss what had happened at the end.

Satisfied with this decision, McMahan turned his attention to other matters.

Chapter 18

The Battle of Beijian

Seated in the Viking boat, Claire and Jason spent some time plotting and arguing about the mission. For Claire, it was simple. She wanted to destroy the shark fins, plus any other contraband they could find, and confront Lau about her father. But she couldn't hold Jason's gaze when he asked her to define "confront".

"You can't simply barge in there and kill him," he reasoned. "That just makes you an assassin, exactly like the men who killed your father, and that's not what you are."

"Come on, Jason. We've both done this sort of thing before. What's the difference?"

"Before, any actions we took were official and sanctioned, as you well know," he argued.

"Fine, then please stay out of it and just cover my back," she said crossly. "But I have a score to settle, Jason, and I'm doing this, with or without you. Besides, I'll be hitting back for many other people who are in no position to confront these criminals."

Claire paused before continuing, more quietly this time. "I know it may sound stupid to you, but I also do this for the countless sea creatures being decimated for profit by Lau and people like him. Whales, dolphins, tunas, sharks, they're all being slaughtered. Someone needs to try to stop it, or at least slow it down, before it's too late, and there's nothing left."

They debated back and forth until Jason's arguments weakened and he conceded. "Okay, Claire, I'm with you. You're right. They're scum and need sorting. Let's get this done."

132

*

A partly haze-obscured moon struggled to caste its light onto the water as the Viking boat slowly approached the southern tip of Beijian Island. Claire had selected a small cove in which to anchor the vessel. Landing anywhere on the island posed problems, especially when unfamiliar with the area. Most of the coastline consisted of jagged cliffs rising straight out of deep sea. But the cliffs looked only moderately high and modestly steep, so maybe not insurmountable for two ex-Special Forces soldiers moving carefully.

The invaders used a combination of anchors and long lines to secure the boat and then prepared themselves for action. From Jason's seemingly bottomless supplies, they extracted figure-hugging, black jumpsuits and masking paint for their hands and faces.

"How did you know my size?" asked Claire as she changed, marvelling at Jason's foresight to compile so much gear in such a short time.

"Lucky guess," Jason replied mysteriously.

Once ready, they dropped soundlessly into the cold water and, ignoring the chill, half-swam and half-waded a short distance to the shore, their bags, bulging with weapons and more, raised above their heads. They needed only 15 minutes to scale the cliff, at the top of which they paused to let their night visions settle and ensure that no guards lurked nearby.

The island measured three kilometres end-to-end with the main buildings roughly two-thirds of the way to the northeast tip. A central rocky ridge ran along most of the island's length, largely covered in short, coarse, matted undergrowth. Claire

133

and Jason kept just below the ridge's southern eyeline and set off at a pace as fast as the scrub allowed.

They soon reached the first watchtower, circumventing it soundlessly, but ready to silence anyone who challenged them. At this stage, they wanted to avoid raising alarms. They continued on, treating two more guard posts the same way. The guards were not at all vigilant and, in one case, seemed concerned mainly with the screen of a mobile phone. Lau's complacency to tolerate such poor discipline worked to their advantage.

Barely half an hour after reaching the cliff-top, Claire and Jason rounded a large rock and saw before them the collection of buildings that formed Lau's centre of operations. They settled down back behind the cover provided by the rock and took time to peer out and study the triad headquarters using their AN/PVS-14 night-vision devices, which transformed the scene into stark relief.

Light spilled from the windows of a single-storey building, inside which people could be seen moving about. Claire and Jason figured it was probably a barracks and, as they watched, two men came out talking together. Each of them held a machine gun slung over a shoulder, and they walked casually towards what looked like the main house some 100 metres up the slope.

That more-distant building was grandly constructed on two levels, mostly out of wood as best the observers could tell, with a surrounding balcony on the higher floor and a flat roof. They saw many large, mostly shaded windows and several doors.

Another structure, 200 metres down the slope and smaller than the barracks, showed no light from inside, but bars covered the windows. A guard sat smoking in front of the single door, leading Claire and Jason to decide it must be a cellblock of sorts.

Halfway between the cells and the barracks stood a two-storey warehouse, windowless and with another guard posted at the front sliding doors, which were closed. A generator and other bits of equipment sat in what looked like an open-plan works area partially visible, but perhaps mostly behind the warehouse.

Amid light spilling from the main compound, Claire and Jason spotted a Bell Jet Ranger helicopter sitting on a flattened pad of rock near the house. Just beyond, a track wound down toward the sea, where a low concrete jetty jutted into the water to provide shelter and moorings for boats. They saw two large fuel-storage tanks near a shed of sorts at the start of the jetty. The end of the jetty was strewn with clutter, mostly old lobster pots and tattered nets. Tethered near the junk, which they knew about, were two skiffs and a large Sunseeker yacht. A small cargo boat rode at anchor a few hundred metres offshore.

"We seem spoilt for choice of targets," observed Jason. "Do you want to scuttle the lot before we go after Lau?"

"Absolutely! But should we keep the Sunseeker as an alternative to the Viking if we need a quick getaway?"

"Trouble with that is if we can't get back here, it leaves Lau and his buddies with something very fast to catch us," advised Jason. "Better to return to the Viking, which they don't know about, and make sure they can't get off the island at all. Same goes for the chopper."

"How about using that to get away? I'm sure you can fly it easily enough."

"Maybe, but choppers take so bloody long to warm up before they can take off that we'd be sitting ducks," observed

Jason. "Let's just fix everything and then work our way up to the main building."

"Okay," agreed Claire. "Before we do the main house, though, it'd be sensible to recce the outbuildings. It looks like Lau has a lot of backup there, and we need to know as much as possible about our odds."

Jason concurred so they set off again, skirting the compound and descending the small hill to the jetty, slinking as they went parallel to the track. There seemed to be only four sentries at the jetty. Claire and Jason waited more than 10 minutes to see if any others appeared. The shed they'd noticed earlier was really a small, open-sided hut adjacent to where the track joined the jetty and served as a guardhouse. Two men sat at a table there, smoking and talking idly, while the other two lazily paced the jetty.

After a few quick whispers, the intruders decided they could take out the four men and deal with any boat crew they found afterwards. They split up. Jason circled behind the hut and waited for Claire's signal.

She had the harder and longer job of quietly reaching the far side of the guardhouse and entering the sea. Once immersed, she swam quietly with powerful strokes, mostly underwater, to the far end of the jetty and, finding there a rusted ladder set into the concrete, pulled herself out soundlessly.

Crouching behind some lobster pots, Claire waited patiently for the nearest guard to close on her position and also watched for any signs of life from the nearby junk. With the guard just a few metres away, she rose and hurled her knife. The guard barely had time to register surprise before the knife buried itself in his throat, dropping him as he gurgled quietly. Claire followed the knife's flight and within seconds had removed her weapon and blended again into the shadows of the cluttered jetty.

The guard's fellow sentry had reached the end of his stroll in the other direction, and turning, saw his colleague in a heap at the jetty's end. He called out and walked quickly towards him, not actually sensing danger, but rather thinking that his companion had fallen or taken ill.

Even the sentry's sudden mild concern alerted the two men in the guardhouse, who looked up and began to rise. Now Jason sprang onto them, also using a knife. He stabbed one in the throat, and leaving the blade embedded in the soundlessly dying guard, wrapped a large arm around the other's neck while pulling his body in the opposite direction. In an instant, the man's neck snapped, and Jason allowed him to drop.

Claire, meanwhile, had one last sentry to handle. As the man approached his fallen comrade, he looked up and gasped in fright as she rose from hiding and charged at him. He carried a rifle strapped over a shoulder and wasted time trying to point it, but before he could grasp the weapon, his crazed assailant was on him and kicked him hard in his groin. As he doubled over, she delivered a fearsome chop to the back of his neck. He sank to the concrete, the only noise being the clatter of his gun dropping onto the jetty.

As Claire kneeled to check on the final guard, a male voice called out from inside the Sunseeker, startling her. She froze. Then she heard steps inside the unlit boat and more talk, this time from another man, followed by laughter. She supposed that the sounds came from the boat's crew, who probably stayed aboard.

Nothing more happened, so Claire grabbed the fallen guard by his collar and dragged him to the edge of the jetty before lowering him quietly over the side, allowing the sea to conceal his corpse. She repeated the process with the other guard and, looking up, saw that Jason had disposed of his opponents in the same way and now approached her along the jetty, carrying their two bags of kit and weapons.

Silently, Claire signalled, indicating the presence of people on the Sunseeker. Jason nodded that he understood, and they wordlessly decided to attack the boat together. As they crept aboard, Claire screwed the suppressor into her Sig Sauer. They moved silently to the open hatchway leading to the sleeping quarters below.

Descending, they heard the earnest grunting of two people having sex in a forward cabin. Jason went ahead and opened the door from behind which the noises emanated. A startled cry preceded two spits from Jason's silenced pistol. He closed the door again and joined Claire in the main cabin.

Already she had foraged in her bag for the explosive to scuttle the Sunseeker. Watching her, Jason thought she looked distressed. "Are you okay?" he asked anxiously.

"Yeah, I'm fine. I'd just prefer not to be killing everyone, and then I think of my Dad…." She paused, took a deep breath and then squarely faced him. "I'm fine, Jason, really. It was just a moment."

Seemingly satisfied with her answer, he watched as she set about cutting a piece of the C4 from the main block. She returned to the deck, lifted an access panel and lowered herself into the engine space. Working from the light of a small pencil torch clamped between her teeth, she folded the malleable, putty-like C4 explosive into a space between a propeller shaft and the engine cowling. She placed a detonator carefully into it and connected that to a timer, which she set for two hours. Extinguishing the torch, she pulled herself back on deck and then joined Jason, who by then was on the jetty keeping guard.

They moved quickly and quietly onward to the junk, which they boarded expecting maybe to find more crew. The actual quarters below deck were quite small. No one was there, but they descended into an appalling smell of bilge water, stinking fish and excrement. "While you sort the charges, I'll check elsewhere," said Jason, hastily leaving the sickly confines below deck.

Claire looked around, but found no way into the engine space. She'd need more time and light for that, neither of which she had. Going back on deck, she prepared the explosive there before slipping over the side of the junk, easing back into the water. She angled around to the single-screw propeller and wedged a C4 bundle against its shaft where it entered the boat.

When she returned to the side of the jetty, Jason pulled her up onto it. "Now it's you who looks sick," she observed. "What's up?"

"That smell," he grumbled.

"What of it?"

"It's human waste. There are chains in that hold, Claire. I reckon they use that junk for human trafficking. Makes me wonder about that coaster sitting offshore too."

"Bloody hell," was all Claire could respond. "The triads are known for that so I suppose I'm not surprised."

"Shall we go after the ship as well then?" Jason asked.

"Let's leave it for now. It would take a while to swim over there, and we'd have to use up most of the C4, which we might need later."

"Makes sense," Jason agreed, as Claire dropped into the first of the skiffs and, with remarkable ease, pulled what amounted to little more than a plug from the boat's base and, jamming a screwdriver that she found by the steering column into the gap, watched as water began pouring inside. The second skiff was similarly dealt with, leaving just the two fuel tanks. After setting charges there, they made their way cautiously back towards the compound.

*

Even when Kim and his men finally had docked at the jetty and delivered the shark fins, Lau remained in a foul mood. He needed to keep the fins on this island now before sending them to the Chinese mainland for distribution via a more-circuitous-than-usual route to avoid possible, albeit unlikely, attention from the authorities. He was alarmed to hear from Kim about the gunfire back in Kowloon. But nothing much seemed to have come of it, and so far, no police enquiries had reached his ears, so he put it down to other triad activities. Members of the 14K Triad always shot things up, so maybe it was them, he reasoned.

As for the nonsense with the Armstrong woman, he felt glad in a way that McMahan had promised to handle her, giving him one less potential headache. Still, the loss of face involved upset him a lot.

All these issues were inconveniences for which he blamed Kim. If and when Simon completed his contract to kill Armstrong before Huang and his men did, Lau would do away with Kim and promote Simon. The latter man was less imaginative, little more than a street thug, but he showed total loyalty and obedience and, in Lau's business, those traits held value above all else.

For now, Lau needed to focus on a far more profitable enterprise. He had forged an extremely lucrative deal with Kage Kuraim, a Yakuza chieftain in Japan, to supply women from across Southeast Asia and Eastern Europe for Kuraim's clubs and brothels across Japan. Hong Kong provided a fertile hunting ground where naïve single-female tourists or contract workers could be lured into triad traps and, before they knew it, shipped in Lau's junk to his holding station on Beijian and then onward to Japan. Usually their families and friends never saw or heard from them again.

Human trafficking formed a big global business, and Lau towered in the midst of it, securely in partnership with one of the most feared and ruthless *oyabun* of any Japanese Yakuza syndicate. This was yet another profitable arrangement brokered by Demesne.

*

Arriving at the top of the track, Claire and Jason crept carefully to a window at the back of the barracks and peered tentatively inside. The whole place was open-plan with curtains to pull at strategic points for privacy as needed. They saw a latrine, next to which was a small kitchen. A thin, sweaty man stirred the contents of a pot on a gas ring, and his vacant expression and staring eyes indicated drug use. Beyond, they observed two rows of bunk beds. They counted 20 berths, which suggested the size of the triad force. At the far end were tables, chairs and five more men sitting around talking or cheering at the on-screen antics in a porn film playing on a small television.

Stepping away, Claire and Jason went behind the warehouse and saw that the open area was indeed a work space. There were two large generators, one toiling at full capacity, presumably serving the entire compound. Nobody else was there, and they considered destroying the generators so as to operate more effectively in the dark.

"Thing is," reasoned Claire, "once these blew, we'd have the whole garrison down on top of us. I reckon there may be about 16 men left. We saw two on guard duty at the next two buildings, there are four watchtowers and two guys walked towards the main house. Six more are in the barracks, and let's assume that Lau has a few goons in the house with him."

"Don't forget the six guys who arrived on the junk. Probably some servants stay in the house with Lau too. I think we should expect nothing less than 25 to 30 people. That stacks the odds too heavily against us."

"You're right, but that needn't stop us from getting Lau. Let's see what's in the warehouse and in that cellblock, if we can. There must be something worthwhile to warrant the guards. Then we'll decide what to do next."

"Suits me," said Jason, "but we'll need to take out the two guards. You deal with the warehouse one. I'll handle the cellblock guy and then come back to join you." Without waiting for a reply, Jason melted into the darkness.

Silencing the guards proved easy and, after dragging both gangsters into the shadows, they reunited just as Claire quietly opened a Judas gate in the warehouse's sliding door. They slipped inside and, keeping their torches masked, began looking around.

In the centre of the floor rested the bags of fins they had followed here. More searching revealed other contraband, notably hundreds of crates of unlabelled bottles of red wine and, on a nearby table, piles of counterfeit *en primeur* claret labels. These would be destined for fine restaurants and private cellars on the Chinese mainland, where prices spoke louder than understanding or quality in the consumption of wine.

Claire and Jason found an even bigger haul on a mezzanine floor: row upon row of stacked packets of white powder. "No prizes for guessing what that is," observed Jason. "Bloody hell, there must be a fortune's worth."

"Let's set a charge in here to coincide with the boats. I saw some petrol cans in the work space outside, so we can soak all this and then let the C4 do the rest after we're gone."

"I'll fetch them," Jason said, disappearing out through the Judas gate. Moments later he returned with a jerry can in each hand. They soaked the drugs and the fins first, and then splashed the remnants around the warehouse walls. Next, Jason set an explosive charge positioned to bring down the mezzanine on top of the contraband below and set the whole lot ablaze.

Then they approached the cellblock. Although their suspicions had remained unspoken, they both half expected to find what they did. At least 30 girls, dishevelled and dirty, with any open eyes showing expressions of dull apathy and listlessness, sat or lay in foul-smelling, abject misery on the floor of the one-room building. None of the captives moved much, nor indicated any real interest in escape. Clearly, they were drugged and in grim shape.

Retreating outside and closing the door behind them, Claire and Jason looked at each other, dumbfounded. They had seen much suffering and brutality when in the Special Forces, but the scene inside Lau's cellblock hit a new low for them. Even worse, they could do nothing to help the captives right now. Instead they needed to complete their own mission and then call in the cavalry to clean up.

"Come on," said Claire, leading off up the incline to the main house.

Nearing the elaborate building, they heard two voices from inside arguing loudly in Cantonese. Through an open window, Claire recognised Kim's voice, but the other man did most of the shouting.

Creeping around the house's exterior, Claire and Jason glanced through a back window and saw a kitchen. Then a door suddenly opened, and a cook and a guard emerged, the former carrying a packet of cigarettes. Seeing nothing amiss in the darkness, they each took a cigarette and lit up. By now, Claire and Jason had no qualms about harming anyone associated with the triad. Without hesitating, they used their silenced pistols to kill both men.

"Smoking can be such a deadly habit," Jason whispered, drawing a grim smile from Claire.

"Worse than chocolate," she whispered back. "Now, follow me."

Warily, they entered the house. Inside servants' quarters next to the kitchen, they found four guards and dealt with them summarily. The noisy argument a few rooms away continued, rendering the muffled spits from their guns nearly inaudible.

Claire and Jason approached a closed door opposite and cautiously opened it. They discovered two maids, judging by the uniforms, sitting on a sofa, talking and smoking. Startled by the arrival of intruders, the women froze, staring fearfully.

Jason pointed his gun at the maids while Claire, after raising a finger to her lips for silence, asked quietly in Cantonese if any other staff members were in the house. The older maid gabbled a reply, trembling and shaking her head, but mentioning a butler and a cook, plus the guards, and no one else.

Suddenly the younger woman produced a pistol from her side on the sofa and brought it to bear on Jason. But she moved too slowly, and Jason shot her in the head with a double tap. The other maid rose, hissing, and charged at Jason, but Claire dropped her with yet another silenced gunshot.

"Bloody hell, why did they do that?" asked Jason.

"Don't worry about it," replied Claire indifferently. "They're just as much triad gangsters as anyone else here. Look at the tattoos on their arms."

As they left the staff quarters, a butler appeared. Seeing the two black-clad figures, he cried out and ran back the way he had come. Jason, who stood the nearest, shot him in the back and, as he fell, an empty tray that he'd carried clattered loudly on the tiled floor.

The cry and then the clatter abruptly ended the argument between Lau and Kim, who both fell silent. For a few seconds, quiet prevailed.

Claire and Jason stood motionless, listening intently. An authoritative voice called out from behind a closed door, followed by the sounds of chairs being pushed back, wood on wood, as the occupants rose to investigate.

Taking the initiative, Claire and Jason rushed forward, together kicking the door hard and forcing it open. With guns extended, they entered the room where Lau and Kim had been quarrelling.

"Sit down, both of you, and say nothing unless I tell you to," ordered Claire in English. She regarded her Cantonese as insufficiently fluent for an interrogation.

Kim dropped into the nearest chair, but Lau, pretending not to comprehend, remained standing. Stepping forward, Claire pistol-whipped him in the face, sending him sprawling backwards onto the floor. "Now do you understand?"

Lau did. Nodding, and suddenly nursing a bleeding cheek and an aching jaw, he sullenly pulled himself up and sat heavily.

With Claire pointing her weapon to keep the two men in place, Jason restrained them with plastic double-locking zip ties, securing their hands behind their backs and their feet to the chair legs.

145

Despite Claire's blackened face, Kim recognised her and said so to Lau before receiving the same treatment as his boss had moments earlier. He shrieked in pain, but drew no sympathy.

"I said to say nothing," Claire told him. "Next time you disobey me, I'll shoot you."

Peering into the set faces of their attackers, the two Chinese men believed her. Failure to comply would be folly.

Then Claire addressed Lau. She almost whispered so pent up was her fury, but she commanded herself to stay calm. "I came here with one question, and now I have a few more. First question: why did you kill my father?"

"I don't know what you're talking about…." began Lau, just as Claire's pistol jerked, its soft spit followed by a howl of pain as Lau's left knee disintegrated in an explosion of blood and bone. She waited for his initial bellows to fade and then repeated the question, while a visibly shaken Kim watched.

Concerned by the noise, Jason looked out into the hallway, but spotted no response to the cries. Nonetheless, he waited quietly and watchfully by the door.

"Still on the first question, why did you kill my father?" said Claire, her weapon pointed squarely at Lau. "Stick to the truth this time."

Between gasps of pain, Lau spluttered, "It was business. He interfered in our shark fin business… needed to be stopped."

"And why are you following and threatening me?" The answer was obvious, but she wanted to ask anyway.

"Same reason," gasped the triad dragon head, "and McMahan said you were a threat and…." He suddenly stopped and looked to the floor. Overwhelmed by pain, he unintentionally had revealed a sacred name from which there was no turning back.

Sensing an important revelation, Claire pounced on the name. "Who is McMahan?" she demanded, but Lau said nothing more.

Claire looked at Kim, redirected her weapon and asked him the same question, but he swore that he didn't know. He was pale and shaking, and had wet himself when Claire shot his boss, so Kim definitely looked vulnerable and pliable.

Changing tack, Claire looked hard into Kim's frightened eyes. "Where are the girls in the cellblock here going?"

Lau looked up, hissed at Kim and earned a bullet promptly delivered to his other knee. This time the triad chief's screams lasted much longer, echoing through the house, and ended in sudden silence as he lost consciousness.

Returning her icy glaze to Kim, Claire repeated her question. "Answer me," she ordered.

"They will kill me," moaned Kim, vigorously shaking his head.

The pistol spat once more, this time at Kim, who looked in horror at his destroyed right knee before bellowing in pain and straining at his bonds. Claire waited for him to settle down. "Again, where are the girls going?"

"Yakuza," whispered Kim. "Japan…."

"Who specifically takes them?"

Kim shook his head pleadingly. "Please, don't…." Claire raised her gun, but this time she didn't need to fire it. "Kage Kuraim. It's Kage Kuraim," shouted the once-proud triad deputy.

Then Kim quietly pleaded, "Please, don't shoot me again, please don't…." His voice trailed off, and he wept.

"Who is McMahan?" Claire demanded again of Lau, who had regained consciousness.

Looking at Kim and ignoring Claire, Lau began ranting hoarsely at his deputy, a guttural tirade that brought flecks of blood and spittle to his lips. Kim took no notice, merely whimpering in shame and pain.

Claire looked dispassionately at Lau, the triad's so-called "mountain master". She felt entirely finished with these two vile people and all the misery and sorrow that their activities and lawlessness brought to so many individuals, humans and sea creatures alike. Justice needed serving, and she knew with absolute certainty that no such justice would happen in any Hong Kong law court.

Coldly, Claire raised her gun and pointed it at Lau's head. Dispassionately, she squeezed the trigger.

Kim looked up, knowing he would be next, but he no longer seemed to care. Recognizing this indifference was his last thought.

"Feel better?" asked Jason from the doorway, but his words failed to penetrate Claire's swirling thoughts. She knew of the Yakuza chieftain Kage Kuraim, and the name McMahan rang a bell too, but she couldn't quite place it.

Jason repeated his question a little louder. This time he broke her spell.

"Better? Not really," Claire replied. "It never is better, not for long anyhow."

Then she snapped back to the mission at hand. "Let's take care of the barracks," she said. "I think we've accounted for most of the other guards so a few well-thrown grenades might finish this business."

"I think we should just go now, Claire," Jason suggested. "We've done enough killing for one night."

"The trouble is that when any gangsters still here find out what has happened, they may want to take it out on the girls,

148

who won't be safe until we call in the authorities and they arrive. Most triad soldiers behave just as badly as these two bastards here did."

"That's true, I suppose. I'll do what you want, but let's still tread carefully. We may have missed some gangsters."

"Right," said Claire, "you go ahead, and I'll fix the house for demolition. Strike quickly, Jason, and then we'll yomp back to the Viking. We'll take out the watchtower sentries as we go."

"Gotcha," said Jason. He retreated back through the house headed for the barracks.

There, the same five men remained fascinated by the moans, groans and yells of pleasure emanating from their movie, none the wiser about the mayhem that had engulfed their comrades. They looked up, seemingly bemused, as one grenade, and then another, was lobbed through the barracks door, landing in their midst. As grim realisations dawned, they all leapt to their feet, shouting and scrambling for the doorway. But they reacted much too late, and the only man still standing once the dust settled was the cook, who, in his drug-induced daze at the end of the building, stared on into his pot, seemingly oblivious to what had happened.

As Jason sprinted back to find Claire, he diverted just long enough to lob another grenade, this one into the helicopter. He flattened himself to the ground just in time before the machine disintegrated, its pieces going airborne contrary to the usual way.

Feeling triumphant, but still vigilant, Claire and Jason hustled back across the spine of the island, caring less for cover than speed. At each watchtower, the sentries stood more alert than earlier, having heard the exploding grenades. Yet they failed to suspect any real attack, feeling mostly curious, and were easily lured into view and dispatched with calculated efficiency by the silenced pistols.

The fourth and final tower was more distant, and so Jason attended to the guard there while Claire climbed down the cliff and swam out to the boat to prepare for their departure. Once Jason joined her, they slipped the mooring lines, pulled up the anchor and soon coasted slowly away from the island before looping around it to the north.

"Do you want to nobble that coaster now?" asked Jason as they approached the darkened ship.

"I think we've probably had enough excitement, don't you?" Claire replied, just as an explosion erupted.

The impact lifted the Sunseeker into the air an instant before its fuel tank disintegrated in a larger, secondary explosion. The once-fine yacht settled back onto the water and promptly sank.

Two more blasts erupted in quick succession, one from the junk and one from the fuel tanks by the jetty. Then two buildings exploded. Being higher up, the warehouse and Lau's mansion could be seen ablaze long after the sounds of the blasts died away.

"Yes, that's definitely enough excitement," Claire repeated as they slowly made off across the darkened sea, their navigation lights extinguished for the moment. Then she thought again about the girls left behind.

"Those explosions and the fires should attract someone to call the authorities, so the girls will be fine," said Jason reassuringly. Then he suggested enjoying the beers that he'd noticed earlier.

Moments later, they knocked two cool cans together in a toast. "That was a decent night's work, Claire," Jason said, "but we need to plan our next moves very carefully and pretty damn quickly."

"My thoughts too," she said. "Have you any proposals because, frankly, I'm feeling a bit wasted?"

"For starters, I don't think we should return to Hong Kong right now. We need to hole up somewhere safe and then take stock. When deciding what to do next, we don't want to be looking over our shoulders all the time for the police or more bandits."

"I hadn't thought about that, but you're right. Got any ideas?"

"Yep, actually, I do. You're coming home to my place in Macau. That's where we can talk through all this bloody mess."

Claire looked at Jason quizzically and then smiled. "Sounds like a plan," she responded. "Why not hand me another beer, and then take the wheel. I don't know the way."

Chapter 19

Putting the Toothpaste Back in the Tube

News of the conflagration on Beijian spread across Hong Kong like wildfire. The authorities received an anonymous tip at about the same time as Huang heard from his contact on Miaowan. Others, including the *SCMP* newspaper, had the scoop minutes later. Most media outlets assigned news crews to learn and report what they could. Soon the leaders of rival triad societies gloated, taking delight in visualising how best to carve up the decapitated Xuè yuèliàng empire. But the news reached southern China's Guangdong Province significantly later.

With Lau being always of interest, the Hong Kong police arrived on site fast, first with a squad from the Special Duties Unit delivered by an AS322 Super Puma helicopter. Half a squadron from the same unit followed, coming at speed on 17-metre RIBs (rigid-hulled inflatable boats).

The awaiting scene looked chaotic and chilling. In the early-morning darkness, the main buildings, such as remained standing, still burned and cast eerie shadows across the compound. When the only undamaged building was opened, the sight of the enslaved women inside haunted the responders even more. With the growing light of dawn, medical teams arrived to care for the women, who soon rode together on a commandeered ferry to Kowloon for protective care.

A large forensic force began the challenging process to work out exactly what had happened. The only potential witness, a confused cook, said little and appeared to be completely impaired. Early conclusions suggested a gang turf war. Even when standing amid the destruction, no one on-site felt very sorry that the Xuè yuèliàng Triad seemed to be eradicated.

After hearing the news, Huang reacted immediately. Already having placed various boats in the Hong Kong approaches, he dispatched a fast motor launch to Beijian, carrying his people to evaluate the situation first-hand. Barely able to assess the destruction before the police helicopter arrived, these gangsters needed to withdraw to avoid entanglement with the authorities, but they left a spotter, who observed the police activities from a safe distance until he too fled as the authorities began sweeping the island. The launch picked him up and retreated to Miaowan, where its occupants telephoned a report to Huang.

*

Early media bulletins also alerted McMahan. He received a preliminary briefing from Huang before sitting down with Campbell over steaming cups of coffee in the chairman's office.

"What the hell's going on out there, Billy?" demanded Sir Iain unhappily. "Is there a triad turf war starting up that we didn't know about? I thought you had all that business settled and under control."

"No, it wasn't the triads, Sir Iain. It was Armstrong," stated McMahan bluntly. "I told you she was dangerous, and now she has destroyed an entire society."

Campbell couldn't believe what he heard. "For goodness sakes, Billy, how could one woman, however strong and resourceful, do that? It's impossible."

"Well, it appears that she did have one other person with her, an equally capable man, presumably also Special Forces-trained. We're trying to identify him."

"Even so, two people then. I just can't believe it." Campbell remained incredulous and then had an alarming thought. "Where are they now? Is Demesne safe?"

"Last question first, yes, Demesne remains perfectly safe," replied McMahan, wishing he felt as confident as he tried to sound. "As for where they are, we don't know yet. Huang has stretched a net of informants over the sea approaches and around Hong Kong's outer islands. His entire network is focussed on finding them, so sooner or later we'll nab them."

"And then what will you do with them?" asked Campbell.

"What I have wanted to do all along, get rid of them," said McMahan sulkily.

"Okay, okay, you told me so, I know. Is there anything else I need to hear?" Sir Iain noticed McMahan shifting uneasily. "What?" he demanded.

So, McMahan updated him about Claire's visits to Kim and later to the Environment Directorate and about the recordings she made. He reported his conversation with the editor-in-chief of the *SCMP*. "Unfortunately, now he probably can't ignore the events at Beijian and may link Armstrong's recordings to the whole affair."

"Did you threaten him or schmooze him to drop the story?" asked the chairman, knowing full well the probable answer. Billy didn't do much schmooze, he thought.

"What do you think?" asked McMahan, somewhat disrespectfully. "Newspaper people respond only to force and threats. But now I think we'll need to silence this particular one permanently before he prints anything harmful."

"I fear that you're right, but it must happen today," said the pitiless head of Demesne. "The story from Beijian erupted after this morning's newspapers went out, but tomorrow the pages will overflow with speculation about everyone and everything."

"I'll get onto it right away," said McMahan, rising.

"You do that, Billy, and get this bloody mess contained and buried fast." Campbell's steely eyes blazed at his deputy. "I am very unhappy."

McMahan retreated to his own office. He'd seen his boss sulk like this a few times before, but never directed at him. The implied threat behind Campbell's words sent shivers along McMahan's normally stiff spine.

Just one solution sprang to mind. McMahan called for Huang.

Chapter 20

Claire and Jason Arrive in Macau

Hints of dawn painted the low clouds on the horizon pink as Claire and Jason motored towards Macau. Jason had chosen to head southwest into open, deeper water, giving the clutter of islands between Beijian and Macau a wide berth. He wanted to keep out of sight and avoid fishing boats returning to their home ports after a night's work. His strategy rendered the trip longer, but safer. After passing well south of Dawanshan Island, the Viking turned north toward Macau's southern tip.

Although daylight reached Macau before Claire and Jason did, it remained early, with few people in sight, as the Viking approached the small harbour of Cheoc Van, a short distance from the better-known and older town of Coloane. The two battle-weary travellers tied up at the quayside and, lugging their bags, walked to a cluster of new houses overlooking the harbour.

Producing a key, Jason opened a door to a dwelling amid the cluster. Bowing slightly to Claire, he said, "Welcome to my humble abode."

Actually, it was far from "humble". Set on three spacious levels with stunning south-facing views, the place was tastefully decorated and appointed in a very masculine way with comfortable furniture. Some decent art adorned the walls.

"This looks all very nice," observed Claire. "It's quite a bachelor pad."

"Yeah, I suppose so," said Jason with a sigh. "Truth is, though, usually I'm bored out of my wits here. I've had more fun in the past few days with you than in the entire previous year."

156

"I'm not sure that I'd call the last 48 hours fun, Jason, but I suppose I know what you mean."

"Right then," he said, remembering his role as a host. "First things first, there's a spare bedroom upstairs with a shower and fresh towels. Why don't you freshen up while I go out and get us something to eat? After that, we'll need to lose the Viking, although I expect that the police may have more pressing concerns than searching for missing boats."

"Let's hope so," said Claire, peering steadily at Jason. "Look, before much else happens, don't you need to get back to work? Your casino bosses must miss you."

"Maybe, but I've decided to quit my job. I earned good money there, but the work was so dull. Spending time with you reminded me that life is too short to squander."

"That's as may be, Jason, but this escapade will end soon, one way or another, and then what will you do?" Although secretly pleased that he wanted to stay with her, Claire felt pangs of guilt for taking him away from stable employment.

"Seems to me there are always good causes to fight for Claire, and that's what I'm trained to do. The decision's made; there's nothing more to discuss."

"Well, in that case, expect no more arguments from me," she said, much relieved. "Let's consider our next moves."

"Not so fast, girl!" he declared authoritatively. "You need to go upstairs and clean up while I run some errands, so be off with you. I'll return soon."

*

Once outside the house, Jason telephoned a local man, a small-time crook in Coloane who did odd jobs for him, some less legal than others. He explained about the Viking boat and

157

asked the man to take it from the harbour and return it to the old China Ferry Terminal in Kowloon, knowing that the absence of keys posed no obstacle to this fellow. Jason asked him to wipe down the boat and clear all prints and any other "evidence". As usual, the man's services would bring a healthy reward.

Next, Jason strolled to a store, arriving just as it opened for the day, and bought some basic food supplies. A few street stalls nearby sold everything from clothing to knock-off handbags, jewellery and assorted junk that usually only the deluded tourists wanted. Visiting several stalls, Jason selected some clothes that he hoped might fit Claire.

Arriving home, he found Claire sprawled asleep on a living-room sofa. A long bathrobe that she wore had parted well above her knees. A towel surrounded her hair, and her face glowed.

Not for the first time, Jason felt stirrings of arousal as he observed this lethal and exciting woman. Suddenly she opened her eyes and saw him watching her. Hastily he turned away and went into the kitchen.

Claire considered his reaction. Another time, she thought, another time. An age had passed since she'd indulged in an amorous relationship with anyone, and if she was honest with herself, she wasn't an easy person for any man to relax with and enjoy real intimacy. Now was not the time, she knew, but was it ever?

With a sigh, she rose from the sofa and followed Jason into the kitchen to find him unpacking his purchases. He gave her a bag of clothes, saying, "I wasn't sure if you had many spare garments wrapped up in that bag of yours, so I bought some T-shirts, jeans and stuff. Sorry it's nothing fancy." He blushed, not used to such domesticity. "Anyway, I hope something fits if you need it." He hastened to start preparing an omelette.

Claire smiled at him. "That was very thoughtful, Jason. Thank you. As it happens, I do need a few things."

She took the bag up to her room and opened it, grinning hugely at his selections. Inside, she found T-shirts, jeans and underwear, all of it fitting well enough.

"Perfect choices and good fits," she reported upon returning to the kitchen. "Mind you, the passion-killers were a bit big so I've left them off."

Jason turned purple with embarrassment, but she patted one of his arms. "Don't worry. I'm only teasing. Thank you."

They gulped down a substantial breakfast of eggs, sausages, croissants, some egg tartlets for which Macau is famous and lots of strong coffee, finally feeling replete. Jason told Claire what he'd arranged for the stolen Viking boat, and then he went to clean up and change clothes too. After that, they settled down to discuss their next priorities.

*

Searches on Google provided a good place to start. Soon Claire and Jason zeroed in on William McMahan and Campbell's Trading Company. They read about a firmly established enterprise with deep roots in Hong Kong and China and, although some of what they perused inferred links to organised crime, especially the triads, nothing sounded proven. A picture emerged of an extremely powerful organisation and a well-protected pillar of the community, one with which it was imprudent to clash. As the longstanding company CEO, McMahan undoubtedly towered as a powerful and influential figure.

They researched more about the company's chairman, Sir Iain Campbell, and found a correspondingly ruthless and determined individual. He, or Campbell's, seemed to own almost everything, from the largest utility company in Southeast Asia to a massive global shipping line, not to mention a small, but prestigious, hotel company, major shareholdings in no less than three regional airlines and a truly global real-estate portfolio with large investments in China, Japan, Russia, North and South America and Europe. Campbell's even held a majority stake in the *SCMP* newspaper, Claire noticed, a detail that alarmed her.

Curiously, Campbell's Trading Company's own website was small and uninformative. It simply referred anyone with genuine enquiries to initiate contact through a set of subject-related telephone numbers and e-mail addresses.

The two former soldiers felt somewhat dazed by their study. Obviously, this was no enterprise with which to trifle. Although the link between Lau and McMahan could not be confirmed, all the circumstantial evidence pointed that way. Likewise, the Yakuza, including Kage Kuraim's name, had resurfaced in the same context.

Since Claire's earliest briefing to Jason, they had discussed little about her activities in Costa Rica and in Japan. For reasons of survival, they had focussed on the issues facing them in Hong Kong and on Beijian Island. But her previous instinct, the hunch she had discussed with Bennett, that the various criminal syndicates seemed connected somehow to a larger parent organisation, gathered momentum. Could such a parent organisation be a global business, perhaps one called Campbell's Trading Company? She shared her troubled thoughts with Jason.

He sounded surprisingly comfortable with the notion. "In a way, it makes things easier for us if everything is controlled from a head office. Maybe we can take down the leader, and everything else collapses."

"That could be true, but overly simplistic," Claire retorted. "Each crime syndicate is a large and determined organisation in its own right. I can't imagine that a man like Kuraim would feel bothered at all if his so-called 'boss' in Hong Kong fell under the proverbial bus."

"Correct, but the business of organised crime on this massive scale involves coordination, transport, communication and contacts at the highest levels of government and society. Hell, it needs sales, banking and corporate organisational expertise applied to its activities."

Jason paused to refine his thoughts. "It's like you said, Claire. Essentially, we're talking about a huge trading company, but along with divisions to handle electronic goods, pharmaceuticals and other normal retail commodities, it also has sections within its structure and chain-of-command to trade in drugs, people, weapons, extortion and terrorism."

"And shark fins, dolphins and whales," said Claire bluntly.

"Those too," he agreed.

"So, what will we do about it?" she asked challengingly.

"You mean, other than reporting them to the police?" He ducked as she hurled a sofa cushion at him.

"Okay, okay," Jason said. "As an immediate priority, I think we should leave this part of the world for a while. After last night, a lot of frantic people are busy trying to connect dots, and some mysterious bad-asses out there, ones we haven't fully identified yet, still seem to have it in for us."

"And?"

"And so we should head to Japan and rattle some cages there. We need to lure Campbell, McMahan and their cronies out from cover, if it really is them, and the best way may be to go after another part of their organisation. We certainly trashed the one here for now."

"Agreed," said Claire flatly. "Let's grab onto Kage Kuraim's cage and give it a good shake, but which part?"

"Well, he's trafficking girls, which means the seamy nightlife in Tokyo's clubland and elsewhere. Same with drugs. Japan's a big, unfamiliar place, though, not like Hong Kong. We'd be out of our depth."

"We know he's into illegal whaling too, don't we? Why not go after the whaling fleet?"

"Good grief, Claire, how do you propose to do that? Anyway, isn't that what Greenpeace does?"

"Absolutely, but Greenpeace plays a disrupting game. At least, that's what it used to do. While that attracts some media attention, it doesn't stop much. The whaling fleets present themselves as victims and continue the killing. No, I'm thinking about sinking some whaling ships."

"You mean like piracy?"

Claire grinned at him. "Exactly, and we have a pirate of our very own in Taiji ready to help us."

PART 2

*

WHALES

Chapter 21

Whales Are Hunted

The small pod of humpback whales felt tired, especially the older female. She had not eaten, yet she had suckled her calf for most of the 4,000-kilometre journey from the warm waters of the central Pacific where she gave birth.

In their yearly migration the whales travelled north to cooler and food-rich waters in the Gulf of Alaska. The calf soon would build reserves of blubber to protect him from the cold and then could be weaned onto herring and krill. Next the mother would introduce him to the serious business of survival, like how and where to feed, what predators to avoid, including hunting packs of orcas, and, eventually, the complex process of mating, although a few years needed to pass before he'd be eligible for any potential and willing partners.

Cooler waters provided much-needed food. The pod ate greedily and collectively. Diving deep, the whales surrounded their prey, mostly herrings, by blowing air into circular cages of bubbles, which confused and entrapped the fish. Then the whales rushed with open mouths up through the middle of the bubbles, consuming huge quantities of precious food in a single ascent. At first, the calf felt perplexed, but soon got the hang of it, following his mother through the maelstrom of bubbles gathering what he could.

Members of the pod ate until the shoal of herring largely was decimated, and only swooping gulls stayed behind to mark the feeding frenzy while clearing up the remains. Now replenished, the whales prepared for the next part of their annual cycle.

The pod consisted of five whales, including the mother and calf, two young males and another adult female. Another pod soon joined them, and the serious business of courting began.

*

Seventy kilometres away to the west, five Russian whaling ships, supported by a huge processing factory ship, cruised through the northern waters in search of early arrivals in the migration. Although the sailors knew that the whales would be far from at their fattest after a long journey north, they wanted to catch as many of the creatures as possible before a rival Russian flotilla arrived.

Long gone were the days of human lookouts posted at elevation to watch for the whales as they broached. In those times, sailors located these ocean mammals by the sight and smell of their "blows", the spray bringing with it a strong, swamp-like odour that carried for kilometres downwind. Today, modern watchmen monitored state-of-the-art underwater radars with detection capacities vastly superior to any human eyes or noses.

The nearest of the whaling vessels, the *Mira*, picked up a faint signal at the edge of its radar screen, and the eager watchman alerted the captain, who immediately ordered engines full ahead with a course due east. The signal grew as the ship closed on its target.

In the vessel's bow, the harpoon master and his team prepared, clearing the protective coverings from around their gun and their armoury of harpoons, lines and explosives. Other crew members, tasked with securing and pulling in the injured or dead whales once they were speared, went enthusiastically to their stations. They all awaited their first kills of the season, and the more whales they killed, the more money they earned.

*

When whales are spotted, a whaler engages in pursuit, leaving the mother factory ship. Crew members on the hunting vessel fire a grenade-tipped harpoon at the target whale. Rope trails from the harpoon to prevent the whale from being lost. If the whale is struck and not killed instantly by the explosive-tipped harpoon, a second one may be used, or the whale may be shot with rifles until dead. The IWC forbids a past method of using a second harpoon to electrocute whales. Environmental groups even report incidents of whales being dragged backwards and drowned.

Each caught whale is secured to the ship's side with ropes. Later these lines are used to transfer the whale to the factory ship where it's winched through a slipway at the stern. Then on the flensing deck, several workers use specialised tools to butcher the carcass. Usable product is delivered to the lower decks for more processing and refrigerated storage. Non-usable product gets dumped back into the ocean.

*

Normally alert to underwater "noises", such as ship propellers churning through the water or radar "pings", the whales instead were preoccupied with their courting rituals. They registered the unfamiliar noises, but being distracted, they made no immediate moves to flee. At that belated stage, it hardly could have helped them if they had.

By the time the whales realised the immense danger and began to dive, it already was too late for one of the larger male suitors. A harpoon plunged into his flesh just behind and to one side of his enormous head. Although that alone was fatal, a small follow-up explosion destroyed what remained of his brain. He floated lifeless on the surface, ready to be tagged and collected alongside the whaler.

The ship slowed and followed the combined pod with radar as the whales dove deep. Larger adults can stay under for up to an hour, but the juveniles can't, and the mother, sensing her calf's distress and keen to help him, began ascending long before she needed to, despite her better instincts. He broached first, vented his stale air in a huge blow, took in another breath and dived again.

On the bridge of the *Mira*, much more sensitive radar was now in play, and the captain easily identified whales of different sizes. He instructed his gunner to hold fire and let the calf go. The mother whale would make a much richer prize.

Just as she broached, another harpoon flashed through the air, but a large wave had lifted the ship's bow just a fraction. The potentially lethal spear flew harmlessly over the top of the whale. By the time the crew had reloaded with another one, the female had vented, breathed and dived after her calf, safe again for the moment.

Disgruntled, the captain verbally blasted his gunner over their two-way radio and rejected the retorted excuses about sea conditions and lack of practice. For each miss henceforth, wages would be deducted. Seething in the cold air and determined not to let another whale escape, the gun crew waited as patiently as possible for the next broach.

By a half-hour later, the ship had followed the pod for several kilometres and noted that the whales were splitting up.

Several of them, though, also climbed towards the surface, so the captain tracked the largest one and directed his gunner accordingly.

As the large adult male surfaced, a harpoon took flight and found its mark halfway down the great creature's back. It was not a killing shot, and the explosive charge maimed, but did not stop, the whale. A second harpoon plunged into his thrashing body. Only then did he lie still, surrounded in a growing pool of bubbling blood.

Then the gunner's attention was called to another broach at the extreme range of his weapon. A harpoon tore into another whale just short of its tail and went right through the animal's body, the explosive charge detonating in the water beyond. The whale began to dive, but was hindered both by its wound and the cable attached to the harpoon that had torn through its body. It struggled to descend, but to no avail as the cable reeled backwards to the ship. As the whale surfaced, on the point of drowning, another harpoon found its mark, killing the creature.

The *Mira* killed one more victim from the pod before the remaining whales scattered, which made chasing down individuals impractical. But the four giant mammals taken so far launched the whalers' season to a decent start. As the crew hauled in the last of this initial catch, the captain ordered a return to the factory ship to deliver the cargo and prepare for more hunting.

*

Mother and calf had survived, and the youngster learned valuable lessons to beware of the strange and unfamiliar echoes that foretold of killing. To stay alive, they both needed to remain highly vigilant, ever alert to the dangers of this awful and ruthless predator, mankind.

Chapter 22

Demesne and Whaling

With the economic miracle of the new China, exciting business prospects and hitherto unimagined possibilities arose for many organisations, some less reputable than others. Demesne certainly capitalised on the opportunities, and Sir Iain Campbell had been surprised and delighted at the results of his exploitation of the shark finning programme, among others. This astonishingly lucrative trade almost matched his well-established engagement with the whaling industry.

*

Whaling has continued for centuries. Traditionally, oil boiled off from the enormous creatures' blubber formed the most precious part of any catch, and hunters gave chase from all over the world. It was hard and dangerous work, but for considerable rewards.

In many countries, including Norway, Iceland, Great Britain, Russia, the US, Canada and Japan, commercial whaling long formed a major industry. Even Australia and New Zealand engaged in whaling before taking leadership roles among the first nations to discontinue the practice. Nowadays, the remaining whaling fleets focus not on whale oil, but on culinary opportunities these extraordinary animals offer for willing-to-pay consumers.

As whaling ships added more sophisticated gear, the ability to find and kill the creatures, using radar and other advanced techniques, increased. By the mid-20th century, whales of all species became endangered with many on the critical list for extinction.

Eventually, governments heard the furious voices of environmentalists. In 1946, the IWC took shape to regulate and limit whaling catches and locations while prescribing quotas and seasons, but the whalers paid little heed. By 1982, the world knew that without a total embargo on whaling, many critically endangered species would vanish. The IWC imposed a total ban, with a moratorium issued to all whaling nations. This was neither well received, nor fully accepted, especially by Japan and Russia.

After silent and unpublicised intervention by Demesne, a clause appeared to allow certain quotas of particular species to be caught by approved countries. The reason finally given by the authorities to sanction such a copout was that the whales were needed for scientific research. Once this ridiculous notion took seed, it grew into an authoritative concept that nobody could overturn.

Worse, many industry participants still gave scant attention to the quotas, and the whaling fleets carried on much as before, knowing that support by the Yakuza and the Russian Mafiya meant that no force on earth could stop them. Japanese and Russian whalers committed the most abuses. Fights at sea between the whalers and Greenpeace became front-page news. The Southern Ocean, North Pacific and Japanese and Russian extended coastal waters became the new hunting areas to remorselessly attack beluga, gray, minke, sei and Bryde's whales. Larger and less-populous humpback, sperm and blue whales were targets too, increasing their extinction odds.

Through the crime syndicates, Demesne gained a stranglehold on much of the whaling industry. To increase profits, it suggested to the Yakuza to hide and freeze the catches before gently drip-feeding whale meat onto the market. That way, it would appear that fewer whales died, creating a false sense of short supply all the better to titillate Japanese demand and inflate prices for this specialty food.

Everyone gained, except for the whales, while hunters assailed them with savage purpose and inadequate oversight.

Chapter 23

Claire Reunites With Teach

Although absent from Hong Kong where the search for them raged, Claire and Jason decided for personal-safety reasons to follow a circuitous route from Macau to Japan. They wanted crowds of people around them so they could lose themselves in the throngs and expect limited customs scrutiny at borders.

From an arsenal of military hardware stashed in a closet of Jason's home, they chose some formidable weapons for their Japanese crusade. None of these would clear through any airport so they caught a train to Guangzhou in southern China before changing onto a bullet train to Shanghai. The ensuing 1,800-kilometre ride lasted just seven-and-a-half hours to reach China's largest city, where they stayed overnight in a small hotel near the main passenger-ferry terminal.

The next day Claire and Jason barely squeezed onto an overbooked weekly ferry to Osaka, Japan. This leg of the journey would last for two days and two nights, and after much bargaining and outright bribery, they secured a twin-berth cabin suite, the booking agent apparently being mortified that all other options had been sold out for days. It cost them the equivalent of US$2,000-plus, but knowing the contents of their carry-on bags, they made no fuss.

Only highly creative imaginations could regard the two-bed cabin as a "suite", but it was clean, comfortable and allowed Claire and Jason to discuss their plans more thoroughly and without interruption. For the first time, they also talked in detail about their personal histories and got to know each other better. When the ferry glided into Osaka after a smooth and uneventful crossing, they emerged as firm friends, not just comrades in arms. Yet despite sharing a cabin, they had avoided plunging across the line of intimacy, although both privately had considered it. The mission kept their relationship strictly professional, at least for now.

Clearing customs was simple, fast and clinical with no bag checks, and they passed into the arrivals hall to be greeted by John Teach. Claire had called ahead asking for him to meet them. He looked as weathered and swarthy as ever, and the huge bear-hug that he bestowed upon Claire reflected his obvious delight to see her again. He greeted Jason equally effusively and bade them to follow him to his car.

They set off for Taiji as Teach showered the newcomers with questions about all the commotion reported in the news from Hong Kong. Claire and Jason stayed somewhat guarded with their answers, which Teach understood, and they arrived at the POSC cottage in Taiji as the sun descended. It wasn't too dark for the host to point proudly towards the upper deck of a large ship sunk in the harbour mouth below them and around which salvage operations continued. As Jason surveyed all the idle fishing boats tied up at the inner-harbour quays, he had to concede that it looked like an outstanding sabotage job.

After going to their rooms and freshening up from the journey, the three ex-soldiers met again in the kitchen. There, Teach opened a bottle of wine.

"Where are the others?" asked Claire, referring to Namika and the students who were there during her last visit.

"The kids have gone," explained Teach. "They were here to observe and count the dolphin culling, but since the whole thing stopped literally overnight, they had nothing left to do, so I let them go. Namika is around though. I expect her back shortly with our dinner."

175

On cue, the front door opened, and Namika bustled in, laden with bags of shopping. She, too, was thrilled to see Claire again, and after greetings were exchanged, she set about preparing dinner. They talked more about Hong Kong, and Teach updated them on the relevant news reports, of which they'd seen little since leaving Macau.

The official line touted by the Hong Kong authorities, and those on the Chinese mainland too, was that the shooting incident at the China Ferry Terminal in Kowloon and the slaughter on Beijian Island in Guangdong Province had resulted from a triad turf war. News of the Xuè yuèliàng Triad's near-eradication pleased many people, but most of its activities were taken over by the 14K Triad, headed by the notorious Wan Kuok-koi, or "Broken Tooth Koi" as he was known.

After finishing a 14-year prison spell in 2012, Koi had kept a much lower profile, and some observers even wondered if he remained active in the triad society. But now he appeared to have eliminated his main 14K rival and climbed back into the saddle. The police suggested that Koi also must have masterminded the destruction of Winston Lau. Understandably, the 14K boss did nothing to dispel this myth.

The news that most shocked Claire related to the death of *South China Morning Post* newspaper editor Chris Turner. Supposedly, intruders had shot him at his home, a scenario that reminded Claire of the home invasion that killed her father. Speculation swirled that Turner had been working on a major political-corruption scandal. The scandal angle came forth from a junior intern at the *SCMP* newspaper, who then disappeared and whose parents were raising merry hell with the authorities about her whereabouts. The head of the ICAC denied knowledge of any such scandal or investigation, and the matter looked likely to dissipate as the rumour mill continued to spin.

176

"That's my fault," muttered a troubled Claire. "I sent the *South China Morning Post* a copy of my recorded chats with Kim, Wong and Ma, and I made no secret that I would go to the press and the authorities. Kim and Lau died before the hit on Turner happened, so either Ma or Wong must have arranged it."

"Or maybe that McMahan character," offered Jason.

"Whoever it was, don't beat yourself up over it, Claire," said Teach. "I'm afraid that Turner was a casualty of war, and a war of sorts is exactly what's happening."

"Agreed," put in Jason. "It's not your fault, Claire, and besides, why don't you send another copy of those recordings to the authorities? Perhaps even suggest some connections between McMahan, shark finning and the recent triad bloodletting. That should stir things up."

"It certainly would," she agreed. "But where should I send it? Who can we trust to act on such sensitive material? Maybe that guy Tsang at the ICAC?"

"I don't think so," said Teach. "From what I gather, the people at the ICAC are as bent as the crooks they're meant to chase. But I do trust one man in Hong Kong. We served in the Regiment together, and later he joined the police. He ended up in Hong Kong, did well and is a senior assistant commissioner and the director of B Department, which, in layman's terms, means fighting serious crimes, triads and all that sort of stuff. We haven't had much contact in recent years though. I'm afraid he doesn't entirely approve of my chosen career." Teach ended with a sheepish grin.

"You're talking about James Russell, right?" asked Jason, and Teach nodded. "I got to know him a little through the casinos in Macau. You're right. He's a good man and straight."

"So let's get a message and the recordings to him," said Claire. "But we need to be very careful about how we do it."

"Leave that issue with me," offered Teach. "I'll find a way."

"Okay, thanks, John," Claire replied. "You go ahead with that. I'll give you the USB stick and some words later. Now let's consider other plans."

Claire paused, and one-by-one she looked directly at each of them, including Namika, who was fully in the loop at Teach's insistence. "About this whaling business…," she began.

Chapter 24

James Russell Receives a Letter

By the time that James Russell left the British Armed Forces, he'd served with distinction and become the youngest full colonel to command the 22nd Regiment, more commonly known as the SAS. With such impeccable credentials, he had no trouble in joining the Hong Kong police, where he rose rapidly through the ranks.

These days, Russell enjoyed a reputation as a firm, but fair, man and perhaps most importantly, as unfailingly honest. Over the years, many less-reliable characters had tried to bribe him, and most of them ended up behind bars. Russell was not a big man, but his square jaw, compact torso and short-cut, silver hair gave an impression of fitness and resolve.

No fan of paperwork, Russell reluctantly waded through a stack of it in his office when his personal assistant (PA), May Kwok, brought in a special-delivery letter marked for his personal attention. May was a generously proportioned woman, unusually large for a Chinese lady, and absolutely dedicated to her work and to Russell personally. Very bright, meticulous and reliable, she thrived in her role and had been at his side as he rose through the ranks.

Normally, May opened Russell's mail so he felt surprised that she had made an exception. His surprise vanished when he saw an insignia stamped on the back of the envelope, a distinctive pair of wings bracketing a dagger, and an inscription below stating "Who Dares Wins", the crest and motto of the SAS.

Russell thanked May and waited until she stepped well away from his desk, only then turning his full attention to the envelope. Rather than opening it immediately, he carefully felt across its entire surface. The content was spongy with a small, hard object inside. The package had no apparent wires and no sinister smell, not marzipan, for example, which would have suggested explosive contents.

"What the hell?" Russell muttered and sliced the padded envelope open with a commando dagger that he routinely used as a letter-opener. Inside he found a USB stick and a printed letter addressed to him.

To: Senior Assistant Commissioner James Russell,
Director, B Department

Salutations, Boss.

I present to you the following solid information for you to do with as you will.

1. *Enclosed are some recordings made by Claire Armstrong, of whom you are probably aware, covering two conversations and a video of shark fins drying on a rooftop on Cameron Road, Kowloon. One conversation is between herself and a vanguard of the Xuè yuèliàng Triad, Mr Kim, and the other is between herself and the director of environmental protection, Philip Wong, and his deputy, Ronald Ma, the latter man apparently responsible for closing down the local office of POSC, the NGO long operated by Claire's father.*

2. *Earlier, a copy of this USB stick was given to Chris Turner at the SCMP newspaper shortly before he was assassinated!*

3. *Before dying at his headquarters on Beijian Island, the dragon head of the Xuè yuèliàng Triad, Winston Lau, admitted that David*

Armstrong was killed for interfering with triad business. For the same reason, a contract to kill Claire Armstrong was issued by someone named "McMahan".

4. *Further research identifies this individual as likely being William McMahan, the CEO and deputy chairman of Campbell's Trading Company.*

5. *The captive girls discovered on Beijian were intended to be trafficked to Kage Kuraim, oyabun of the Boryokudan Yakuza syndicate in Japan, with whom the Xuè yuèliàng Triad had close ties.*

6. *Kuraim controls much of the Japanese fisheries, notably the dolphin cull in Taiji and the country's entire whaling industry. The Russian Mafiya allegedly controls the Russian whaling industry, most of the catches from which sell to Japan and China through the Yakuza and the triads.*

7. *The drug cartel Barrio 18 in Central America is the principal syndicate involved in coordinating shark finning in the Eastern Pacific and Caribbean, channelling the product through Costa Rica and, until recently, on to the Xuè yuèliàng Triad in Hong Kong.*

8. *In the past few months, Claire Armstrong has violently encountered the Xuè yuèliàng Triad, Barrio 18 and the Boryokudan Yakuza syndicate.*

Questions: Is there a "parent company" coordinating these crime syndicates? Campbell's perhaps? How can we help to rectify matters? I'll be in touch.

Blackbeard

Russell showed the letter to May. When she'd finished reading it, he asked, "Please find me the exact location and contact details for John Teach, also known as Blackbeard." Seeing the bemused look on her face, he added, "No, I'm not joking. That's really his name."

Once May had returned to her desk, Russell read through the note several more times before inserting the USB stick into his personal laptop and playing the recordings. He replayed them a few times and then sat at his desk thinking.

Again, May entered the inner office. "That wasn't hard to find, sir," she said as cheerfully as ever. "John Teach works for the NGO, Protection of Sea Creatures, which David Armstrong ran. He leads its Japan branch based at Taiji. That's the place where the dolphin culls happen each…."

"Yes, I know where it is. Thank you," interrupted Russell, more testily than he intended. "It's also where a ship recently sank, stopping this year's cull dead in its tracks.

"Now listen to this." Russell played the recordings for May. "This is highly confidential," he warned her. "Got it, May? Not a word to anyone."

"Understood, sir. This is explosive stuff," she commented.

"Yes, quite literally," he agreed, rubbing his hands together in delight. "I want you to collect whatever information you can find for me about POSC, John Teach and Claire Armstrong. Presumably, POSC has modest resources and capabilities, yet it seems to have declared a global war on the crime syndicates. How remarkable is that?"

Chapter 25

Everybody Looks For Claire

Although McMahan disliked small talk, he needed to try being courteous when dealing with the Japanese. Among all the nationalities with whom he interacted, he knew that using his usual blunt and brutal approach to business didn't work with these people, and so he composed himself before calling Kage Kuraim.

The man in question was enjoying himself at one of his clubs in the Roppongi district of Tokyo. The club offered attentive, attractive and available hostesses, mostly from Russia or the Philippines, exotic cabaret shows, music, discreet dancing and decent, if expensive, champagne. One of many such clubs in Tokyo's notorious red-light district, it appeared to operate generally within the spirit of the law.

But on two hidden basement levels, the club also provided more extreme services by special order and introduction. These involved violent bondage and even more depraved experiences for discerning clients who paid vast sums for such entertainment and to indulge in their perversions. The women, and occasional men, who "entertained" there usually did so against their wills, representing the worst side of sex trafficking, an industry in which Kuraim led the market.

Although it was only mid-afternoon in Tokyo, Kuraim played host to some senior officials from the Fisheries Ministry, two men he was setting up to blackmail and extort significant favours from during the whaling season. The hapless object of the men's attentions was slim, blond and hogtied on a pedestal before them, with three local men taking turns to penetrate and brutalise her. The assault had persisted for more than an hour, and the girl no longer screamed, her eyes blank in dull acceptance of her fate. As spectators, the much-inebriated government officials were ecstatic, encouraging the assailants with lewd suggestions and sometimes reaching out to touch or slap the victim, unaware of the invisible, rolling cameras recording their enjoyment.

An attractive female aide brought a message to Kuraim that "Mr McMahan from Hong Kong" was on the telephone, and so he testily left the room to answer the call. He disliked leaving the government officials beyond personal view, but at least his cameras continued to keep tabs on them. Definitely, a phone call from Demesne was not one to ignore.

After exchanging a few pleasantries, McMahan came to the reason for his call. "I expect that you've heard about the death of your triad colleague, Winston Lau," he began.

"Of course, but not yet the precise details," answered Kuraim politely in his impeccable English. "I was sorry to hear about it because we did much business together. Can you tell me exactly what happened, Mr McMahan? It seems all rather mysterious, if the rumours are credible."

"What happened was a woman named Claire Armstrong."

"I've never heard of her," replied the *oyabun*, surprised and curious.

"Actually, you have, by her deeds if not by name," said McMahan, rather enjoying himself when dropping a bombshell. "She's the one who halted your dolphin cull in Taiji harbour."

"Just one woman did that? I don't believe it," Kuraim answered incredulously. If true, it made the incident even more embarrassing. Many rivals in the Yakuza took a smug satisfaction in Kuraim's discomfort about the sunken boat and its impact.

"You'd better believe it because she also just wiped out most of the Xuè yuèliàng Triad, and now she may be headed your way again."

"Well, it would give me great pleasure to meet her, I'm sure," said the gangster hopefully, "but why do you think she may return to Japan? That seems foolhardy."

"She's on a mission to protect the seas and everything in them," said McMahan tiredly. "Her father ran the NGO called Protection of Sea Creatures and was killed here after condemning the shark finning business. It seems that she has taken over his goals, just working rather more violently."

"Okay, I recognise the name of that misguided group," said Kuraim. "But what does this have to do with me?"

"For God's sake, don't be so bloody naïve, Kage," snapped McMahan. "Just think about it. She challenged the shark finning operations in Costa Rica, trashed your dolphin cull in Taiji, where incidentally POSC has representation, and removed an entire triad society from Hong Kong because of its links to these activities. I would expect whaling to rank rather high on her agenda, wouldn't you?"

Kuraim bridled at being spoken to so disrespectfully, but maintained his poise. "Where is she now?" he asked bluntly.

"We're not sure. There's no sign of her in Hong Kong, yet she hasn't left by any legal transit point, so she must have fled by other means. We believe she's travelling with a similarly dangerous man, and she, at least, used to be a soldier in the British Special Forces, so you've been warned."

"Well, thank you for the timely warning," Kuraim replied with exaggerated courtesy. "We'll hope that she does come to visit us in Japan, and when we find her, you may be assured that we'll provide her and her companion with an especially warm welcome. Goodbye, Mr McMahan."

185

Without speaking words of farewell, the man from Demesne already had disconnected. Knowing the head of the Boryokudan as he did, McMahan expected that if Armstrong did dare to surface in Japan, then it would be her undoing. The thought pleased him.

*

Much time had elapsed since Claire last talked to Chuck Bailey of POSC, their most recent conversation having ended discordantly. Although the NGO shouldn't consider itself any longer associated with her or her activities, she deemed it only fair to connect with him. She also wanted a favour. Calling from the kitchen table at the cottage in Taiji, she quickly reached him.

"Well, hello stranger," offered Bailey when he picked up Claire's call. There was little warmth in his voice.

"Hi, Chuck, how have you been?" she asked, already noticing the frostiness in his tone.

"Oh, we've been busy closing offices, relocating and paying off staff, that sort of thing. Nothing as exciting for us as the time you seem to be having, young lady."

"Look, Chuck, I haven't called to argue." Claire started to feel angry and to regret the call. "I'm trying to do something positive, something that actually lives up to our name. You know, saving sea creatures and all that."

"Oh, yeah, I forgot. Thanks for reminding me, Claire," he replied sarcastically. "Judging by what I see in the news, does that include taking unilateral action on a military scale against the triads?"

"For God's sake, Chuck, stop bitching and bloody well get onside with me here," snapped Claire. She'd had enough of his fence-sitting. "I need some information. Will you help me or not?"

"Depends on what you need," he answered sulkily. "You know, we've taken a lot of heat here, Claire."

"Oh really, Chuck? Well, if you can't take the heat, get out of the kitchen." Disgruntled, she slammed down her mobile phone, nearly breaking it against the table.

"So that went well," observed Blackbeard sardonically. He was about to comment more when Claire's phone rang, and she saw that it was Chuck Bailey calling back. She answered using the speaker function.

"Claire, look, I'm sorry," he said, his more familiar kindly and paternal voice now putting her more at ease. "I know you've been having it pretty rough. We're very worried about you, you know?"

"Okay, Chuck, no hard feelings. This is just the way I'm wired, I suppose," said Claire, more contritely. "Look, I need as much information as you can email to me about the Japanese whaling industry…."

"Oh, please, Claire," Bailey interrupted loudly, "you're not going after them too, are you? You'll get yourself killed."

"Don't worry, Chuck. This is just for general research."

"Where are you anyway? Not cooking up more trouble with that pirate Teach, are you?" This brought grins from the others listening in the cottage.

"Wouldn't dream of it," Claire lied smoothly. "I just want to understand what's happening because it seems to me there's a lot going on that's illegal, and someone needs to say something."

"Greenpeace and others say, and do, a lot, Claire," replied Bailey. "They're champions, but they're up against a complicit Japanese government and a major industry, so it's tough to make much progress."

"So it's back to public-relations work, is it?" she asked.

"There's little else, I'm afraid."

"Well, if you could send me some data anyway, Chuck, I'd be most grateful. At least I'll be better informed. Any introductions to people trying to fight the same battle would be great too."

"Ships from the Sea Shepherd Conservation Society's fleet no longer engage whalers in the Southern Ocean because the Japanese vessels are too well protected now, but I'll get you information if it helps for background."

Bailey knew that Claire was up to something, but what could he do about it? He reasoned that if he'd failed to dissuade her from a perilous quest, then maybe he should try to support her. In some small way, his assistance could help to keep her alive.

He simply gave a last caution. "The police and intelligence officers from MI6 have been here asking us questions about you, Claire. Of course, there's nothing much we can tell them because there's nothing much that we actually know, but please be careful. You've chosen very large and powerful enemies, you know."

"Don't worry. I'll behave sensibly," Claire assured him, bringing more smirks from the listeners in the Japanese kitchen.

"Please email me information. It might help. Take care, and thanks, Chuck," she said, ending the conversation.

*

No sooner did Claire finish her call than Teach's mobile phone rang. It was James Russell.

"Blackbeard, me ol' mucker, James Russell here. I got your note. Whatever are you doing?"

"Hi, Boss, it's been a while," responded Teach, somewhat lamely. "I said that I'd be in touch. Really didn't expect to hear from you so quickly."

"Well, you know how it is. Things have gotten a bit explosive here lately, and your letter lit another fuse. Now, is Ms Armstrong with you? I need to talk to her, please."

This phone was on speaker mode too, and Teach looked enquiringly at Claire, who nodded and took over the conversation. "Commissioner Russell, a pleasure. How may we help you?" she said crisply.

"I'm not the commissioner yet, Ms Armstrong, or should I call you Captain Armstrong?"

"Just call me Claire," she said bluntly.

"Claire it is, then. The pleasure is all mine, I think. As to helping me, I'm curious to know where you're going with this deadly crusade of yours. Whilst it all may be very comforting for the general public to see criminals and gangsters receive their violent comeuppance, what you've done completely violates the law."

"Well, it seemed to me the law wasn't doing very much about anything," Claire snapped, "so I figured that I should avenge my father myself."

"Yes, I get that, but the body count now stands at triads one, Avenging Angel, somewhere north of 30. Not precisely balancing the books," observed Russell.

"You know how it goes. One thing leads to another. There are some very bad people out there, and they're away ahead of conventional law enforcement."

"So, if this is no longer about your father, then what is it about, soldier?" asked Russell, speaking more as a previous colonel and SAS commanding officer than as the head of Hong Kong's B Department.

189

Claire needed to pause. The question made her uncomfortable, and she felt her resolve waver. Finally, she answered. "You saw the girls on Beijian Island, right? They all form part of the human-trafficking and sex-slavery chain. And you know all about the drugs, extortion, coercion, protection rackets and assassinations. Police forces worldwide work hard in a never-ending game to confront and stop all these activities and to protect ordinary citizens, yet usually the authorities are playing catch up." She stopped for a moment to gather her thoughts.

"But do you know what?" Claire continued. "No law-enforcement agency stands up for our oceans. These same crime syndicates rape and pillage the seas and slaughter the precious animals in them. They wipe out entire species for profit, completely disregarding the laws and treaties put in place to stop them. Realistically, what law-enforcement team can spend months at a time on the Southern Ocean and apprehend the whalers? No police force can prosecute the tens of thousands of impoverished fishermen around the world, the powerless people who cut off shark fins on orders from their overlords or else risk dismemberment themselves."

"So I ask again," Russell said, "where are you going with this?"

"I'll tell you exactly where I'm going, Colonel, if that title suits you better," Claire said in little more than a whisper. "I'm going to destroy as many of these sons-of-bitches as I possibly can and put more of them out of business. I'm going after the whalers, the finning boats, the tuna fleets, the dolphin cullers, the bottom trawlers and the electrofishing boats. All of the evil bastards clubbing together to promote their own greed are going to be in my crosshairs, and they're going to know it. I realise that one person, or a few people, can make only a small

190

difference, but when I'm done, they'll all be looking over their shoulders and, with any luck, there'll be enough public support to shut them down, or at least to dramatically reduce the demand for what they do."

"And Blackbeard's going to help you?"

"And me," piped up Jason.

"Ah, the mystery accomplice! And who might you be, soldier?" asked Russell.

"You already know me too, Boss. It's Jason Chan."

"Well, well, Jason Chan. My word, Claire, that's quite an outfit you've assembled."

Russell paused and took a deep breath. "You people know that eventually this all will end badly, don't you? You simply can't take on the world's most violent and notorious criminal organisations and expect to get away with it for long. I daresay that you'll all be killed, and if you're lucky, which is unlikely, it may happen quickly."

"Well, thanks for the vote of confidence, Colonel," said Claire. "In the meantime, can we pool our resources? Will you help us?"

"You're kidding, right?" sighed an exasperated Russell. "You know that I can't possibly condone your actions."

He went quiet for a moment. Then he said, "Maybe I could assist you with a little intel though."

This brought smiles to the group, and Claire replied, "That'd be good. Thank you. Does that include keeping us in the loop about Campbell's?"

"Bloody hell, Armstrong," erupted Russell, "you really do push your luck, don't you?" This brought fresh smiles all around in the cottage's kitchen.

"At this point in time, there's no 'loop'," Russell said. "Just making the most basic enquiries about the leader of that particular organisation could get me the sack or worse."

"So, you're not going to follow up on the leads we gave you?" asked Claire, accusingly.

"I didn't say that. Now if there's nothing else, I have a plane to catch."

"Where are you going, Boss?" asked Teach.

"As a matter of fact, you bloody pirate, I'm booked on the next flight to Tokyo to discuss your plans with you. Meet me in the lobby bar at the InterContinental Tokyo Bay Hotel at 2200 hours this evening."

The call disconnected, and members of the group in Taiji looked at each other with uncertainty. Was Russell coming to try arresting them or to help them? Until they knew, they decided to err on the side of caution. Carefully, they began to plan an immediate trip back to the Japanese capital.

Chapter 26

Hatching a Plan in Tokyo

From Claire's previous visit, she knew they needed at least seven hours to drive to Tokyo, and she wanted enough time before the meeting with Russell to explore the hotel and thoroughly recce the area. That made flying their only travel option, which also meant leaving behind all weapons.

At this point, Namika, as a locally hired POSC employee who routinely handled transport issues, came into her own, explaining that three flights per day flew to Tokyo's Haneda Airport from Nanki-Shirahama, a regional airport a 90-minute drive from Taiji. She proposed to deliver Claire, Jason and Teach to the smaller airport and then drive to Tokyo with their gear the following day to rendezvous with them at the hotel.

The flight would take a little more than an hour, and then the InterContinental Tokyo Bay Hotel was just a short ride away. They all needed to bustle, but Namika dropped off the three passengers at the domestic terminal in the nick of time for the next flight. Unable to book seats together, they took what they could get and made their journey, each mulling intense personal thoughts.

Regrouping at Haneda Airport, they shared a taxi and soon checked into the hotel with Claire continuing to pick up all the room, flight and taxi bills. Once settled into three rooms on the sixth floor, they reconvened in the main lobby. It was 8 o'clock, leaving them with two hours to prepare for the encounter with Russell.

Since Teach knew Russell the best, they decided that he should meet first with the incoming police official. Claire and Jason would stay out of sight, ready to run for it if the meeting turned out to be a trap. They considered this unlikely, but believed it wise to be prepared.

Without weapons, they all felt vulnerable, but Jason had placed a call to an associate in the gaming business, and they were promised a special delivery to the hotel before the meeting. Jason asked the concierge to page him immediately when the "important package" arrived.

Then the three newly arrived guests entered the hotel's all-day restaurant, Chef's Live Kitchen, for some food and to focus on their plans. As they finished eating, the concierge called.

After collecting the package, they retreated to Jason's room where he opened the special delivery. They were surprised and delighted to find three Sig Sauer P229 automatic pistols. Each was loaded and came with suppressors and two spare 15-round magazines.

"Nice to have friends in low places," quipped Blackbeard. "D'you suppose they'd like to join our gang?"

"I'll ask them," said Jason. "But the perceived wisdom in Japan is not to mess with the Yakuza, so I expect it's unlikely."

Claire holstered her pistol to wear behind her back, leaving it easy to reach, but well concealed under her floppy shirt. The others did likewise, and the spare magazines went into the small backpacks they carried.

Then Blackbeard left for the rendezvous in the New York Lounge bar just off the hotel lobby. Without two-way radio devices to keep in touch, they instead used their mobile phones, leaving a line open. They agreed that as soon as Teach deemed it safe for Claire and Jason to appear, he'd simply invite them to join the meeting. However, if the invitation included the words "POSC team", they would understand that it was a trap and not show. All rather too simple, as tradecraft went, but there was no time to prepare otherwise.

*

Being 20 minutes early to meet with Russell, Teach perched in a comfortable corner armchair at the far end of the lounge. Few people were present, and from this position he'd be able to see Russell coming, or anyone he might rather not encounter. Before sitting, he took note of a back way out through a staff-service door. He then settled down and ordered a favourite cocktail, one of his own inventions, although he doubted if the bar-staff would be able to produce it successfully.

"I'd like a Blackbeard's Treasure, please," he told the attractive waitress who came to take his order. Her nametag identified her as Miko.

"To be honest, I'm unfamiliar with that drink," she confessed in excellent English, "but if you describe it to me, I'll do my best. We're very proud of our liquor collection, and we always try to attend to our customer's needs." At this point, she raised an eyebrow flirtatiously and awaited his response.

"It's two shots of Pusser's Rum, a splash of fresh coconut water and a squeeze of raw sugar cane, all on ice and stirred. There, now you've got a challenge," he declared, offering back his own raised eyebrow together with a cheeky grin.

The waitress smiled. "As you say, sir, it's a challenge. Let me see what we can do."

Teach watched her leave and considered what to order instead when she returned, inevitably to disappoint him. He wasn't surprised when she came back a few minutes later, dismay visible on her face.

"I'm so sorry, sir," the waitress said coyly. "But we seem to have completely run out of ice!"

Teach burst out laughing, and the waitress giggled too at his reaction. It was a nice way to say they lacked the ingredients, he thought.

"That's very good, Miko," he said. "Okay, give me a Dark 'n' Stormy instead. But gosh darnit, please try to find some ice!"

The girl smiled again. "That one I know," she said before leaving to concoct his dark rum and ginger ale on the rocks. She had just delivered it, along with a bowl of mixed nuts and rice crackers, when Russell entered the lounge.

Looking around, the police executive spotted Teach and approached purposefully, carrying a large travel bag. Teach felt relieved to see that Russell appeared to be alone.

As Russell reached the table, Teach rose, and they warmly shook hands. They'd been comrades in arms, and that sort of bond never breaks.

"It's good to see you again, John," said Russell as he sat down. "It's been a very long time, and you don't look like you've changed much."

"Well, I'm a bit slower on the pins and thinner on top, Boss," Teach replied. "But thanks anyway."

"Yeah, tell me about it. Sitting at a bloody desk all the time slows you down more than you can believe, and it turns you grey too."

Russell paused, looking up as Miko appeared at his side. "I'll have whatever he's having," he ordered, with a nod towards Teach.

When Russell turned back to their conversation, the benign, chatty façade had gone, and he was all business. "Where are your new chums, John? I don't have too long, and we have a lot to get through."

"They're a bit shy, Boss. They wanted me to meet with you first, sort of see what the score is."

"Don't play silly buggers with me, Teach. I came to help you lunatics, remember, so if they're not sitting here within five minutes, then I'm off back to Hong Kong."

"Okay, okay, Boss. They'll come and join us now, won't you, guys?" Teach said, addressing the unseen mobile phone.

Russell rolled his eyes and took a pull on his drink.

Claire and Jason had waited nearby, watching Russell arrive and go straight into the bar. Seeing that he was unaccompanied, they were ready to join the meeting instantly when Teach signalled.

"Well, well, here's the dynamic duo, Claire Armstrong and Jason Chan," exclaimed Russell as they approached and shook hands with him. "Good to see you both. What'll you have?" They each ordered a beer and made small talk until the drinks arrived.

"Right, let's get down to business," began Russell, reaching into his bag and extracting a large brown envelope. "Here's a file on Kage Kuraim. It's not pleasant reading. His syndicate, the Boryokudan, is probably the most feared of all the Yakuza gangs. He, himself, has a reputation for cruelty and ruthlessness that his rivals don't quite match. He's alleged to have been behind some high-profile assassinations and kidnappings, as well as extortion cases, human trafficking and drug shipments, you name it."

"If you know all this, why hasn't he been arrested and prosecuted?" asked Claire reasonably.

"That's simple enough," Russell said. "The authorities here are frightened of him. Potential witnesses tend to disappear, and he has much of the judiciary in his pocket, scared stiff of his power."

"I pointed him out to Claire at the fish market when she last visited," said Teach. "She saw how well protected he was."

197

"Would that happen to be at about the same time as when you sank a ship in Taiji harbour and stopped the annual dolphin cull?" asked Russell innocently.

"I wouldn't know about that," replied Claire vaguely. She still wondered how far the lawman could be trusted.

"Anyway, you're right, John," Russell said. "Kuraim is well protected, but whereas the authorities must play by the book, a freelance team like you guys just might be able to take him down."

"Really, Colonel?" asked Claire. "Are you suggesting that we actually turn into some sort of mercenary unit to clear up the mobsters that your people can't? We have a mission, sure, but we set the objectives and the targets, not you or anyone else."

"Understood, but if our goals coincide nicely, then it's to our joint advantage to work together, right?"

"Perhaps," she replied guardedly. "What else?"

"Our problem in Hong Kong is that Kuraim lives outside our jurisdiction," said Russell, ignoring Claire's bluntness. "His reach and influence, though, are extraordinary, especially in a crime world already controlled by triads. You've discovered his drugs and human-trafficking links, but we're uncertain to what levels his extortion and influence reach in our business and political spheres."

"Which supports our theory that a master criminal organisation controls everything," Claire stated.

"It would seem highly likely," confirmed Russell.

"Campbell's!" declared Jason.

"Hold on there," said Russell, raising his hands. "We can't jump to conclusions. We must be very circumspect about this."

"It seems to me," riposted Claire, "that if you can't 'jump to a conclusion' like that now, you never will." She wondered if the meeting had become pointless.

"We need to make the masterminds break cover," said Russell, ignoring her. "If we can rattle their cage enough, it could force them to show their hands, to make a mistake."

Jason picked up the thread. "And if we go after Kuraim and panic him, then you reckon he'll turn to Campbell's or whoever, and then the people there will stick their heads above the parapet?"

"Exactly! Whether we catch a glimpse of heads or hands, the point is that we want them to reveal themselves."

"And then what?" asked Claire. "Have us return to Hong Kong and assassinate them? Come on, Colonel, we're not vigilantes. I'd remind you that our central mission is to protect sea life."

"How else can you help us?" Jason asked. "I hope you've got slightly more than a file because otherwise we're wasting our time here."

"As for not being vigilantes," said Russell, becoming testy with these unruly ex-soldiers, "you've given a pretty good impression of being exactly that in recent weeks. As for help, yes, I do have something else, and if you'll stop being so bloody-minded and confrontational, I'll tell you what it is!"

Russell reached for his nearly untouched drink, drained it in one long swallow and signalled across the room to Miko for another. The others traded understanding looks and silently agreed to let Teach pick up the discussion.

"Okay, Boss, point taken. We're all ears."

"Thank you, John. Right, would a boat help you?" That settled them down, Russell thought, studying their faces.

"What sort of boat are you talking about?" asked Claire cautiously.

"A damn good one that could follow the whaling ships and mess with Kuraim's control on the fisheries," Russell said. "In

199

and of itself, a disruption to Japanese whaling wouldn't be a catastrophe to him, but it would signal a huge loss of face, especially after the Taiji affair. Assuming he does report to a 'head office', so to speak, any disruption to his whaling interests definitely counts as loud 'cage rattling'."

"I'd have thought that going after his drugs and trafficking interests would have a higher-value impact," suggested Claire.

"Well, if you can manage that too, Claire, I'm sure we'd all be most grateful," replied Russell with a cold, humourless smile.

She stared back at him before saying, "Okay, tell us more about the damn good boat."

Altogether, they talked for more than an hour before Russell finally stood, looking at his wristwatch. "I have to get back to Hong Kong," he said. "You guys need to be very careful. After the big show you put on against the triads, it's more than likely by now that Kuraim already is on the lookout for you, so watch your backs."

Russell picked up his heavy travel bag and passed it to Teach. "You may find some useful items in here to help you on your way."

"How on earth did you get all that here?" asked Claire, glimpsing the contents. "That looks like enough explosives to sink a battleship."

"Not so loud, please, and never you mind how," replied Russell. "Let's just say that certain travel benefits come with my position. Anyway, you'll also find a few small limpet mines, so please use them wisely."

Teach looked delighted and thanked Russell on behalf of the team.

"A pleasure, you old pirate," came the reply. "Now take care, and if I were you, I'd stay away from Taiji. Your adversaries must have made the connection to POSC by now so it won't be safe for you."

"Bloody hell, you're right," exclaimed Teach. "I just hope that Namika is okay. I must call her now."

Despite it being almost midnight, Namika picked up on the second ring, and Teach felt much relieved to hear her voice. He told her in no uncertain terms to pack a bag for them both, lock the cottage and drive to Tokyo immediately.

"Good, she's on her way," said Teach after ending the call. "That's a relief."

He, Claire and Jason saw Russell into a taxi and then went to their rooms, agreeing to meet for an early breakfast. Jason took the bag of explosives with him because he wanted to examine the items, being perhaps the most experienced among them at demolition work.

*

The anxious late-night call from Teach scared Namika nearly out of her wits, but she followed his orders. She put Claire and Jason's bags into the car and, after packing another for herself and Teach, locked up the cottage and drove off into the night.

In Namika's haste, she failed to notice two shadowy men watching from a vehicle parked across the road. Alerted by her sudden departure, they called in and reported to their boss.

After hearing from McMahan, Kuraim had sent men to watch the POSC cottage in Taiji. He'd ordered them simply to observe and report anyone coming or going and anything unusual. They'd arrived too late to see everyone leave for the regional airport, but a sudden departure so late at night surely counted as highly unusual.

When they informed Kuraim, he told them to follow the departing car, no matter where it went, and continue to report. He would dispatch other men to cover an ongoing surveillance on the cottage.

*

Claire struggled to sleep. Her mind churned and, for the first time in memory, she grappled with doubts about her chosen course of action. Eventually she rolled out of bed and walked to the closed connecting door leading to Jason's room. She paused briefly, and despite wearing only a short night slip, knocked on the door.

"Come on in," Jason called. "I can't sleep either."

"Sorry to disturb you, Jason," she said as she entered the room and began pacing blindly in the darkness. "I'm just wondering where all this is headed and how it'll end."

Usually she seemed so confident, but now Jason detected the corrosion of self-doubt. "I know," he said. "We've been pretty lucky so far, and it's understandable to be anxious."

"It's just that this is my fight, and I'm dragging you and John into a mess that looks more suicidal all the time."

"Come here, and sit down," he said, sitting up on his bed and reaching out to her in the darkness. "This isn't just your fight, Claire. We joined you happily and voluntarily. John shares your passion for the oceans, and I just happen to like taking down bad guys."

Jason took her hand, squeezed it, and she sat on the side of the bed. "You're not alone," he murmured.

Unexpectedly, emotion overwhelmed Claire. She always was a bit of a loner and really never had settled into any long-term relationships. Then with the death of her father, she had bottled up all of her feelings, determined to exact revenge for him.

Suddenly she felt a need to let everything out, to unburden. "Thank you," she whispered as she leant towards him and tentatively pecked his cheek once, then again, and after a pause, moved to his mouth, which opened. Then they were kissing each other with hunger and yearning.

Jason reached out, tugged off her slip and then pulled her in tightly, furiously caressing her and kissing her face, nuzzling her neck. Claire responded with equal urgency, touching, kissing, licking and biting him.

Already naked, he rolled on top of her and pressed her down, his hands exploring her taut body as he continued his barrage of kisses. But she would not stay on her back and, in turn, rolled over on top of him, and their foreplay became more of a wrestle, as each dominating character sought control over the other. They pawed, grabbed and held each other in alternating positions of submission, placing licks and kisses as and where they could.

They panted heavily and emitted little gasps and cries as they eventually found a compromise, sitting face to face with Claire astride Jason, her legs wrapped tightly behind his back. Jason thrust up as Claire sank down onto him, and soon they heaved with effort, his one hand lifting her bottom while the other stroked her hair, caressed her breasts and cupped her chin for occasionally snatched kisses.

She, in turn, rode him hard, pumping up and down in an ever-increasing rhythm. Suddenly he cried out, exploding inside her with all the pent-up passion that had simmered within him since joining forces with this astonishing woman.

A strangled cry came from deep inside Claire as she climaxed immediately after Jason. As the shared frenzy abated and their breathing slowed, they eased their iron-like grips on each other and began to uncoil.

Quietly they lay side by side, their held hands forming the only point of contact. Claire was not used to this, and her mind reeled.

After a few minutes, Jason rolled onto his side and studied the dark outline of her face. Tentatively he traced a finger down her forehead, then her nose, mouth and chin. "Now why don't we try that again, only this time like civilised people?" he whispered.

She grinned in the darkness and said, "Sure, if you think you're up to it."

Hardly had she finished speaking before he again rolled on top of her. This time he was supremely gentle, and she let him take the lead.

*

"What the bloody hell happened to you two?" asked Teach as they convened for breakfast. "You both look like you've been in a prize fight."

Claire and Jason each sported a few small bruises, burns and scratches from their night-time antics, fortunately mostly unseen beneath their clothing. Blushing slightly, they muttered some feeble excuses. Teach quickly interpreted the situation for what it was and left the matter alone.

Instead of asking more questions, he confirmed that Namika had just arrived and crashed out in his room. Briefly, he had explained their concerns to her, and then she'd collapsed, exhausted from having driven through the night, and fell straight to sleep on his bed.

The three of them ate a quiet breakfast. Then Claire announced that it was time to go and check out the boat that Russell had mentioned.

When returning to their rooms to collect their gear and leave Namika a note, Jason took Claire aside. "Are you okay?" he asked uneasily.

"Absolutely," she replied with a sparkle in her eyes and a smile on her lips, both the likes of which he hadn't seen previously and which relieved his anxiety. "I know we probably shouldn't have done what we did, but what the hell? It was the best time I've had in months, so yes, I'm definitely okay. Now let's get busy and prepare to crack some more heads."

Chapter 27

Down to the Docks

Maintaining a mistrustful level of caution, the three campaigners decided to split up temporarily. Claire and Teach would leave first by taxi, going straight to the dock where the so-called research vessel, *R/V Seven Seas*, was located. There, they would contact the man Russell had called simply "the captain" and then assess the situation. Jason would follow separately and observe the vessel from a safe distance. If something went wrong, then he would become the cavalry.

*

The two watchers who had trailed Namika all the way from Taiji observed Claire and Teach depart, but they weren't looking for another team member and so failed to focus on Jason, who left a few minutes later. After updating their boss, they received instructions to access the targets' hotel rooms and await their return, when they'd subdue the two former British soldiers and bring them before Kuraim. He'd send reinforcements to help too. Under no circumstances should they fatally harm the prisoners. Kuraim wanted that pleasure for himself.

Members of the hotel's reception staff knew enough to easily recognise Yakuza and the associated potential trouble. So they complied readily when confronted with fierce demands for two particular room numbers. The tall, black-bearded man and the athletic, young woman who had just left together were easily placed and their room numbers provided.

Forceful orders came next for the two rooms not to be serviced or otherwise disturbed today. The receptionists, with their heads deeply bowed in respect and fear, watched the two gangsters take the key-cards for both rooms, walk arrogantly to the hotel's main lifts and disappear.

When the gangsters opened the first door, they found the room to be beyond tidy, with few personal items present. A connecting door was locked, so they left and advanced to the second room across the corridor.

There, they momentarily were taken by surprise to find someone asleep in bed, a young Japanese woman, the same person they had followed all night, who suddenly woke up and, startled to see them, began to scream. One man strode over and slapped her hard across the face, knocking her back against the headboard. She slumped, moaning in semi-consciousness as blood from a split lip dripped onto the sheets.

The gangsters lifted a lamp from the bedside table, tore off the flex and used it to bind the woman while she remained groggy. They stuffed a flannel from the bathroom into her mouth as a gag. When she revived, with her eyes watering, barely able to breathe through the gag, they showed complete indifference to her discomfort.

After telephoning in another status report, the two henchmen soon were joined by four others. Crowding into the two rooms, they all settled down in luxury-hotel comfort to await the return of their quarries.

*

Shiohama district lies about as far from the mouth of Tokyo Bay as it is possible to berth any ship with deep-sea capabilities. Little trade happens there. Generally, it's a quiet place compared to the frenetic bustle elsewhere along the bay's docklands.

Easily locating the dockside, Claire and Teach arrived there an hour after leaving the hotel. In part due to an astonishing lack of customs and control gates, they immediately spotted the *R/V Seven Seas* tied up halfway along the wharf. They strolled slowly towards the vessel, noticing that two men standing at a safety rail above the bridge warily watched them.

Making mental notes as they approached, Teach calculated that the ship measured 50-60 metres long and displaced maybe 675 tons. Although not large, it was stocky with maybe a 10-metre beam. Its broad, raised bow suggested capabilities as an ice-class vessel.

Reaching a gangway leading onto the ship, they stopped and hailed the men above the bridge. "Hello! We're looking for the captain," called out Teach. "James Russell from Hong Kong suggested that we call on you."

After trading wary glances, the two men invited the visitors aboard. Both sailors vanished momentarily and then reappeared at the top of the gangway as first Teach and then Claire boarded. Everyone introduced themselves before the newcomers were led to the spacious bridge where four chairs surrounded a large map-table covered with used drinking glasses, coffee mugs and full ashtrays. No refreshments were offered.

One of the seafarers, the captain as it happened, was a dark-complexioned, grizzled, tough-looking Australian called Andy Tyler. He had dark blue, penetrating eyes sunken under heavy eyebrows, and his rolled-up sleeves revealed thick, muscular, tattooed arms. The other man, Olafur "Olly" Jonsson, a huge, craggy, blond Icelander, was introduced as the first mate. Together, they formed a very capable-looking pair.

Tyler started the conversational ball rolling. "I understand from Russell that you guys are looking to make a nuisance of yourselves with the Japanese whalers," he began in a broad Australian accent. "Now that's exactly what we do, but I have to tell you, it can get pretty rough, and we're sometimes gone for up to four months at a time. So, the big questions are, do you have experience at this sort of thing and have you got the time and stamina for such an adventure?" When asking, he looked pointedly at Claire.

"Well, we certainly do rough," said Claire. "As for experience, I was with the British SBS for six years, and Blackbeard here was SAS." Normally she wouldn't admit so readily to their military service, but she wanted to gain Tyler's respect quickly. They had no time to waste on proving their mettle.

"Hold on, did you say 'Blackbeard'?" Jonsson snapped his fingers in recognition while grinning at Teach. "I thought that maybe I recognised you somehow. You're one of the guys who sank the whalers in Reykjavik some years back, right?"

"A lot of years back actually, but guilty as charged," confessed Teach.

"Yeah, and the authorities back home still want to talk to you about that," said Jonsson lugubriously. "What've you been doing since then?"

"Well, most recently I helped Claire to sink a whaler in Taiji before she took down a triad society in Hong Kong, so as she said, we do rough well enough."

"Strewth, that was you two?" exclaimed Tyler, excitedly rubbing his hands together.

"Along with our partner, Jason," added Claire. "He has similar credentials. But as for time frames, we have no intention of staying at sea for anything close to four months. Our plan is simple and quick, and then we all come home."

"Oh yeah, and what plan is that?" asked the captain.

"We find the whaling fleet's factory ship as soon as possible, attack and sink her," she replied succinctly.

Tyler and Jonsson looked at each other without a word, and then back at Claire. "Exactly how do you intend to do that, Claire?" the captain asked. "That's a bloody big ship we're talking about, you know, and the Japanese Navy now protects her. Shit, they even track us by satellite. That's why the Sea Shepherd vessels stopped chasing and disrupting the whalers. It got too bloody dangerous."

"So why are you still doing it?" asked Teach.

"Fucked if I know really," declared Tyler with a laugh. "Truth is that Olly and I used to sail in the Sea Shepherd fleet. We both sailed on the *Farley Mowat*, a sister ship to this one, so we know what it can do. Anyway, we wanted to be more aggressive and have more action. We broke away, found a sponsor, got hold of this old tub, put a crew together, and here we are, ready to go and do battle to save some whales, come what may."

"How are you going to 'do battle' in such a small ship?" Teach queried. "A lot of the whalers must be vastly larger and certainly faster."

It was Jonsson who answered. "Being small is actually an advantage," said the big man incongruously. "Because we're low in the water, we're harder to spot. We also have a reinforced bow for ice-breaking, but it works well for ramming too."

"What's with the '*R/V*' designation in the name?" asked Claire.

"That's our cover," answered Tyler. "If anyone stops us to enquire, we're on a research vessel, and before you ask, we've got a lab and all sorts of stuff to prove it."

"By a 'lab', he means an old microscope and a laptop together on a table," said Jonsson. "But back to you guys, how do you plan to sink the mother ship? There would be five whaling ships all told, plus whatever naval or other security vessels that could be around."

"We have mines and explosives," Claire said. "We'll need to get scuba gear, but that shouldn't be difficult, and I assume that you have a sturdy inflatable with a fast motor."

"We certainly do, two RIBs, in fact. There's a big Apex A24 with a 300-horsepower inboard engine. It serves as a crew run-around and also as the main lifeboat. Then there's a smaller Apex A18 with a 150-horsepower inboard engine. It's very quick and nifty and the one we mostly use to harass the whalers. It'll do tops about 35 knots, takes up to eight people and so should be ideal for you."

"Sounds perfect," Claire said. "So we use one of the RIBs and go after the factory ship. Once it goes down, the other whalers should call it a day and, meanwhile, we're getting the hell away."

"It's certainly bold," said Jonsson, "and, you know, it could work. But it's really high risk, Claire. The seas out there are cruel and dangerous and don't take kindly to people swimming in them. Attaching explosives on a moving vessel in those waters could be suicidal."

"Well, let us worry about that," said Claire, wanting to seal the deal for an alliance. They could settle the details later. "So will you take us and, if so, when do we leave?"

Again, the two sailors traded looks, and Jonsson nodded before Tyler replied. "Sure, we'll take you. We leave tomorrow. Be here by noon and bring your gear. It'll be pretty cramped, and you'll need to share berths so don't expect much in the way of comfort."

"Suits us. We're not looking for a luxury cruise," confirmed Claire, "and remember there'll be three of us. What about payment, contributions for victuals and so forth?"

"No worries about that," Tyler said. "You just sink us a whaler or two, and that'll be more than a fair contribution."

*

Claire and Teach reunited with Jason at the end of the wharf and briefed him on the arrangements while they all waited for an Uber taxi.

"Incidentally," Claire told him, "we didn't discuss the Yakuza side of this. We're simply extreme anti-whale-hunting activists."

"Makes sense for now," said Jason.

"We left the bag of explosives with Tyler and Jonsson so they'll know we're serious if they go through it, which they likely will. Now let's find enough wet-weather and scuba gear while considering what else we may need," said Claire.

"Are you sure we can trust these guys?" asked Jason. "They sound pretty rough and piratical."

Teach answered this. "Honestly, anyone active in this game to the degree they are will be a bit crazy. But if Russell reckons on them as a good outfit to work with us, that's more than good enough for me."

"Well, I guess that it takes a pirate to know pirates," teased Jason as they climbed into the taxi and set off to buy high-quality scuba-diving equipment.

Chapter 28

Confrontation With the Yakuza

After a successful shopping spree, Claire, Jason and Teach returned to the hotel in the late afternoon. They had found everything they needed and, after calling Tyler, arranged to send their purchases directly to the ship.

None of them had eaten since breakfast so they wanted some food and refreshments in the New York Lounge. Immediately, Miko approached them and whispered in urgent tones to Teach. This time she was not smiling, nor bubbly, instead acting very nervously. Then she turned and walked away without taking drinks orders and leaving Teach looking decidedly worried.

"What gives?" asked Jason. "You don't look happy."

"I'm not. Apparently, the hotel-staff rumour mill places a bunch of Yakuza gangsters waiting in your room, Claire, and in mine. Damn it! Namika was sleeping in there."

"Shit! Hey, don't worry, man. We'll get her out of there," Jason said.

"Seems like Russell was correct, and we may be under surveillance right now," said Claire, looking idly around. "Probably the men upstairs already have been alerted that we're back at the hotel, so let's keep it cool, guys. John, why don't you go out back and see if you can learn anything more from your waitress friend? We'll wait for you here."

Teach rose and left the lounge through the staff door. Claire told Jason to order a round of beers while she went to the reception desk to begin their counter-offensive. That meant spreading disinformation. She noticed that the reception staff also looked very edgy and anxious, but she ignored that irregularity and began asking questions.

"We need a nice place to eat an early dinner, a good restaurant not too far from the hotel," Claire said, addressing the nearest receptionist. "Where can you recommend?"

The receptionist promptly provided two suggestions, from which Claire selected one, asking him to make a reservation there for three people to arrive 30 minutes later. She asked for walking directions, which he supplied, and then she returned to the lounge just as Teach reappeared.

Trying to look calmer than they felt, they all sipped their beers while Teach updated Claire and Jason on the little extra he had heard. "Seems like there are six Yakuza, split between Claire's room and mine," he said. "For some reason, they didn't ask about Jason so there's no one waiting in his room."

"When we left this morning, I locked the connecting door leading into Claire's room," said Jason, "so with any luck that gives us a surprise entrance."

"They know about Claire and me through Taiji, I suppose," observed Teach, "and they probably saw us leave the hotel together this morning. So that leaves Jason as a free agent for now, which is good."

"Absolutely," said Claire. "Now I've asked a receptionist to reserve a table for us at a nearby restaurant where we're due in about 20 minutes, so let's make like we're headed there. The people at the reception desk look so terrified that I'm sure they'll report our movements, so again it may be best if Jason leaves separately. Then no one upstairs should expect us for an hour or more. Once we're all outside, we'll double around to the back, come in again through a staff entrance and take a service lift to the floor above ours."

"We may have problems using the staff entrance," suggested Teach. "Hotel management can be pretty strict about who waltzes in and out of there, you know."

"If anyone tries to stop us, we simply show them the Sigs," said Jason. "That'll get us through, and then the hotel employees will be calling for security and the police, which suits us fine. But I doubt if they'll alert the thugs in our rooms. We may have just enough time to deal with them."

"I agree," said Teach, "but there's going to be only one way for this to end, with bodies hitting the floor. After that, we'll need to disappear in a hurry."

"We'll discuss more details about the rescue when we're outside. Any questions here first?" asked Claire. Hearing none, she rose from her chair and Teach followed her.

The two of them left the lounge, conversing loudly as they crossed the lobby and stepped out through the hotel's front doors. As expected, they noticed a receptionist reach for a telephone, presumably calling upstairs to one of their rooms. Moments later, Jason followed them.

Once outside and regrouped, Claire, Jason and Teach talked briefly before walking quickly to the rear of the hotel and pushing through the staff-entrance door. Inside, they found a chaotic din and a general air of excitement as many staff members appeared to be leaving, with others arriving for night shifts.

The three determined guests felt gratified not to be challenged, and they moved purposefully through the melee, soon finding a service lift. When they pressed its call button, the lift doors promptly opened.

They reached the seventh floor, pistols now drawn and with suppressors attached. Each of them also carried a large, new diving knife, kept back from the bag full of purchases sent earlier to the boat.

Using a fire-escape stairway beside the lift well, they cautiously descended one level and peered warily into the sixth-floor corridor. Seeing no guards there, they walked quietly and purposefully to Jason's room.

They had agreed that the two men would access Jason's room first before Claire knocked on her own door and called out, "Housekeeping". Her presence, with repeated knocking if needed, could distract enough for Jason and Teach to charge through the connecting doorway and shoot the gangsters on sight. They needed to be careful in case Namika or other "civilians" were present, but otherwise they felt no qualms.

Delicately, Jason unlocked his connecting door. Once they heard Claire's call from the corridor, they burst through into her room with Jason leading.

As expected, three gangsters occupied the room. One stood by the main door, and the other two sat in armchairs. They were totally unprepared and died before fully realising they were under attack, a series of double-tap, silenced rounds seeing them off quietly and quickly. Moments later, a third bullet was administered to the head of each gangster to make sure.

Jason opened the door to let Claire inside and quickly closed it again. So far, the whole engagement had lasted less than a minute and, as best they could tell, the other Yakuza thugs in Teach's room across the corridor had not been alerted.

But the next move looked likely to be altogether trickier and more risky, especially because they didn't know exactly where Namika was. Cautiously, they withdrew to Jason's room and considered their options.

"We need to lure at least one of them out without unduly raising his suspicions," suggested Teach. "I can speak a little

Japanese and probably could fake a call on one of these guy's mobile phones to bring them out. What do you think?"

"Well, we sure as hell can't swing through the window on ropes," said Jason, "so that works for me."

"What'll you say to them?" asked Claire.

"Something like, 'Just had a call from the boss. New orders. Two of you get over here quickly, one stay and keep an eye on the woman,' and then hang up."

They exchanged looks before nodding. "Okay, John, you and Jason stay in my room with the door ajar to make the call," Claire said. "As they come in, you take them between you. I'll be down the corridor pretending to enter another room. As soon as they go to you, I'll breach your room and take out the remaining guard."

She saw a look of concern cross Teach's face. "Don't worry," she added. "Namika will be fine. I'll make sure."

"Well, it's not a perfect plan," bemoaned Jason. "But it's the best we can do, I reckon, so let's get cracking."

Returning to Claire's room, they pulled the three corpses out of immediate sight and frisked them for mobile phones and anything else of potential use. Each gangster had carried a variety of unpleasant-looking weapons, which they ignored.

Teach examined the "contacts list" on each man's phone, but, of course, it was impossible to know the names of the three men in his room. Simply guessing at any of the listed names might alert others nearby and jeopardise their mission.

Using a different tactic, Teach identified the names of the phones' owners. Then choosing the device belonging to the best-dressed of the three thugs, on the assumption that fellow may have been a leader of sorts, he called the hotel's main phone number and, speaking Japanese in a guttural voice, demanded to be put through to room 610, his own room.

Claire, meanwhile, had left and, three doors down the corridor, she could just hear Teach shouting authoritatively into the mobile. Whatever he said, it seemed to work. Almost immediately, the door to his room opened, but only one gangster emerged. He looked suspiciously up and down the corridor, seeming to sense no danger from the distant woman trying to open her door. He marched straight into the room opposite, and Claire barely heard the muted spits of several shots fired.

The gangster had left Teach's door open. As Claire hustled towards it and prepared to enter, Jason joined her, and they burst into the room together. Their training years before had been exhaustive, and an ability to select and shoot at "hostiles" while not injuring "innocents" was ingrained into them. The remaining gangsters were positioned nowhere near Namika, who was tied up and lying on the bed, and they both died in a hail of bullets.

But one gangster had held his silenced gun in hand, and when they entered the room, he raised it and fired a shot before falling in the onslaught. The bullet grazed Jason high on his left arm, producing a rapid trickle of blood, but seeming not to faze him in the least.

Teach joined them and rushed to the bed to assist Namika. Tenderly, he pulled the gag from her mouth, and she immediately began sobbing and shaking uncontrollably. He untied her and held her tightly, whispering soothingly to her as she eventually began to calm.

Meanwhile, Jason closed the door. He and Claire checked the dead men's pockets, again seeking anything useful, but to no avail.

"Sorry, guys," Claire said to her companions, "but you've got no more than two minutes to grab your things. Then we're out of here."

Somewhat defying her own deadline, she took Jason back to her room to check on his wound, which she hastily cleaned up, although it looked like a mere scratch. Lacking proper first-aid items, she tore a strip from a bedsheet and wrapped it around his arm.

"Good to go?" she asked.

"Never better," he confirmed with a grin. "I'll get my gear, and then

They regrouped, with Namika now more composed, and headed this time for the guest lifts, which they rode to one level above the lobby. There, they smashed a fire-alarm call-point and set off the alarm before descending by the fire-escape stairway to the lobby. Staff members rushed around trying to act in their official capacities while guests milled about waiting, as always in such situations, to receive instructions.

Amid the confusion, nobody gave the departing foursome a second glance, and they slipped out through the hotel's front doors into the night, walking away rapidly to find a restaurant to establish an alibi. Obviously, they wanted to avoid the two restaurants suggested to Claire earlier. Probably the receptionist would tell both the Yakuza and the police where he had suggested that they dine. Luckily, it was getting late so they had no trouble finding an available table elsewhere, and they settled down to a somewhat rushed meal.

*

Kuraim's *saiko komon*, or deputy, was a quick-tempered and singularly nasty, sadistic individual known simply as Rai.

Although slight in stature, he was wiry and proficient in the martial arts. Yet whenever a chance arose, Rai preferred to use knives, weapons with which he could enjoy inflicting immense suffering.

Right now, Rai's thoughts turned blacker with each passing moment as he tried to raise one, then all members, of the team he had dispatched to the InterContinental Tokyo Bay Hotel. Receiving no replies, he called the hotel directly and demanded to be put through without delay to first one room, and then the other, where his men had waited to ambush the *Shiroi yūrei*, or "white ghosts", as Caucasians in Japan frequently are called. Still unable to contact his henchmen, Rai understood beyond doubt that something had gone badly wrong. He summoned six more of his men, and they all sped off in two black SUVs bound for the hotel.

On arrival, Rai and his underlings saw a fire engine just leaving the street in front of the hotel. More concerned than ever, Rai raced to the reception desk to ask what had happened.

"Just a false alarm on the first floor, sir," said a receptionist meekly, his head bowed respectfully low. Members of the hotel staff all knew Rai, by reputation if not by sight, and were terrified of him.

"Give me the keys to the rooms," Rai growled. Such was his arrogance that he perceived no need to elaborate as to which rooms, and he was right.

The receptionist knew exactly and handed over two key-cards. "Sixth floor, sir, rooms 610 and 611," he said.

Trailed by his anxious men, Rai commandeered a lift, forcing out a startled young couple who had just entered its cabin, and rode to the sixth floor, where they proceeded cautiously to the two rooms. They first knocked and then, using the key-cards, entered each room in turn.

None of these men were in any way squeamish by nature, but they all paled, stunned by the scenes before them. All six of their cohorts had been shot dead, neatly and with no signs of much struggle. The hostage's restraints remained as they had fallen, discarded on the bed.

"Kuraim won't be pleased about this," Rai whispered to himself as he tapped at his mobile phone to place a call to his boss.

*

"Every minute counts," Teach told his colleagues, all gathered around a restaurant table, its surface now replete with empty dishes. "We need to get under cover quickly. The Yakuza will mount an all-out search starting the moment they discover what happened."

"You're right, John. Any ideas?" asked Claire.

"I reckon the best thing for us is to go straight to the ship and see if we can leave early," Teach replied. "That should get us out of harm's way, at least for now. Even if the captain doesn't want to leave pronto, we'll probably be safer there than anywhere else."

"Makes sense," said Claire. Then turning to Namika, she asked. "Is there somewhere you can go, Namika, out of Japan, I mean? It's going to get pretty dangerous where we're headed, and it's certainly no place for you."

Namika scowled. "You can take a running jump, Claire, if you think I'm bailing out now," she replied indignantly. "I've worked at sea conservation for a bloody lot longer than you have, and besides, this great ox here needs me to look after him." She elbowed Teach in the ribs as she spoke. "I'm coming with you, and if you try stopping me, well, maybe you'll learn that the Yakuza aren't the only fierce people in Japan…."

"Okay, okay, Namika, I get the picture," interrupted Claire, amused at the Japanese woman's accented use of colloquial English. "It's good to see you so spirited."

Then Claire turned to another of her dining companions. "Jason, let's give these two some space for a moment while we pay the bill. Everyone, we're out of here in five minutes."

They left Namika and Teach, who whispered animatedly, at the table. When Namika stood and visited the Ladies room, Teach meekly approached Claire and Jason.

"The thing is, Namika has no real family, except for me and POSC," Teach explained. "I know she's not trained for military situations like we are, but she can help out a lot, and I don't want to leave her behind. I'd just worry about her."

He paused, looking down, away from their faces. "So if it's all the same to you guys, she'll come with us, and I'll be fully accountable for her." Then he looked up and asked, "What do you say?"

Claire wasn't entirely happy, but acquiesced. "Alright, you crazy pirate, but she's your responsibility. Got it?"

Just then, Namika reappeared, and Claire said, "Welcome to the gang, Namika. Now let's get going." Namika beamed back at her.

Once outside, they found a taxi, piled into it and rode in the direction of the Shiohama district. They paid off the driver a half-kilometre before reaching the docks and walked the rest of the way to the ship.

By now, it was past midnight, but a light still glowed on the bridge. They agreed that Claire would go aboard first and talk to Tyler.

"Requesting permission to come aboard the *Seven Seas*," she yelled from the top of the gangplank. A window on the bridge opened, and Tyler's head appeared.

"Hey, Andy, it's Claire," she said. "Can we have a word?"

If the ship's captain felt surprised to see her again at such an offbeat hour, he hid it well and told her to come up to the bridge. He and Jonsson had been playing cards. On the table between their chairs stood a bottle of Pusser's Rum looking decidedly the worse for wear.

"Blackbeard will be happy to see that," Claire said, indicating the bottle. "That is, if your supplies are up to it."

"Oh, they're up to it alright," said Tyler, producing a glass from a cabinet and pouring her a large shot unbidden. "Here you go, Claire. Cheers." He tossed back the rest of the contents in his own glass, as did Jonsson, and together they regarded Claire until she did likewise.

The liquor burned Claire's throat. But she was damned if she'd show any reaction to these two blokes.

"So what brings you back here at this prime time of the night, Claire?" Tyler asked casually.

"Truth is," she replied, "we've had a spot of bother with some locals and would prefer to depart as soon as possible."

"Define 'spot of bother', can you?" asked Jonsson.

Originally, Claire had thought of making up some story, but she'd decided against spinning a yarn and to trust the men before her. If they were sailing into harm's way together, they all needed complete trust. So she told them about the Yakuza, and when she'd finished, Tyler was grinning from ear to ear.

"Bloody heck, woman, you're some piece of work. I'll say that," he declared.

Tyler freshened up the contents of their glasses and, as they toasted each other again, he threw back his drink in a single gulp. Claire and Jonsson nursed their drinks more slowly.

"So where are the others?" Tyler asked finally.

"Just a call away," she said vaguely.

"This Namika…," Jonsson said. "Is she going to be up for what we have planned?"

"She's pretty tough and very determined," replied Claire. "She won't get in the way."

"Maybe it's for the best," said Tyler. "We haven't been able to get a hand for the galley since the last one went AWOL a few days back, so it looks like Namika's much needed. She'll be just as busy as the rest of us."

"What about the other crew members?" Claire asked. "You haven't told me much about them. How many are there, and what are their backgrounds?"

Jonsson fielded this query. "There are six more of us. A mad Scottish engineer called Jock and his mate, Kevin, two general deck hands, Miles and Chris, an IT and communications guy we call Knowledge, and someone else we loosely term as a 'security man'. He's named Muscles, and you'll see why later. They're a good bunch, tough and capable, and we've been together for a few seasons so we all know how each one of us ticks."

"Olly, there's nothing to stop us from leaving tonight," suggested Tyler. Then he switched his attention to Claire. "We'd hoped to pick up a new cook tomorrow morning, but since your Namika is coming along, we can be away as soon as the other crew members return from the nightclub they went to visit."

"They'll have sore heads and maybe a little blurred vision, Andy," said the first mate. "But yes, I suppose we could leave right away once they get back."

"Claire, why don't you summon your pals and bring them aboard?" suggested Tyler. "We can get to know each other a little better before the others turn up. Suit you?"

Claire agreed and phoned Jason, and soon they all came aboard, with Jason and Namika being introduced and everyone being obliged to down at least one shot of Pusser's. The only person who appeared totally undaunted by the liquid hospitality was Teach, whose history of anti-whaling exploits seemed to make him the stuff of legends. A real spirit of camaraderie prevailed.

Chapter 29

Everyone's Angry

As Rai anticipated, Kuraim sputtered in fury. When news stories appeared the next morning, his mood deteriorated even more. Extravagant headlines focussed on the bloodbath in two rooms at the InterContinental Tokyo Bay Hotel, complete with speculation about a Yakuza gang war. Media reports expressed concern as to the whereabouts of some foreign nationals who had occupied the rooms where the carnage happened. Tattoos on the dead gangsters' bodies indicated their affiliation with the Boryokudan syndicate, and so Kuraim's face looked even more blemished to his rivals.

Rai already had instigated citywide searches for Claire, Teach and Namika, and he suspected there must be others in the same group for them to outmanoeuvre his men so easily. A sizeable reward was offered for information leading to their capture, and gang members all across Tokyo scoured hotels, clubs and bars for any signs of the foreigners brazen and foolhardy enough to inflict damage on the Yakuza.

Kuraim was still hissing and spitting with rage when a phone call reached him from Hong Kong. It was McMahan, who had noticed the hotel-shooting story on the early news there and wanted to know what the hell was happening.

"It's that bitch, Armstrong," shouted Kuraim. "And so as you know, it's not just two people, but a larger force of at least six or seven soldiers." He exaggerated to salvage as much face as he could.

The sinister *de facto* head of Demesne remained unimpressed. "Rubbish!" exclaimed McMahan. "There may be three, four tops. In any case, I warned you they were coming, and you screwed up badly. So where are they now?"

Kuraim felt unnerved by the man's harsh tone. "We're looking for them," he replied more contritely. "They cannot escape us for long. You may be assured of that."

"Bollocks," spat back McMahan. "They're probably halfway to Antarctica by now, preparing to disrupt your whaling activities. What are you going to do about it?"

"The whaling fleet sails in a few days," Kuraim replied uncertainly. "The captains will be briefed and the ships accompanied by some of my best men. If Armstrong foolishly shows up, she will be killed, along with her companions, and their boat sunk without trace."

Unconvinced, McMahan rang off without another word, leaving Kuraim to stew in his wrath and dented pride. The Yakuza *oyabun* had been badly dishonoured, and his loss of face required a brutal response.

*

Sir Iain Campbell showed no hesitation when issuing orders. "Billy, I want you to travel over to Tokyo and keep an eye on Kuraim," he said. "Kill him if you must. Take Huang with you."

McMahan sat in front of the big desk in Campbell's office, and he, like Kuraim far to the north, simmered in a towering bad temper. "What's the point of me going there? We could just send Huang?" challenged McMahan hotly.

"It delivers the right message, Billy. We want to show that we have a firm grip on things and are leading from the front. Syndicates around the world need to remember that they never should try to get away with any lapse of respect or fealty towards us. If it's known that death remains the standard penalty for failure to perform or show proper deference, then things will settle down quickly."

"What's brought this on?" asked McMahan, curious. It was unlike Campbell to get this involved in Demesne's day-to-day administration.

"'What's brought this on?'" repeated Campbell, suddenly yelling. "I'll tell you what's bloody well brought this on. Claire bloody Armstrong has brought this on, and if you'd taken proper care of things as I'd expected you to do earlier, we wouldn't be in this damn mess."

"I don't deserve…," started McMahan before being interrupted by his infuriated boss.

"Billy, don't you dare say a fucking word to argue with me! Just listen. This Armstrong bitch needs to be stopped once and for all before our entire network unravels. The people at Barrio 18 in Central America are pissed off that the shark fin supply chain got interrupted, so they've started dealing directly with the Chinese mainland, trying to bypass us. Here in Hong Kong, the 14K Triad flexes its muscles, striving for supremacy and whispering about independence from us. From Vancouver to San Diego, the 14K's North American triad offshoots openly question the point of our association. So Demesne faces its greatest challenges ever, and I have no intention for everything we've built up so carefully to be destroyed because of one pissed-off bitch who likes big fish."

McMahan had never been spoken to in quite this way by anyone. It was a measure of the power exuded by Campbell that McMahan did not lash out and hit him, or at least turn and walk out of the office.

Telling his boss "I told you so" would gain nothing, McMahan supposed. Instead he suggested, "Maybe we should just kill Kuraim anyway, and while we're at it, perhaps also Miguel Sanchez of Barrio 18."

"Then we'd have more power vacuums and, in Kuraim's case, no means to channel all the takings from the upcoming whale hunt. Come on, Billy. You can do better than that," spat back Campbell.

"I'm pretty sure that Armstrong's going after the whaling fleet," offered McMahan. "We should be able to arrange for something unpleasant to happen to her and her friends at sea."

"That's all very easy to say, but how do you intend to find her first?"

"We don't. Instead we let her find the whalers, and then we hit her hard. No messing around, simply sink her vessel. We can get Kuraim to coordinate the action."

"We'd need to be careful," cautioned Campbell. "If the Japanese Navy goes along to guard the whaling fleet like last year, it'll be difficult to do anything untoward."

"Maybe we can have a word with the right person and make sure the Navy stays away this year. You have connections there," McMahan said.

Campbell rose from behind his desk and strode around his office thinking. McMahan sat quietly. They both mulled the logistics of waging such a sea battle and reinforcing Demesne's position as a ruthless, unforgiving ruler. Eventually, Kuraim would need to go, but perhaps it worked better to wait until after the Armstrong woman died.

At last, Campbell stopped pacing and stood in front of his deputy, who also stood to face his boss. "Okay, Billy, let's do it. I'll make a call or two, but you just make sure this all gets cleared up quickly. We need to bring total order and stern authority back to our business fast."

"Does this include hitting Sanchez?"

"No, not yet. Let's sort out one fuckup at a time, and Kuraim currently qualifies as the bigger one."

"I'm on it, sir," said a much-chastised McMahan, making for the exit.

"Billy," called Campbell. McMahan stopped at the door and turned towards his scowling boss.

"No more mistakes, my friend. Not a single one."

The menace behind Campbell's words was palpable as McMahan left to clear his desk and to fetch Huang.

*

Sir Iain still fumed when his personal assistant announced that James Russell, a senior assistant police commissioner, was outside and hoping to see him, despite having no appointment. The angry business titan felt tempted to tell the policeman to get lost, but on reflection decided it might be prudent and useful to hear what this fellow had to say. Campbell did not know Russell well, but the latter's reputation was solid enough that this lawman, unlike most others, commanded some respect for integrity, efficiency and effectiveness.

Campbell's assistant ushered Russell into the inner office where the two men cautiously shook hands and sat in comfortable armchairs facing each other. Then the assistant poured coffee for them and left the room.

"Thank you for seeing me without an appointment, Sir Iain," began Russell deferentially.

"You're lucky to have caught me, Russell. I have an appointment shortly, so you'd best make it quick."

"I'll do that," said Russell, keeping a neutral expression. "I'm sure you are aware of the recent triad-related violence in Hong Kong and on Beijian Island. Yesterday some shootings

231

happened in Tokyo too. You may have heard about these incidents."

"Of course, I'm aware of all this from news reports, but I'm not sure what it has to do with me or Campbell's. It's just gangster turf wars getting out of hand, surely?"

"Well, as a matter of fact, it is not. Have you heard of Claire Armstrong?"

Campbell was surprised, but revealed nothing. "Claire Armstrong, let me think. It rings a bell.... Why?"

"She and her father, the well-known oceanographer, were attacked, killing him, during a triad home invasion some time back."

"Ah, yes," said Campbell, pretending now to recall her name. "She had some special training and killed the attackers, as I recall. So what's the relevance?"

"Well, Ms Armstrong is also the person who almost single-handedly took down nearly the entire Xuè yuèliàng Triad and killed its dragon head, a man named Winston Lau. Perhaps you know this?" baited Russell.

"Why ever the hell would I know that?" demanded Campbell, becoming agitated. He forced himself to calm down and not let this bloody cop rattle him.

"I just assumed that someone as highly placed and well informed as you undoubtedly are, Sir Iain, would know. In any event, Armstrong also was responsible for the killings in Tokyo yesterday, and while we're making lists, she even brought a rapid and sudden end to this year's Japanese dolphin cull in Taiji."

"She sounds bloody dangerous and in need of locking up then. I hope you're close on her trail," suggested Sir Iain, looking pointedly at his wristwatch. "Anyway, interesting as all this is, why have you come here, Russell?"

"Ah, yes," said Russell, collecting himself to drop his bombshell. "It's just that a surprising name has come up in our investigations of all this, along with the murder of the *SCMP* editor recently. Specifically, it's the name of your CEO, Mr William McMahan. I wondered if you could throw any light on that turn of events for me."

Give the man credit because he didn't even blink, thought Russell.

"No light at all, I'm afraid," Campbell said. "You'd better take the matter up with McMahan directly. Now if you'll excuse me, I really must proceed to my next meeting."

Sir Iain Campbell rose from his chair and extended a hand. At the same time, he called for his assistant to escort Russell out of the room.

"I will speak to Mr McMahan soon," said Russell as he departed. "Perhaps, though, if you think of anything that might be related, would you give me a call? I'd be most grateful."

The chairman of Campbell's was left feeling uncharacteristically rattled and uneasy. He debated whether to tell McMahan about this discussion with Russell. The way things looked to Sir Iain now, if his deputy could take care of Armstrong and get the Yakuza back on an even keel, then things would settle down. If not, then even McMahan would need to be sacrificed.

Campbell ordered his assistant to call McMahan back in and, while waiting, he thought of another sacrifice that needed to be made – Russell himself, who also posed a serious threat. With that in mind, he called a very private telephone number, one known not even to McMahan.

"I need you to arrange a fatality," he told the man who answered his call. "The victim's details will be forwarded to you shortly."

Then Sir Iain Campbell sat back and waited for McMahan to return.

Chapter 30

The R/V Seven Seas Departs

Dawn was breaking by the time Claire and her team had settled into their quarters and grabbed a few hours of sleep. They all were squeezed into two tiny cabins, with Claire and Jason in one and Teach and Namika in the other. Sleeping and washing facilities were very basic. But at least everyone was safe for now and had the time and opportunity to consider future moves in detail.

The ship's crew members finally had returned from their nightclub excursion, mostly the worst for wear. Then Tyler gave orders to cast off. With a throaty rumble from below deck, the powerful engines fired up. Next, Jonsson, assisted by a slightly inebriated deckhand, raised the gangplank and slipped the lines, and they were away.

Claire considered it a bit odd that the *Seven Seas* apparently needed no customs or other formalities to depart, but she wasn't complaining. Probably this represented just one more among many mysteries surrounding the captain. Soon the ship moved slowly away from the dockside and out towards the harbour entrance.

By now, Claire had patched up Jason's injured arm more properly. Then they both joined Tyler on the bridge and watched as the shore slipped past in the gathering light.

The air felt chilly, but not uncomfortable, and a light wind blew from dead ahead. On the starboard side, they passed the huge US naval base at Yokosuka, home to the US 7th Fleet. Next they bounced over the choppy shoals near the mouth of the bay before passing the Sunosaki Lighthouse to port. Then only the open sea beckoned ahead, and both Claire and Jason felt as if great weights had lifted from their shoulders.

Tyler noticed their demeanours change and commented, "There's nothing quite like the sea to elevate a person's spirits."

"That's a fact," agreed Claire. "So where are we headed, Captain?"

Tyler surrendered the wheel to Jonsson and took them to the map-table, now tidied up and covered with sea charts instead of mugs, glasses and ashtrays. He selected a large chart showing the Western Pacific, stretching from the Arctic, along Russia's eastern seaboard, past Japan and then showing the Philippines, Papua New Guinea, Australia, New Zealand and even down to Antarctica.

The captain pointed out New Zealand's South Island and said, "At our cruising speed of 10 knots, we'll take about three weeks to get down there. Then, depending on the weather and where the whales are, about another week to reach the hunting grounds." He looked at them, hoping for a reaction, but seeing none continued his briefing.

"The *Nisshin Maru* is the main factory ship and the head of the whaling fleet. She's based in Shimonoseki and due to head out any day now, followed maybe a week later by the four, faster whale-catcher ships, the *Yushin Maru* series, and probably a few private security patrol vessels. There may be a naval escort too. They'll all follow pretty much the same route and rendezvous maybe 1,000 kilometres southeast of New Zealand. Then the hunting will begin." He paused again, but his audience stayed mute.

"Okay, so our plan is to try getting into place ahead of them and to disrupt them as much and often as we can. When they're hunting, the *Nisshin Maru* stays pretty much in one place so she could be easy to target. That's probably the best time for you to play with your fireworks. But she's increasingly well defended, and the Japanese play rough now. No longer do they rely on just water cannon to discourage us. They also shoot at us with live ammunition, use grenades, ram us, throw acid and lob Molotov cocktails, all those sorts of things. So we'll kind of wing it, and see how we go. Any questions?"

"It seems to me," observed Claire after a pause for thought, "that the sooner we attack the factory ship, the better. We should try and take her in the calmer northern waters of the Philippine Sea, say around the same latitude as Okinawa, before the rest of the fleet catches up to her. Her crew won't expect trouble so soon, and with any luck, if the Navy plans to protect her, its operations wouldn't begin for at least another fortnight. By then, the *Nisshin Maru* should be resting on the bottom of the Pacific."

The captain looked incredulous. "Fuck, you guys don't mess around, do you?"

"No, sir," Claire replied.

"With the factory ship gone, what will the other whaling vessels do?" Jason asked Tyler.

"They can't do a lot because they don't have room on board to hold many carcasses or to process them. Frankly, it'd be a waste of time and money for them to mount a trip at all."

"So our main problem comes down to making sure that we're in the right place at the right time to nobble her," declared Claire. "What do you think, Jason? Should be a piece of cake, right?"

Her flippancy was mostly for Tyler's benefit. She and Jason both knew this would be an extremely dangerous and complicated action with the outcome by no means assured, including questions about their ability to survive the engagement.

"A doddle it will be, Claire," said Jason, exaggerating what little remained of his Chinese accent.

Then turning serious again, Jason asked Tyler, "Can we have a sit-down with Knowledge as soon as possible? This whole plan hinges pretty much on his ability to place us in just the right spot."

"Agreed," said Claire. "Which raises another question, Andy. Just how much do the crew members know about us?"

"All I've told them so far is that we're taking along a few extra activists, which should be enough for the moment. But we'll need to fill them in sooner rather than later, especially with what you're talking about now."

"Alright, let's get them together, introduce ourselves and have a briefing before it's too late for any of them who may want to bail out."

Tyler snorted in derision. "I can promise you that none of them will want to bail out, Claire. The only grief I ever get from them is that we don't do nearly enough to stop the whaling bastards. When they hear what you're planning, they'll be ecstatic."

"Okay," proposed Jason, "so we'll get a bit farther out to sea and let them get over their hangovers first. Let's present the details to everyone this afternoon when they're all awake, alert and have eaten."

"Fair enough," said Claire. "Then we'd better make sure that Namika excels in the galley."

Tyler turned and looked at Jonsson, who had listened to every word of the conversation from his place at the wheel. The two men swapped grins, excited at the prospect of real action with this strangely forceful group of people who seemed to care little for the consequences.

238

*

The crew members sat around the packed galley, all in high spirits and in general agreement that the meal they'd just eaten ranked as the best they'd ever consumed aboard the *Seven Seas*. Immediately, Namika became everyone's favourite crewmate, and she blushed happily in a corner, perched on Teach's lap.

"Let's start with introductions," began Tyler when they all were settled. The captain first presented "the famous Blackbeard", outlining a little of Teach's background as an activist and a recent hero of Taiji. This brought cheers and applause, as did Namika's formal introduction.

Next it was Jason, of whom Tyler could say rather little, but concluded with, "All I know is that he's a tough bugger so best not to mess with him." There were nods of greeting, but the reception wasn't as gushing, which suited Jason fine.

"And last, but not least, meet the boss of this outfit, Claire Armstrong. Guys, you really don't want to mess with her." This brought back some smiles.

Claire and Jason had advised beforehand how much Tyler should tell the crew, ideally omitting certain details. So his next words really caught everyone's attention.

"Not only are Claire and Jason both former British Special Forces soldiers, but they're the people responsible for that triad showdown a few weeks ago in Hong Kong." He paused to let this sink in for his audience. "Claire was with Blackbeard in Taiji, and she's been busy since causing trouble for the Yakuza in Japan."

"Actually," broke in Teach, "Claire did all the real work in Taiji. I just went along for the ride."

239

"You got a death wish or something, Claire?" piped up one crew member, and the others laughed, but only a little. Clearly, this was a scary woman, someone best not to risk offending.

"Look, guys," said Claire, now standing beside Tyler, "this isn't about me or any heroics, whatever you may think. My main purpose is the same as yours, to disrupt and, if possible, stop the terrible abuses against our oceans and the remarkable creatures living in them."

"Hear! Hear!" chorused the crew members, thumping the galley table with their plates and crockery. This was their common goal, and hearing it so eloquently stated, they instantly accepted the new team members as soulmates.

A few questions were batted out and fielded, but then Claire called for attention again and began to outline their plan. The details caused jaw-dropping disbelief, and Chris, a deckhand, voiced what others also thought.

"What you're proposing, Claire, is a big step up from what we've done before," he said. "I mean, it's one thing to be disruptive and a pain in the ass to try reducing the catches. But you're talking about sinking an 8,000-plus-ton ship and, very possibly, killing some people. Nobody's done that to the whalers for maybe 40 years. I mean, it's like piracy."

"Well, that's exactly why I'm here," said Blackbeard to lighten their concerns. A few people chuckled, but they remained thoughtful.

"Seriously, this will be dangerous for all of us," interjected Muscles. As his nickname suggested, he was a great bull of a man, yet also softly spoken. "As you can probably tell, I'm always up for a scrap, but this will be different." The others laughed at this because Muscles sported a black eye from his misadventures out on the town the night before.

"What Claire hasn't told you yet," broke in Tyler, "but I may as well, is that there's a Yakuza element to all this too. It seems that the Japanese whaling industry is underpinned by the mobs. If not for them, the industry probably would have folded under public pressure years ago. Same with the killings of dolphins, tuna and God knows what else. Mind you, if we can put the factory ship permanently out of business, there's a chance that Japanese commercial whaling might stop completely."

"From where I'm sitting," said the ever-doleful Jonsson, "it makes sense to go along with Claire, support her team and sink the bastards once and for all. Are you with me?"

Another chorus of table-thumping followed this call to arms, and when the noise subsided, Claire picked up the briefing. "In point of fact, if things go the way that I hope, none of you should need to get too close to the *Nisshin Maru*. It'll be just Jason, Blackbeard and myself."

She had wanted to allay their fears, but instead stirred a spirit of rebellion. The crew members were damned if they'd miss all the action and said as much.

Again, Tyler interceded to calm everyone. "Don't worry. There'll be plenty of aggravation for everyone to dish out. You'll be as busy as ever, only this time we have a specific agenda. We'll fill you in on more details when we have the plan fully fixed, okay? Meanwhile, are there any more questions right now?"

There were a few, but mostly everyone wanted to talk among themselves and get to know the new arrivals. It was a bit early to start drinking, but never mind, the captain broke out the beer rations, and they drank and talked for hours.

241

With Jonsson back at the helm, the *Seven Seas* gently ploughed on towards the dusk. On board, a sense of celebration and keen anticipation prevailed.

*

Later that evening, Claire, Jason and Teach met with Knowledge and Tyler on the bridge. The time had come to discuss their plans in more detail, and the IT guru was critical to the mission's success. Knowledge seemed quite unfazed by the plan that Claire outlined and, after posing a few pertinent questions, he stepped away with his laptop to work on his brief.

Then Claire asked Tyler about the departure schedule for the *Nisshin Maru*. "Don't worry about it," he declared cheerfully. "The Sea Shepherd Conservation Society – hell, what a mouthful of a name that is – has a few people based at Shimonoseki to observe the whaling fleet. They don't engage in protest activities or anything, but just keep a reliable record of what's happening. I've asked them to let me know the very minute the old bitch casts off."

"I thought you weren't on speaking terms with the Sea Shepherd people," said Jason.

"Yeah, well, it's true that we had a bit of a falling out, but we're still basically friends and still talk to each other. They just don't want me on their ships anymore."

"Why the hell not?" Teach asked mischievously, for he already knew the answer. It was the very same reason for which he could no longer sail with Greenpeace.

"Because, as you bloody well know, you pirate, I kept breaking them!" Tyler declared, and they all laughed and clinked bottles together in a toast.

"I don't know about you guys, but I notice that the sun long since has sunk below the yardarm, and that means it's time for Pusser's on parade," Tyler observed. "Olly, get Miles up here to relieve you and then join us."

Soon all their glasses were full, and they rose as one in another toast. "To the *Seven Seas* on the seven seas, and to all who sail in her and on them!" they proclaimed.

Before long, Teach left for the galley to help Namika. Later, Claire and Jason grabbed some food before heading to their cabin. They had two bunks, one above the other, and hardly space to move, but they somehow managed.

Without knocking their heads too often on the higher bunk, they made love unhurriedly and tenderly, rocking to the gentle rhythm of the boat. Afterwards they fell into a deep and contented sleep.

Chapter 31

The *Nisshin Maru* Prepares For Sea

Daybreak on the second day of the journey found the *Seven Seas* in open, blue water, motoring along at a steady 10 knots on a southeasterly bearing. The vessel had covered some 250 kilometres and reached the halfway point, well on schedule for its planned rendezvous.

The *Nisshin Maru*, the factory ship that the crew of the *Seven Seas* intended to meet, remained tied up alongside the wharf at its home port of Shimonoseki. It was due to leave that evening and was loading final provisions and crew for the coming long voyage.

The ship's captain, a man named Saito, was a highly experienced sailor who had worked on whaling ships all his adult life. He had a haggard appearance, accentuated by a black-stubble buzzcut, and he favoured his left side in a permanent and slightly bent posture, the result of a collision many years ago between a recovery boat that he piloted and a whale. But he had good connections where it counted, and so he was kept on the fleet, earning his captaincy some 10 years later.

With character traits to match his looks, Captain Saito had a reputation for driving his crewmen hard in all weather and conditions. His job was to hunt and catch whales and turn in profits as big as possible to his employers, the so-called Institute of Cetacean Research (ICR). To this end, his sailors often considered him a tyrannical taskmaster, but he knew who his real boss was, someone meaner and nastier than anyone.

Saito stood on the flying wing of his bridge and watched the bustle of dockside activity through his small, barely visible eyes.

Suddenly his attention clicked onto four black SUVs in a rapidly moving convoy that braked near the gangway, stressing their arrival with a needless squeal of tyres, scattering workers aside. The captain felt no surprise to see this, the procession of his "unofficial" boss. News of the man's recent troubles had reached Saito's ears, and the boss must have decided to pay a visit to ensure that nothing went wrong on the coming expedition.

Men clad in black climbed out of the vehicles, peering around warily, even expectantly, for signs of danger. A moment later, Kage Kuraim emerged too and ascended the ship's gangway, leaving the goon squad, as Saito thought of them, on the dock. With raised eyebrows, the captain noticed the absence of the despicable Rai, who usually trotted along at Kuraim's heels. Probably the underling had been left behind to tidy up problems back in Tokyo.

Saito left the bridge and descended quickly to the main deck to meet the *oyabun* and escort him to the captain's day-cabin, where tea was ordered and served amid exchanges of facile pleasantries. When the two stewards in attendance finally left them alone, Kuraim got down to business.

"We believe you will encounter some unusually aggressive interference on this voyage," he began. "As a precaution, I'm leaving four of my best men on board this vessel for the protection of the ship and her cargo. They will be armed with machine guns, a sniper rifle and a shoulder-mounted, surface-to-surface Stinger missile system."

Silently, Saito looked at his boss. Consistent with his usual practice, a matter of self-preservation, he believed, the rugged seaman regarded the powerful crime boss with an inscrutable expression that seldom changed or revealed thoughts.

"These extra men join your mission with specific orders from me," Kuraim continued, "to adopt any means necessary to repel attacks and, if required, to kill anyone or to sink any vessel attempting to divert you from your purpose. Am I clear?"

"Very clear, as always, sir," replied the captain carefully. "May I ask, what about the Navy? Will it also accompany us this time?"

"No, it will not," said Kuraim. "The Navy no longer anticipates a sufficient threat, now that the Sea Shepherd fools have been chased away with their tails between their legs. We also advised the Navy that you and your crew have been sufficiently effective in safeguarding our assets."

Then, with a tone of genuine respect entering his voice, Kuraim added, "You have played a pretty rough game at sea in the last few years."

This brought the first slight movement to Saito's inexpressive face, which Kuraim rightly interpreted as a gratified smile. "In any case, our two security patrol vessels still will go along in support of your mission," the crime boss continued.

Saito finally spoke. "Well, it's a good thing the Navy will not be there if your men are going to kill people and sink ships," he said. "We want no extra witnesses to that, do we?"

"Indeed, Captain," agreed the *oyabun*. "There's also something else we don't want the Navy to see. You must kill as many whales as possible this season. Don't concern yourself with quotas or even species. Just take as many as you can."

"That will be a pleasure," remarked Saito. "The crews will be most pleased since, as you know, much of their pay is commission-based, according to the number of kills. Do you have any information about the ships or people we may encounter or when they plan to attack us? It would be most helpful to know these things."

246

Kuraim produced several photos and displayed them. "This woman is Claire Armstrong. She was previously with the British Special Forces and has made a lot of trouble here in Japan and in Hong Kong. The other picture shows someone you may have come across before, John Teach. He has been an activist since leaving the British Army, where he also served in the Special Forces. There are probably a few other misguided fools with similar backgrounds and ambitions to obstruct you, but we have no more details."

"Yes, I have come across Teach a few times," confirmed Saito. "He has spelled trouble for the whaling community for much too long. I would be pleased to feed him to his precious fishes." Again, a slight smile cracked Saito's face.

"There was a ship last year, the *Seven Seas*, that became quite a nuisance, I gather. Maybe Armstrong and Teach are hooked up with its crew, but we can't be sure."

Saito thought for a moment. "This is true. The *Seven Seas* harassed us constantly in the Southern Ocean and became very adept at keeping us distracted. That's why I have arranged for more powerful water cannon and some extra surprises on this voyage, but if your men will protect us, then we have no cause for concern, do we?"

"No, you don't. Just do your job, and bring me back as many whales as you can catch," ordered the Yakuza chieftain. "The ICR can handle any questions about exceeding quotas that may spew from the mouths of curious busybodies."

Kuraim then rose and left the captain, who bent in a deep bow of respect. Returning to the dock, the crime boss gave curt orders to see to the embarkation of the extra men and their weapons.

Next, Kuraim climbed back into one of the four black SUVs, and the entire convoy sped away from the dock as hurriedly as it had arrived. The *oyabun* needed to fly directly back to Tokyo and deal with William McMahan, who had just announced an intrusive visit.

*

Accepting the four mercenaries created serious headaches for Captain Saito. Kuraim's "best men" all were arrogant and demanding, insisting to sleep in the best quarters. Before the *Nisshin Maru* even left port, tensions simmered between these mobsters and the whaling crew.

Adding extra men caused a delay too, not only to rearrange the sensitive issue of sleeping billets, but also to procure more supplies. Although a supply ship would service the *Nisshin Maru* at sea from time to time and also take away processed whale product, Saito and his sailors still needed ample supplies on board at the outset.

By early the next day, the *Nisshin Maru* finally was ready to sail. As was traditional, families of the crew members flocked to the docks to wave farewell. Everyone on board would be away from home for at least four months. For some people, therefore, especially many of those standing at dockside, this turned into a tearful occasion.

Mingling amid the watching and waving crowd stood a young couple employed by the Sea Shepherd Conservation Society. Security measures were tight at the docks, but these two people discreetly had recorded all the pre-departure activity involving the *Nisshin Maru* and fed the information to their relevant headquarters, currently in Melbourne, Australia.

Sea Shepherd also operated a base in the Canadian city of Vancouver, which hosted the organisation after its forced departure from a previous office in nearby Friday Harbour, across the US border in the state of Washington. However, for the southern-hemisphere whaling season, Australia was better positioned strategically to monitor events, even without plans to run direct interference on the whaling fleets.

During recent seasons, ships in the Sea Shepherd fleet had endured so much interference and so many assaults that it became too dangerous for them to operate at sea. The Japanese Navy acted to protect the whalers and to deter protesters, and two privately contracted security patrol vessels joined the whalers too. In 2013, three Sea Shepherd vessels suffered serious damage in a major collision with the vastly larger *Nisshin Maru* factory ship. Recently, the whalers also had shown no hesitation to shoot live ammunition or use flashbang grenades. So most protesters now considered overt action against the whaling fleet nearly impossible.

For old time's sake, the Sea Shepherd couple watching the *Nisshin Maru* at dockside liked to keep Captain Tyler informed too. Details about the extra crew and slightly delayed departure promptly reached the *Seven Seas*. Talk on the dockside suggested that the smaller, faster whale-catchers and one security vessel would depart a week later. Another security ship would accompany the *Nisshin Maru* all the way, with the two vessels meeting at the mouth of Tokyo Bay. Clearly, someone wanted to take no chances.

*

The news from Shimonoseki caused mixed feelings on the bridge of the *Seven Seas*. There, Knowledge was busy sharing his ideas with Tyler and the team about exactly where and how best to snare the *Nisshin Maru*. They had reached the rendezvous zone and started a waiting game.

"That's great," said Knowledge, reacting to the incoming details. "We'll have extra time to get ready." He looked at his wristwatch. "So let's say that we'll expect our target to come through at about dawn tomorrow."

"I wouldn't call it great news, Knowledge," said Claire. "No security patrol vessel (SPV) at all would have sounded much better. Anyway, the timing is good so we'll be able to attack at dawn and intercept the factory ship out of the sunrise."

"Rather poetic as it sails from the Land of the Rising Sun and all that," said Tyler. This elicited grins all around before everyone turned serious again.

"Back to business," Tyler continued. "The whalers probably won't be too alert, given the time of day. With their proximity to Japan, they shouldn't expect trouble yet. They also won't be on any regular shipping lane so, with luck, they will not be glued to the radar and may not spot us too early."

"That's an awful lot of luck we need to rely on," noted Teach, "but I guess there's not much choice, is there?"

"Not really," said Claire, "but as long as we're in our RIB to the southeast of the factory ship and the SPV in plenty of time and ready to go, we should manage okay. Even when they pick up a diversion coming out of the southwest, our RIB shouldn't show up on radar immediately. With its speed and agility, I reckon we have a good chance to get the job done and to move well away before they even know what hit them."

"Amen to that," said Jason. "So why don't we go through things once more, and then let's get that RIB into the water and try it out?"

Chapter 32

Demesne Gets Rough

"I want you to fix a meeting with Kuraim as soon as possible," demanded the CEO of Demesne. "Make it somewhere public, where we'll be safe and he won't feel threatened, but not here in the hotel."

Together, McMahan and Huang had arrived in Tokyo on the Campbell's Trading Company's private jet. They had just checked into the Peninsula Hotel, McMahan to his usual deluxe suite with fabulous views of Hibiya Park and the Imperial Palace Gardens, and Huang into a regular room, which by any standards was also special in this most luxurious of hotels. In truth, McMahan, being the snob that he was, would have preferred to place Huang somewhere else entirely, but he did recognise the prudence of keeping his security man nearby.

Huang seemed only too eager to please. He still smarted from the shame of having allowed the Armstrong woman to slip away from him again. Unless he quickly redeemed himself, he knew that his days with Demesne would be numbered, and a rather small number too.

"Certainly, right away, sir," said the security chief. "Is there anything else in particular you want me to do?" He knew that Kuraim had tumbled in status, falling into McMahan's bad books, and wondered if perhaps his own purpose in visiting Tokyo was to terminate the troublesome *oyabun*.

"Who do you think was behind the shootings at the InterContinental Hotel here?" snapped McMahan.

"I assumed it was a Yakuza squabble," offered Huang, before another possible answer dawned on him. "You think it was Armstrong?"

"Of course, it was bloody Armstrong, you moron," McMahan shouted. "And if you had done your job like I told you, she wouldn't have been there causing yet more trouble. She'd be dead. So if you want to do something really useful, find her and kill her."

With those furious words ringing in his ears, Huang left McMahan's suite. He went to his own room to call Kuraim.

McMahan felt unusually anxious and had since his last meeting with Campbell. "How could my name have arisen in police circles concerning anything?" he wondered aloud.

Only one explanation made sense. The Armstrong woman must have extracted secrets from Lau before executing him. She truly needed to die before she destroyed the entire Demesne organisation, for that looked like her intention. Now that she had taken on Kuraim for a second time, she must be found and stopped.

"Ideally stopped by a bullet," McMahan mused. "And if a hail of bullets happens to hit her, so much the better."

From his room, Huang tried to contact Kuraim several times, but without success. Finally, he connected with Rai, a man he despised, but with whom he sometimes needed to conduct business. Rai indicated that his master had left Tokyo, but would return that evening. As a meeting venue, they agreed on a popular restaurant in the Ginza district.

*

Not daring to be late, Rai met Kuraim at the airport. As the two men rode together in the backseat of a luxury limousine toward Kuraim's even-more-luxurious home, the deputy briefed his boss about the proposed meeting.

At first, the *oyabun* seemed uninterested and detached. Then a pleasant thought occurred to him. He gazed directly at his second-in-command and asked in barely a whisper, "How would you like to assassinate the esteemed Mr McMahan for me?"

This request came as a big shock to Rai. He did not know all the details of the business arrangements between his boss and the mysterious organisation represented by McMahan, but he did know that this man was among the few to whom Kuraim ever had shown much deference.

Regardless, Rai recovered quickly and replied with enthusiasm. "It would be my honour and pleasure, Master," he said, bowing awkwardly while still seated in the moving car.

"Good, then do it. Go to the meeting, inform McMahan that I'm running a little late and then kill him. Probably he'll have Huang with him, but handle it as you wish. Then come to my home and report in person. No phone calls about this, understood?"

"Understood, Master."

With one issue settled, Kuraim advanced to another of similar importance. "What about the hunt for Armstrong and her people? Obviously, you didn't find them, or you'd have told me. Well?"

"They seem to have just vanished, Master. After they left the hotel, they visited a nearby restaurant. There were four of them, Armstrong, Teach, the woman we had taken hostage and…."

"And all of whom you lost," interjected Kuraim. "Who was the fourth person?"

"Yes, unfortunately so, Master. The fourth person was a big man, very strong and able apparently, so we can assume he's part of their gang. Then they left, and we've found no signs of them anywhere since."

Now the car arrived at Kuraim's deluxe apartment block, all of which he owned, and in the penthouse suite of which he lived in solitary and secure isolation. "Keep searching for them," he ordered. "I believe they'll target the whaling fleet next, so if they haven't left Japan already, they will very soon."

Two armed security guards stepped forward, one pulled open a back door of the limousine and they both escorted Kuraim into the apartment building. Other brawny security guards kept their wary eyes directed at the street and the surrounding area. None of them paid the slightest attention to Rai, who directed the driver to take him to a popular restaurant.

*

Rai barely had enough time to place an urgent phone call and arrange for two of his most reliable men to rush to the restaurant, pose as diners and provide him with backup. He himself sat down at a strategic table just in time to peer out a window and see McMahan and Huang descend from a taxi and walk to the eatery's entrance.

From his table, Rai watched as Huang slowly led McMahan in rehearsed order towards him. They were both on edge and highly mistrustful, wary of deceit or betrayal. At no time as they approached did Huang stop surveying the room suspiciously.

"Where is Kuraim?" demanded Huang anxiously, reaching the table. Neither man from Hong Kong looked very happy. McMahan already began to back-step towards the restaurant's entrance.

Standing to greet the guests, Rai began, "So sorry. Mr Kuraim asked me to tell you…." He already had cocked his pistol, keeping it concealed on his lap. When rising, he brought the weapon to bear on Huang and fired.

To Rai's astonishment, Huang and McMahan dived sideways in opposite directions with the speedy reactions of wild animals sensing imminent danger. Seeing the targets no longer aligned, Rai delayed a split second, deciding which one to shoot at next.

As Rai pointed the gun at McMahan, his accomplices fired two shots. This distracted Rai, costing him time and adding to the pandemonium that engulfed the restaurant as guests and staff frantically tried to run for cover or take refuge on the floor.

A yelp of pain indicated a hit, and Rai saw a red stain blossom on Huang's shirt high up on the right shoulder. Again, Rai sought out McMahan, who showed remarkable speed in hurtling towards the door.

Still aiming his pistol, Rai readied to fire when the still-standing Huang shot at him, three rounds in rapid succession, one of which hit his outstretched right arm just below the elbow. He cried out, dropping his weapon, as more shots erupted and slammed into Huang, who toppled lifeless to the restaurant floor.

Trying to refocus through the pain, Rai looked for McMahan, his main target. But Huang's gunfire had bought his boss precious seconds, and the surprisingly fleet-footed executive had reached the door and vanished into the night, apparently unscathed.

Rai and his two men raced outside, but saw no sign of McMahan. How remarkable that such a big man accustomed to a life of luxury could show such athleticism! Apparently, the survival instinct overcomes much.

McMahan had been lucky to flag down a passing taxi instantly. Now he fled back to the airport, phoning instructions to the jet's crew to prepare for immediate departure. He had neither the time, nor inclination, to worry about the fate of his security chief. Already he planned the details of gruesome retaliation against the leader of the Boryokudan Yakuza.

*

In different cities, news of the restaurant shootout reached Campbell and Kuraim at almost the same time, and both were livid. A clear pronouncement of war had been declared, which meant that Demesne needed to act fast before its credibility endured more and prolonged scrutiny.

In a sense, Kuraim felt more pressure because he wielded less influence outside Japan. Even there, he had been embarrassed again, this time by a very public, botched assassination attempt. Unless his whalers excelled with big catches and a successful hunt, then his remaining days of clout and command would be few.

After failing so badly, Rai now stood before Kuraim in the *oyabun*'s penthouse apartment, a bloody bandage wrapped around one arm, which hung in a makeshift sling. Rai's head drooped in shame and misery.

Merciless as always, Kuraim felt tempted to order the inept assassin to commit *seppuku*, or ritual suicide. The process involved plunging a short blade into one's own belly and drawing the weapon from left to right, slicing open the torso and then up diagonally across the intestines. But now was not the right time, the *oyabun* decided.

More than ever, Kuraim needed support from his right-hand man for the inevitable confrontations ahead against Demesne, against Armstrong and likely against other Yakuza gangs.

Facing war on multiple fronts, he craved help from every able man he could muster.

Campbell, in contrast, commanded a truly global reach and fully intended to use it to destroy the upstart Yakuza chieftain. He would reach out to the rival Yamaguchi-gumi syndicate, led by an *oyabun* named Kenichi Shinoda, who had expanded most effectively despite hindrances by Kage Kuraim. It was an open secret that Shinoda had plans to muscle in on Japan's lucrative fisheries operations. Well, now was as good a time as any for a change, Campbell decided.

Meanwhile, the Demesne boss awaited confirmation of Russell's removal, and then very possibly Sir Iain might deal the same way with his own long-time deputy. He and William McMahan had developed and expanded Demesne together, but now Billy seemed to have gotten sloppy. He'd failed to contain Armstrong, leading to the loss of the Xuè yuèliàng Triad, attracted unwelcome police interest with his handling of the *SCMP* editor and an intern, and now starred in a bungled homicide attempt on him in Tokyo.

What a shame, Campbell thought dispassionately, but only one solution really existed. Reaching a decision, he summoned the late Clement Huang's deputy chief of security, Kevin Lim, into his office and gave the fortunate fellow both a promotion and some very detailed instructions.

*

Sometimes when Russell faced a knotty problem, he took his trusted PA out for after-work drinks and used her as a sounding board for his ideas. The as-yet-classified enquiry into Campbell's Trading Company certainly qualified as a knotty problem, so they left the office early, hopped into a taxi and rode a short distance to the Grand Hyatt Hotel where the Champagne Bar was a favourite haunt. Neither of them noticed another taxi that pulled away from the curb behind them and followed their progress to the hotel bar.

Actually, the second taxi wasn't available for public hire. Instead it served as a private run-around vehicle for the man to whom Sir Iain Campbell had reached out. His driver dropped him at the hotel's front entrance, and he followed Russell and the woman through the lobby and into the bar. He settled into a comfortable chair, from which he could watch both the entrance and his target, and nursed a glass of champagne.

Normally, Russell stayed alert to his surroundings, but this time he felt preoccupied and failed to spot the man following them. When their drinks arrived, the senior policeman began to talk, telling May of his suspicions about Campbell's being a front for a huge criminal enterprise and speculating about its activities.

May listened attentively, offering a few comments, but mostly staying silent and sipping her champagne. Once when Russell paused for thought, she said worriedly, "If what you suspect is true, then you've shown them your cards. You could be in danger, James."

"The thing is that I needed to visit Campbell," Russell said. "It was necessary to rattle his cage, and it looks like it worked, what with McMahan rushing off to Tokyo and getting mixed up in a Yakuza shootout. That ties in nicely with what Claire Armstrong and her pals are suggesting. Incidentally, since talking to me, Team Armstrong has survived another attack and caused more of a firestorm with the Yakuza, but there's nothing yet linking it all to Campbell's. Trouble is, Claire and her group are at sea, and nothing looks likely to happen until they confront the whaling fleet. That's going to get pretty rough and dangerous. Meanwhile, the top people at Campbell's can just sit tight and watch things unfold."

"So what can you do?" asked May.

"Having already rattled the cage, it seems to me that now I need to poke Sir Iain Campbell's nest with a big stick and stir up all the hornets inside. I'm just not sure exactly how yet."

"You'll figure something out," May said, glancing at her wristwatch. "Sorry, boss, but I should go now. I need to do some shopping and stuff."

Russell accompanied May outside to a taxi before returning to the bar. In passing, he noticed that a man who had been sitting nearby was leaving too, but thought nothing more of it. After sitting back down, Russell slowly finished his drink before paying the check and leaving.

When strolling through the lobby again, he saw the same man, now apparently browsing magazines in the hotel's lobby shop. This time Russell studied him more closely, not in alarm, but because that's what he did automatically. The man appeared quite ordinary, Asian and perhaps in his forties. He looked to be in decent shape, and he dressed smartly in open-necked shirt, blazer and slacks.

Without pausing, Russell walked outside and waited for another taxi. Within five minutes, he was homeward-bound to Happy Valley, where he lived along one of the quieter backstreets near Hong Kong Island's famous horse-racing course.

When paying his taxi driver, Russell noticed another taxi approach behind them. A backseat passenger stared intently at him. It was the same man from the hotel.

Instantly alert, Russell moved quickly, just as the other vehicle accelerated towards him, a passenger window down and the barrel of a compact machine gun protruding. The weapon fired before the moving taxi came fully alongside him, spraying bullets onto the pavement and into the walls behind him. His own taxi took a hit, and glass rained down as he crouched for cover.

The taxi carrying the shooter stopped, as did the gunfire, and the assassin briefly inspected his work. Russell always carried a concealed Heckler and Koch, a 9mm USP compact automatic pistol, and during the pause he raised his own weapon and directed two bursts of double shots at the unknown attacker. He was an expert marksman, and all four bullets found their mark.

As the fake-taxi's driver tried to speed away, Russell took a bead on the fleeing car's tyres, firing four more rounds. With an explosive report, the vehicle swerved violently, crashing into a parked van.

A front door opened, and the driver scrambled out. He began running, but Russell moved quickly and ordered him to stop or be shot. It took the driver a split-second to decide, and he skidded to a halt, raising his arms in surrender.

After forcing the captured man to lie on the pavement, facedown with hands behind his head, Russell carefully checked on the shooter. Astonishingly, the would-be assassin remained alive, but bleeding heavily from four wounds, two on his arms, one on his shoulder and a graze to his neck.

While covering both men with his weapon, Russell called an emergency number on his mobile phone. Despite heavy evening traffic nearby, two police cars full of armed special-response officers arrived promptly. They took control of the scene just as an unmarked ambulance appeared and removed the gunman. More police converged. Rapidly they sealed off the area, and a massive investigation began.

Russell's taxi driver was very shaken, but unharmed. As a key witness, he was taken to the nearby Wan Chai Police Station, as was the assassin's driver, the first to a comfortable room with coffee and polite questioning, the second to an altogether-less-pleasant environment.

Meanwhile, the man Russell most wanted to question underwent emergency surgery in the nearby Adventist Hospital, but the doctors expressed confidence that he'd survive. From a police perspective, the shooter, and whatever he knew, needed to wait slightly longer.

As Russell finally arrived home again, this time accompanied by a protection detail, he thought of May Kwok's prophetic words from earlier in the evening about placing himself in danger. Absolutely, his efforts to jolt the people at Campbell's had worked. Now he knew for sure that he was onto something big.

Chapter 33

Action at Sea

Running dark, the *Seven Seas* maintained slow headway on calm waters in the Philippine Sea, due south of Tokyo and due east of Okinawa. The sky took on a faint red glow in the east, and a gentle, lazy breeze heralded a quiet dawn. It was six o'clock, and the crew members were keyed up and ready for action. A final briefing had taken place two hours earlier, and now they all were at their stations.

Claire and Jason stood in the bow of the smaller tender, the Apex A18 RIB, with Teach at its wheel and the RIB still tied up alongside the *Seven Seas*. They were fully kitted out in diving gear, except for the bulky air tanks that they would put on later, and just had run the last checks on their equipment.

On the other side of the *Seven Seas*, three crewmen, led by Muscles, had settled into the larger inflatable, the Apex A24 RIB. The people in both speedy boats waited patiently for a signal to interpret as a green light.

Knowledge bellowed down from the bridge that he detected two vessels on his radar, both headed directly for them. The approaching ships were a little ahead of his anticipated schedule. Now he calculated that they would converge with the *Seven Seas* in about 45 minutes. There were no other contacts to be seen.

So informed, team members on the two RIBs let go their lines and headed off in opposite directions away from their ship to take up strategic and pre-determined positions. The smaller tender moved east into a brightening sky, and the larger one went west.

Some 30 minutes later, the crew members still on the *Seven Seas* spotted running lights of the oncoming ships. The *Seven Seas* powered up to full speed and set a course directly towards the larger of the two radar contacts. The crew began receiving radio calls demanding identification and a change of course, but ignored them.

The A24 RIB also increased speed and ran parallel to its mother ship. Meanwhile, the smaller RIB waited patiently in its agreed position, the occupants fretting anxiously. If the diversion that Tyler and his crew had in mind to slow the *Nisshin Maru* to little more than a fast-swimming pace failed, then the entire plan probably would need to be aborted.

*

Both officers of the night watch on the *Nisshin Maru* had not yet settled into the rhythm of the voyage and so felt sleepy. Suddenly a radio message from the security patrol vessel three kilometres to the west squawked at them, bringing them fully awake. A ship had appeared on radar headed directly towards them. The intruder showed no running lights and ignored their radio calls. The SPV would go to intercept and advised the whaling factory ship to sound general quarters (action stations). This looked like the first contact with anti-whaling activists.

The factory ship's senior watch officer agreed and dutifully sounded the alarms. Within what seemed like little more than seconds, Captain Saito arrived on the bridge fully dressed. Other officers followed minutes later. After being briefed, Saito talked by radio to the captain of the SPV. Just then, a second and much smaller radar contact was reported to the west, moving parallel to the larger one.

It was most unusual to encounter protesters at this juncture of the voyage, and Captain Saito considered his options. He could accelerate to maximum speed and hope to outrun the oncoming boats, leaving the SPV to do what damage it could to them. Alternatively, he could stand and fight, demonstrating right away to the troublesome attackers that they would be punished heavily if they tried to disrupt his whaling operations in the coming months.

At heart, Saito was a warrior so the decision to make an example of the campaigners came easily, especially since he had no other whaling vessels along to worry about at this stage. As Tyler had predicted, the Japanese caption opted to slow down and fight. Saito relayed his decision to the escorting SPV and adjusted his speed and course towards the unknown ship.

The crew members stood ready at their stations. Despite the *Nisshin Maru* being a factory ship, it had been fitted not only with extra-high-powered water cannons, but also two modified harpoon guns, these set on each side and a little aft of the bow. The harpoons were distinct in that they had no attached cable and carried explosive charges decidedly larger than those used to kill whales, making them offensive weapons intended to significantly damage any would-be attacker's ship. Saito even had placed amidships what looked like mortars, devices firing small and potent tear-gas bombs with options for more lethal ordinance. Being so well prepared, the captain and his crew looked forward to engaging the enemy.

Kuraim's four mobsters eagerly anticipated the coming encounter too. The one carrying the Stinger missile system jostled with the harpoon gunners for position on the foredeck, while his cohorts equally tried to assert themselves over the crew. Saito furiously shouted orders and directed his senior officers to intercede before chaos and internal fighting erupted, but they could establish only an uneasy peace.

Dawn slowly dispelled the darkness, and the crew of the *Nisshin Maru* could see the *Seven Seas* as the two vessels closed on each other. The SPV also raced towards the unwelcome ship, momentarily ignoring the smaller, but faster, RIB that remained difficult to spot in the early light.

Although the *Seven Seas* had a reinforced hull for ice-breaking, a head-on collision with a much larger ship was never a good idea. When the two vessels were little more than a half-kilometre apart, Tyler spun the wheel of his ship to veer off at a 90-degree tangent, apparently fleeing.

As the *Seven Seas* turned, a loud report, followed by a smoke trail, erupted from the bow of the whaling factory ship, followed by another missile. Both narrowly missed, but the loud double explosions, completed when the missiles hit the water, showed beyond dispute that the whalers on the *Nisshin Maru* meant serious business.

The much more manoeuvrable A24 RIB, ignoring the SPV, headed straight for the *Nisshin Maru* on what looked like a suicidal course. Saito felt tempted to run down the RIB, which most likely would kill the people on board, but he baulked at the last moment and steered his heavy ship away.

Still, the captain wanted to inflict damage and, with the RIB now close enough, he ordered for his nearest water cannon to douse the tender and those within it. A flooded inflatable tender would cause no one any trouble. But the well-driven little craft was highly nimble and, like an annoying mosquito at night, danced around the cannon's powerful jets of water, taunting and teasing the factory ship's crew members and, most importantly, distracting them.

The anti-whaling protesters pulled back fast, though, when what sounded like machine-gun fire opened up on them. This was a shocking development for which they were unprepared.

Meanwhile, the SPV changed course to chase the *Seven Seas*, extending its gap from the factory ship. Tyler waited for as long as possible and, with the patrol craft almost upon his vessel, turned again, this time aiming directly at the much smaller and lighter pursuer.

The SPV captain recognised the looming danger and hastily turned his wheel to avoid a collision. He nearly made it, but his manoeuvre had the temporary effect of presenting his vessel broadside to the *Seven Seas*, forming a larger target. The old icebreaker caught the SPV in the stern with a terrible impact, the sound of rupturing steel overriding cries of dismay from the SPV crew.

An eerie silence settled in after the crash as the two ships drifted apart. The *Seven Seas,* with its powerful reinforced bow looking unscathed by the encounter, reduced power and slowly began to circle the rival vessel. Similar positive news did not apply to the SPV.

Being smaller and less sturdy than the *Seven Seas*, the security patrol vessel had sustained serious damage. The collision had disabled its rudder and, more importantly, cracked and displaced the propeller shaft. This, in turn, opened up a large gash in the stern through which water poured into the engine room. Within minutes, the damaged ship showed a notable list, and its stern settled lower in the water.

Shocked and dazed by the sudden turn of events, the SPV captain heard the alarming damage reports from his frightened officers. The ship was sinking! He sent out a Mayday call to the *Nisshin Maru* and, in a haze of disbelief, gave the orders to abandon ship.

It wasn't a large complement of men. The SPV's 15 shocked crew members climbed into their life raft before watching their ship slip quietly backwards below the ocean's surface, the bow pointing skywards at the last moment before disappearing from sight. No one had been hurt, a fact that gave the captain his only consolation. For the SPV, the whole destructive encounter had lasted less than 15 minutes.

Tyler and his crew felt equally shocked at the result of their actions, although quietly elated too. They continued to circle the area slowly, prepared to pick up the survivors, but their offer of assistance was rejected in favour of the factory ship, so they idled nearby and waited.

*

As a diversion, the whole episode worked perfectly for the three militants in the smaller RIB. They had watched the events unfold through powerful binoculars, and when the *Nisshin Maru* had turned to avoid running down the larger RIB, they accelerated towards the factory ship at top speed from their position hidden against the rising sun.

Approaching the massive target vessel, Claire and Jason strapped on BCDs (buoyancy compensation devices) with their dive tanks already attached and made final adjustments to their gear. By radio, Tyler updated them on the engagement with the SPV, its result and the gunfire that had come from the main ship.

Teach reported back that the factory ship appeared to be headed to the scene of the sinking. That counted as good news because it meant that the big vessel would heave-to when it picked up survivors from the life raft, or at least it would move very slowly.

Claire's main concern always had been the difficulty of attacking the whaling ship if it moved at speed, so the circumstances unfolded perfectly for the attack. The news of gunfire, however, was deeply worrying. If spotted, they'd make easy targets for anyone on deck.

The *Nisshin Maru* slowed greatly as it approached the SPV's life raft. All the available crewmen, wary of more provocations, kept sharp eyes pointed at the *Seven Seas* as it hovered safely a kilometre away, now joined there by the larger RIB.

No one aboard the whaling factory ship looked behind them as the small RIB quietly pulled up and ran alongside its midsection. Jason leant out towards the big vessel and placed a large mooring magnet on the hull. A line was attached, securing the RIB to the ship's side as it moved slowly towards the stricken escort crew still floating helplessly on the opposite side.

Without time to tarry, Claire and Jason flipped backwards over the side of the RIB into the chilling water. They each were attached to a line on the inflatable because they couldn't afford to get anywhere near the big propeller of the *Nisshin Maru*. Nor could they risk floating past altogether, so they paid out the line until they were positioned about 15 metres before the stern.

There, the keel began to taper towards the ramp, up which slaughtered whales normally were dragged for processing. The two ex-soldiers repeatedly collided with the keel, their tanks making alarmingly loud bangs that echoed inside the ship, but this problem lessened as the *Nisshin Maru* continued to bleed off speed. The pull on their lines also caused discomfort as they were hauled through the water, trying their best to maintain control of their positions. It was no easy task.

Strapped to their belts, Claire and Jason each carried a small Maindeka Advanced Limpet Mine measuring a third of a metre in diameter and weighing just six kilograms. More commonly, these would be used against stationary targets in harbours or at anchor because their suction capability became compromised if the vessel to which they were attached moved at speeds in excess of about eight knots.

Claire and Jason waited uncomfortably as the *Nisshin Maru* slowed. After what seemed like ages, but in reality, was less than five minutes, the engines stopped. The factory ship began to drift, preparing to pick up the stricken SPV's anxious crew.

Wasting no time, Claire and Jason affixed the two mines a metre apart and three metres below the waterline, the idea being to create one large hole into the engine room. Each mine held a kilogram of a high-explosive composition mix of RDX and TNT, giving maximum blast and cutting effect. At the very least, the anticipated explosion should severely disable the factory ship and disrupt the whale-hunting expedition.

The saboteurs set the mechanical timers for 20 minutes and then cut their attaching lines to the RIB. They needed to fin strongly to pull away from the huge ship's suction as it drifted through the water, and they only surfaced at a safe distance.

Teach, meanwhile, had cast the RIB free and was idling some 100 metres away, keeping a sharp lookout for the divers. He promptly spotted them and brought the RIB in to pick them up quickly. As they flopped into the inflatable, he slowly and quietly steered the RIB away from the factory ship so as not to alert those on board. At an appropriate distance, he powered up the engines and sped away at full throttle.

Claire and Jason collapsed in exhaustion to the floor of the fast-moving craft. Although in good physical shape, they lacked the same level of fitness as when on active service. The constant battering and bruising against the factory ship's side had drained their reserves. Despite their dry suits, if they had needed to stay in the cold water much longer, their strength would have been entirely sapped, leaving them in serious trouble. As it was, though, they had placed the mines and now needed to return to the *Seven Seas* to watch events unfold.

*

On the *Nisshin Maru*, the crew brought the survivors of the SPV aboard up the ramp at the stern of the ship. Captain Saito stood on the flying bridge looking at the *Seven Seas* in the distance when he noticed another inflatable, a smaller one, running at speed in its direction. The larger one still idled near its mother ship. He wondered where the second RIB had come from and what its occupants had been doing.

What Saito knew for sure was that he felt distinctly uneasy and had a deep sense of foreboding. This attack had been highly coordinated, and the tormentors' actions were much less random than it first seemed or was usual with these irritating activists. The whole episode would delay his expedition because now he must return to Shimonoseki, spend time with the authorities and appease the inevitably infuriated Kuraim. But was this attack simply a delaying tactic or something else?

Saito barked out orders to the recovery team to hasten bringing the SPV survivors aboard. He wanted to get under way and leave the scene as quickly as possible.

Another 15 minutes, give or take a few moments, saw everyone safely aboard, and so Saito issued orders to return to the home port at full speed. The big ship's variable-pitch propeller churned the water, forming a thick, creamy wake, and the *Nisshin Maru* slowly began to pick up speed.

*

The three assailants in the small RIB looked anxiously towards the *Nisshin Maru* as the factory ship accelerated away to the northwest. Within another minute or so, pressure on the limpet mines would become unsustainable, and they would detach from the hull and sink uselessly to the ocean floor.

Just when the dangerous mission looked likely to fail, a mighty double explosion erupted from below the waterline near the stern of the departing factory ship. A huge waterspout rose at the ship's side, and as it fell, the colossal vessel slewed around drunkenly, its speed falling off rapidly.

Another explosion ensued, this one internal to the big ship, quieter and muffled. At the waterline on the ship's side, a large hole appeared from which billowed thick, black, oily smoke.

Cheers of elation broke out on the *Seven Seas* and on the two RIBs. Both inflatables were pulled aboard, and the one ship still seaworthy after the decisive conflict prepared to head off to the southwest.

The *Seven Seas* needed to flee before naval and patrol vessels arrived. By now, the authorities would have received not only distress calls, but also some details about the attackers and their apparent acts of piracy. For the culprits, lingering would mean certain arrest and probably much worse.

Yet thoughts of leaving the scene caused a moral dilemma aboard the *Seven Seas*. Abandoning a stricken vessel, even an enemy one, violated all maritime codes of conduct. Claire, Jason and Teach discussed this on the bridge with Tyler and Jonsson.

For the moment, they decided to stay on station and observe from a distance. In doing so, they kept a sharp lookout on the radar and listened to all radio transmissions.

*

271

Never before had the *Nisshin Maru* faced such serious trouble. The limpet mines easily had breached the hull, and their position had been adjacent to one of the engine room's fuel tanks. Shrapnel from the first blasts had penetrated the tank, which began spewing its contents onto nearby super-heated pipes. The result was instantaneous combustion, and the tank blew itself apart, spraying burning oil all over the engine room. As heat built up in the blazing space, pipes and plant began melting, bearings and lubricants overheated and the main prop shaft ground to a screeching standstill of shredded metal. Seawater rushed in, turning instantly to steam, and the whole place became an inferno.

But fire needs oxygen, and with the hatches having sealed automatically, that was quickly consumed. As the flames died down, seawater could come in without instantly vaporising. Soon what little remained of the engine room was completely flooded. Fortunately, no one had been in there at the time of the explosions, all hands having been summoned on deck to repel the attackers and then to help pick up survivors from the sunken SPV.

On the bridge, Saito spoke urgently to his chief engineer, who reported that all the engine-room controls were inoperable, including the pumps. The fire teams reported that they couldn't access the area at all to assess damage because they dared not open the hatches. Meanwhile, the sea filled the entire engine room, and pressure built on the hatches, which as sturdy as most of them were, had not been designed to withstand such punishment.

The ship's stern rested low in the water, and the encroaching sea had climbed nearly to the top of the ramp. Suddenly the crew heard a loud report, sounding like another explosion, only this time it was a small inspection hatch that had blown out. Immediately water poured through into the corridor beyond, and a fire team trying to inspect the damage nearby only just managed to evacuate the area before it too flooded.

*

Observers on the *Seven Seas* knew the *Nisshin Maru* was sinking. Tyler announced that he felt obliged to offer assistance, despite the anxiety about staying in the vicinity. No one objected enough to stop him, so he radioed the factory ship and offered help.

When the call came in, the radio operator looked to Saito for instructions. The captain seized the mouthpiece and began a tirade of verbal abuse, denouncing the activists and threatening that if they came within range, he would shoot them. Help was not required under any circumstances.

Reluctantly, Tyler accepted the rebuttal. Yet the *Seven Seas* still held station at a distance, and the crew members continued their subdued observations.

*

The chief engineer on the *Nisshin Maru* conferred again with the captain, who now faced the grim decision most dreaded by all seafarers, whether to abandon ship. Gloomily, the chief engineer reported that likely the mother ship and long-time champion of the Japanese whaling fleet would founder, and that he could do nothing about it. As if any doubt existed, another explosion signalled the inevitable breakup of Saito's ship. His decision was made for him.

A distress call had been transmitted after the initial explosions, so it just remained to ensure that everyone on board evacuated safely into the lifeboats. For 15 of the disheartened sailors, it was their second time to abandon ship within an hour, giving them a fireside story to tell for the rest of their lives.

For Saito, the enormity of the situation left him shocked and appalled. Cranky protesters long had beset these whale-hunting expeditions, but these people today were of an altogether different breed. They had shown great resourcefulness, determination and courage, and these traits he grudgingly admired.

No matter how the captain calculated, for him the entire incident added up only to a dismal outcome. He felt like the culprits had destroyed him personally and as completely as if they had put a gun to his head and pulled the trigger. Then and there, he decided to go down with his ship rather than bear the shame of being defeated by three people in a small inflatable RIB.

Saito saw personally to the departure of the ship's company into the lifeboats, commanding them to leave without him, despite the protestations of his officers. Then he returned to the bridge and, with the sun rising higher for the new day, he stood firm, unflinching, as water rushed in and took him and the *Nisshin Maru* gently spiralling to the ocean floor more than 4,000 metres below.

*

Aboard the *Seven Seas*, all crew members looked on in awe as the huge vessel vanished below the surface. Their earlier elation had soured somewhat at the enormity of what they had done.

Through binoculars, Tyler could see that the *Nisshin Maru's* lifeboats appeared seaworthy and under control. When he had made a second offer of assistance, the reply again was one of vigorous rejection. He conferred with his own crew on the bridge, and they agreed on the need to leave the scene before rescue services arrived.

Jonsson pointed the ship southeast, and the *Seven Seas* made off at full speed.

Chapter 34

Heads Roll

News of the calamity spread rapidly. This was a huge story for environmentalists worldwide, and they ensured that major news networks covered the double ship-sinking in detail. When carefully prodded, investigative journalists linked the latest attack to the earlier one in Taiji, and then the commentaries began to occupy unprecedented airtime. Hailed as "environmental vigilantes", the activists, whoever they may be, were deemed heroes, and since they'd killed no one, at least not in these two incidents, they were idolised worldwide.

Public opinion swung, even in Japan. Most people polled now claimed to support a total embargo on whaling and dolphin culling. Bloody and distressing archive photos repeatedly appeared. Expert witnesses delivered their learned opinions on the distressing state of the oceans and endangered sea life. Officially, governments and global organisations condemned the sinking of ships as blatant piracy. Arrest warrants, ready to be enforced when the culprits were identified, appeared for anyone involved. Yet millions of people across all continents openly applauded the supremely disruptive actions.

When news reports highlighted that some whalers not only had hunted in contravention of the IWC's original ban, but also consistently exceeded quotas, an outcry rippled around the planet. An early casualty, with many to follow, was the chairman of the Institute of Cetacean Research in Japan, who hastily resigned to avoid being turfed from office. The sense of scandal deepened when ties to organised crime became public knowledge. Rumoured links to some recent shootings in Tokyo hotels and restaurants simply embellished the story.

In his solitary Tokyo penthouse, Kage Kuraim fumed, consumed by impotent fury. Naturally, he blamed everyone else all around him and vented his near-constant bouts of rage on the hapless staff members who serviced his apartment. He knew that this latest debacle might trigger his permanent downfall, and he noticed that even Rai now tried to avoid him. This fed his intense paranoia, and so he pulled himself deeper into his shell, surrounded by frightened bodyguards and plenty of guns.

Within days, the Japanese government felt obliged to announce at least some action in response to the groundswell of public opinion. At a huge press conference, government officials ordered a national moratorium on all whaling by Japanese ships until a comprehensive public enquiry could take place and report its findings. In the Japanese manner, a long row of officials bowed deeply in unison before the assembled media to show "sincere remorse" for past inaction.

Widespread public protests demanded better ocean conservation, including by Canada, whose northern native peoples by tradition hunted and killed many whales, and even by countries like South Korea and Indonesia, whose citizens caught relatively few. Russia used police violence to try suppressing the protests, but almost everywhere, people took to the streets and made their voices heard. Whaling must end, they insisted.

*

Kenichi Shinoda, *oyabun* of the Yamaguchi-gumi Yakuza syndicate, received William McMahan's phone call whilst out on a golf course. He played regularly as a member of the Tokyo

277

Golf Club, one of Japan's most expensive and exclusive clubs. Not a very good player, he was known to cheat, but his playing partners never challenged him, rightly deeming it imprudent even to consider calling out a Yakuza chieftain.

McMahan placed the call at Campbell's behest. The recent incidents with Kuraim, culminating in the assassination attempt and the whaling fiasco, necessitated a change of allegiance and support, and Shinoda was the natural choice as a successor. He and the Demesne leadership had met informally a few times and, although never mentioned, each side knew substantial details about the other's most secretive business operations.

"Mr McMahan, what a pleasant surprise! What can I do for you?"

Shinoda spoke excellent and almost accent-free English. In his late fifties, he was elegant and well groomed, purveying a false air of urbanity that could fatally deceive. Actually, he was utterly merciless and had carved out a crime empire that now placed his syndicate firmly atop the felonious tree.

"Good day, Mr Shinoda," replied Demesne's chief executive. "We need to talk in person. Please name the time and place."

Shinoda knew all about the attempted slaying of McMahan and the difficulties faced by Kuraim, his own long-time rival. "Would this have anything to do with our mutual friend, Kage Kuraim?" he teased.

"No friend of mine," replied McMahan tersely. "Well?"

"I imagine that you may prefer not to visit Japan again for a while so why don't I stop by to see you and Sir Iain Campbell in Hong Kong? It's been an age since I was there, and I'd like to break the news of Mr Kuraim's tragic death to Sir Iain personally." Orders had been issued to dispose of Kuraim, but not yet enacted, so Shinoda spoke well ahead of the curve.

McMahan sounded totally unperturbed. "I'll tell Sir Iain, but I cannot answer for his schedule. Let me know when you're coming."

As was rather usual, McMahan then disconnected before awaiting a reply. He had wearied of trying to behave courteously towards the Japanese.

Not at all offended, Shinoda smiled as he pocketed his phone. Then after hastily glancing around, he blatantly kicked his golf ball out of the rough and re-joined his fellow players.

Coming events will be good for me, Shinoda thought.

*

No sooner had McMahan ended his conversation with Shinoda than someone knocked at his office door. His secretary had gone to lunch so he barked out, "Come in."

He recognised Clement Huang's former deputy as the person entering the room, but failed to recall the fellow's name. The man bade him "good afternoon", confidently approached the desk where McMahan sat and leaned over it. He was a big brute, like his ex-boss, and could be most intimidating.

"Do you mind?" McMahan erupted. "Stand up straight when you're in my presence. What do you want?"

Kevin Lim smiled down at McMahan and simply said, "You, sir."

Suddenly waves of fear rolled through McMahan's body. Knowing that he was alone, he reached for a panic button under his desk and jabbed it several times, but heard no alarm bells.

Smiling faintly, Lim circled the desk and grabbed McMahan in a steely clamp around the neck, lifted him out of the chair and began dragging him towards the large floor-to-ceiling window overlooking the harbour. McMahan tried calling out, but the grip around his throat prevented sound from emerging.

When Lim reached the window, he briefly relaxed his grip to hit McMahan on the back of the neck, just hard enough to subdue the man whilst leaving him still conscious. Lim let the CEO drop to the floor and slowly opened the window as wide as it allowed.

The office was situated on the 23rd floor of Campbell's Tower. Immediately the open window attracted a rush of wind that wailed as it tore through the room, lifting papers in its path.

In a foggy mental state, McMahan realised what was happening and struggled to move but lacked the strength, his muscles feeling like lead. Lim bent down and heaved the reluctant CEO into the window frame.

McMahan began to cry out, but the howling wind rendered him inaudible. He braced his hands against the window frame to halt his forward momentum, but Lim just karate-chopped them away and forced him out farther, farther… and farther.

At last, gravity took its relentless grip. A grunt from Lim preceded a final shove that sent McMahan falling, with his limbs flailing as he descended to his death, slamming onto the paving below.

Moving quickly, Lim left McMahan's office and returned to his own, from where colleagues soon summoned him to assist at the front of the building. There, it appeared that the company's troubled CEO had taken his own life by jumping from an office window, a method of suicide all too common in Hong Kong with its abundance of skyscrapers.

Employees duly informed the apparently distraught Campbell's chairman about the demise of his second-in-command. Then the police arrived and began to investigate.

*

"Bit of a coincidence, I'd say, Mr McMahan jumping. Why do you think he did that?" Russell asked.

Once again, the senior policeman was visiting Sir Iain Campbell's office, confronting the chairman. The two men now behaved towards each other with open hostility. Campbell had tried to brush off the police official, refusing to meet with him. But when told that failing to cooperate would mean being taken to the police headquarters for questioning, he capitulated.

"I have no idea why," replied Campbell testily. "And what do you mean, 'coincidence'?"

"When we last spoke, I indicated that our sources had mentioned Mr McMahan's name in connection with the triads. Then he suddenly takes flight and goes to Tokyo, where the Yakuza tried to kill him. He returns here only to get shoved out of a window, which in my book all looks like a big coincidence."

"What do you mean, he was 'shoved out of a window'?" demanded Campbell. "It was a suicide, plain and simple. He'd been under a lot of pressure, and I suppose maybe the assassination attempt on him was the last straw."

"Good job that we don't all commit suicide after someone tries to kill us and fails," Russell said. He had just come from the hospital, where his own would-be assassin still refused to talk.

When Campbell ignored him, Russell continued stonily. "We are watching you very closely, Sir Iain, and seeking to establish links between your company and organised crime. When we do, as I fully expect that we will, please be assured that all of your grand and doubtlessly well-paid-for connections will count for nothing. Good day."

*

Shinoda had instructed his men to avoid subtlety when eliminating Kuraim. He wanted the assassination to be seen as bloody and brutal, thus serving to warn other crime lords that any moves against him would be met with extreme violence.

When the time came, Kuraim never stood a chance. He'd always liked to regard himself as being impregnable when fortified inside his penthouse apartment, surrounded as he was by so many of his men. But overwhelming forces, armed with heavy weapons and explosives, came after him. Ruthless men cut a blood-slicked path through his defenders. When the assailants reached Kuraim and his obnoxious deputy Rai, they carefully set upon them with knives, making their deaths as gory, drawn out and spectacular as time allowed before the authorities arrived.

Almost overnight, Shinoda's Yamaguchi-gumi syndicate gained the undisputed leadership of Japan's criminal underworld. The next day, a jubilant Shinoda celebrated his ascent with another round of golf.

Chapter 35

Claire and Jason Head For More Choppy Waters

On the *Seven Seas*, the crew members' initial euphoria about a spectacularly successful mission continued to wane. Their goal always had been to disrupt whaling ships wherever they sailed. Usually they enjoyed reasonable success at this. But never before had they sunk one, let alone two, and the full ramifications slowly dawned on them.

But Claire, Jason and Blackbeard all felt a great sense of accomplishment and remained highly exhilarated. This was the sort of thing they did best, and the mission had unfolded perfectly for them. In one offensive action, they'd disabled the entire Japanese whaling fleet, scored a major victory over the Yakuza and, most importantly, saved possibly thousands of whales from hideous, unnecessary deaths. This last fact also lifted the spirits of the other crew members.

Immediately after leaving the scene of the double sinking, the crew members who had ridden in the RIBs took showers and warmed up, soon clutching mugs of steaming hot coffee provided by Namika. Gradually they joined Tyler and Jonsson on the bridge. There, despite the morning hour, they found the inevitable bottle of Pusser's Rum fighting a losing battle to survive against the captain and his mate.

"So, m' hearties, where do ye want to be headin' now?" asked Tyler, rendering his idea of pirate-speak. This inevitably attracted a quip from Blackbeard.

After some idle banter, the captain turned serious. "Guys, we need to decide quickly where we're going. Lots of people will search for us now, and we all need to get as far away as possible."

"Speaking for myself," said Claire, "I want to return to Hong Kong and link up with Russell. There's still the matter of who pulls the strings behind all this, and I need to see it through."

"Same goes for me," said Jason. Since he'd resigned from the casino operations in Macau, he felt like he had little to lose and enjoyed the action. In all honesty, he also wanted to stay near Claire for personal reasons.

Teach sounded less certain. "I'm still employed by the people at POSC. At least, I hope that I am, so I reckon that Namika and I will touch base with them and see what they want us to do."

"That's fair enough," said Claire. "If Chuck Bailey's still talking to me, which is a big question mark, I'll have a word with him."

She paused and looked around the bridge, her gaze lingering on every person there. "You guys all have been great, but I must take total responsibility for sinking those ships. There should be no blame attached to any of you, and certainly no legal actions taken against you."

"Hold on there just a damn minute, lady," said Tyler, glowering. "That's a very honourable notion, I'm sure, but you're not going to hog all the credit. This was a team job, and we've got our reputations to consider too. We're all in this together, got it?"

"Bloody right," added Jonsson, doleful as ever, speaking up from his place at the wheel.

"Okay, okay, I surrender," said Claire, raising her hands into the air. "I only want to protect you from possible prosecution, but have it your own way."

A few grins circulated on the bridge amid the process of refilling beverage glasses. After various toasts to the successful mission, and then more to the prosperity of whales, the conversation reverted to escape plans.

Tyler picked up the thread. "I'm going to contact the Sea Shepherd guys, maybe head up north and see if we can make ourselves useful to them in the North Pacific, chasing the Russian whalers. In which case, we probably can get you to Hong Kong in, what, three or four days?"

With raised eyebrows, he directed his query to Jonsson, who simply nodded. "We'll drop you off first and then sail north," the captain told Claire and Jason. "Does that suit you?"

"Sounds good," answered Jason. "Macau may work better as an access point, but we'll sort that out as we go. For now, I'm going to crash out. After all the fun and games, no sleep last night and then all this rum, I've had it. Coming?" he asked Claire.

"You go ahead. I'll join you soon," said Claire. She remained on an adrenaline high and knew from experience that she needed more time to unwind before sleep would come.

"I'm with you, Jason," said Teach. The two men rose and left the bridge, accompanied by Jonsson, who had needed relief at the helm and so handed over to Tyler. All three headed to their respective bunks.

Claire stayed and talked to the captain until Muscles joined them and took the wheel. Then Claire and Tyler also went to their cabins for some much-needed sleep.

*

The *Seven Seas* and its crew approached the Luzon Strait, halfway between Taiwan to the north and the Philippines to the

285

south. They passed the Batanes Islands on their starboard side at night and continued unchallenged into the next day on calm seas and with a mild following wind.

As it turned out, Teach and Namika opted to stay on the *Seven Seas* and travel north with the ship for new adventures. They had failed to reach Chuck Bailey, and suggestions from the ship's crew, who had taken to the POSC pair as two of their own, swayed the decision. Teach remained popular with his tales from the early days of anti-whaling protests, and Namika's gastronomic creativity in the galley made her a sweetheart to her shipmates. They really had nowhere else they wanted to go, so the arrangement pleased everyone.

Claire and Jason decided to jump ship on Lamma Island to the south of the more populous Hong Kong Island. They knew that Lamma was an altogether quieter place, with less officialdom and a distinctly more serene way of life, than the bustling main-island or Kowloon.

They planned their landing for after midnight. Following final drinks of Pusser's Rum, they bade especially fond farewells to their comrades in arms, Teach and Namika. They had formed a close bond and were sorry to see each other go their separate ways. Then it was farewell to Tyler and his crew, all of whom turned out to see them depart. The two ex-soldiers climbed into the smaller RIB, and Muscles drove them quietly ashore to a beach at an uninhabited spot near the island's south end.

Once Muscles had returned to the ship, the *Seven Seas* vanished into the darkness. Although nobody on board could see them, Claire and Jason each waved a final goodbye.

They rested on the beach for a while and snacked on sandwiches and coffee prepared by Namika. Then they trekked north across difficult and hilly scrubland, moving carefully in the murk of night. Soon they picked up a narrow walking trail and followed it for more than an hour as it led them, first up into the hills and then down again, all the way to Yung Shue Wan, Lamma's largest village and the site of a ferry pier.

Claire and Jason had decided to ride a ferry to Aberdeen on the southern side of Hong Kong Island, the first sailing for which would leave at six in the morning. They arrived at Yung Shue Wan in plenty of time and strolled through the awakening community, grabbing some soup (absolutely not shark fin soup) from an early vendor by the harbour.

They were the first passengers to clamber aboard the ferry and promptly placed their heavy backpacks on the floor beside their seats. The ride to Aberdeen took just 30 minutes, and then they easily caught a taxi to Claire's home at Shek O. They felt reasonably confident that no furtive characters still watched the place, but stayed alert and ready in case they were mistaken.

Once they'd arrived and dropped their gear, Jason followed Claire on a tour of the property. "This is a lovely place you have here," he said.

Everything was clean and tidy, evidence that David Armstrong's faithful amah, Queenie Ho, continued seeing to the house. Jason noticed a shadow pass over Claire's face as she showed him where she had fought and killed the intruders, now seemingly so long ago.

Feeling hungry, they entered the kitchen. "The fridge shelves are bare, except for a few beers and some decent wine," announced Claire, peering inside the appliance. "What do you say that we wander down to the village, have something to eat at Ben's Back Beach Bar when it opens and then shop for supplies?"

"Sounds like a plan," agreed Jason. "And speaking of plans…."

287

"Yes, I know. We need to plan the next stage. But let's just chill for today, shall we? I don't know about you, but I could do with a short break."

"Agreed."

They spent the rest of the day and that evening relaxing, eating and drinking, absorbing the sights, sounds and smells of the village and of Claire's home, acting as if they hadn't a care in the world. It was a special time together, and they cherished it, almost hoping it never would end.

But at 9 o'clock the next morning, a scream of startled surprise from the kitchen disturbed their peace. They leapt out of bed, grabbed guns and marched naked and purposefully to the source of the alarm. Another scream followed when the amah saw the two of them burst into the kitchen pointing weapons at her. Embarrassed apologies followed as the gunslingers threw on some clothes, and Claire introduced Jason to the disconcerted Queenie.

"I was scared, Miss Claire, because right away after I came inside, I saw that someone had been in the place," said Queenie. "I'm so sorry, but I didn't know you were coming, or else I'd have prepared some food and filled the fridge for you."

"Please don't worry, Queenie. Everything is fine, and I should have called to let you know," Claire assured her. "Jason and I have been quite busy chasing down my father's killers, you see, and we didn't know we'd be coming here until yesterday. I'm so sorry we frightened you."

"This ruckus in the news, Miss Claire, about the triads and the Yakuza and the whaling, is that all your doing?" asked Queenie.

"Good gracious, no, not really," Claire answered evasively. "We simply helped the authorities with their enquiries. Anyway, we'll be around for a few days, I expect, so we can catch up after Jason and I finish getting dressed."

"Great," declared Queenie, not quite believing her. "I'll fix you a nice, big breakfast." She peered towards a doorway through which Jason had retreated and then said with a knowing smile, "From what I saw, your friend looks like he needs feeding. There's no fat on him anywhere, huh? And the same goes for you too, Miss Claire."

*

The telephone rang, startling Claire and Jason as they enjoyed Queenie's vast breakfast. The amah answered it, told the caller to wait, and then asked them, "Are you here for a Mr Russell?"

They traded looks of surprise. Then Claire rose from her seat at the table to take the call.

"James?"

"Thought I might find you there…. Jason and Blackbeard with you?" the police official began cheerfully. "My word, you lot have been busy. How about if we meet for lunch and you tell me all about it?"

"Just Jason. Where?" Claire still felt disinclined to be very communicative with the police about their activities, no matter how friendly anyone from the authorities might sound.

"Could you arrive at the Mandarin Grill in Central district at 12:30? There's someone I'd like you to meet there."

"Is it safe? Aren't we wanted by the authorities to assist with their enquiries or something?"

"No, actually you're not. The Tokyo police would like to hear from you to clarify some details about a Yakuza turf-war shooting in your room after you left the InterContinental Hotel, but that's about all, as far as I know."

"You mean they have no clue about who conducted any mysterious acts of piracy on the high seas?" she asked, amazed. Queenie, who pretended not to listen, raised her eyebrows at this.

"None at all. The authorities are searching for a ship active in some anti-whaling activity, albeit quite extreme, that led to two Japanese whaling vessels sinking. But the ship had no visible name or registration, and it seems to have vanished anyway. Haven't you followed the news reports?"

"No, we haven't had time. Are you saying that nobody's looking for us?" Claire hardly could believe it.

"Well, I wouldn't go so far as to say that, but since you've destroyed most of your adversaries, it's really just the big boss left to worry about, hence my invitation to lunch."

"Okay, we'll be there."

Claire hung up rather abruptly and looked at Jason. "We've got a lunch meeting at the Mandarin Grill in less than three hours, and we need to find you some more clothes before then, so we'd better skip the rest of our breakfast and get moving."

"Yes, ma'am," he replied, standing. "Sorry, Queenie, but we must go. It's the boss's orders!"

"No problem, Mr Jason. Also, Miss Claire, another man has called here a few times asking for you. He was a friend of your father's, Mr Chuck Bailey. He said that if I see you, I should ask you to call him back please."

"Sure, thanks, Queenie. I'll try him later." Claire felt as if she owed it to Chuck to at least call and assure him that she was okay. Probably he was worried sick, believing she'd been involved with recent events.

But talking to Chuck needed to wait a little longer. Claire and Jason had an important lunch meeting.

*

After arriving at the restaurant with 10 minutes to spare, Claire and Jason sat in the bar and ordered drinks while perusing the menu. No sooner had the drinks appeared than Russell did too, and they all went through into the restaurant, their drinks following with a waiter.

Quickly they ordered food. Then Claire and Jason began to brief Russell about the events since they last met. They told him about Namika's kidnapping and subsequent rescue, their "cruise", as Jason called it, and their return to Hong Kong. Russell listened attentively, grinning hugely when they relayed the details of demolishing the *Nisshin Maru*.

Food portions at the Mandarin Grill are typical of many Michelin Star restaurants, delicious but tiny, and certainly inadequate to sustain battle-hardened ex-soldiers. They finished the meal and the briefing within an hour, and Russell posed a few queries.

Then Claire asked the questions that she and Jason most wanted answered. "Have you had any luck enquiring about McMahan and Campbell's Trading Company? And who do you want us to meet?"

In response, Russell looked at his wristwatch before asking, "Do you know of Sir Iain Campbell?"

"As in McMahan's boss, the chairman at Campbell's?" answered Jason. "Sure, he's a heavyweight in Asian business circles, owns and runs a multi-faceted company and, apparently, wields far more influence than he should, both politically and industrially. You want us to meet him?"

"Exactly. He normally dines here at about 1:30, and so he'll arrive any minute. Once he settles down, we'll go and introduce you. He'll hate it, and it all will get highly awkward, but just stick with me, say nothing much and enjoy the ride. Ah, here he comes."

Claire and Jason swapped puzzled looks, but moments later they rose with Russell and followed him to Iain Campbell's table. Campbell himself had barely sat down, chatting with his three guests, when Russell forcefully interjected.

"Hello, Sir Iain! How nice to see you again so soon after our last little chat!"

Campbell was about to protest at the intrusion, but Russell continued talking. "I'd like to introduce you to some wonderful friends of mine, Mr Jason Chan, and someone whom I believe you know all about, Ms Claire Armstrong."

At first, Campbell froze. Then, still seated, he glared at Claire who, totally unfazed, leant forward and gripped his reluctant right hand, shaking it firmly. Her eyes matched his for iciness as she said, "A real pleasure to meet you face-to-face, Sir Iain. I've heard so much about you and about many of your associates too."

In turn, Jason then grasped the business titan's right hand and shook it, painfully for the recipient, in a steel-like grip, simply acknowledging the man's name. "Sir Iain."

Campbell made no move to introduce his own guests. All three of those men took their lead from Sir Iain and stayed in their chairs. But they looked acutely disconcerted and uncomfortable, sensing serious tension in the air.

Russell then cheerfully bade them farewell. "Alas, we can't linger now, but I'll be in touch again very soon, Sir Iain. I promise. Good day."

Turning, Russell marched out of the restaurant followed by the clearly puzzled, but faintly amused, Claire and Jason. Not really in such a rush after all, they stopped in the bar and ordered coffee, where Russell explained about his curious behaviour just now, his recent interactions with Campbell and the suspicious death of McMahan.

Astonished, Claire summarised, "So after you rattled Sir Iain's cage, someone tried to kill you, and because you were closing in on McMahan, they topped him? Wow!"

"Yes, 'wow' indeed. Meeting you here, right inside one of his regular hangouts, will offend Campbell enormously and make him even more anxious, so we need to see what he does about it."

"Great, thanks a lot," said Jason haughtily. "You've just set us up as bait and in front of a nasty predator too."

"And your problem with that is…?" questioned Russell, feigning innocence.

"Let's cut the crap, James," said Claire. "You've made your point. Now tell us what happens next."

They talked for another hour before Russell took his leave, and Claire and Jason returned to Shek O. Needing to be on their guard once more, they checked their inventory of weapons and prepared again for battle.

*

Following the attack on the Japanese whaling ships, law-enforcement authorities worldwide grilled NGOs and environmental protection agencies for information. Chuck Bailey had been interviewed again by the UK police about his organisation's global activities, especially in Asia. But he had nothing new to tell. In truth, POSC struggled these days, with

293

official operations at three of its key locations having ended since David Armstrong's death. If the NGO couldn't stay relevant and active where it mattered, then its future looked bleak.

After a tedious morning, Chuck felt restless and decided to head off for a late lunch. As he was about to leave his office, the telephone rang. He considered ignoring it, but duty prevailed, and he picked up the call. Hearing Claire's voice, he was overjoyed.

"Hi, Chuck. How've you been?"

"My dear girl, thank God. Are you okay, and where are you?"

"I'm okay, Chuck. Thanks. I'm in Hong Kong, back at Dad's place. How's everyone at POSC?"

"We're all fine, but we've been worried sick about you, Claire. You've been out of contact for so long that we started to think the worst had happened. Then we kept reading news reports about triads being wiped out and Yakuza shootouts, all somehow linked to illegal fishing, and Gaby Saunders insisted that it must be you behind it."

"How is Gaby? I behaved a bit unsympathetically to her in Costa Rica, I'm afraid."

"She's good. We had to close down our office there. It became too dangerous to stay on so Gaby's back with us here in the UK while we figure out what to do. The future's not looking too bright for us, you know."

"You mustn't say that, Chuck," said Claire vehemently. "The Japanese whaling industry is all but over, and that's a massive leap forward. Other whaling fleets will fold too if the pressure continues. You must fight on, Chuck. Work the public-relations angles."

"We guessed you were behind all that, but I won't ask anything about it now. Is that pirate, Teach, with you? The Taiji station has been unresponsive for a while. Is he alright?"

"He's on great form. I know that he tried to contact you recently…." She stopped herself in time from revealing that he'd been at sea with her, and she smiled as she thought of Blackbeard. "He and Namika had some issues with the Yakuza after the dolphin cull got stopped, so they had to take off for a while. Last I heard they were headed for the North Pacific to give the Russian whalers bloody noses."

"So much for peaceful protest, I guess," bemoaned Chuck. "You may get things done your way, Claire, but it's damned dangerous and, sooner or later, you're going to get hurt, along with any other mugs you have tagging along."

"Trouble is, Chuck, the bad guys play rough, so unless we play even rougher, we're just wasting our time and effort. Look at what happened to Dad."

They both fell silent for a moment before Chuck asked, "So what are your plans, Claire? We'd love to see you back here and, incidentally, so would your mother."

"I've got some unfinished business here, Chuck. But when I'm done, I'll let you know. Look, I must go now. Take care, and please say 'hi' to Mum for me."

Before he could reply, she disconnected. She wanted to hear no emotional plea, however well intended, for her to desist in her quest.

Next, Claire grabbed a beer from the fridge and joined Jason on the balcony. It was dark now, and they gazed out over the sea into the night, the countless lights of Hong Kong's famous skyline unseen farther around the island, but projecting a glow in the ever-hazy sky.

Soon they strolled together to the Shek O Country Club for a casual dinner, walking in companionable silence and mentally bracing for inevitable dangers. They ignored the four plainclothes police officers, part of a protection detail assigned to watch them, who followed at a discreet distance.

Despite using Claire and Jason as bait, Russell wanted to take no chances with their safety. They disliked having police protection, believing that they themselves could repel any attacks. Nevertheless, they went along with Russell's demands.

Chapter 36

High Noon in Hong Kong

Leading one of the world's most prosperous and successful criminal corporations brought many benefits, not the least of which was plenty of assassins at one's disposal. Three people posed increasing threats to Sir Iain Campbell's security and position, and he needed all three eliminated. He had tried using local talent, which usually proved highly competent and trustworthy, but recently the locals had failed him. Now he needed an altogether more reliable solution, and he wanted to be absent from Hong Kong when it took effect.

Sir Iain turned to his international connections and travelled to Marseilles to meet some old confrères in the Union Corse, an expansive criminal enterprise based in southern France. Years ago, he had masterminded the French Connection with these very same acquaintances, establishing a pipeline for them in what became one of the world's greatest heroin-smuggling enterprises, sourcing from the Golden Triangle in Southeast Asia.

With minimal fuss, Sir Iain provided his acquaintances with detailed files on his assassination targets and, in no time, a contract with a small squad of expensive, but dependable, mercenaries had been arranged. The men were veterans from the French 2nd Circle. Officially unrecognised, this unit forms the elite of the French Special Forces and loosely follows the same structure as the UK's SAS. If Sir Iain's enemies came from elite military backgrounds, then it made sense to battle them with people of similar capabilities and talent.

From Marseilles, Sir Iain travelled to Paris, where he ensconced himself in the opulent Royal Suite of the Hôtel Plaza

Athénée. There, he proceeded to entertain lavishly, publicly and generously.

Now Claire Armstrong, Jason Chan and James Russell were marked for death. Furthermore, Sir Iain had forged a cast-iron alibi to establish his presence elsewhere, and therefore his innocence, should his intentions ever be questioned.

*

During a 12-hour period, the three hitmen arrived on different flights into the Hong Kong International Airport. They were large men, strolling with the easy and confident gait of the physically fit and self-assured. All of them dressed casually. Each seemed slightly tanned and wore his dark hair short, military style. They took taxis to the Crowne Plaza Hotel in the Causeway Bay district on Hong Kong Island. There, they checked in and waited patiently in their rooms.

Russell had placed all entry points into Hong Kong on high alert since his encounter with Campbell at the Mandarin Grill restaurant. He rightly expected more attempts on their lives and probably by outside players, since the local talent had failed on previous missions. If Campbell could afford no more botched efforts, then he'd bring in some big guns. When Russell learned that Campbell had left town to flaunt himself around Paris, his instincts pricked up, and he doubled the number of protective watchers.

This intuition reaped results. One arriving mercenary was identified, namely Olivier Viger, who was accordingly followed as he progressed through customs inspection and left the airport.

*

The hit-squad members assembled that evening in the Pavilion, a trendy and popular bar with panoramic views on their hotel's 27th floor. Kevin Lim, who had been instructed by Campbell to act as their liaison person and facilitator, met them in the bar. He updated them on the whereabouts of their targets, pointing out that all three now had 24-hour, special protection details. Armstrong and Chan seemed to be remarkably relaxed and taking life easy, while Russell was another matter, usually hard at work inside the Police Headquarters Building in nearby Wan Chai.

The three mercenaries took it all in, asked some questions and gave Lim a shopping list of weapons and ordinance that they required, which he promised to deliver to them the following day. They took little notice of a young couple at a nearby table who seemed obsessed with each other, chatting, groping and giggling as they consumed one cocktail after another.

After Lim left, the three men under contract downed a few more beers and then headed off to the nearby red-light district in Wan Chai, noting with amusement its close proximity to the police headquarters. Tomorrow, and as many days ahead as needed, would be all about business, but tonight they would play.

The giggly "lovers" at the nearby table watched them go, reported in to their controller and passed the baton to other police officers to follow the mercenaries.

*

"They're here," said Russell over breakfast. Having called ahead, he sat with Claire and Jason on their balcony in Shek O.

In the background, Queenie hovered attentively, again pretending not to listen.

Russell described the would-be assassins, what the police knew about them so far, and the clincher, their meeting with the Campbell's security man, Kevin Lim. The "lovers" in the Pavilion surreptitiously had taken some decent photographs of them. Along with the name of the man spotted at the airport, these had been run through the extensive database that Russell had at his disposal.

"They're pros, originally from Tier 2 in the *Commandement des Opérations Spéciales*, the COS, of which surely you're both familiar. The senior man seems to be Bertrand Favre. The others are Olivier Viger and Philippe Lapointe. They're part of a well-established unit within the Union Corse and do mercenary work at high prices anywhere they're needed. They're a bit older than you two, and after leaving the military, they carved out quite the reputations. Even by your standards, they're mean, callous and bloody dangerous. If there was just one, or even two, of them, I'd be less concerned, but three assassins may tip the scales against us. It means they outnumber you."

All this sounded worrisome, but hardly unexpected. Claire and Jason brooded silently, mulling over the news, and then both started talking at once. "Ladies first," Jason offered.

"Thanks!" Claire said. Then she addressed Russell. "Since your people did such a good job of spotting these guys and tracking them, and we know where they're staying, I think we should go on the offensive, the sooner the better. The longer we leave it, the better prepared they become."

"My thoughts exactly," agreed Jason.

"That makes sense, but even with my men backing you up, it's still extremely dangerous," Russell said. "What do you plan to do?"

"Kill them all!" Claire and Jason replied in unison. Those three forcefully spoken words seemed to bring on an uncomfortable bout of coughing in the adjoining kitchen where Queenie had gone.

Oblivious to the coughing, Claire continued. "No chitchat, no questions, let's just take them out wherever and whenever we can. They won't give us extra chances, nor should we with them."

"Where are they now?" asked Jason.

"They were last seen returning to their hotel at about three o'clock this morning after an energetic romp in one of Wan Chai's seedier establishments," reported Russell. "Hopefully they have huge hangovers because they haven't emerged since, and we have surveillance in place for when they do."

"Don't count on them being hungover, or even tired, from any nocturnal exercises," cautioned Jason. "We underestimate them at our peril."

"Agreed. I think we should get going," said Claire, rising. "Can you drive us into town, James?"

"Yes, of course," replied Russell as he lifted his mobile phone to take a call. His expression indicated bad news, and his response confirmed it. "Well, you bloody well better find them."

Ending the call, he addressed the two expectant faces in front of him. "Evidently our French visitors never actually went to their rooms when they returned to the hotel. We have a housekeeper on the hotel staff, and she just inspected their rooms, all empty. I'm sorry, guys."

"Not your fault," said Claire, shrugging. "So much for going on the offensive. Last night's seedy fun may have been just a ruse to shake off anyone who might be following them, whether they spotted a tail or not. Frankly, it's the kind of thing I'd have done too."

"Agreed," said Jason. "But this means we need to wait for them to come to us. Where's the best place to make a stand, do you think?"

"We need to pick a place where collateral injuries to the public can be avoided," said Russell.

"The trouble with that is, if it's too remote, maybe they can pick us off with a sniper rifle without even getting close," argued Claire.

"And if we go for a confined space, they'll expect a trap and avoid it," countered Jason.

For a moment, they all thought in silence, and then Claire said, "Let's take another boat trip. We can charter a junk for a pleasure trip to one of the outlying islands, but it'll be a decoy, and we won't be on it. Instead we'll follow at a distance in a fast motor launch and watch for anyone following the junk. When the assassins appear, we go in hard and fast and sink their craft with a Stinger or whatever else you can get for us. Once they're in the water, we clean up loose ends."

"And how are they supposed to know about this 'pleasure trip'?" Russell was sceptical. Action at sea also could create difficulties for his officers to provide discreet support.

"We should be able to plant a message for them through Lim's people," suggested Jason. "Almost certainly, he's still in touch with them. They need to have someone managing their logistics."

"I don't like this," said Russell. "So much could go wrong. Still, I can't think of anything better so let's go for it."

*

Favre and his men rested in the comfort of a serviced apartment in Repulse Bay on the south side of Hong Kong Island, a place that Lim had arranged for them before their arrival. Their pre-paid rooms at the Crowne Plaza Hotel and their late-night visit to Wan Chai all had been a subterfuge, exactly as Claire surmised, designed to see if they had been marked, which they had. So when they returned to the hotel in the early-morning hours, they took measures to lose their tails and did so easily. Then an evasive series of taxi rides took them across the island to their current, lower-profile address.

By mid-afternoon, they grew restless and impatient. They disliked relying on strangers and, being in the trade they were, they didn't fully trust the big Chinese man assigned to assist them.

As the daylight started to fade, Lim finally contacted them. He rang their doorbell and was greeted with a volley of abuse, entirely in French, which he didn't understand. But Lim recognised the sentiment, and, being no pushover himself, he snarled back in Cantonese at the three disgruntled Frenchmen. Tempers simmered, and it took Favre to shout everyone down in English, their language of mutual understanding, and to bring them all to order.

"Do you have our supplies?" Favre asked once Lim had entered the apartment.

Lim glared sulkily at him and the others, but nodded. "I have everything in my truck outside. You want it, come down and get it."

"We need to keep out of sight now, Lim," said Viger. "So why don't you go fuck yourself and bring it up here for us?"

They resumed bickering until Favre interceded again. "*Mon Dieu!*" he grumbled, before nodding towards his two colleagues.

"Both of you, go down and help *Monsieur* Lim to bring everything up," he ordered.

Reluctantly, Viger and Lapointe followed Lim outside. From past experience, they knew better than to argue much with their leader.

As the three contractors examined their new gear, Lim told them that he had picked up a nugget of information from one of his many sources, learning that Armstrong and Chan had chartered a junk from the Aberdeen Boat Club for a pleasure excursion the next day. This opportunity seemed too good to be true, and Favre instantly turned suspicious.

"How come you just happen to have a source who told you this?" he demanded.

"Since Armstrong and Chan returned to Hong Kong, we've had everyone watching for them and reporting to me," Lim said. "That includes 14K Triad members, who now are the ruling society here and ultimately report to Campbell's."

"Maybe so, but it seems just a little too convenient for my liking," persisted Favre.

"You know, Boss, I think maybe we should take this chance," said Lapointe. "There likely won't be a better way to get them without lots of witnesses. If Lim here can find us a fast boat, we can come up behind and blast them to shreds."

"Better still," suggested Viger, "if we can find out which junk they're renting, we could plant a bomb on board tonight and detonate it remotely when they're at sea."

Both ideas had merit, so after dispatching Lim to secure a fast launch and identify the junk, they weighed their options. Favre remained somewhat reticent, but conceded that perhaps the others were right. It was too good a chance to miss. However, they needed to erase Russell too, which would get that much harder once the other two died because the police official would go to ground.

"We could split up," proposed Lapointe. "If we take them all at about the same time, then no one gets a warning."

"How would you handle Russell?" asked Favre.

"I'd prefer to get in close and stab him," Lapointe said. "No noise that way. But it would depend on where he is. If he's holed up in a police station with others nearby to help him, then I'd use a gun."

"That's all fine, *mon brave*," conceded Viger, "but how will you get close enough even to shoot him? If he's being guarded like Lim says, you won't stand a chance."

"As always, a good diversion helps. I'm sure that the danger of a fire, or some other distraction, at the police headquarters would bring out even a senior assistant commissioner."

The three men looked at one another, and finally Favre nodded. "Okay, it sounds good, Philippe. You take care of Russell while Olivier and I handle the others. Now let's consider the details."

Chapter 37

Ice Is Just Sleepy Water

The *Seven Seas* had made a smooth and relatively calm journey to the North Pacific. Assisting the ship was the Kuroshio Current, also known as the Black Stream or Japan Current, a north-flowing current on the west side of the ocean, part of the North Pacific Ocean Gyre.

As Blackbeard explained to his crewmates, this circular body of currents helped to form the misleadingly named Great Pacific Garbage Patch. More than 90 per cent of the "patch" actually consisted of microscopic plastic particles in suspension, creating new hazards for sea life and making a successful clean-up nearly impossible.

When sharing his impassioned insights to a captive audience in the ship's galley, Blackbeard lamented the lasting damage caused by water pollution. "Most humans don't see the results of their mindless littering," he said, "but sea organisms ingest the mess, which enters the food chain and poisons countless creatures, including people. Humans really need to manage their waste better and stop using the oceans as giant garbage dumps. As a species, we've got to smarten up."

"And the sooner the better too," chimed in Namika, who sat in her usual spot beside Blackbeard.

"We can only hope," declared Knowledge, sitting across from them.

"There's got to be hope," said a sombre-looking Namika, her voice lowering to little more than a whisper. "That's what keeps us going, right? It's why we try to create positive change."

"Exactly correct, my dear," Blackbeard agreed, his voice also dropping a few decibels.

*

Ten days after delivering Claire and Jason to Lamma Island, Tyler received word of a Russian whaling factory ship operating with five supporting hunter-vessels. Having been chased out of US and Canadian waters, these ships searched for grey and beluga whales near the pack ice, several hundred kilometres north of the Andreanof Islands.

Tyler conferred with his crew, and they agreed to search out the whalers and cause as much aggravation and disruption as possible. As they continued north, the cold began to bite. Although the steel-grey sea remained placid, it seemed somehow sinister in its calmness and everyone knew that exposure in these frigid waters would lead to hypothermia and a quick death.

The *Seven Seas* and its crew passed to the west of the Rat Islands and far into the Bering Sea. As they neared the ice sheet, they picked up the Russians on radar and began to prepare.

Among the crew members, the collective mood was thoughtful, even meditative. They all had experience, to a greater or lesser extent, at troublemaking against whaling ships, but they still wished that their previous extraordinary passengers had stayed with them. The younger crew members idolised Blackbeard, but they all had venerated Claire and Jason. Still, when they sighted the first of the Russian ships, they all felt fully committed and ready.

*

Despite an occasional miss, the harpoon gunner aboard the *Mira* had been enjoying a good expedition and so far, had killed

307

278 whales. The other ships in the Russian fleet had caught similar numbers, and they were only halfway into their expedition.

The *Mira* and its sailors had picked up two distinct targets at the full range of their radar. One reflection came and went, possibly indicating a pod of whales swimming near the surface, but the other stayed strong and came straight towards them, clearly another ship. It wasn't one of the *Mira*'s sister ships. They all were to the northeast, queuing to unload freshly killed beluga whales onto the factory ship, so this coming contact was something different.

Before long, people on the opposing vessels could see each other, and the Russian ship hailed the other by radio. When repeated calls were ignored, the whaler's captain ordered all his crew members to their stations and alerted the captain on the mother factory ship that they likely faced anti-whaling protesters. His suspicion was confirmed when he saw two inflatable RIBs launch from the mystery vessel and speed ahead towards his ship.

The entire whaling community knew about the fate of the *Nisshin Maru* and its SPV, so these whale-chasing seamen viewed the approaching craft with a measure of respect. Still, they were all big, solid Russian sailors unwilling to be intimidated by busybodies in two inflatables.

Russian crewmen manned their water cannons, and the gunner in the bow prepared extra explosive charges that he fitted onto several harpoons before removing their cables. He would shoot these at the mystery ship when it came into range. The harpoons might not sink the intruding ship, but with the attached explosives, could cause enormous damage.

The *Mira* and the *Seven Seas* continued to close on each other. Meanwhile, the RIBs began running circles around the Russian whaler at a distance of about 200 metres, moving gradually closer with each circuit.

Even while concentrating on the action ahead, the whaling captain noticed that the other radar contact had disappeared, and he cursed aloud, realising that probably he had lost the pod of whales for good. He returned his attention to the forthcoming scrap.

When the captain perceived that the range allowed, he gave an order for his water cannon to open up on the small craft. The targets resembled troublesome insects, he thought. Flying vermin could avoid insecticide spray for a while, but eventually succumbed. So it was with the water cannon. His men rarely made direct hits with the powerful jets of water, but little by little, the inflatables filled up and lost manoeuvrability. Soon the RIBs retreated to safety to pump out the water taken aboard.

All observers could see that the *Seven Seas* looked bent on a collision course with the *Mira,* and the captain of the latter lost his nerve first, steering his big ship away barely in time to avoid a dangerous impact. This was the moment the gunner had waited for, and as his ship turned, he fired a harpoon at almost point-blank range.

The spear flew to the bridge of the *Seven Seas,* piercing the roof at an angle. Such was its velocity that it flew straight through and out the far steel wall. Just as it exited from the bridge, the explosive charge detonated, sending shards of the harpoon all over the deck.

On the bridge, the harpoon narrowly had missed Tyler and Jonsson. Fortunately, no one on the deck was hurt, a result of good luck, not good judgement.

The two vessels pulled away from each other as the Russian gunner reloaded and tried to fire off another round while the target ship remained close enough. But in his haste, he narrowly missed his target altogether, and the second harpoon exploded harmlessly in the sea.

By now, the two RIBs had returned to the fray, teasing the water-cannon crews with nimble charges and feints. Their occupants were so preoccupied with avoiding impact from the water cannons that they failed to notice two Russian crew members aiming shotguns at them.

The blast of a gun's discharge rose over the engine sounds, and rock-salt shot peppered the smaller RIB and its crew. For the crew, this was extremely painful, but not fatal, and the shot merely bounced off the RIB's toughened rubber.

But with the next gunshots, real cartridges were used, and two large holes appeared almost simultaneously in the smaller RIB's stiffened sides, instantly causing half the boat to deflate. Seawater rushed in, and the little craft lost way.

Aboard the whaler, the two trigger-happy Russians slapped together their raised right hands in a gesture of achievement. Then they lifted their weapons again.

Blackbeard, in his usual place at the inflatable's wheel, had been hit too. A large and growing red stain appeared on his left arm and started to seep through his tattered thermals, windbreaker and outer oilskins. He struggled to pull the crippled RIB away from the *Mira*, just as another round of gunfire hurtled towards him, but the latest shots fell short.

Everything had happened so quickly and with such unwelcome results that Tyler became deeply concerned for the safety of his people. He ordered Muscles, in the larger RIB, to break off the engagement and to assist Blackbeard, while he used the *Seven Seas* to distract the *Mira*'s crew.

Safely away from the harpoon gunner in the whaler's bow, Tyler brought the *Seven Seas* up behind the *Mira* and rammed it into the rival's stern, the solid bow of his icebreaker crashing up against the bigger vessel's rudder and screw. The speeds of the two ships were similar, so the damage to the *Mira* perhaps was less than Tyler might have hoped, but still enough to cause the whaler to heave-to while its crew members inspected and assessed the results.

The *Seven Seas* peeled back out of range and made for the two RIBs, now tied together with the larger one slowly towing the damaged smaller inflatable as far away as possible from the whaler. Willing hands helped to pull everyone back aboard the *Seven Seas*. As the next priority, Blackbeard was taken below deck for a distressed Namika to attend to his injury.

As soon as the RIBs were stowed and secured, the *Seven Seas* beat a hasty retreat. Its grim-faced crew watched as the stationary *Mira* gradually disappeared from view.

*

On the *Mira*, an inspection by the crew revealed that damage to the vessel would require a visit to a dry dock to fix. The ship could maintain slow headway, but the rudder had been bent and its housing compromised. Also, one propeller blade had sustained damage and needed replacing.

The captain cursed at length and, after reporting in to his counterpart on the mother ship, started his vessel limping off towards the home port in Vladivostok. For the sailors on board, their anticipated salary bonuses had vanished, prompting much more cursing throughout the ship.

*

On the *Seven Seas*, a similar damage assessment took place. The bridge needed repairs, and the small inflatable required a new side section. Apart from that, plus a gunshot wound, the anti-whalers had fared better than the whalers did. Still, it seemed that any more disruptive actions needed to wait. Such encounters simply got too dangerous and, probably sooner rather than later, someone would die. This time Blackbeard had been lucky and looked likely to recover.

Tyler contacted some friends in Washington State. Although he did not report to them, they were all of one fraternity, and so they suggested that he bring the *Seven Seas* in for repairs and replenishment. Everyone agreed that the crew had done a fine job, but with the Russians playing such hardball, the risks of serious injuries or fatalities were unacceptable. Recognising this as the best advice, Tyler set a new course and steered into the gathering dusk to the southeast.

Seated in the galley, most of the crew members reviewed a video, soon to be posted online, that Muscles and his team in the larger RIB had taken of the skirmish. Broadcasting the behaviour of commercial whalers formed a key part of the public-relations war against them. The latest footage showed Blackbeard being shot, followed by close-up views of his wound as Namika gently patched him up and a voiceover explained what had happened.

Blackbeard enjoyed watching the video. Although feeling a bit weak from loss of blood, he soon reclaimed his usual position as the centre of attention. Everyone in the galley raised their glasses to him and downed yet another tot of the rapidly depleting stocks of Pusser's Rum.

Chapter 38

Extreme Prejudice

To all intents and purposes, Claire and Jason looked just like any other couple enjoying a few after-dinner drinks in Ben's Back Beach Bar. The place featured several televisions, used mainly to view sports events, but now CNN covered the story of a confrontation between Russian whalers and anti-whaling protesters in the Bering Sea.

Claire and Jason watched with interest when suddenly John Teach appeared on the screens, all bloodied and battered, in a video clip from the engagement. His two former shipmates in the bar raised their glasses in a silent toast to Blackbeard and his crewmates before leaving for their own rendezvous on the beach.

Bobbing on the waves and waiting just offshore, they found one of the latest in the Sunseeker range of motorboats, a sleek Hawk 38. Essentially, this was a day-boat, but because of its extraordinary high performance and speed, the Hong Kong police had bought a special version to use in B Department's anti-smuggling operations. With a top speed of 62 knots, the Hawk 38 easily outpaced the main police patrol vessels and, more importantly, the powerful cigarette boats used by triads.

The Hawk carried no tender, so Claire and Jason waded into the surf carrying their gear over their heads. They threw in their equipment before climbing aboard at the stern on either side of the twin Mercury 400R outboard engines.

Russell had waited for them in the boat, along with the Hawk's regular police crew, a very-capable-looking woman, who was the boat's captain, and an equally competent-looking young man. The senior assistant police commissioner offered strong drinks, which Claire and Jason declined, opting instead for piping-hot coffee, since they were now operational.

As they stowed their equipment, the captain guided the Hawk quietly away from the beach and into open water, the only sound being a deep rumble from the two outboards. Initially they did not have far to go, and 15 minutes later, they moored alongside the Po Toi ferry jetty in Stanley, still on Hong Kong Island.

There, Russell conducted a briefing. The hired junk would be manned by two of his agents, assuming the roles of Claire and Jason, who would meet at the Aberdeen Boat Club at nine o'clock the next morning and set off straight away. They would maintain radio contact with the Hawk while taking a circuitous route towards Po Toi Island, placing them in open water and off the main shipping channel, making an attack more tempting for the assassins. The Hawk would be positioned strategically to approach the junk from the south side of Lamma Island, staying ready to accelerate into action.

To Claire and Jason's disappointment, Russell had failed to source any surface-to-surface missiles, however lightweight. There just had not been enough time. He did provide them with two M4 carbines equipped with M203 grenade-launcher attachments. Each of these submachine guns had an accurate range just shy of 500 metres, but needed to be much closer to use the grenade launcher with its 150-metre effective range, which might not be a great benefit depending on what the assassins used to fire back. The magazines carried 30 rounds, and Russell provided 10 spare clips each. As he reasonably pointed out, anyone needing more ammunition than that probably wasn't up to the job anyhow.

"Where will you be when everything goes down," Claire asked Russell after the briefing.

"I'll be in my office, preparing to coordinate and wrap up the fallout from a shootout at sea, from which it emerges that bandits attacked a young couple trying to enjoy a nice, quiet junk charter," he replied. "When the action ends, we'll get in touch by radio and extract you."

"Sounds good to me," said Jason as he carefully studied and checked the guns. "We'll see you tomorrow afternoon then."

"Take care," Russell cautioned as he left. "These people mean business, so watch out and make sure to hit them first."

"As the unwritten 11th Commandment would have said," claimed Jason, "do unto others before they do it unto you!"

*

The Hawk was designed for fast daytime leisure cruising, not overnighting, but Claire and Jason did not want to leave it unguarded for fear of any unforeseen developments. Accordingly, they stayed aboard and spent a rather chilly and uncomfortable night under cloudy skies before gladly welcoming a breakfast of warm doughnuts and hot coffee that the boat's crew brought along at dawn.

Then everyone kitted up, which at Russell's insistence included wearing body armour. With Claire and Jason acting in more of an official capacity than previously, there were some rules they needed to follow, like it or not, and one such decree meant taking this "reasonable" precaution.

The Hawk's crew wore helmets and bullet-proof vests, together with extra protection for necks and upper arms. Claire and Jason put on just the main vests, part of the newest range from Virtus. Although this gear felt remarkably lightweight, they still believed that anything more might limit their freedom of movement, to which Russell reluctantly had agreed.

315

Soon the heavily armed squad cast off and motored purposefully to the ocean side of Lamma Island. There, the Hawk slowly cruised around, its occupants waiting.

*

Campbell's Trading Company owned many boats, ranging from large hospitality junks to run-about speedboats and medium-sized cabin cruisers. Sir Iain even had a super-yacht that stayed mostly in the Caribbean.

Lim considered every company vessel available to him in Hong Kong. Favre had insisted on having a boat with speed and manoeuvrability, so Lim provided the three assassins with the latest addition to the Campbell's fleet, a Stingray 250LR sports boat. It was a compact vessel with a small cabin and a top speed of 50 knots.

Collecting the hitmen early as requested, Lim drove them first into the Wan Chai district. There, he dropped off Lapointe, who was stylishly dressed and carried a large rucksack.

Intent on preparing for all eventualities, Lapointe wanted to observe the morning shifts arriving at the police headquarters, and he was pleased to see Russell appear earlier than most. The Frenchman even thought of attacking his target then and there, but he knew that his team's plan called for the "hits" to happen almost simultaneously to avoid alerting anyone. So Lapointe lingered in the vicinity and waited patiently for a call from his companions on their closed-circuit radio link.

Favre, Viger and Lim headed back across Hong Kong Island to Aberdeen, where the Stingray was tethered to a far-off jetty belonging to the Aberdeen Marina Club. They pushed their gear in a jetty buggy and felt relieved finally to stash it all aboard. Lim then slipped the lines, and they motored slowly around the outside of the marina, keeping a lookout for the rented junk and their targets.

They spied the junk already tied up alongside the boat club. Eventually a carefree-looking couple strode arm-in-arm down a flight of stairs to the quay and stepped aboard. The woman wore a floppy hat almost completely hiding her face, while the man, defined mainly by his bulky build and general physique, sported dark glasses and a baseball hat, its peak pulled low. A crewman carried their bags and, in almost no time, the junk pulled out of the harbour.

Unable to make a positive ID on the two targets, Favre relied on Lim to confirm their status. The team leader felt altogether too dependent on this unfamiliar man. Happier when personally holding total control at all times, Favre wondered if he soon might regret going along with this less-than-ideal situation.

In Favre's judgment, Lim already had failed. They had hoped to plant a bomb at night in preparation to kill the junk's passengers with minimal effort today, as Viger had suggested, but Lim somehow lacked the proper know-how or connections to confirm in time exactly which vessel would be chartered. This left them no choice but to fall back on the plan to launch a merciless attack at sea.

The junk passed 100 metres away from the Stingray, and the assassins heard faint laughter coming from its covered aft deck. Favre remained unable to verify his targets satisfactorily, but at least they appeared relaxed and unsuspecting of trouble. This task should be quick and easy, he thought.

Being at the wheel of the Stingray, Lim let the junk motor well away before slowly picking up its wake and following it out of Aberdeen, holding back a good half-kilometre.

With the day's events off to a satisfactory start, Favre radioed in to Lapointe, and they exchanged the latest information. At both ends of the conversation, the situation looked similar. "So far, so good," they agreed.

*

The junk's skipper talked on his radio too. He updated the Hawk's crew about his boat's departure, stressing that a small, but powerful, Stingray motorboat appeared to be following about a half-kilometre behind. Using binoculars, he reported seeing three men on the Stingray, although he couldn't identify them individually.

This report also reached Russell, who spoke anxiously to Claire from his office. "I'd have anticipated four people in pursuit, including someone to manage the boat. So maybe one of them is missing, in which case, what's that guy doing?" he asked.

"I don't know, but whatever it is can't be good," replied Claire. "It also could mean this isn't them. We won't assume it is, not yet anyhow."

"You're right," Russell agreed. "Until you're certain, you can't attack."

Russell sounded distinctly uneasy, thought Claire. She felt uneasy too. "James, remember that you're still a target too. Are you safe?" she asked.

"Of course, I'm safe. I'm in a bloody police station," he replied gruffly. "As it happens, every officer in the building is on alert just on the chance that someone nasty comes to pay me a visit."

"Okay, so we just need to let things play out. Keep in touch."

After disconnecting, Claire updated Jason and the crew. Then she asked, "Did police officers thoroughly search the junk? I'm wondering about bombs."

"They were going to, but I'll check again to make sure," said the police captain. Moments later she confirmed that the junk had been well searched with nothing untoward being discovered.

*

In Wan Chai, Russell renewed his directions that all personnel in the police building should stay on high alert. After a few moments of extra thought, he also issued orders to post guards outside at every entrance to watch for one of the three French assassins. But he acted too late.

Moments earlier, Lapointe had entered the building, blending in with the station's ongoing morning arrivals. His self-assurance and well-dressed appearance deceived the duty officers at the front desk when he calmly approached them, claiming to have an appointment with Senior Assistant Commissioner James Russell. They mentioned the appropriate floor number and directed him to the lifts.

When those same officers at the front desk then received the latest alert directive, one of them promptly reached for a telephone, just as the piercing wail of fire alarms sounded. A rush of enquiries immediately distracted him, and several minutes passed before he again thought to contact Russell's office upstairs.

Amid the racket of the alarms, May Kwok needed to speak loudly when answering the incoming call. "Good morning, Senior Assistant Commissioner Russell's office."

Wasting no time in reacting to what the officer downstairs told her, May ended the call and then yelled out to Russell just as the outer office door swung open. A huge, well-dressed man appeared there pointing a gun with a large suppressor attached.

Petrified, May could not move or say anything more. She froze to the spot where she sat.

The gunman quickly brought his pistol to bear on her. May watched in horror, but still failed to move.

From behind May, a deafening report sounded, followed by another, both all the more jolting amid the blaring fire alarms. Frosted glass from a connecting window to her boss's office showered all over her.

May saw two dark holes appear on the intruder's chest. As he crumpled to the floor, she finally screamed and didn't stop until after Russell marched into the room and shot the man again, this time in the head.

Kneeling, Russell checked the man's life signs, but knew it was an academic gesture. People didn't survive a double-tap to the chest followed by a third shot to the head, nor should they.

On the chance there was another attacker, Russell kept his weapon in hand, but also reached for May and hugged her, whispering for her to calm down. She stopped screaming, but remained emotionally shaken.

After Russell reported the attack and the fire alarms fell silent, a medic led May away. She'll be okay, her boss thought, but in all fairness, he really needed to consider arranging a pay increase for her.

"That was close," Russell murmured to himself. "One assassin down, two to go." Then he made a radio call to the Hawk and the junk.

*

The junk made steady progress. Having passed a conspicuous power station on Lamma Island's northwestern edge, it moved south along the coast, preparing to steer southeast for open water.

Advised accordingly, team members on the Hawk positioned their boat in Sham Wan Bay to the south, where it could remain unseen, but close enough to intercept the Stingray if necessary. Their strategy assumed the likelihood of an attack on the junk as far from land as possible, although they still hoped to take the initiative and attack first.

The Stingray had followed the junk at a sedate pace, still staying a half-kilometre behind. But now it slowly began to close the distance, a move noticed by the junk's crew. Both vessels remained near the Lamma shoreline. After what Russell had reported, everyone on the junk and on the Hawk felt on edge, nerves tingling more than ever as the waiting game continued.

Suddenly the Stingray opened up its throttles and roared up behind the junk. The slower vessel's occupants, now clearly seeing a Chinese man at the Stingray's controls and two Caucasian passengers, called for the Hawk to "come fast". But as the accelerating speedboat overtook the junk on the seaward side, it abruptly veered off, heading out to sea at speed.

This move surprised Claire. After initially speeding forward, she and her teammates had received another radio call from the junk, prompting them to slow down and discuss the implications.

Jason wasn't surprised or bothered. "Probably they're just testing to see if a security ship's trailing the junk," he said. "Remember, these guys are professionals so it makes sense."

Claire agreed. "In that case, they likely will sweep back in very soon, and that's when they'll attack. Let's advance quietly, and get ready."

Already, Claire and Jason had positioned themselves on the Hawk's foredeck for uninterrupted fields of fire. Their biggest problem might be for the boat to stay steady enough when they fired, a difficulty they both recognised.

As the Hawk rounded the headland of the bay, yet another call came in from the junk. "The Stingray looks dead in the water about a kilometre out from us. Thick smoke is billowing from its stern."

Suddenly both vessels picked up a Mayday call from the Stingray declaring an engine fire and requesting immediate assistance. Warily, Claire ordered for officers on both boats to acknowledge and confirm that they'd stand by to assist, arriving in about five minutes.

The Hawk then accelerated forward and, when just 200 metres short of the Stingray, hove-to in the water. "Let's see what happens now," Claire murmured.

*

On the Stingray, everything had appeared to be going nicely to plan until a second vessel confirmed an offer of assistance. The three men were burning oily rags in a drum on deck to simulate an engine fire and lure their prey into close contact.

Annoyed at the extra boat's intrusion, Viger and Lim cursed, one in French, the other in Cantonese, and then deferred to Favre for instructions in English. They all had Heckler and Koch MP5A2 submachine guns ready to shower the junk when it arrived, but now an unknown player had appeared.

Favre's finely tuned survival instinct tingled at this new development. He sensed a trap and, when he aimed binoculars at the newly arrived boat, his suspicions gained instant confirmation.

Bellowing for Lim to evacuate them from the area at top speed, Favre raised his machine gun. The MP5's effective range was just 150 metres, but he fired off a few rounds to discourage pursuit. He and his team had grenades and other explosives too, but their armaments all worked best for combat at reasonably close quarters.

Claire ordered for the junk to fall back, well out of harm's way. Then the Hawk again advanced at top speed, moving in eccentric semi-circles to avoid being hit as its pilot tried to close on the target.

Fleeing in a straight line, the Stingray at first extended the gap between the two boats, despite not quite matching the Hawk's maximum speed. But when Claire ordered a straight course, the Hawk, with its superior pace, closed in quickly.

The pursuers began taking fire, which although inaccurate at high speeds, was still very dangerous. As they drew closer, Jason yelled for Claire to maintain suppressive fire with one M4 while he propelled some grenades with the other.

Much less than 150 metres now separated the two boats and punishing bullets impacted both. Suddenly the Hawk's skipper staggered back from the controls and slumped to the deck, her face obliterated by a random bullet from the Stingray.

The Hawk slewed wildly, but being in the bow, neither Claire, nor Jason, could help much without completely exposing themselves to the enemy's steady gunfire. After a moment of horror, the remaining crew member unsteadily took the wheel, and the Hawk continued to close the distance.

So far, all the grenades that Jason fired had landed in the sea, each causing a sizeable eruption of spray, but then one found its mark as the Hawk moved within 100 metres of the Stingray. The result was spectacular with the fleeing launch seeming to fall apart before tripping and somersaulting into the air. It landed upside down and began to sink.

The Hawk pulled up to within 10 metres and held station while Claire and Jason, standing in its bullet-shredded bow, covered the scene of destruction, their weapons held at the ready. Their caution proved well founded for abruptly, out of the flotsam, a man rose above the water's surface wildly firing a semi-automatic machine gun. Somehow Favre had survived the crash and made a final effort to complete his mission. Claire and Jason fired back, and the assassin vanished underwater, the sea now stained with his blood.

They waited considerably longer, until well after the Stingray sank with no more signs of life, before standing down and climbing back to assist the surviving crewman. He had conducted himself well, but was badly shaken by the fate of his colleague who had died instantly when shot. Now the young policeman vomited over the side of the boat into the sea.

Moments later, all three of them knelt beside the fallen police captain. Solemnly they covered what remained of her head with an oilskin jacket.

Then Jason noticed that Claire was bleeding from a wound high on her left arm. "Hey, Claire, you're hurt!" he exclaimed.

As he moved close for a better look, her eyes rolled up into her head, and she collapsed. He grabbed her, broke her fall and prevented her from sliding into the sea.

Momentarily panicked, Jason hastily examined the injury and saw that a bullet had passed right through Claire's bicep muscle, but appeared to have missed both her artery and the humerus bone. She may have lost considerable blood, but it wasn't pumping out, and the damage looked survivable.

Reassured, Jason urged the crewman to take them at full speed to Aberdeen and the boat club while he radioed in a status report. The Hawk turned north, again moving at near-maximum velocity.

An ambulance met the battered launch at the quayside, as did Russell and the officers from several police vehicles. Claire just had regained consciousness and, to her fury, was taken away for treatment.

Sombre arrangements were made for the dead skipper. The Hawk's remaining crewman, having broken down now at the loss of his partner, tearfully accepted an embrace and words of comfort from Russell. Then his police colleagues guided him away, leaving Jason together with Russell, just as the junk docked nearby.

"We're really sorry about the loss of your skipper," offered Jason. "She was very brave to keep her nerve and steer into gunfire, as was the young lad."

"Yes, thanks, Jason," replied Russell glumly. It always brought pain to lose an officer, and he felt the tragedy deeply. "I guess that we all had close calls today, and frankly, Claire's lucky not to have cashed in too."

"That's a fact," observed Jason.

Russell shook his head while surveying the Hawk's bullet-ridden and chipped hull and superstructure. Turning, he clapped Jason on the back. "Remind me never to lend you a speedboat again," he said before moving away towards his car.

Under the circumstances, Jason didn't laugh.

Chapter 39

Curtain Call

In Paris, the occupant of the Plaza Athénée's Royal Suite attracted unfavourable attention. Housekeepers had reported angry shouts and the sounds of breaking glass coming from inside the unit. Ignoring a "Do Not Disturb" sign dangling on the main-entrance doorknob, a hotel executive reluctantly knocked, received no reply and then entered.

The place was a mess. Someone had knocked most of the furniture askew. Shards from a mirror and a china lamp-stand, both in pieces on the floor, provided more evidence of serious mayhem.

Unfazed, the assistant manager, who had seen worse disarray at times in his career, called out for Sir Iain, asking about his health.

The gentleman in question, wearing just a linen dressing gown, stormed out of the master bedroom. Purple with rage, he bellowed, "Who the fuck are you, and what the hell are you doing in my suite?"

"I'm the hotel's assistant manager, Sir Iain," said the hospitality executive, quite unperturbed by the human tornado standing before him. "We wanted to make sure that everything's alright. There were reports of yelling and fighting here, which made us concerned for you."

"Well, there's no bloody fighting, and I'm fine, so get the fuck out of here," bawled Campbell.

"As you wish, Sir Iain," replied the assistant manager calmly, moving to depart. "Please let us know if you need anything."

"Get out!"

The assistant manager obeyed. Campbell slammed the door behind him and double-locked it.

*

After the unwelcome invasion of privacy, Sir Iain returned to his laptop on a table in the hotel-suite bedroom where he had been conducting a Skype meeting with his chief operating officer, Stanley Fong.

Although never part of the Demesne structure, Fong was a highly capable person, and since McMahan's sudden departure from the ranks of the living, effectively had been running the massive Campbell's Trading Company. At the beginning of their online meeting, Fong had briefed his boss on the latest news about the surprising circumstances surrounding another death within Campbell's, that of Kevin Lim.

The information had triggered an epic tantrum. Although Sir Iain abruptly moved away from the computer and Fong couldn't see much of how the boss reacted, he did hear plenty of screaming and other sounds pertinent to the mishandling or destruction of hotel furnishings.

"What else have you got to tell me?" barked Campbell when he reappeared to continue the long-distance meeting.

"There's one other issue, sir," Fong said. "We had a visit from the police, specifically a senior assistant commissioner, one James Russell…." That was as far as Fong got before being interrupted again.

"What does that bloody man want? He's become a real pest."

One more interruption ensued when Sir Iain saw off someone who had entered the hotel suite. Thousands of kilometres away in Hong Kong, Fong heard more yelling, presumably from Campbell again.

When the boss returned, Fong resumed. "James Russell, sir. He wants to see you urgently, something to do with the David Armstrong murder case and more recent events concerning the triads. Can't think why."

Fong reflected for a moment before continuing. "Anyway, I said you were out of town and that I wasn't sure when you planned to return."

"Did you tell him where I was?" asked Campbell icily.

"Well, I'm afraid he was most insistent, Sir Iain, so yes, I did."

"How long ago did this happen?"

"Must be a couple of hours...." The Skype call disconnected.

Fong's efforts to raise his boss again failed. Finally, he closed his laptop and went home, having endured a long and very strange day.

*

Hastily, Campbell dressed and gathered up anything essential. He called his driver, telling him to prepare to depart immediately. Pausing only to kick over one more chair in a final display of annoyance, the Demesne boss left the suite.

In the lobby, the assistant manager saw the hotel's esteemed guest hurry past the reception desk and dash out the front doors to a waiting Rolls Royce. The luxury vehicle's driver stood respectfully beside an opened rear door, which he gently closed once the passenger had climbed into the heavily cushioned backseat. Then the driver slid behind the steering wheel, and the car quickly departed.

Minutes later, two official-looking men approached the assistant manager. Identifying themselves as criminal-investigation officers with Interpol, they asked to be taken to Sir Iain Campbell's suite. The news that Campbell had just left was not well received.

When the officers examined the suite, they found only some clothing, a few personal-hygiene items and various misplaced or broken furnishings, fixtures and fittings. They had arrived too late.

*

Once more, Claire and Jason dined as guests of James Russell, this time in the more relaxed environment of the Lobster Bar and Grill in Hong Kong's Shangri-La Hotel. At least this time the portions were generous, and they both ate rib-eye steaks. After everything they had done to protect ocean creatures, it never would feel right to eat fish, no matter how successfully any restaurant might strive to offer only sustainably sourced seafood.

Russell reported that Campbell had vanished without a trace, although Interpol remained on his trail. With search warrants in hand, B Department's IT and serious-fraud people had started to examine every aspect of Campbell's Trading Company. It was early days yet, but already, thanks largely to Stanley Fong, the company's chief operating officer, they had found significant irregularities and links to organised crime. For a long time, Fong had grappled with concerns about certain aspects of his employer's activities, and so he willingly assisted the police. Arrest warrants followed, and the company's suspension on the stock market drove it inexorably towards ruin.

Claire asked, "What about those two little bastards, Ma and his boss Wong, at the Environmental Protection department? For me, this all started with a meeting there."

"Too right," Russell said, nodding and grinning as he spoke. "Yesterday we arrested both of them for links to organised crime. They squealed like pigs, each trying to cut a deal by blaming the other."

"Good," Claire exclaimed, "and may they rot in hell."

"More likely, they'll rot in jail cells," corrected Russell somewhat humourlessly. "We also picked up someone else, although he wasn't directly involved with you, namely Albert Tsang, the boss at the ICAC."

"That's a big fish, although not one that we care to protect," observed Claire. "What did he do?"

"It seems he's been on Campbell's payroll for quite some time," said Russell. "Time will tell us who else was corrupted by this monster."

"You've got your hands full," observed Jason.

"Too true, too true," Russell mused. "Anyway, what plans have you two made, now that the war seems to be ending?"

"Calling it a 'war' is correct," Claire answered, wincing from a stab of pain, not unusual from her left arm since the shooting. She looked over at Jason.

He finished the reply to Russell. "We'd like to go somewhere far away, not tell anyone where and have a really good break."

"That sounds like an excellent idea," said Russell, raising his glass to them. "We have quite a job here, untangling this mess, but thanks to you two, at least we know about it. Quite incredible just what Campbell and McMahan were doing, but it looks like you were absolutely right. One central criminal organisation, apparently called Demesne, coordinated and controlled so many other lawless enterprises. Really quite staggering...." Russell's words drifted off as he considered the sheer gall of Campbell and the enormity of the crimes.

When they left the restaurant, Russell cautioned: "It's a miracle that you survived at all, and the triads and the Yakuza have long memories. You two stay safe, okay? If you ever need anything in the future, just call on me."

They parted on the sidewalk. Russell strolled back to his office while Claire and Jason humped their limited gear into a taxi and rode to the airport.

Chapter 40

The Prisoner at Châteaux Sermet

Referred to simply as "Monsieur Le Count", the mystery guest at the Châteaux Sermet had arrived late one night some weeks ago escorted by staff members and a company of plain-clothes French Legionnaires. The peaceful community of Villefranche-du-Périgord in southwestern France buzzed with speculation. The Châteaux had languished empty for several months, and the arrival of a large contingent of new occupants, however enigmatic, came as good news for the village because it meant a boost in local trade.

The staff members and Legionnaires mostly kept to themselves, but when they did venture into the café in the village square, they were surly and uncommunicative. The mayor had given notice that these people should be left alone and that no one should visit the Châteaux unless invited.

A short man who spoke little French, the "Count" paced restlessly and continuously through the rooms and corridors of the Châteaux. His untidy, long, grey hair and penetrating, blue eyes gave the few people who saw him the impression of a caged beast of prey. Such perceptions came close to the truth.

After fleeing from Paris, Sir Iain Campbell had sought refuge with his companions in the Union Corse. They owned many properties in France and beyond, but the Châteaux Sermet was a favourite, secure enough to safeguard fugitives of high rank and status. This likely would be a temporary stay. With Interpol searching for him, Campbell needed to keep moving, but for now, it sufficed.

The Châteaux stood solidly atop a small hill, surrounded by thick woods and accessed by a single spiralling track. Its other security features included cameras, strategically located tripwires and pressure pads and dog patrols. As if that wasn't enough, the guards of Legionnaires on permanent loan to the crime syndicate lacked any reputation for kindness. Effectively, Campbell had become a prisoner in his own fortress, but at least he avoided jail.

He spent his days and some nights plotting how and when to take revenge on the person most responsible for his downfall, one Claire Armstrong. Using underworld connections, he amassed a thickening file on Armstrong and her known companions, dispatching investigators to find them. If a day came when he located them, then he planned to issue decisive new orders.

For now, Sir Iain bided his time in the solitary comfort of the Châteaux. Gradually he accepted that his freedom had fluttered away, turning into an elusive luxury, one that he'd never experience again.

Epilogue

Consequences

Events in the Philippine and Bering seas galvanised even more individuals to stand up against the abuse of the ocean's great animals. People had heard too much of the ludicrous excuses for whaling; scientific research, indeed! The NGOs and other groups devoted to protecting marine environments leveraged global indignation in ways never before dreamed possible. Protest marches filled the streets of capital cities, both in nations that still practised whaling and in those that did not.

Finally, with a receptive audience for data, NGOs quenched the public thirst for facts and figures, which made for some upsetting news reports, TV shows and online documentaries. The whaling issue merged with the shocking practice of shark finning, and an increasingly curious public also learned that dolphin hunts extended beyond mindless cruelty in Japan, also happening in the Faroe Islands, Solomon Islands and Peru.

Some governments hastily curried favour with their electorates by denouncing various hunting practices, but in one spectacular case, this backfired. When the French government lambasted anyone complicit in slaughtering so many cetaceans, public protesters clamoured that France had championed bottom trawling and electrofishing, both enormously destructive to the underseas environment.

Then the fate of Atlantic bluefin tuna attracted attention. These huge and endangered fish remained prey for an organised slaughter each May and June as they migrated past Carloforte in Sardinia, Italy. Clubs, harpoons, guns, nets and electrodes, everything imaginable, came into play for *"la Mattanza"*, the killing, directed at the magnificent, but disappearing, fish. In the shadows behind these fishermen lurked the sinister presence of the Union Corse, yet another example of organised crime running roughshod over law enforcement and public opinion.

*

Buoyed by public interest, the International Whaling Commission organised a convention to piggyback on the 2018 Florianopolis Declaration, in which 40 non-whaling nations agreed to safeguard marine mammals in perpetuity and to allow for the recovery of all whale populations to pre-industrial-whaling levels. The IWC targeted 27 whaling nations that had neglected to sign the previous declaration or subsequently withdrew from it. This time, the IWC wanted a formal treaty enforceable by international law. Diplomatic battle lines were drawn.

Protection of Sea Creatures (POSC), the NGO led by Chuck Bailey, intensified its work and gained massive new support. By all indications, its founder, David Armstrong, and his extraordinary daughter, Claire, had changed the world. With luck, maybe the tide had turned in favour of oceans and the creatures within them.

*

On a distant tropical shore, two lovers held hands and strolled along a beach. It was midnight, and a vast canopy of stars above them competed for attention with a full moon.

The lovers stopped, sat on the sand and watched as gentle waves broke onto the beach, each producing a magical display of green, sparkling lights as plankton tumbled and frolicked in the surf. It was enchanting.

Both people knew that this profound sense of peace could not last. Soon they would begin the task of hunting down a tyrant, one who had sought their destruction and ended, or ruined, so many other lives. Having evaded capture, he still might come after them again. Such monsters in human form never rested without taking revenge on anyone who crossed them.

The lovers felt resigned to facing more dangers. But for now, they enjoyed happiness in each other's company and in the peaceful harmony with nature afforded by their island retreat in the Indian Ocean.

Shining impressively, the moon rolled out a brilliant white carpet of light, stretching out across the indigo sea towards the settled pair. The light rippled with the gentle swell; the setting dreamlike, even hypnotic.

Suddenly, Claire gasped and pointed out into the night, startling Jason. "There, look. Do you see her?"

"See who, where?" asked Jason, somewhat alarmed.

"Out there, about 100 metres. Can't you see her, Jason?"

"I can't see anyone, Claire," said Jason, now standing and anxiously casting his sight across the water. "Are you sure you're not imagining things?"

Claire stood and hugged him, laughing softly and still pointing. "If you look very carefully, you always will see her in the wash of a full moon," she said.

"See who? I can't see anyone," he replied, beginning to feel silly. He prodded Claire in the ribs. "Who is she?"

Claire leaned close and whispered in his ear. "She's a mermaid."

The End

Acknowledgements

❖ John Cairns, an author and editor, who edited this novel and who always has reviewed my manuscripts and given me so much encouragement. Thank you, John.

❖ Claire Nouvian, the founder of Bloom Association, who first introduced me to the issue of shark finning. A truly inspirational person and champion of the oceans and the wonderful creatures within them.

❖ ♯ ME TOO, a justly rousing movement and not before time.

❖ Stan Shea, the marine programme director at Bloom Association, Hong Kong, who reviewed my manuscript for accuracy and gave me many valuable insights into marine conservation.

❖ Burt Kirschner, a kindly and gentle man with a love of the sea and the creatures within it, who taught me to scuba-dive many years ago in the Caribbean and imbued in me a love of the undersea world.

❖ Sir David Attenborough, whose teachings and presentations about our world, and the creatures we share it with, are a constant motivation and inspiration for us all.

❖ Jacques Cousteau, a French naval officer, conservationist, filmmaker, innovator, scientist, photographer, author and researcher, who studied sea life in the earliest days of underwater exploration. He developed the diving regulator to complement the self-contained underwater breathing apparatus (SCUBA) which we use today.

❖ Yulia V. Ivashchenko, a Ph.D. associate scientist at the US National Marine Mammal Laboratory, Alaska Fisheries Science Centre, who provided helpful insights into the whaling industry.

❖ The general managers and directors of private members' clubs and hotels in Hong Kong, who first made a stand and removed shark fin soup from their menus before rolling out a campaign to the Chinese mainland.

❖ Rose Gater, a much-travelled environmentalist who provided valuable ideas and feedback.

❖ Max Vine, a retired airline pilot and book reviewer, whose perceptiveness and feedback helped greatly to refine this book.

❖ Steven Thompson, the owner of Hua Hin Divers, a scuba-diving centre in Thailand, who helped with some technical details.

❖ Philippa Southwell, a specialist lawyer and managing director at the Human Trafficking and Modern Slavery Expert Directory.

Bibliography and References

1. *Moby Dick* by Herman Melville

2. Beyond the Cove by Keiko Yagi

3. Project Dolphin – Ric O'Barry

4. Bloom Association – Claire Nouvian

5. Save Our Seas Foundation

6. Greenpeace

7. Sea Shepherd Conservation Society

8. *Sharkwater* by Rob Stewart

9. **RTHK-HK** – Article on shark fin seizures, 06 May 2020
    <u>https://news.rthk.hk/rthk/en/component/k2/152457</u>
    <u>5-20200506.htm</u>

10. South China Morning Post newspaper

11. BioExpedition.com

12. Fishbase.org

13. United Nations Convention on the Law of the Sea 1982 (UNCLOS)

14. International Whaling Commission (IWC)

15. Worldwide Fund for Nature (WWF)

16. International Union for Conservation of Nature's Red List of Threatened Species

17. "A Record Fuelled by Scarcity" by Rupert Wingfield-Hayes, a report on the 2019 New Year tuna catch in Tokyo, January 2019

18. "Too Much Is Never Enough: The Cautionary Tale of Soviet Whaling", *Marine Fisheries Review 76*: 1-21", Yulia V. Ivashchenko

19. "Russian Whale Jail", CBS, March 2019

20. *A Whale of a Tale* by Megumi Sasaki

21. Ocean Wise, a Canadian organisation promoting healthy and flourishing oceans

22. The Convention on International Trade in Endangered Species (CITES), August 2019

23. The Independent newspaper

24. *MailOnline* newspaper

25. Assets Publishing Services, UK

26. Quora information platform

27. ThingsAsian Press

28. Hong Kong Government and Administrative Structure

29. "Organized Crime the Nordic Way", Lars Korsell and Paul Larsson

30. *Crime and Justice*, August 2011, University of Chicago Press

31. Independent Commission Against Corruption (ICAC), Hong Kong

32. "Transnational Organized Crime in Asia and the Pacific", UNODC (United Nations Office on Drugs and Crime), April 2013

33. "Asian Organized Crime and Terrorist Activity in Canada, 1999-2002", Canadian Federal Research Division, Library of Congress, July 2003

34. "Yakuza: The Japanese Mafia", Nabanita Dutt, July 2002

35. "Human Trafficking and the Sex Trade in Japan", Martha Mensendiek, Global Ministries, May 2014

36. "Organised Crime in China", Stratfor, August 2008

37. "Investigation and Analysis of Organized Crime", InsightCrime Foundation

38. Kung Fu Tea – Martial Arts History, Wing Chun and Chinese Martial Studies

39. Eliteukforces.info – British Special Forces and Elite Units

40. Formal announcement in October 2018 by the chief of the defence staff, General Sir Nick Carter, along with the Ministry of Defence, concerning the inclusion of women in British Special Forces

41. Military.com (US)

42. Army Times (US)

43. Special Operations Command, French Special Forces

44. Heckler and Koch Group

45. Sig Sauer

46. Colt's Manufacturing Company

47. Apex Boats

48. Sunseeker International

49. Wikipedi

About the Author

The author on a rooftop in Hong Kong

An experienced hotelier and motivational speaker whose business and career spans the globe, Charles Barker has worked in ten countries on five continents and likes to explore the cultures and environments of where he has lived. These have notably been in the Caribbean, Russia, the Middle East and Southeast Asia. Formally educated in the UK, he has run hotels and clubs for InterContinental Hotels, Peninsula, St James's Clubs, the Leander Club, the Hong Kong Club and other enterprises.

Like Claire Armstrong, he has a passion for oceans and the undersea world. In Hong Kong, he actively engaged with Bloom Association, an anti-shark-finning NGO. As chairman of

The Club Manager's Association of Hong Kong, he organised several environmental and sustainability conferences. He also works with other charitable institutions.

His first novel, *The Brown Envelope Club*, appeared in 2010 and concerned two entangled stories of revenge following the first Gulf War. A second, *The Iraqi Deception*, followed in 2018 and dealt with weapons of mass destruction in Iraq before the second Gulf War, how they were acquired and what happened to them. Both books sell on Amazon and Kindle.

Follow the author on: **www.charlesbarker.club**

Printed in Poland
by Amazon Fulfillment
Poland Sp. z o.o., Wrocław

58462921R00211